Salt of the Earth is the story of one woman's determination to rise above the harsh circumstances of a working class family struggling against poverty and hardship in Britain's industrial heartland. Given strength by the indomitable support of a close-knit family she endures tragedy and heartbreak to see her dreams become reality — but there is an emotional price to pay . . .

Sally Spencer was born and brought up in Marston, Cheshire, but now lives in Spain.

By the same author

Up Our Street
Old Father Thames
A Picnic in Eden

SALT
of the
EARTH

Sally Spencer

ORION

An Orion paperback
First published in Great Britain in 1993 by Orion Books Ltd,
Orion House, 5 Upper St Martin's Lane, London WC2H 9EA

A CIP catalogue record for this book is available from the British Library

Typeset by Datix International Limited, Bungay, Suffolk
Printed in England by Clays Ltd, St Ives plc

For Lanna

AUTHOR'S NOTE

The places described in this book did, and do, exist. There was an Adelaide Mine in Marston and the house in which Becky Taylor — and I — were brought up, was a chip shop in my great-grandfather's time. Equally, many of the events in the book — the collapse of the canal bank, the flooding of Ashton's Mine etc. — did actually occur, though I have taken the liberty of moving their occurrence by a few years. All the characters in the book, however, are purely the result of my own imagination. I have no idea, for example, *who* was the landlord of the New Inn in 1870, but I'd be willing to bet that his name wasn't O'Leary.

Sally Spencer

PROLOGUE
1871

Ted Taylor covered the ten feet from his back gate to the corner of Ollershaw Lane, then, as usual, stopped and tried to force himself to feel at least a little enthusiastic about the fourteen-hour shift which lay ahead.

Looking down the lane, into the darkness, he could make out the glow of cigarettes, bobbing about like fireflies as they hung loosely in the mouths of other men on their way to work. He could hear familiar sounds, too – the click of clogs on the cobbles, the rasping of early morning coughs, the mutterings of others as reluctant to get to work as he was.

'Still, there's no getting round it,' Taylor said with a sigh, stepping out into the road.

The moon was shrouded with cloud that early morning, and though Ted could have trodden his way to work blindfolded, he couldn't help wishing that there were gas lamps to light his way, as there were in Northwich. But it would have been too dangerous to install gas pipes in Marston. The ground below the village had been mined for over half a century and was a honeycomb of current and abandoned workings.

And that's why you can never bloody trust it, Taylor thought grimly.

Sometimes the ground gave way suddenly and dramatically, as it had the year before.

He'd been having his supper at the time, Taylor remembered, and the first indication that anything was wrong had been an angry growling noise, like a wounded animal might make.

'What's that, Dad?' young George had asked, frightened.

'It's nothing to worry about,' his father told him as the crockery rattled furiously on the table.

And as it happened, it wasn't — not for the Taylor family. But for the people on Cross Street it had been a different story. Slates had fallen, windows and doors had buckled, cracks had appeared in walls and — in one case — a whole gable end had fallen down, leaving the roof it had been supporting hanging precariously in the empty air.

Of course, it wasn't always like that. Often, the ground was more cunning, waiting until night when everyone was asleep, and then slowly — almost gently — beginning to give way. Houses often sank several feet overnight — with the occupants knowing nothing about it until they tried to open their back doors the following morning.

Aye, it's a bugger, Ted Taylor thought to himself.

Halfway up the humpbacked bridge over the canal he heard footsteps behind him and turning his head saw the silhouette of a lanky figure doing its best to catch up with him.

'Is that you, T . . . Ted?' the pursuer asked.

'Yes, it's me,' Taylor replied, and slowed down to allow Harry Atherton, known since their days at infants' school as Ha-Ha-Harry, to draw level.

'How's your M . . . Mary?' Atherton asked.

'The size of a house. But she's as pale as anything, and not eating enough to keep a sparrow alive,' Taylor told him.

'The b . . . baby's due soon, isn't it?'

'Soon enough. Some time next week.'

The two men continued to climb the bridge.

To their left was Worrell's Salt Works. Ted Taylor remembered Len Worrell when he'd been nothing but a boiler-maker. Then Worrell had come up with his invention — a special valve or summat — and, to give him credit, he hadn't blown the money as some men would have done, but had bought the salt works. Now he was sitting pretty — and good luck to him.

Taylor turned his mind back to his wife. He was worried about her, and there was no point in denying it. Seven kids, he'd given her, and none of them seemed to have caused her anything like as many problems as this one. It wasn't just that she had no appetite — his Mary who could normally eat a horse. She looked tired all the time, and once or twice, when she'd thought he wasn't watching her, he'd noticed a twinge of pain flicker briefly across her face.

'She'll be all right,' he said, though he'd never meant to voice his thoughts out loud.

'You m . . . mean your M . . . Mary?' Ha-Ha asked.

'That's right,' Taylor agreed. 'I mean, Ma Fitton'll be looking after her, and you can't go wrong with Ma, can you?'

'M . . . midwife to royalty,' Ha-Ha said, and both men laughed at the old joke, even though it was no joke to Mrs Fitton who continued to claim, despite the ridicule heaped on her, that she had once assisted in the birth of a German princeling − 'almost a cousin of the Queen's.'

At the top of the bridge they paused for a second. Just ahead of them, before the National School, lay the Adelaide Mine, their place of work. They could hear the winding engine clanking as the engineers built up a head of steam. They could see the black smoke, swirling like a malevolent snake, up towards the moon.

'It's dark when we go down there, an' it'll be dark when we come up again,' Taylor said.

'True enough,' Harry Atherton agreed philosophically.

Mary Taylor had got up early, as usual, to make her husband's breakfast − a big mug of hot, sweet tea and a piece of bread. She'd watched him spread the bread thickly with lard and wished he'd try that newfangled margarine stuff, which was all the rage now. But Ted was a creature of habit, always had been and always would be, so there was really no point in arguing with him.

She shouldn't really complain, she thought, as she pushed the hob over the blazing fire. Ted *was* a bit set in his ways, but then what man in Marston wasn't? And if it hadn't been for him, she'd still have been a maid of all work − scrubbing and polishing in someone else's house till her hands ached, ironing the master's shirts well after midnight and knowing that she'd have to be up again in a few short hours to light the fires. All that for £10 a year plus her keep!

She looked up at their wedding photograph, which dominated the centre of the mantelpiece. He'd been a good catch, she decided. He had a hard, compact body which many other men would have envied, and even if his forehead was perhaps a little too broad and his chin a little too square, he was *almost* a handsome man.

Not that Ted had done badly out of the deal either, she thought in fairness to herself. She'd been something of a beauty when she was younger, and even now, though she had a few grey hairs, her chin was as firm as it had ever been. Her breasts had not lost much of their firmness, either, she reflected, and a burning on her cheeks told her that she must be blushing. And her eyes were still as deep green and sparkling as the day she'd married.

Yet she felt tired. Seven children she'd borne Ted. Little Walter had died almost as soon as he'd come into the world, and poor Clara hadn't lived to see her fourth birthday. But that still left five kids to look after. A real handful. And there was another baby well on the way.

Ted didn't seem to realize how painful giving birth could be. Nor did he appreciate how dangerous it was.

Just look at Peggy Larkin, Mary told herself.

Strong as a horse Peggy'd been, but two days after her time came they'd been laying her in a hole, with the infant beside her.

And she wasn't the only one – not by a long chalk.

There was that Mrs Worrell, too. Her husband had plenty of money for fancy doctors, what with running the salt works and all, but that hadn't saved her, had it? She'd died giving birth to her second child.

'And this will be my eighth,' Mary groaned.

The kettle was boiling fiercely and as she bent over to pick it up, Mary felt a stab of pain.

The baby?

It couldn't be. The head hadn't even dropped yet.

'No more after this one,' she said aloud as she poured the hot water into the teapot.

Mary waddled to the foot of the stairs.

'The tea's made,' she called out. 'Get up right now, you lot, or you'll all be late for school and then Mr Hicks will have something to say, won't he?'

The problem was, she told herself as she returned to the kitchen, she didn't really feel ready to give birth right then.

If only I'd had time to build me strength up, she thought.

But there never was time, was there? How could she ever expect to get stronger when there was so much work to do? The only rest a woman got was a few days after the baby was born, when the neighbours pitched in and helped a bit. Otherwise, no matter how pregnant you were, there was still the washing to do, the house to be cleaned, the meals to be cooked.

'I've warned you kids,' she shouted. 'If I have to come up there and get you out of bed you'll feel the back of me hand.'

Not that she had the energy to climb the steep, narrow stairs and carry out her threat. It was as much as she could do to struggle across to the kitchen chair and lower herself clumsily onto it.

As the sat there, doing her best to regain her wind, Mary listened to the sound of the children moving around in their bed-rooms.

'Hurry up, Jessie!' she heard Eunice say loudly.

'I'm being as quick as I can,' her younger sister protested.

'Well make sure you are,' Eunice told her. 'It'll be me what gets in trouble if we're late — 'cos I'm responsible and you're not.'

'Oh, stop being so bossy,' Jessie said.

Despite her discomfort, Mary caught herself smiling. Eunice had become a *little* bossy, but that was understandable now she was a monitor and had the education of the smaller pupils in her hands.

A pounding on the stairs told Mary that Jack was on his way down, and a second later he burst into the room, looking as fresh and alive as if he'd been up for hours.

'Morning, Mam,' he said as he rushed across the crowded kitchen to the back door.

'Have you combed your hair?' Mary asked, looking at the mass of curls which crowned Jack's head.

'Yes, Mam,' Jack replied, shaking his head so that the curls seemed to swirl.

'Well, it doesn't look like it to me,' his mother told him.

Jack grinned guiltily. 'I'll just get a bucket of water for me wash,' he said, and before Mary had time to say any more, he was out of the door and heading for the wash-house.

There were new footsteps on the stairs — slower, more deliberate ones. That would be George. He did *everything* slowly. Some people said he was a bit slow himself, but Mary knew that wasn't true. If little George took his time about doing things, it was because he always thought a lot about them first.

The two girls arrived last, Eunice bustling self-importantly, Jessie still looking a little resentful at her sister's high-handed treatment.

Minutes earlier the kitchen had been a quiet, still place. Now the whole family was there with the exception of Ted — who would already be down the mine — and little Philip, who was sleeping peacefully in his crib in the front room.

A sudden scream told Mary that Philip was far from asleep.

'Go and see to your brother will you, love,' Mary said to Eunice.

Her eldest daughter pulled a face.

'Do I have to, Mam?' she asked. 'He's always whining.' And then she noticed the look of pain on Mary's face and her tone changed from irritation to concern as she said, 'Are you all right, Mam?'

'Of course I'm all right,' Mary replied, forcing herself to sound cheerful. 'I've just got a bit of indigestion, that's all.'

'I've never seen you look like that with indigestion,' Eunice said worriedly.

'Well, that's all it is,' her mother insisted. 'Now go and see to our Philip. You know he won't quieten down until somebody's had a word with him.'

As Eunice turned to go and comfort her brother, Mary felt

another spasm of pain. Eunice was right, she thought. This was a lot worse than even the most painful indigestion. But it couldn't be the baby, she told herself. The head hadn't dropped yet, and the baby couldn't possibly be coming if its head hadn't dropped.

'I allus feel like a p ... pile of bloody washing in this thing,' Harry Atherton complained.

Ted Taylor laughed. The tub they were standing in did look a bit like the one Mary did the family's wash in every Monday. But Mary's tub stayed firmly on the ground, while this was being lowered, slowly but surely, down a shaft which was a hundred and twenty yards deep.

The tub touched the floor and the men climbed out. They were in a large cavern. The anteroom of the mine, one of the gaffers had called it — whatever that meant. The ceiling was sixteen feet high and supported by pillars of rock salt thirty feet in diameter. The pillars hadn't been put there, at least not by man. Rather, they had been carved out, allowed to remain standing when all the salt around them had been blasted away and shipped out.

Taylor looked around the cavern. He'd been told by his father that when the Tsar of Russia had visited Marston just after the turn of the century, owners of the mine had held a ball for him on this very spot, complete with orchestra and sumptuous banquet. And probably it had looked very attractive, Taylor thought. What with the candles shining on the browny-silver rock salt crystals, it must have been a bit like holding a dance in the middle of a diamond. Aye, but if the Tsar had had to work the salt, day after day, it would soon have lost its appeal.

'Ready, Ted?' Harry Atherton asked, as he did at the start of every working morning, and Taylor, as *he* did every working morning, replied, 'In a minute. I'll just have a word with me mates first.'

He walked over to a fenced-off area which was strewn with straw.

9

'How you doin', Beauty?' he asked the nearest animal, a jet-black pit-pony with a white star over its eyes.

The pony ambled over to him, an expectant look in its eyes.

'Didn't manage to get anything for you today,' Taylor told the pony.

Beauty snorted in disbelief.

'One of these fine days my missis'll catch me doing this,' Taylor said, reaching into his pocket for the twist of paper he'd put there earlier, 'and then we'll both be in trouble.'

The pony whinnied as if to say that it was sure he was far too clever to get caught. Taylor opened the twist and poured some sugar onto his hand. Beauty quickly licked it clean, then raised her head and gazed hopefully at him.

'Don't be greedy,' Taylor admonished. 'There's others want their share.'

He had a few words – and a little sugar – for all the ponies.

'How are you today, Snowdrop?' he said to an almost pure white animal.

'We're bursting to get to work, aren't we, Hercules?' he said to a dappled grey, and when the animal shook his mane as if in agreement, Taylor added, 'We're bloody liars – the pair of us.'

Though he could not see Harry Atherton, Taylor could feel the other man's impatience. Well, that was only natural. Atherton was a ferrier, one of the blokes whose job it was to fill the pit-ponies' trundles with rock salt, and he couldn't do that until his mate Ted Taylor – who was what was known as a rock getter – had drilled or blasted the crystals from the salt face.

'Ted . . .' Harry said tentatively.

'I know, I know,' Taylor replied. 'I've never met a feller as keen to get to work as you are.'

'We *are* p . . . paid by the t . . . ton,' Ha-Ha pointed out. 'And I'd have thought that with a new n . . . nipper on the way, you could use all the money you could make.'

A new nipper! Soothed by his time with the ponies, Taylor had temporarily managed to put his wife's condition to the back of his mind, but Ha-Ha's words brought all his worries flooding back.

She's got to be all right, he told himself desperately. If she's not all right, I don't know what I'll do.

Len Worrell eased his cut-throat razor over his cheeks, scraping away the foam and revealing the face beneath – large hard eyes, big autocratic nose, a wide mouth which in anger could set as tight as a drum.

He was getting fat, he told himself. Well, not exactly fat – but he could certainly do with losing a bit of weight. And had his cheeks always been so red, or was that something new, too?

In the old days he'd been leaner and harder, he thought. Back then, when he was a boiler-maker, he could have taken anybody on – and often did. Then he'd come up with the idea for his pressure valve. It was a good idea, and they were sure they could find a use for it, his employers had told him as they'd encouraged him to sign his rights away for a few hundred quid. It had been a good idea all right. Thousands it had made for them – thousands!

Still, that had been the last time anybody had ever taken *him* for a ride, he reflected as he wiped away the remaining soap. Ever since he'd bought the run-down salt works, he'd made damn sure that nobody – *nobody* – got one over him.

Having finished his toilet, he rang the bell to summon his valet.

His valet!

Who would ever have imagined that Len Worrell would have servants waiting on him hand and foot? He'd had no idea how to handle them at first, but Caroline, in her clever, unobtrusive way, had slowly steered him in the right direction.

It had turned out to be a surprising marriage, he thought as his valet helped him on with his jacket. He'd married Caroline because he was ambitious, because her family, though technically 'in trade', were a considerable cut above his. He'd married her for the sake of the children he hoped she would bear him – for the dynasty he wished to establish.

Love had never been part of his plan, yet love had come unbidden, and when she'd died – giving birth to their second son, Michael – it had hurt him more than he'd ever imagined possible. Now his sons – and his hopes for them – were all he had left. Caroline had given up her life for his dynasty, and whatever else happened he would see to it that her death hadn't been in vain.

When Worrell entered the breakfast room his sons were already seated but jumped to their feet the second they noticed his arrival.

'Good morning, Father,' said Richard, the elder one.

'Good morning, Father,' echoed Michael.

Father! Worrell relished the sound. 'Dad' was what he'd called his old man – it would have been unthinkable to call Ebenezer Worrell anything else – but his own children were different. Richard and Michael didn't have to rough it as he had – they had a governess and when they were old enough they would attend one of them expensive public schools. Richard and Michael would grow up to be gentlemen.

Worrell helped himself to some food from the buffet – kidneys, sausage, scrambled egg with salmon – and sat down facing his sons. As he tucked into his food with the enthusiasm of one who knows what it's like to have gone hungry, he thought about how different his sons were from each other.

Richard, now aged eight, had inherited his father's rugged handsomeness. Michael, just past his sixth birthday, owed much more to the mother he had never known. He wasn't effeminate – far from it – yet looking at him now Worrell could discern a delicacy in his appearance that definitely didn't belong to his side of the family.

And it was not only in their looks that they differed, Worrell reflected. In almost everything they did they were poles apart. Take eating, for example. Richard loved kidneys, but rather than start on them he had pushed them to the side of his plate. As he ate the rest of his food, his eyes never left them, and it was kidneys – not bacon or egg – he was tasting.

But Worrell knew that when his elder son did finally come to the kidneys, he would find them a disappointment — just as he found most things in life a disappointment once he had attained them.

Michael, on the other hand, worked his way through his breakfast as though he regarded food as nothing more than fuel — or as though he were eating it only to please his father.

Yet Worrell did not find it easy to be pleased by his younger son. Michael tried too hard to be amenable, as if his whole life were dedicated to proving his own worth. How much easier it would have been to take to him if he had been more like his brother — charming, witty, easygoing.

'May I be excused, Father?' Michael asked.

Worrell glanced at his son, and saw in the boy's face a look which reminded him so much of his dead wife — a wife who would still be alive but for Michael.

'No, you may not be excused,' he said harshly.

At ten o'clock Mary Taylor told herself that she'd feel better after she'd had a little sit-down. When eleven struck, and the pains were worse than ever, she was finally forced to admit that even though it shouldn't be, the baby was definitely on the way.

Grabbing the edge of the kitchen table for support, she pulled herself to her feet. Standing was agony, and for a second she was tempted to sit down again. But she knew if she did that she would never get up again — and then both she and the baby were as good as dead.

She staggered over to the fireplace. Gritting her teeth, she bent down and picked up the poker. The thing seemed to weigh a ton, she thought, as she made her way groggily across the room to the wall which divided her home from the next-door neighbours'.

Lifting the poker was a tremendous effort for Mary, and as she struck the wall several sharp blows with it, she felt as if her stomach was on fire.

The poker fell from her hands, and she knew that even if

they had not heard her next door she did not have the strength to pick it up again.

When Clara Gibbons answered the urgent summons on her wall, she found Mary Taylor back in her seat and looking as pale as a corpse.

'Is it the baby?' she asked.

'I think it has to be,' Mary admitted.

'Is there anything *I* can do?' Clara asked worriedly.

Mary shook her head. She was a nice girl, Clara Gibbons, but that's all she was – a girl, with no experience of having children.

'Just get me Ma Fitton,' Mary gasped. 'Everything'll be all right if you just get me Ma Fitton.'

Nellie Fitton was sitting in the best room of the Sportsman's, one of Northwich's busiest pubs. She'd only meant to call in for a quick drink after picking up the lace she'd ordered, but then she'd met this very nice young woman who seemed very interested in her life in midwifery, so naturally she'd stayed a little longer.

'You were going to tell me about your princess,' the young woman said.

'I was in service at the time,' Ma Fitton told her. 'Sir Robert Aspbry, I was working for. Well, this lady – I didn't know she was a princess at the time – came to stay for a few days, incognito, as they say. She thought she wasn't due for a week or two, but I could see different. Well, when she started getting her pains, they all fell into a panic. There they were, in this big country house, miles from the nearest doctor, and they didn't know what to do. "You leave it up to me," I told Sir Robert. "I helped deliver three of me brothers and this one, for all that's it going to be royalty, shouldn't be no different."'

'Was it a difficult birth?' the young woman asked.

Ma shrugged. 'I've known worse,' she said. 'But then, when you've delivered half a village, like I have, you seen just about everything there is to see as far as babies are concerned.'

'And when's the next one due?'

'Some time next week. A lass called Mary Taylor.'

'Well if it's not until next week, you might as well have another milk stout, mightn't you?' the young woman said jokingly as she opened her purse.

'That's very kind of you,' Ma Fitton said.

Clara Gibbons had made up the bed in the front parlour and helped Mary Taylor into it – but that was about as much as *she* could do.

'I need Ma Fitton,' Mary groaned. 'I've *got to have* Ma Fitton.'

'Stop worrying,' Clara said reassuringly. 'Everybody's keeping an eye out for her, and if she's anywhere in the village she should soon find out she's wanted.'

Jack, her eldest, had been a difficult birth, Mary thought, but after him it got easier and easier, and she'd hardly noticed she was having Philip. But even the pain of having Jack had been nothing like this – nothing at all.

She was going to die! She knew she was going to die! But what about the child she was carrying?

'Where the hell are you, Ma?' she screamed. 'Come and save my baby!'

Ted Taylor looked at his pocket watch in the light of his helmet lantern. Six o'clock. Another day over, another bloody long shift completed. The tub arrived and he and the other men stepped inside. Overhead, the steam engine hissed, the machinery groaned and the tub began to rise.

'How come it always seems to take about twice as long to haul us out of the bloody mine as it does to lower us in?' Taylor asked grumpily.

'You're in a b ... bad mood tonight,' Harry Atherton said.

Yes, he was – and not without cause. When the basins had been lowered down the shaft at twelve o'clock his had not been among them. Which meant that instead of tucking into the food his wife had cooked for him that morning, he'd had to scrounge — a bit here and a bit there — from the other workers.

The tub reached the winding shed. Taylor stepped out and looked up through the skylight at the stars.

'When a man's down the mine for fourteen hours, he's entitled to a decent meal in the middle of the day,' he said.

Mary, who knew how much he needed a good hot dinner when he was working down the pit, would never have forgotten to prepare it. So the fault must lie elsewhere — with whichever of his kids had been given the job of delivering his basin. Yet he couldn't really believe that, either. Eunice had always been a very responsible girl, and hadn't put a foot wrong since she'd become a school monitor. You could always rely on Jessie, too. And as for Jack — well, he might be a bit wild, but he'd never see his old dad go hungry. And little George, for all that he was only five, was the most serious of the lot of them. Still, it had to be one of his children who was at fault, and when he found out *which* one, the young bugger would feel his belt.

Most nights Ted would walk home with Harry, but tonight he didn't feel like it, and before Ha-Ha had a chance to fall in step with him he was striding off towards the bridge over the canal.

By the time he reached Worrell's Salt Works the men were already knocking off, and the evaporation pans, which had been bubbling and steaming all day, lay still and empty.

It's a good business Len Worrell's got himself, Taylor thought.

But he did not envy Worrell his wealth. What was the good of money, after all, when you had no one to share it with?

The rest of the family would already be home, including the one who had failed to deliver his basin. The offender would have to be punished — spare the rod and spoil the child. But Taylor was not really looking forward to it, and so instead of heading straight for his own kitchen as he normally would, he found himself being pulled towards the light shining from the bar of the New Inn.

On the doorstep of the pub he stopped and checked through

his pockets to make sure that he had enough coppers on him. A pint now would mean no pint later – he knew that – but there were times when a man really felt like a drink. Pocketing his change again, he pushed open the pub door.

The room which he entered was so familiar to him that only if it had been changed around would he really have noticed it at all. But there had been no changes: the leather settle still ran around the sides of the wall; the round tables, with their wooden tops and cast-iron legs, stood where they had always done; the oak bar counter, set against the far wall, continued to dominate the whole place.

Taylor looked around him. The bar was empty, but through the hatch to the best room he could hear a strident female voice which told him that 'Not-Stopping' Bracegirdle was holding court.

'How are you tonight, Paddy?' he asked the man behind the bar.

'Fine,' Paddy O'Leary replied as he automatically reached for a glass to pull Taylor's pint. 'And how's yourself, Edward?'

Taylor strode over to the counter, placed one foot on the brass rail and rested his elbow comfortably on the oak top.

'I mustn't grumble,' he said, although he'd been doing little else – in his head, at least – since his basin had failed to turn up.

Still, things were looking up at last. Taylor picked up his pint and took a measured sip. That was better.

Elsie Bracegirdle had earned her nickname of Not-Stopping by her habit of following her announcement that she was 'not stopping' with at least half an hour's juicy gossip. She was not a natural beauty. She had a large nose and that, plus the fact she kept her black hair in a tight bun, made her a little like a crow. And she was crowing now, over yet another domestic tragedy she claimed to have predicted with accuracy.

'I warned Jennie Becket right from the start,' she told her listeners. 'I said, "He's bought that animal as a fighting dog. You can tell just by looking at it. And where there's fighting, there's betting." And was I right? I was!'

'Any news on poor Mary Taylor?' asked Dottie Curzon, obviously bored with the subject of dogs.

'You might well ask,' Not-Stopping replied. 'She sent for Nellie Fitton this morning. Well, they couldn't find her, could they. She was out boozing in Northwich. And all the time, Mary Taylor's lying there and ...'

'Are you talking about my missis?' asked an urgent voice from the bar.

Not-Stopping raised herself up off her seat until her eyes were level with the hatchway.

'Oh hello, Mr Taylor,' she said ingratiatingly. 'I didn't notice you'd come in.'

'My missis,' Ted Taylor persisted. 'Were you talking about my missis?'

'Well, yes, we were,' Not-Stopping admitted. 'Poor girl.'

'What's ... what's happened to her?' Taylor said faintly.

'Don't you know?' Not-Stopping asked. 'That is surprising. Fancy nobody bothering to come and tell you.'

'You tell me!' Taylor said, suddenly angrily. 'You bloody tell me!'

'Well, she started her labour pains this morning, so she sent for Ma Fitton right away and ...'

But Taylor was already out of the door and running frantically towards his back gate.

'Typical of a man, isn't it?' Not-Stopping said to her drinking companions. 'They ask you a question and then they never wait around for an answer.'

Taylor burst into his kitchen to find Ma Fitton drinking tea with Eunice and Jessie.

'Where is she?' he said frantically. 'Where's my Mary?'

'She's in bed,' Ma Fitton said. 'Where else would you expect her to be when she's just given birth?'

'Is she ... is she all right?' Taylor gasped.

'She is now,' Ma Fitton said, 'and so is the baby, but for a minute it looked like we were in trouble. The nipper's head was the wrong way round, you see.'

'Head?' Taylor said. 'Wrong way round?'

'You men!' Ma Fitton said in disgust. 'You know nothing, do you? You have your pleasure then you think your bit's done. The baby was going to come out feet first. I had to turn it round.'

'Can I . . .?' Taylor asked. 'Can I . . .?'

'Yes, you can go in and see her,' Ma Fitton told him. 'But if I was you I'd try and calm down first. After what she's been through the last thing she wants is you charging round like a bull in a china shop.'

Mary looked pale and strained. The baby lay by her side. Its head was as red and wrinkled as those small sour oranges the fruit man sold at three a penny, but to Taylor it seemed the most beautiful child ever to have been born.

'It's a girl this time,' Mary said.

'Is it?' Taylor replied, feeling slightly abashed by his earlier behaviour now that he could see the crisis was over. 'A girl, by gum.'

He realized he was still wearing his cap, took it off immediately and twisted it awkwardly in his hands. The corners of his wife's mouth began to crinkle as they always did when he'd amused her.

'So what are we going to call her?' Mary asked.

'Rebecca,' Taylor said firmly, though he had no idea what had caused him to pluck that particular name out of the air. 'We'll call her Rebecca.'

And Rebecca it was.

PART ONE
1874–81

CHAPTER ONE

'You've been nothing but a pest since the day you were born,' Mary Taylor said good-naturedly to her youngest daughter. 'Since before you were born, as a matter of fact.'

'Why, Mam?' Becky asked.

'Because you're full of questions for a start,' Mary told her. '"What's that for, Mam?" "How does that work, Mam?" "Why do our Philip and George have to go to school?" I tell you, that curiosity of yours will be the death of me yet.'

'But how could I be a pest *before* I was born?' Becky wondered.

'See what I mean?' her mother asked triumphantly. 'Nothing but questions!'

But it was hard *not* to ask questions when the world — which stretched all the way from the canal at one end of the village to the railway line at the other — was such a fascinating place.

At first, expeditions into this magic kingdom were only undertaken at her mother's side. Hand in hand, mother and daughter would walk down the lane to Mr Cooke's shop.

'When you're a little bit bigger I'll let you do this by yourself,' Mary promised.

And Becky looked forward to that day with eager anticipation.

'What say we get six penn'orth of pieces?' Mary would ask her in the butcher's shop. 'Make a nice meat pudding, that would, with lots of gravy, just like your dad likes it.'

'Just like he likes it,' Becky would agree.

'And what shall we put in the roly-poly pudding today. Apples or currants?'

Becky would give the matter her serious consideration.

'I don't know,' she'd say finally.

'If it'll help you make up your mind, we've got apples at home, and if I don't have to buy currants, there might just be enough money over for a bottle of lemonade.'

The game always brought a grin to Becky's face no matter how many times they played it.

'Apple might be nice for a change,' she'd say.

'Yes,' her mother would reply. 'It'll make a real change. Not had apples since – oh – yesterday. I don't know, our Becky, you're more spoiled than the Prince of Wales' children – and them royalty.'

Once the shopping had been done, the cleaning had to be attacked. Though the front door was used only for weddings and funerals the step still had to be donkey-stoned so regularly that it always gleamed in the sunlight. And just as the step had to be whitened, so had the grate to be darkened until it was as black as coal.

'You watch this,' Mary advised her daughter as she applied the black-leading liberally. 'Some day you'll have to do this in a home of your own.'

Nor was this the only cleaning which went on around the oven. The brass rods which ran across the hearth and along the mantelpiece had to be polished until they shone like gold.

The part Becky liked best was dusting the ornaments. Each of these would be taken down from the mantelpiece individually and handled with great care, like the precious treasure it was.

Every ornament had its own story.

'That glass vase came from Venice.'

'Where's Venice, Mam?'

'A long, long way away.'

'Near Manchester?'

'Much further than Manchester. You have to cross the sea to get to Venice.'

'And have you been there?'

'Course I haven't, my little love. What would I be doing going abroad? No, Master Peter brought it back from the tour he took just before he went to university.'

'What's university, Mam?'

'It's a school for grown-up rich people.'

It didn't make sense to Becky that people should need to go to school once they'd grown up – after all, children in the village left school when they were ten – but she didn't press the point, because there were more ornaments and more stories.

There was a pottery horse, covered with a bright chestnut glaze.

'Your dad bought that for me from a man who came round with a wagon. We'd only just starting walking out together then, and he was trying to soft-soap me, you see. Two and sixpence it cost him. Think of that!'

'You said it cost two shillings last time you told me.'

'Did I, my little princess? Well, perhaps I did. When you get to my age, you start forgetting things. You'll find that out yourself, one day.'

There were other animals in the mantelpiece menagerie – a rabbit with an almost human face; a gun dog, set to spring the moment the rifle was fired. Becky used to make up stories about them, but she never told these stories to anyone else, not even her mother, because it was a private game.

The china mugs were the most precious objects of all. There were two of them. One read 'A Souvenir of Blackpool' and the other 'A Gift from Southport'.

'Your Uncle Reg gave me the one from Blackpool,' Mary told her daughter.

'Did he, Mam?'

'He did indeed. But I bought the other myself,' Mary said with some pride. 'Right on the seafront.'

'Can we go to the seaside, Mam?'

'Perhaps one day, when I've fewer mouths to feed.'

When time could be snatched from her other tasks Mary would pick up her needle and thread. Most people in the village either bought their clothes from the second-hand stalls in Northwich or else wore the hand-me-downs of the gentry which came to them through their daughters in service. But though Becky's sister Eunice was already an under-housemaid, none of the Taylor girls ever wore dresses which had once graced the backs of their betters.

'Other people's clothes make me itch,' Mary would explain. 'I had enough of that when I was in the workhouse.'

When Becky turned four Mary decided that her daughter was finally big enough to run short errands on her own.

'Watch out for the traffic,' she cautioned.

Not that there was much. An occasional gentleman's coach passed through the village on its way to the Lake District, farm wagons would lumber up the lane at harvest time, once in a while the accountants to the salt workings would appear in their dog-carts – but that was about all the four-wheeled traffic Marston ever saw.

Still, there were other dangers.

'And keep an eye open for men on penny-farthing cycles,' her mother would warn her. 'They belong to clubs, you know, and they race each other.'

'Why do they do that, Mam?'

'Because they're nothing but a load of mad buggers – and that's swearing. According to *Lloyd's Weekly News*, they're always killing innocent people who are just out for a walk. I don't know why the government doesn't build special roads for them so they don't have to bother ordinary, peaceful folk.'

'I'll be careful, Mam,' Becky would promise her mother at the same time as she promised *herself* that if she *did* see one of these riders she'd be sure to ask him if he really was a 'mad bugger'.

'And don't go anywhere near that canal. Nellie Green-Teeth lives there, and there's nothing she likes better than eating little girls.'

So Becky was *very* careful when she went near the canal, pausing on the bank for only a second, then looking over her shoulder as she ran away in the hope of seeing Nellie rising out of the water in an attempt to grab her.

Whatever the errand she was to be sent on – whether it was

to pay a penny into the boot club at the cobbler's or buy a *Northwich Guardian* from Mr Cooke's shop – Becky would dawdle at home until she could be sure that she'd be in the street when the train from Northwich crossed the village on its way to the Pool Mine.

How cunning she was in delaying her departure.

'I can't find me boots, Mam.'

'Why don't you look under the table. That's where I saw you put them five minutes since.'

'I need to go to the lavvie, Mam.'

'Yes, I thought you might.'

And her mother would smile as if to say, 'I know your game, my girl.'

What a joy it was to watch the arrival of the train. The first sign it was on the way would be when a man dressed in a smart blue frock-coat with shining buttons came out of the railway house. Anyone dressed like that had to be important, Becky thought, and indeed, from the way he glanced up and down the lane, it seemed as though he owned the whole village.

The railwayman carried a red flag in his hand, and on the rare occasions when a brewer's dray or a carrier was approaching, he would wave the flag to make it stop.

'But they'd have lots of time to get across before the train came,' Becky protested once.

And the man in the blue frock-coat had looked at her very coolly and said, 'I'm only following railway regulations.'

Having once brought the street to a standstill, the man would begin the process of swinging the railway gates across the lane. Usually he did this as if he resented it – as if he felt that such a lowly task should be left to someone else. But occasionally, if he was in a good mood, he would let Becky climb onto the gate and swing across with it.

Once the gates had been clicked into place Becky would turn her eyes towards the track. It was the smoke she'd see first, great billowing jets of it, climbing high in the sky. And then the train would appear, puffing and panting, as it pulled a load which even fifty strong shire horses could never have hoped to shift.

As the train thundered past Becky would wave to the driver and the fireman and they would wave back. Sometimes, if she was lucky, the fireman would throw her a couple of boiled sweets, and once she'd brushed the soot from them, Becky would pop them into her mouth, well satisfied with life.

At first it was a little cramped in their small house. The three girls slept in the front bedroom, the boys in the back. Ted and Mary had a let-down bed in the parlour. Washing caused endless complications, far beyond the mechanics involved in heating the water for the tin bath. It didn't matter to Becky who saw her bathe, but as the other children grew older, so they became increasingly self-conscious. Eunice and Jessie refused to take a bath with any of the male members of the family present, which meant confining their restless brothers to their bedroom for at least an hour. The boys on the other hand, didn't mind their mam and dad being in the same room, but even Philip drew the line at Eunice and Jessie joining them.

'It'd be easier running the Great Western Railway than it is organizing you lot,' Mary complained.

Yet she supposed that the children *did* have some right to privacy when they were washing. Goodness knows, they got little enough at any other time.

Eventually, the situation eased. Eunice gave up her school monitoring and went into service, soon to be joined by Jessie. Then Jack was taken on as an apprentice by one of the steam packets which sailed from Winsford to Liverpool with cargoes of salt, and there were days at a time when he was away from home. With three children working, there was a little more money coming into the house too, and Mary began to look forward to the day when they could afford to buy an upright piano.

But before that could be purchased there were more pressing demands to be met. Philip and George were still at school, and soon Becky would be joining them. That didn't come cheap – fivepence a week for each child, it cost her, one shilling and threepence in all – to be found out of each and every one of Ted's wage packets.

Perhaps if we can't have the piano, we can at least manage a day at Blackpool soon, Mary thought. It'd do the little ones good to get some sea air.

The air around the pan was as sticky-hot as usual, and sweat patches had already formed on the flannel vests of the lumpmen who were working there.

'This is what's called a "fine" pan,' Len Worrell said to his two sons. 'We produce a better grade of salt in a fine pan than we do in a common pan. You'll notice it's shorter than a common pan, only about sixty feet long, 'stead of around a hundred.'

Michael Worrell watched as one of the lumpmen stretched forward and pulled his long-handled rake across the sea of bubbling brine in order to draw the salt crystals to the side of the pan.

'Does anyone ever fall in, Father?' he asked.

'Hasn't happened recently,' his father replied.

Which was just another way of saying that it *had* happened at some time in the past. Michael imagined himself leaning over the pan, losing his footing and plunging head-first into the boiling liquid. He shuddered. No one should ever have to take that risk.

'Wouldn't guard rails be a good idea?' he asked. 'Then it would be impossible to fall in.'

Usually, Worrell's response to his younger son's enquiries was at best a show of mild irritation and at worst an annoyance which verged on rage – so Michael had long ago given up asking questions unless he really needed to know the answer. Today, however, was different. Today, the father was showing the sons his works – his pride and joy – and any display of interest was appreciated.

'Guard rails,' Worrell said reflectively. 'Yes, they would make things safer – but the men'd never stand for it.'

'Why not?' Michael asked.

'Because they're paid on piece rate,' Worrell said, with a little of his customary impatience entering his voice. 'The more they produce, the more they earn — and guard rails would only slow them down.'

'But even so, if it's as dangerous as all that ...' Michael began.

'Look at him,' Len Worrell interrupted, pointing to another lumpman who was using his skimmer to scoop out hot salt crystals and emptying them into an elm tub which rested on a rail inside of the pan. 'We call the tub he's using a sixty.'

'Why's that?' Richard asked.

Michael looked at his brother in amazement. He was enjoying the tour of the works himself, but he'd never imagined that Richard, who seemed to care for little except the most idle pleasure, would express any enthusiasm for it.

'We call them sixties,' said Worrell, beaming at his eldest son, 'because the salt from sixty of them will make a ton. Notice it's got slits at the bottom so the excess brine can drain back into the pan.'

'Oh, I see,' Richard replied, as if it were the most fascinating thing he'd ever heard.

'Just what is he up to?' Michael wondered suspiciously.

Worrell led his sons over to some tubs in the corner. The salt in these had been pulled out earlier in the day and therefore had time to harden.

'Notice how the tubs are tapered,' Len Worrell said. 'That's to make 'em easier to turn out onto the hurdles.'

'Could I try it, Father?' Richard asked.

Worrell laughed indulgently. 'Well, by rights it should spend a few days in the drying room first,' he said, 'but go ahead.'

Richard hefted the tub onto the trundle and tapped its bottom hard. The block of salt slid out.

'Was that all right?' Richard asked.

'You're a natural,' his father told him.

From the pan they went to the hot house which was heated

by flue gases. It was here that the blocks of salt were stored to thoroughly dry out.

'These have been drying for about four days,' Worrell said. He hit one of the blocks with his knuckle. 'Hear that?' he asked his sons. 'Rings like fired pottery, doesn't it? That means the salt's properly stoved.'

'How frightfully, frightfully interesting,' Richard said.

He spoke almost under his breath, so that his father could not hear him. But his brother did.

Now that's the Richard *I* know, Michael thought.

Worrell sat behind his desk with his two sons perched in front of him on visitors' chairs. He was pleased that Richard had shown an interest in the works, because that fitted in perfectly with his plans.

'You've got a long summer holiday ahead of you,' he said to Richard, 'a bloody long holiday. So I don't see why you shouldn't devote a bit of it to learning the business from the bottom up.'

'The bottom up,' Richard said. 'Why on earth should I want to do that?'

'Because everybody in this world'll try to pull one over on you,' his father explained, 'especially the idle buggers who are supposed to be working for you. One day, you'll take over the works, and when you do I don't want the lumpmen running rings round you. I want you to know about every skive and fiddle they've got better than they know 'em themselves. And you can only learn that by starting at the bottom.'

'Could I work on the pans, too, Father?' Michael said.

'Do you really want to?' Worrell asked.

'Yes,' his son replied, quietly but firmly. 'I really want to.'

Worrell hesitated before reaching a decision. Richard was thirteen now, as old as many of the apprentices, but Michael had only just turned eleven, and he had never had anyone that young working for him before.

On the other hand, Worrell was aware that he sometimes favoured Richard over Michael, and whenever he caught himself at it he felt the need to make some guilty compensation.

'Do you really think you can stick it out?' he asked.

'Yes, Father.'

'Because if you start flagging after the first couple of days, you'll lose the men's respect for ever.'

'I'll stick it out,' Michael said earnestly. 'I'll make you proud of me.'

'It's a tricky business working the fine pans,' Worrell said, continuing his sons' instruction as they arrived at the works the following Monday morning. 'If you don't get the rate of evaporation exactly right, you're buggered. And if you don't watch the drying process carefully, you're double buggered. You can't just make anybody a lumpman. It takes years to learn the job properly.'

'Yes, I think we learned something about that at school,' Richard said.

'Did you now?' his father replied. 'Imagine them teaching you about salt in that fancy school of yours.'

'Latin, Greek and salt,' Richard said. 'They're all part of the curriculum.'

Michael looked sharply at his brother. There was just a hint of a sarcastic smile on Richard's face.

Why doesn't Father realize Richard is making a fool of him? Michael thought angrily. Why does he *never* realize?

'Anyway,' Worrell went on, 'the common pans — where you'll be working — are a lot easier to manage. The crystals can be larger, you see, no special drying's necessary and once the salt *is* dry, you can store it anywhere, without having to worry your head about what effect the moisture in the atmosphere's going to have on it.'

'Now I don't think we learned that,' Richard said. 'Maybe we'll cover it next term.'

Cedric Rathbone was a small man with a big reputation.

'He never goes looking for a fight,' people said of him, 'but if there's one in the offing, you won't see Cedric turning his back on it.'

He was, moreover, as free with his mouth as he was with his fists, and he made no secret of his disgust when Michael reported to him at the start of the shift.

'There's no room for passengers on my gang,' he told Michael. 'We're paid piece rate, so if we make less salt, we earn less wages. And times are tough enough without a drop in pay.'

'I'll pull my weight, Mr Rathbone,' Michael promised.

Rathbone looked him up and down. 'Don't look as if you've got that much weight to pull,' he said doubtfully.

For a moment it seemed as if he were about to tell Michael to bugger off, then he shrugged his shoulder.

'I suppose I'm stuck with you,' he said. 'All right — let's get started.'

Michael soon learned that there was a great deal of difference between visiting a pan for a short time and working at it for twelve to fourteen hours at a stretch. After the first hour his throat was as dry and salty as if he'd just crossed the Sahara. After the second hour it was his arms which began to take the strain and every time he lifted the skimmer to pull more hissing brine from the pan it felt as if some malevolent spirit was piling more and more invisible weights onto his aching biceps. After the third hour his skin began to itch, though whether from the sticky atmosphere or because of his flannel vest he could not be sure.

Relief from this sweaty hell came only when the handcart had finally been filled. Then Cedric Rathbone would call for the checking clerk, and once the appropriate tick had been made in the right column he'd turn to his gang and say, 'Right lads, let's get this sod tipped.'

The handcart was tipped in the salt store, which was across the road from the main works. It was a huge wooden building with an arched roof, which from the front looked like a beached whale. But it was not through the front gate that the handcarts entered the store. Instead they were pushed through a side door halfway up the humpbacked bridge — and onto an open platform suspended a hundred feet over the floor of the store.

The first time Michael made this journey the sight of the drop made him feel giddy. With four people struggling with a heavy, awkward cart it would be the easiest thing in the world for one of them to go plummeting over the edge, he thought. A hundred-foot drop — and only a small pile of salt at the bottom to break the fall.

Cedric Rathbone seemed concerned too — though not about the same thing.

'Go easy,' he shouted. 'Lose the bloody cart and we'll be paying it off for a year!'

The men moved the handcart slowly forward towards the void.

'And . . . tip,' Rathbone called out.

Michael, trying his best to forget how close his feet were to the edge of the platform, joined with the rest of the gang in easing the handles of the cart upwards. At first it was harder work than even the pushing had been, but then salt began to cascade out into the empty air and the cart started to grow lighter.

'And . . . back,' Rathbone ordered.

The gang righted the cart and, walking backwards, dragged it out of the store and onto the bridge.

'Frightening the first time, isn't it?' Rathbone asked Michael, not unkindly.

'It is a bit,' Michael admitted.

'You'll get used to it,' Rathbone assured him. 'You can get used to anything if you have to.'

The gang took one last breath of fresh air, then pushed the cart back into the steamy, sticky atmosphere of the brine pan.

Len Worrell was in a foul mood over supper that night.

'I will not be cheated!' he thundered.

'Cheated, Father?' Richard asked.

'There was a guinea on the table in my dressing room last night,' Worrell explained, 'and now it's gone. Stolen!'

'By whom, Father?' Michael said sleepily.

'By whom?' Worrell demanded witheringly. 'I'll tell you by

whom. By one of the bloody inside servants. And I will not have it! Either I find out which one is the thief or I'll get shut of the whole pack of 'em and take on a new lot.'

'But you can't do that,' Michael said, alarmed. 'It wouldn't be fair.'

'Fair!' Worrell retorted. 'Of course it's not fair. Life isn't fair. It's a dog-eat-dog world, and I'm not going to be the dog what gets eaten.'

'But Father ...' Michael protested.

'Father is quite right,' Richard said. 'If you can't rule by fear, then you can't rule at all.'

They were wrong, both of them, Michael thought – but he knew it was pointless to argue. Besides, after his first day on the pans he felt too exhausted to fight. He wondered why his brother didn't seem as tired as he did – didn't seem tired at all. In fact, Richard looked as if he'd spent the day lying in the sunshine rather than sweating over a brine pan.

'By the way,' said Len Worrell, somewhat calmer now, 'I've been getting good reports from your gang boss on the way you've been working, Richard.'

'Thank you, Father,' Richard said complacently.

And what about me? Michael pleaded silently. What about me?

'And I had a word with Cedric Rathbone about you, Michael,' Worrell said.

'Yes, Father?'

'Aye. He says you're shaping, too – but you've a long way to go before you catch up on your brother.'

On the matter of the theft Worrell was as good as his word. The inside servants were questioned over the loss of the guinea and when none of them would admit to having taken it they were all given a week's notice.

'Couldn't you talk to them?' Michael implored Old Sam the groom. 'They respect you. I'm sure you could get the guilty one to own up.'

'Wouldn't be any point, Master Michael,' the groom told him. 'The thief isn't one of them, you see.'

35

'But if you know that, then you must know who really took the money,' Michael said.

'Of course I know,' Sam replied. 'We all know.'

'Then why doesn't somebody tell my father?'

'The Master wouldn't believe it,' Sam said. 'He'd sack any of the outside servants who tried to tell him. And if it was one of the inside ones – well, they've lost their jobs already, so he'd probably have them thrown in clink.'

'Tell me who the thief is,' Michael said. 'I'm not afraid of my father. *I'll* make him listen.'

Sam shook his head sadly.

'You've got a good heart, Master Michael,' he said, 'but you don't understand much about the ways of the wicked world.'

'Then teach me,' Michael demanded. 'Tell me all about it.'

The old man shook his head.

'It's best all round to leave matters as they are,' he said. 'Or there'll be more damage done.'

It was not until Michael had been working with Cedric Rathbone's gang for nearly three weeks that he started to gain some inkling of just how little effort his much-praised elder brother was actually putting into his work.

The knowledge came as the result of a chance meeting. Michael was taking a short cut from the canal back to his own pan when he came across Richard lounging against a stack of lumps in the hot house and smoking a cigarette.

'That's it, hurry up,' Richard said sarcastically. 'You get right back to work.'

'You better go too,' Michael advised him, 'or you'll be having your gang boss reporting you to Father.'

'Oh, there's no chance of that,' Richard said airily.

'I wouldn't be so sure,' Michael cautioned.

'Well, of course you wouldn't,' Richard agreed. 'That's because you don't know how to exploit things to your own advantage.'

'How do you mean?' Michael asked, interested in spite of himself.

'Bert Mills, my gang boss, is smart enough to realize which side his bread's buttered on,' Richard explained.

'I still don't understand,' Michael told him.

'In a few years I'll be running Worrell's,' Richard said, 'and I've made it quite clear to Bert that if he wants to keep his job then, he'll make sure I'm happy now.'

'*You'll* be running Worrell's?' Michael said, unable to keep the surprise out of his voice.

'You think I couldn't?' his brother challenged.

'I don't know,' Michael confessed, 'but I never thought you'd want to.'

'Because I like having fun too much?'

'Well, yes.'

A cockroach scuttled across the floor. Richard placed his right foot in its path, and when the creature turned, he put his left foot in the way. Confused and trapped, the cockroach cowered in the shadow of a pile of salt blocks.

'There's nothing as much fun as having power,' Richard said. 'Nothing in the world.'

He bent down. The cockroach made a frantic dash for freedom, but he was not quick enough. Richard stubbed out his cigarette on the animal's black shiny back.

When he looked up again, Richard was smiling.

'But power isn't just about using the big stick,' he said. 'Sometimes it's wise to throw in a carrot, too. Bert Mills likes a drink, and I see to it that he gets one.'

'But where did you ...' Michael began.

'Where did I get the money from?' Richard interrupted. 'Remember Father's missing guinea?'

'You stole it!' Michael exclaimed.

'Let's just say I needed it, so I took it,' his brother replied.

'The servants lost their jobs because of you,' Michael said angrily.

'Yes, they did,' Richard agreed. 'And all the new servants know it. That's why they're very careful not to upset me.'

'I'll tell Father,' Michael threatened.

Richard laughed. 'He'd never take your word against mine,'

he said. 'Besides, he couldn't allow himself to believe you, because that would mean admitting he'd made a mistake, and that's not in Father's nature.'

He's right, Michael thought. There's nothing I can do.

The realization of his own helplessness only fuelled his anger, and almost before he knew what he was doing, he threw himself at his brother.

The fight was short-lived. Michael had the fury of righteousness on his side, but Richard had the advantage of two years' extra weight and height. It was not long before Michael was on the ground with Richard sitting on his chest and pinning down the younger boy's arms with his knees.

'I hoped you'd try that,' Richard said. 'I really did.'

Other boys at school had talked about their older brothers bullying them and making their lives a misery, but they had never described anything like the look of utter loathing Michael saw on his brother's face now.

'You hate me, don't you?' he said.

'Oh yes, I hate you, all right!' Richard replied.

'But why?' Michael asked.

'Who knows?' Richard sneered. 'Maybe I hate you because we're so different. Or perhaps it's just because you're so stupid. It doesn't really matter *why*, does it?'

He eased himself off his brother's chest, gave Michael one last kick in the ribs and stormed away.

CHAPTER TWO

It had seemed to Becky as if the start of school was so far in the future it would never come, but the weeks slipped by and almost before she realized it, the big day had arrived.

Mary Taylor got up exceptionally early that morning and fussed over her daughter as if Becky were the first child she'd sent off to school, instead of the sixth.

'These clothes are new,' she said as she helped Becky into her long brown dress with its white lace collar. 'And there's not many little girls just starting school who can say that. So no fighting and no rough games. Do you understand?'

'Yes, Mam,' Becky said.

'And don't go fiddling with your hair once you're in school,' Mary said as she pulled her daughter's tresses into a tight plait at the back. 'Because if it comes undone, there'll be no Mam there to tie it up for you again.'

'No, Mam.'

Mary Taylor shook her head disbelievingly.

'Yes, Mam. No Mam,' she snorted. 'You'll say anything as long as it'll shut me up, won't you?'

'Yes, Mam,' Becky replied, grinning.

Mary looked across at her middle son, who was relishing the last few crumbs of bread and marg which still stuck to his fingers.

'I'm putting you in charge of our Becky, George,' she said.

'Me, Mam?'

'No, not you,' Mary told him. 'It's the other George I'm talking to.'

The boy looked hopefully around the kitchen for a second George, and failing to find one realized the awful task was to fall on him.

'But Mam ...' he protested.

'But Mam what?' Mary demanded.

'Well ...' George said uncomfortably. 'I mean ... the other lads will laugh at me, won't they?'

'And what if they do? That's their ignorance, not yours.'

'I know,' George said helplessly. 'But ... but ...'

Mary placed her hands squarely on her hips.

'Look,' she said reasonably, 'I can't ask our Philip to do it, can I?'

'Why not?' George asked.

'Because he's not much more than one of the infants himself. But look at you.'

'What about me, Mam?'

'Well, you're in Standard Four, aren't you? You may not be a man yet, but you're not far from it.'

George's thin chest puffed out with pride.

'Would it be all right if our Becky walked a couple of steps in front of me?' he asked tentatively.

'That would be fine,' his mother replied in the spirit of compromise. 'But mind you watch her right to the infants' gate. And make sure you're waiting for her when she comes out again for her dinner.'

'I will, Mam,' George promised.

'You'd better,' Mary threatened. 'Because if you lose her, you'll have me to answer to. And you wouldn't want that, would you?'

'No, Mam,' George said, sounding as if he meant it.

Becky had always had her doubts about school. Who, after all, would willingly swap happy days around the washtub with Mam for hours spent imprisoned in a grim building with high walls? And would the teacher throw sticky sweets to her as the train's fireman did? She very much doubted it!

But as she trudged up the humpbacked bridge past Worrell's Salt Works her doubts were beginning to multiply. There was this matter of having to dress up for a start. It wasn't just her frock – her boots were new as well, and squeaked with every step.

And why wear boots at all? she wondered.

It made sense to wear them in the winter, when the frost nipped at bare toes. But why should the silly people at the school insist she put them on in September, with the summer hardly over?

What was the point of going to school, anyway? Dad had hardly been at all, yet he managed all right. He could read his Sunday paper. He could add up his wages. What more did he need?

'Watch out, you silly little bugger!' a voice called out.

Becky looked up. She had been so absorbed in her own thoughts that she hadn't noticed she'd drawn level with the salt store, nor that a gang of men had emerged from the works, pushing a heavy handcart.

Becky stopped, and her boots squeaked again. She watched the men strain against the cart. One of them didn't look much older than George.

She let her gaze wander to the other side of the road and saw another boy, obviously the brother of the first, leaning against the doorway and laughing to himself. On impulse she crossed the road to the smirking lad.

'Did you have to go to school when you were little?' she asked.

It seemed as though the boy was going to tell her to get lost at first, then, as she got closer, he began to look interested in her.

'You're a pretty little girl, aren't you?' he asked. 'What's your name?'

'Becky Taylor,' Becky told him. 'Did you have to go to school?'

'I still do,' the boy said with a laugh. 'But mine doesn't start again until next week.'

That seemed like a good idea.

'Can I be your friend?' Becky asked.

'Why should you want to be my friend?'

'So I can go to your school instead of mine.'

The boy laughed again.

'My school isn't for girls,' he said. 'But I'll tell you what. Come and see me in a few years' time, and then we really can be friends.'

Maybe it was the look in his eye, perhaps the gentle, caressing tone of his voice, but whatever the reason, the idea of being his friend delighted Becky.

'When can we be friends?' she asked, trying to pin him down.

'When you're old enough to play big girls' games,' the boy said.

Becky didn't understand him, though from the way his lip was curling, it was obvious that he'd said something very funny. She was just about to ask him to explain when the handcart came trundling back and her attention was caught by his brother, who was pushing on the side closest to her.

The pushing boy smiled at her. He had a nice face, she thought. Not perhaps as handsome as his brother's, but nice ... kind.

'Come on, our Becky!' George called out from across the road. 'If we're late, Mr Hicks won't half give us a leathering!'

So you got leatherings at school, too! Becky was looking forward to it less and less.

'I've got to go,' she said to the boy still leaning in the doorway.

'Remember what I said,' he told her. 'In a few years' time we'll play some really interesting games.'

Mr Hicks had a bristling moustache and wore a black frock-coat. He stood at the front of the hall like the Wrath of God, and addressed the new infants – in a booming voice – on their Christian duty. He seemed to Becky to be the most terrifying man in the whole world, and it was something of a relief when, his harangue being over, the infants were led away by a little, white-haired old lady called Miss Stebbings.

Out of the frying pan into the fire! Miss Stebbings might have looked like everybody's grandmother, but no grandmother ever born could have cracked a ruler across an offending scholar's knuckles with such ruthless accuracy as she could.

'And which of you is Colleen O'Leary?' she asked.

The girl who had been seated next to Becky put her hand up.

'Me, Miss,' she said.

Becky had seen the girl before – she was the daughter of Mr O'Leary from the New Inn – but they had never spoken.

She was a funny-looking girl, Becky thought. Her nose was so big, and her mouth so wide, that there seemed to be very little room in her face for anything else.

'When we have prayers, O'Leary,' Miss Stebbings said, 'or when the Vicar comes to tell us about Gentle Jesus, you are to get up quietly and go into the playground. But you must not play once you are outside. You must stand perfectly still and look at the ground. Do you understand?'

'Yes, Miss,' said Colleen, obviously intimidated both by her teacher and the fact that the eyes of all the other children were on her.

Becky longed to ask Colleen why she couldn't hear about Gentle Jesus, but the thought of Miss Stebbings' ruler coming down on her knuckles was quite enough to restrain her natural curiosity.

'Monitors!' Miss Stebbings called out.

'Yes, Miss,' replied two big girls only recently out of Standard Four, who – for the princely sum of one shilling and sixpence per week – were now employed to teach the 'babies' to repeat parrot fashion the lessons *they'd* learned to repeat themselves only a few years earlier.

'I shall instruct the older children for writing,' Miss Stebbings said grandly. 'You take the new children over into that corner and start teaching them the alphabet.'

'Yes, Miss,' said the monitors – and curtsied.

The monitors herded the babies away from the more advanced scholars.

'Why do you have to go out when we say prayers?' Becky whispered to Colleen O'Leary.

'We're Catholics,' Colleen replied, 'but my mam thinks I'm too little to go all the way to our school in town.'

'No talking!' snapped Miss Stebbings, who seemed to have eyes in the back of her head and ears as sharp as a hunting dog's.

After what seemed like an eternity of 'A is for apple, B is for ball', playtime finally came around. The infants trooped out like well-disciplined soldiers, but once in the playground they went wild, releasing hours of pent-up energy in an orgy of running and shouting.

Becky looked around her. The playground was bounded by tall, intimidating fences. From beyond one came the shrieks of the older girls. Over the other drifted the shouts of the bigger boys. Even though she was surrounded by the other infants Becky suddenly felt lonely.

George and Philip were just the other side of the fence, she thought. If she could manage to climb over she could go and play with them. Then she remembered how unwilling George had been to even be seen walking with her, and realized there were different rules at school to the ones which worked at home.

'Papist, Papist, Big-nose Papist!'

Becky turned round to see what all the excitement was about. A group of bigger infants had formed a ring and were dancing round Colleen O'Leary.

Poor Colleen, Becky thought. She looked as if she was about to burst into tears. It was true she did have a big nose, but it was cruel of them to mention it.

'Papist, Papist, Big-nose Papist!' the children chanted again.

'Stop it!' Becky shouted furiously.

They did – and wheeled round on her.

'What's up with you?' asked a big lad called Toby Hitchens. 'Are you a Papist an' all?'

'Yes!' Becky said defiantly.

'Then we'll get round to you when we've finished with her,' Toby threatened.

'Leave her alone now,' Becky told him.

'Or what?' Toby demanded. 'Do you want a fight?'

In her new dress a fight was the last thing Becky wanted, but despite herself she felt her face turning red and her fists beginning to clench.

'Go on – hit her!' another boy called out.

But looking down on Becky's mounting anger, Toby Hitchens seemed to be regretting his bravado.

'I . . . I don't hit girls,' he stuttered.

'Course you do,' his friend said. 'You hit Maisie Price the other day, didn't you?'

Toby glanced once more at Becky's fists.

'Well, I don't hit girls any more,' he said.

Toby Hitchens slunk away and the others followed him, leaving Becky and Colleen alone. Becky put her hand on the other girl's shoulder.

'Don't cry,' she said.

'I'm not,' Colleen replied unconvincingly.

'Let's be friends,' Becky suggested. 'Would you like that?'

Colleen nodded her head mutely, and the matter was settled.

'So how do you like school, our Becky?' Ted Taylor asked his younger daughter as the family sat around the supper table at the end of her first week.

'It's all right,' Becky said noncommittally.

She looked across the table at her three brothers. There was Jack, fourteen years old, with his curly hair and gypsy eyes. Next to him sat George, just past his tenth birthday, blunt-nosed, square-chinned and already starting to take on the shape of a chunky grown-up. And finally there was Philip, seven years old and as pale and delicate as a girl. They all seemed to have survived two years in Miss Stebbings' class without suffering any real damage – so maybe she would, too.

'I'm speaking to you, Becky,' Ted Taylor said, a little sharply.

'Sorry, Dad. I didn't hear you,' Becky confessed.

'I said, enjoy your schooldays while you can,' her father advised her. 'They're the best days of your life.'

'They weren't the best years of my life,' said Jack. 'The best years of my life have been since I became a flatman.'

'You always were a contradictory young bugger,' Ted Taylor said. 'And you're not a flatman yet, either. You're nowt but a lad, still wet behind the ears, who just might become a flatman *one* day.'

The words might have sounded harsh, but there was no rancour behind them. Now Jack was working on the steam packets, he was entitled to a little more latitude at the table than the other children – and both father and son knew it.

'What do you like best about the job, Jack?' Mary Taylor asked.

'Visiting Liverpool,' her son said without hesitation. He turned to his father. 'You should come down the river with us one day, and see it for yourself, Dad.'

'Oh, I should, should I?' Taylor replied. 'And why's that?'

'It's a real eye-opener,' Jack enthused. 'You think there's some big buildings in Northwich, but they're nothing to what they've got in Liverpool.'

'What would you say is the tallest building in Northwich?' Taylor asked mildly.

Jack thought about it. 'The Sportsman's Hotel,' he said finally.

'Aye, I think you're right,' his father agreed. 'Well, that's big enough for me.'

'It's not just the buildings, Dad,' Jack said exasperatedly. 'They've got parks ...'

'Parks,' Taylor interrupted. 'Yes, I believe I know what they are. I even think we've got one, right here in little Northwich. Verdin Park it's called – at the bottom of Castle Hill. You might have seen it yourself.'

'And they've got trams!' Jack said triumphantly, as if he'd come up with a clincher.

'Trams,' Taylor said, savouring the word. 'And what are they when they're at home?'

'They're like long thin coaches that go up and down the street,' Jack explained. 'They're pulled by horses, but they run on rails just like trains.'

'And what do they carry?' Taylor asked.

46

'People, Dad,' his son told him.

Taylor shrugged.

'What do they want to ride in these trams for?' he asked. 'Don't they have legs in Liverpool?'

'You don't understand, Dad,' Jack said helplessly. 'You'll never understand until you've seen it for yourself.'

'Then I'll never understand,' Taylor said simply, 'because I've never been further than Northwich in me life, and I can see no reason to start gadding about now.'

'I'm going to travel when I'm grown up,' George announced. 'I'm going to join the army and serve in foreign parts – Africa and India and places like that.'

'Are you indeed?' Taylor mused. 'And what about you, Philip? Have you got big plans, an' all?'

Philip shrugged as his father had done.

Becky looked fondly at her youngest brother. Though he was two years older than her, she couldn't help feeling responsible for him, as if he were the baby of the family. And it would *always* be like that, she just knew it would.

'Well?' Ted Taylor said. 'Do you have any plans – or what, Philip?'

'I don't know what I want to be,' Philip confessed, 'but whatever it is, I want to make a lot of money out of it.'

'Make a lot of money!' Ted Taylor said in mock disgust. 'You'll never make much money – none of us will. The best we can ever hope for is to keep our families decently clothed and fed.'

'Let him have his dreams while he can,' Mary said quietly. 'God knows, he'll find out the truth soon enough.'

Right on Becky and Colleen's doorsteps was Worrell's Salt Works – a natural playground.

The hot house and the storeroom, for example, were perfect places for hide and seek. Becky and her big-nosed friend would spend hours there, occasionally hiding from each other but more often pitting their wits against the eagle-eyed checking clerks and gang bosses.

The salt store across the bridge from the main works was another of their favourite haunts. It had obviously been built largely for the pleasure of little girls – why else would there have been a gap between the wall and the main gate which was just wide enough for them to squeeze through?

Once inside the store they were confronted by a mountain of shiny, scratchy salt, which could be anything they wanted it to be. Sometimes it was sand, and they made quickly-collapsing tunnels through it with their tiny, earnest hands. Sometimes it was snow, and they rolled around with abandon, or else pelted each other with it until they resembled Lot's wife who, the Vicar had told Becky – though not the Papist Colleen – had been turned into a pillar of salt for looking back.

Becky often caught *herself* looking back – to her first day at the National School. She remembered the two boys – the one pushing the handcart, the other standing there and laughing at him – and every time she and Colleen played around the salt works she half hoped that she would see them again. But she never did.

'I know where you've been,' Mary Taylor would say as she combed salt out of her daughter's hair. 'You'll be getting into real trouble one of these days, and it'll be no good crying for your mother when the bobbies have got you locked in them cells.'

Yet Becky could tell from her mother's tone that Mary didn't really mind – that the salt store was not one of those dangerous areas little girls could only go to secretly.

Jutting out from the side of Worrell's which faced the canal was a wooden platform, and it was from here that the workers tipped the salt into the narrow boats waiting below. These boats fascinated Becky from the first time she saw them. They were great long things – seventy feet from bow to stern – yet narrow enough to negotiate their way through even the tightest canal lock.

The outsides of the narrow-boat cabins were decorated almost like gypsy caravans, with paintings of castles and flowers. Inside, the wooden furniture and the pots and pans carried the same motif. And tiny as those cabins were – never more than ten feet long – whole families seemed to live quite happily in them.

The boat people were even more exotic than their floating homes. It was almost as if they had studied the way the people on the land behaved, and then decided to do exactly the opposite. Landlubbers fed their horses from nose-bags – very well then, they would feed their horses from a metal bowl suspended from the animal's harness. Landlubbers never decorated their mops and brushes, so the boat people painted the wooden shafts in red, yellow, green and white stripes.

Even in their dress they stood apart. On land the gentry set the fashions and the common people aped them as best they could. On the water there was no fashion at all, only a sort of uniform which had not changed in living memory. All the men wore voluminous shirts – each one made out of at least four yards of cloth and a yard of calico lining. Their trousers were always of pale corduroy and held up by fancy braces with needleworked spider's web designs on them. The women, for their part, wore flowery dresses and bonnets which, like their husbands' shirts, involved yards of material.

But as far as Becky was concerned the best thing of all about the narrow boats was the horses. They were wonderful animals which towered over even the tallest man. Towing a boat weighed down in the water by tons of salt was nothing to them.

'Is this all you can find to tax me with?' their powerful shoulders seemed to say as they began their journey up the canal towards the Mersey. 'I could have handled a load twice this size.'

Becky's favourite was a dappled carthorse called Hereward. She loved the way his ears twitched, loved the way he snorted when he saw her coming. She admired the well-polished brasses which hung from his harness. She complimented him on the brightly-painted wooden bobbins through which his trace ropes were threaded. And she did her best not to laugh at the crocheted ear-cap which he wore to keep the flies away.

It was through the horse that Becky and Colleen got to know the owners, Mr and Mrs Hulse. Mr Hulse was a tall, thin man with leathery skin which was as brown as a berry. Mrs Hulse was a short, fat, jolly person. They had no children, but there was a third member of the family — a scruffy spaniel called Jip.

'He may not be much to look at, but he's right clever, is that dog,' Mr Hulse told the girls.

Colleen giggled. 'Clever?' she said. 'Can he do sums and joined-up writing like us?'

'No,' Mr Hulse admitted, pretending to be offended. 'But I bet there's things that dog can do that you never could — not if you lived to be a hundred and one.'

'Like what?' Becky challenged.

'Oh, I can't tell you,' Mr Hulse said mysteriously. 'You'll have to find out for yourself. If you were to travel up the canal with us for a bit, you'd soon see what I mean. Would you like to do that?'

'We'd love to,' Becky said without a second thought.

The promised excursion took place the following Saturday. Becky was certain that her mother wouldn't mind her travelling a short way on *The Jupiter* — which was what the Hulses called their boat — but just to make *absolutely* sure, she neglected to mention exactly where she was going when she set off that morning.

Mrs and Mrs Hulse were waiting for the two girls under Marston Bridge. Hereward was already in harness and Jip, showing absolutely no signs of intelligence, was asleep on the cabin roof.

'Well now you're here, we'll get started,' Mrs Hulse said. 'We've a long way to go today.'

She stepped from the bank to the cockpit, then disappeared into the cabin.

'Making a brew,' Mr Hulse explained. 'We always have a cup of tea just after we set off.'

He stepped into the cockpit and took the tiller. The two girls followed him.

Mrs Hulse had said they were eager to get started, yet her husband, taking out his pipe and lighting it, did not seem to feel any particular hurry. A minute ticked by, then another. Becky and Colleen, who had been looking forward to the trip all week, were almost bursting with impatience.

'Something wrong, Wally?' Mrs Hulse called from inside the cabin.

'T'horse won't go,' Mr Hulse said calmly.

'Why not?' his wife asked.

'Nobody's told him to,' Mr Hulse replied.

And suddenly, Becky got the hint.

'Gee up, Hereward!' she shouted, and the great carthorse tensed his powerful muscles and moved off.

*

It was wonderful travelling by narrow boat, Becky thought. It skimmed its way over the water as if it were floating on air. And the old familiar buildings — the salt works, the pub, the houses — all looked completely different when seen from the water. It was nice, too, to watch Hereward as he plodded calmly along the tow path.

Only Jip was a disappointment. Instead of showing how clever he was, as Mr Hulse had promised, he just lay on the cabin roof, almost asleep.

They were about half a mile outside Marston when Mr Hulse disappeared into the boat's tiny cabin, and when he emerged again he was carrying a shotgun. At the sight of the weapon Jip suddenly came alive, his ears pricking up, his nose pointed firmly at the canal bank.

'Don't shoot him,' Becky said in a panic. 'Please!'

'You what?' Mr Hulse said.

'Just because he's not been clever, don't shoot him,' Becky begged.

Mr Hulse laughed.

'It's not *him* I'm planning to shoot,' he told her. He pointed to a field on the far bank. 'Look over there.'

Becky looked. A sea of long grass was swaying gently in

the breeze, the odd cuckoo spit stretched upwards towards the sun, a hawk hovered overhead.

'What am I looking *for*?' she asked.

'There! See him?' Mr Hulse said.

'No, I – Yes! Yes I do.'

A blob of brown fur had broken cover and was running furiously towards its bolt-hole. Suddenly, as if sensing danger, it swerved to the right and plunged back into the grass. Mr Hulse raised his gun to his shoulder and fired.

Even before the narrow-boat man had time to lower his weapon again, Jip dived into the water and was swimming furiously for the bank.

'A good dog,' Mr Hulse said with pride. 'The best I've ever had.'

Jip disappeared in the long grass in search of the rabbit.

'How ever will he find us again?' Becky asked.

'He'll find us, don't you worry,' Mr Hulse said confidently.

The dog was waiting at Burn's Bridge, with the dead rabbit in his mouth. When the boat drew level with him he jumped aboard and dropped his prize at his owner's feet.

'He really *is* clever,' Becky said, full of admiration.

'Huh, any boat dog can do that,' Mr Hulse replied dismissively. 'Wait till you've seen his real party piece.' He pointed towards a clump of trees they were just passing. 'Fetch, Jip,' he said, and the dog leapt onto the bank once more.

'But you haven't shot anything else,' Becky protested.

'There's more ways of catching food than shooting it,' Mr Hulse said with a chuckle. 'He's not after rabbits, this time. He's gone down to Forge Pool.'

When the boat reached Marbury Bridge, Jip was sitting waiting on the tow path. He had something in his mouth, but it didn't have brown fur. Instead, it seemed to be white and shiny.

'Good dog,' Mr Hulse said encouragingly.

The last time Jip had climbed on board he had done so with a triumphant bound, but this time he stepped onto the boat very gingerly indeed.

'Doesn't want to break it, you see,' Mr Hulse explained.

'Doesn't want to break what?' Becky asked.

Mr Hulse said nothing, but instead held his hand out, palm upwards, under the dog's muzzle. Slowly and carefully, Jip opened his jaws and the object he'd been carrying slipped into Mr Hulse's hand.

'And what would you call that?' the boatman asked.

'It's an egg,' Becky said in surprise. 'But it looks very big.'

'That's because it's a wild duck's egg, not a hen's,' Mr Hulse said. 'Our Jip's been out nesting. And just look at this egg. He must have carried it half a mile in his mouth, and there's not a single crack in it. Now could *you* have done that, even if your mouth was big enough?'

'No,' Becky admitted. 'I don't think I could have.'

'Rabbit pie and fried duck egg,' Mr Hulse said, licking his lips. 'By, but it's a grand life sometimes.'

'I think it's time we were going home,' Becky said reluctantly, noticing that they were already well past Marbury Bridge.

'Yes, it probably is,' Mr Hulse agreed. 'We don't want your mothers accusing us of kidnapping you, now do we?'

'No,' Becky laughed, thinking it would be a brave man indeed who would risk a kidnapping with a mother like hers to answer to.

The boatman steered the narrow craft close in to the bank and the two girls jumped off onto the tow path.

'Thank you, Mr Hulse,' they chanted in unison.

'My pleasure,' the boatman said. 'You're welcome aboard *The Jupiter* any time.'

The girls did not go straight home, but stood on the tow path and watched the boat until it was out of sight.

''Bye Jip, 'bye Hereward, 'bye Mr and Mrs Hulse,' Becky said when *The Jupiter* was no more than a speck in the distance.

She sighed happily. Mr Hulse was right, she thought – life *was* grand sometimes.

CHAPTER THREE

Gilbert Bowyer was a man of mystery from the start – the start being defined, as far as Marston was concerned, as the moment when the Warrington mail coach had deposited him outside the New Inn one summer afternoon.

He hadn't arrived empty-handed. As he looked up and down the village with obvious interest, the coachmen struggled to unload the large trunk he had brought with him.

The mail coach pulled away, leaving Gilbert and the trunk alone in the lane. Well, not quite alone – Not-Stopping Bracegirdle was standing at her front gate and watching him with undisguised interest. Nor did she move when Gilbert strode, with military precision, to a position just a few feet from her.

'Will you be standing there long, Ma'am?' he asked.

As long as it takes to find out a bit more about you, Not-Stopping thought, but aloud she said, 'Why? Who wants to know?'

Gilbert did not seem to take offence.

'I've had a long journey,' he said, 'and I've worked up a bit of a thirst. Would you mind keeping an eye on my trunk while I go for a drink?'

It was too good an opportunity to be missed.

'Yes, I'll keep on eye on it,' Not-Stopping promised, sounding much friendlier now. 'But you needn't worry – this is an honest village and we keep ourselves very much to ourselves.'

'Thank you Ma'am,' Gilbert said, 'Much appreciated.'

He tipped his hat to her. A gentleman couldn't have done it better, Not-Stopping thought grudgingly.

'So where *have* you come from?' she asked hastily as he began to walk away.

Gilbert turned and smiled at her.

'Today?' he asked. 'From Crewe.'

'No, that's not what I mea . . .' Not-Stopping began.

But Gilbert was already marching back up the lane.

Once Gilbert was safely inside the pub, Not-Stopping grabbed her chance to have a closer look at his trunk. It was a battered old thing, but though the leather was now cracked and the brass fasteners badly scratched, she could see that it must have been expensive when new. It was covered with stickers, too, most of them partly rubbed away by friction, but she could make out the words Bombay and Delhi.

What's a man whose been to India come to Marston for? she wondered.

She lightly touched one of the brass locks – just to make sure it wasn't going to suddenly jump out and spill the trunk's contents all over the lane – and found that it appeared to be securely fastened. Disappointed, though not without hope of learning more later, she made her way back to her own front gate.

The stranger was a man of medium height, Paddy O'Leary noticed as he served him his pint. His hair was white and he had pale blue eyes. A jagged scar ran diagonally across his left cheek. O'Leary thought of him as old, and soon everyone would be calling him Old Gilbert, but in truth he could have been anything from a wrecked fifty to a well-preserved seventy.

'Nice village you have here, landlord,' Old Gilbert said as he picked up his glass. 'Quiet. Out of the way.'

'Kind of you to say so, sir,' Paddy O'Leary replied, though privately he wondered how anyone could find a place so full of smoking chimneys anything even approaching 'nice'.

'I'm looking for some simple, clean digs in this area,' Gilbert continued. 'Could you recommend any?'

'You've got me there, sir,' Paddy confessed. 'Everybody who lives in the village was either born here or married into a

Marston family. There's never been no need of what you might call lodging houses.'

'It doesn't have to be a lodging house,' Old Gilbert told him. 'A room in an ordinary house would serve me just as well.'

'You could try Ma Fitton,' Cedric Rathbone suggested. 'She might appreciate the company and a bit of extra money.'

'She might at that,' Paddy O'Leary agreed.

From her gate Not-Stopping Bracegirdle watched Old Gilbert walk down the lane and knock on Ma Fitton's door. He did not emerge again for half an hour.

'I didn't know you knew Nellie Fitton,' she said to him on his journey back to the New Inn.

'How could you, when I'd never mentioned it to you?' Old Gilbert asked mildly.

She was still glued to her post ten minutes later when two wallers from Worrell's went past her struggling under the weight of Old Gilbert's trunk.

'He's never moving in with Nellie, is he?' she asked.

'He'd better be,' one of the wallers grunted, ''cos for threepence, Ma's is just about as far as I'm willing to heft this bloody thing.'

Well if he was planning to stay, Not-Stopping thought, he wouldn't be a mystery much longer. By the end of the week she'd know all there was to know about him.

Not for the first time, Not-Stopping was wrong. The week turned into a month, the month into a year, the year into two. And still Old Gilbert remained something of an enigma.

'We don't even know where he comes from,' she complained to her cronies at the New Inn. 'But he has to come from *somewhere*. I mean, everybody does.'

'He doesn't sound local,' Dottie Curzon chipped in unhelpfully.

'Well, he might be a stranger to these parts, but he's no stranger to Nellie Fitton's bed, if you ask me,' Not-Stopping proclaimed, her natural venom reinforced by a frustrated curiosity and three bottles of milk stout.

It was not one of her more successful rumours. Old Gilbert and the Midwife-to-Royalty always looked extremely comfortable in each other's company, but no one seeing them together could ever seriously believe that the flame of passion burned between them.

'He claims he's nothing but an old soldier, living on a pension,' Not-Stopping mused.

'Well, maybe he is,' Maggie Cross pointed out. 'He does walk like a soldier – and every week, regular as clockwork, he's down at the post office to collect his envelope. And what's in that envelope, if it isn't money?'

'But what made him decide to settle down in a village where he didn't know nobody?' Not-Stopping wondered aloud. 'What the devil is he hiding from?'

Becky Taylor reacted to her discovery of Gilbert in much the same way as Columbus must have reacted to the discovery of America. Right there, where she'd least expected it, was something strange and wonderful – an old man who knew so much and, more importantly, was prepared to tell a curious little girl all about it.

Gilbert had been everywhere and seen everything. Sitting on his camp stool at the end of Ma Fitton's alley, he would describe to Becky the busy streets of London, or explain to her how sailors navigated at sea. And Becky would soak it all in as a sponge absorbs water.

It was not until she took her brother George to meet him, however, that the subject of Old Gilbert's military career came up.

'I'm going to be a soldier when I grow up,' George announced proudly.

'And why should you want to go and do that?' Old Gilbert asked.

'It's dead exciting,' George explained. 'Have you ever read *The Life of a Soldier*?'

'No,' Old Gilbert admitted. 'I can't say I have.'

'It's all about this soldier called Edred. He travelled all over the world, having adventures. He fought this tribe of infidels and ...' George closed his eyes so he could remember the words exactly, '... *vanquished their leader hand to hand, no common feat o'er one of Eastern Land.*'

'I was a soldier myself,' Gilbert said quietly.

'Were you?' asked George, looking at the old man with new respect.

'Aye, I was,' Gilbert replied. 'I didn't know any better than to join up. I was nothing but a bit of a lad when the recruiting sergeant came to my village and ...'

'Where was it?' Becky asked.

'Where was what?'

'Your village.'

'A long way from here,' Old Gilbert told her evasively. 'A long long way.'

'Stop interrupting, Becky,' George urged. 'I want to hear about the recruiting sergeant. Go on, Mr Bowyer.'

'He was a fine figure of a man,' Old Gilbert continued. 'Well over six feet tall and dressed in a splendid scarlet uniform. He took all us village lads to the pub and bought us drinks. In those days, on a farm labourer's pay, we couldn't afford more than half a pint a night – and we used to have to spin it out. Now there we were, knocking back as much beer as we could drink, and all at the army's expense.'

'But why did the army ...?' Becky began.

'Shut up,' George said, pinching her – though not hard. 'He's coming to that.'

'The drink went straight to our heads,' Old Gilbert said, 'but not as much as his fine talk did. We'd have a grand life in the army, he promised us. Live like kings, we would. Live like convicts more like – and that was nothing fresh to half the men I served with.'

'Convicts!' George said incredulously. 'The men you served with can't have been convicts!'

'Oh yes, they were,' Old Gilbert said firmly. 'Convicts and

the Irish poor. I'm not saying we couldn't be brave when we had our backs against the wall, but there's no doubt about it – we were the scum of the earth. Well, who else'd join up for a shilling a day? And we didn't even get to keep all of that! Half our money went on extra rations – we'd never have survived without them.'

'But ...' George said feebly.

'In some ways we were *worse* off than convicts,' Old Gilbert told him. 'Prisoners have a lot more space in them little cells of theirs than we ever had in barracks. A flogging in gaol was nothing like as vicious as a flogging in the army. And to top it all, convicts only had the prison wardens to put up with – we had our bloody officers, which was a lot harder work.'

'Were they the scum of the earth too?' George asked despondently.

Old Gilbert laughed. 'No, quite the opposite,' he said. 'They were proper gentlemen, they were. Why, until old Gladstone put a stop to it in seventy-two, they used to have to buy their commissions.'

'Buy their commissions,' Becky said, enunciating the words slowly and carefully. 'What does that mean?'

'It means that if you wanted to be an officer, you didn't need any training or anything like that. All you needed was the money to buy your way in. So you could imagine what kind of officers we got.'

'Did they earn a shilling a day, too?' George asked.

Old Gilbert laughed again. 'They got a lot more than that,' he said. 'But they couldn't live on their pay any more than we could. They had more expenses, you see. Dinner parties to give, polo ponies to look after – that sort of thing.'

Becky wondered exactly what a polo pony was, but she didn't want to raise her brother's ire by interrupting again.

'They all had private incomes, you understand,' Old Gilbert continued. 'Soldiering wasn't a job to them, it was more like a pleasant way of filling their time. Until the Crimean War, that is.'

'What was that like?' George asked.

'It was sheer hell,' Old Gilbert said simply. 'We lost more men through disease and the stupidity of our officers than we ever did from the Russkies' bullets.'

George frowned. This wasn't the least like the story of Edred in *The Life of a Soldier*.

'Did you ever serve in India?' he asked hopefully.

The old soldier's eyes suddenly lit up.

'India was different,' he told them. 'I'm not saying it was easy, mind — it could get as hot as hell in the summer, and I've never seen so many flies in my life — but at least out there we could afford to buy some decent grub. We had servants, too — yes, even us common troopers. Punkah-wallahs to fan us, bhisti-wallahs to fetch our water, boys to do the cooking, boys to clean our boots and buttons.'

'Tell us some more,' George said eagerly.

'Then there were the bazaars,' Old Gilbert continued.

'What were they?'

'They were markets, I suppose, but they weren't like any markets you're likely to have seen,' Old Gilbert replied. 'They had miles and miles of little twisted streets. If you weren't careful you could get lost and never find your way out without the help of a nigger. All sorts of people used to go to them bazaars — rich and poor alike — all rushing about, shouting at the tops of their voices and looking for bargains. And the smells! Woodsmoke, exotic spices, cooking meat — all mixing together in one wonderful perfume.'

'It sounds great,' George murmured.

'And then there were the hill stations,' Old Gilbert continued. 'To go up to one of them after the heat and dust of the plains was like arriving in Paradise. It was cool up there. And green. There were flowers all over the place. It was just like being in England, except I've never seen anywhere as pretty in this country as them hill stations were.' A troubled look suddenly crossed his face. 'Yes, I loved India,' he continued, 'but it was my downfall in the end.'

'Downfall?' George said.

'Samuel Quickly,' Old Gilbert said, though it was obvious

that he was no longer talking to the children but to some distant figure from his past. 'Captain Samuel Quickly. He's the one who's responsible. He's the one who did it to me.'

The old man's expression had become a mask of anger and hatred. His hands clenched as if he could see Captain Quickly standing before him at that very moment – and as if he wanted to strangle the man.

'Mr Bowyer ...' Becky said worriedly.

Her words seemed to burst the bubble of Old Gilbert's sudden dark mood, and slowly the frightening look drained from his face.

'Are you all right, Mr Bowyer?' Becky asked.

The pale eyes which were looking at her now were as mild and unassuming as they'd been before the memory of Samuel Quickly had come back to haunt the old man.

'Well, what's past is past,' Gilbert said philosophically, 'and there's nothing we can do about it now.'

He reached into his waistcoat pocket, and held out his hand so the two children could see what he'd extracted.

'What are they?' Becky asked.

'Indian silver rupees,' Old Gilbert replied. 'Two of them – one for each of you.'

'Oh we couldn't take them, Mr Bowyer,' Becky said, although she desperately wanted to.

'Go on,' Old Gilbert urged. 'They used to be my good-luck charms, but they've not done much for me. Maybe they'll bring you better fortune.'

Becky took her coin and George did the same.

'I'll always carry it with me,' Becky promised, as she slid the coin down the side of her boot.

'You do that,' Old Gilbert said. 'And you' – speaking to George – 'mind what I said about keeping away from the army.'

'Just think about it,' George said to Becky as they walked back up the lane. 'Hill stations and bazaars. Doesn't it sound wonderful?'

*

Despite George's burning ambition to join the army it was his older brother Jack who was the first to announce his intention of leaving home.

'I want to be a sailor,' he told the family over supper, one evening shortly after Becky's seventh birthday.

'But you already are a sailor,' his mother protested.

'No, I'm not,' Jack said, shaking his head. 'I'm nothing but a flatman. Where's the excitement in taking a steam packet from Winsford to Liverpool and back again for the rest of my life?'

'You liked the job well enough at the start,' his father said grumpily. 'You thought yourself lucky to get it at the time – and so you were. So what's happened to change your mind now?'

'Liverpool, Dad,' Jack said. 'It's Liverpool that's opened me eyes. We chug into the dock on the steamer and there they are – the tall ships. You should see them yourself. All them masts. All them miles of canvas. Marvellous, they are. Majestic. And I want to work on one of them. I want to be a *proper* sailor.'

'Well you can't,' Ted Taylor said firmly. 'At least, not until you've finished your apprenticeship.'

'But that's too long to wait,' Jack said anguishedly. 'Far too long.'

'You've no choice in the matter,' his father told him. 'You signed your indenture papers and so did I. Seven years you promised you'd give them, and seven years it'll be.'

'Just be patient,' said Mary Taylor, the perpetual peace-maker. 'The ships'll still be there when you come out of your time.'

'That's just it – they won't,' Jack replied. 'Twenty years since, it was all sail, but the steamers have started taking over. It's steamers all the way to India and China now. They've not put them on the grain runs to Australia and San Francisco yet – but they will – and I want my chance to travel under canvas before it's too late.'

'We can't always do what we want,' Ted Taylor said with mounting irritation. 'Do you really think I'd work down the mine if I didn't have to?'

'But you've got a wife and kids, Dad,' Jack pointed out. 'Obligations. I haven't. There's nothing to hold me here.'

'I will not be argued with at my own table,' snapped Ted Taylor, banging his knife down angrily. 'Especially by a slip of lad. When you're twenty-one you can do as you please, but until then you'll do as *I* say. I've told you you're not going, and that's it.'

Becky risked a quick glance around the table. All her brothers were studying their plates, and even Mary was directing her gaze at anything but her husband.

'Am I getting through to you, lad?' Ted Taylor demanded.

'Yes, Dad,' Jack muttered.

'Look at me when I'm talking to you,' Taylor said.

Jack raised his his head. 'Sorry, Dad.'

'Your father's only thinking of what's best for you,' Mary Taylor told her eldest son.

'I know that, Mam,' Jack replied.

'So we'll hear no more about it, will we?' Taylor asked, his voice softening a little now.

'No,' Jack said. 'We'll hear no more about it.'

The tension around the table was broken. Mary smiled and both George and Philip breathed a sigh of relief.

'Well, maybe now that's settled we can all get on with our food,' Ted Taylor said.

But Becky wasn't sure it *was* settled. There had been a moment, just before Jack had looked directly at his father, when she had seen a wild glint in his gypsy eyes – and that glint had told her that Jack was a long way from giving up the idea of sailing under canvas.

It was still dark when Becky heard the bedroom door click softly open and felt a pair of lips being gently pressed to her forehead.

Becky forced her eyes open. She could just make out the dark shape standing over her.

'Wha . . .' she mumbled, still half asleep.

'Shush,' Jack whispered. 'I just came to say goodbye.'

'Goodbye?'

'I'm running away to sea.'

Suddenly Becky was wide away and sitting bolt upright.

'You can't run away,' she protested. 'Dad'll kill you when he finds out.'

'He'll have to catch me first,' Jack replied.

'But I don't *want* you to go,' Becky said, almost crying now.

'And I don't want to leave you,' her brother assured her, 'but if I don't do it now I never will.'

He put his arms round her and hugged her to him.

'Think of it, Becky,' he said. 'The open sea. The kangaroos in Australia. All them cowboys in America. I've got to take me chance while it's there.'

Becky gulped back a sob. If it had been Philip, or even George, she might have tried again to talk him out of it – but once Jack had made up his mind, that was it.

'You will be careful, though, won't you?' she said.

Jack laughed softly. 'I'll be careful, *Mam*,' he said.

Despite herself Becky found that she was laughing too.

'Keep away from fallen women,' she counselled, because although she had no idea what a fallen woman was, she knew they were to be avoided at all costs. 'And look out for the Red Indians.'

'I will,' Jack said. 'Give me your hand. I've got something I want you to have.'

Becky stretched out her arm in the darkness and felt her brother place a cold, round object into her palm.

'What is it?' she asked.

'My watch,' Jack said.

His most precious possession! The watch Dad had given him when he'd started work on the steam packet.

'Keep it,' Becky urged.

'I can't,' Jack said sadly. 'Dad gave it to me because he was proud of me. Well, he won't feel very proud when he finds out what I've done, will he?'

Becky was about to argue, but what would be the point? They both knew their dad.

'If I work very hard at my reading will you promise to write to me?' she asked.

'Course I will,' Jack said. 'Now go back to sleep. And don't tell *anybody* that I came to see you 'cos it'll just land you in trouble.'

He turned and walked to the door. As he closed it behind him Becky thought she heard a low sob — but she couldn't be sure.

Becky slowed counted up to twenty, then climbed out of bed and groped her way to the window. The moon was in its first quarter, giving just enough light for her to see Jack as he stepped out into the street.

He was dressed in his Sunday clothes and was carrying his few possessions in a small sack in his left hand. He had always seemed so big and strong to Becky before — but now he looked more like a frightened, helpless child.

Jack walked to the centre of the lane, then turned and looked back at the house. For several minutes he continued to gaze at his old home, as if he were counting every brick.

Don't go! Becky prayed silently. Please don't go.

Almost as if he could hear her Jack looked up at her window and waved. Then he turned on his heel and started to walk down the lane.

For a few seconds Becky fancied she could hear his footsteps, but after that there was only an awful silence. She pressed the watch against her cheek. It was all she had left of her big brother. She wondered if she would ever see dear, wonderful Jack again.

CHAPTER FOUR

At the Adelaide Mine they worked only a half shift on Saturdays, but even once he was on the surface again there was no peace, Ted Taylor thought cheerfully. Look at him now, standing in the wash-house, trying to have a quiet stripped-off wash, while all the time George and Philip were hanging around like two foxhounds which had picked up the scent and couldn't wait to be off.

'Hurry up, Dad,' George urged.

'I'm being as quick as I can,' Taylor told him.

'We'll miss the kick-off if we don't hurry up,' Philip warned.

'You say that every time we go, and we haven't missed one yet,' Taylor replied. 'Anyway, if you don't stop mithering I'll go on me own.'

It wasn't much of a threat, and all three of them knew it. Taylor enjoyed his football, but it wouldn't be the same for him without his cheering sons standing by his side.

'You're getting too soft with them two lads,' Mary Taylor had started warning him lately.

Well, maybe he was, but it was better being a bit lax than going too much the other way. Spare the rod and spoil the child, they said – but if you used the rod too much, you lost the child altogether.

'The Vics are playing Crewe next week,' George said.

Taylor spread the scrubbing brush thick with soap and attacked his armpit.

'Oh aye,' he said cautiously.

'Can we go and see them, Dad?' Philip asked.

'If they're playing in Northwich, we can.'

'They're not,' George said disappointedly.

'Then we'll have to give it a miss, won't we?'

'But Crewe are a smashing team, Dad,' George said. 'We really want to see them.'

'And so you shall,' Taylor promised as he lathered his arms. 'The very next time the Vics play them at home.'

'But that might not be for ages,' George complained with all the impatience of childhood.

'Well you won't make it come any quicker by dwelling on it,' his father pointed out.

'All their best players will have retired or died by the time we get to see them,' George said gloomily.

'I doubt that,' Taylor told. 'They're as strong as horses, are them fellers from Crewe. Comes of working in them railway yards during the week.'

'If we *did* go and see them, we'd have to go by train,' Philip said.

'Well, if we *did* go and see them, we certainly couldn't walk it,' his father conceded.

'You've never been on a train, Dad. You might enjoy it.'

Cunning little bugger, Taylor thought, but aloud he said, 'Trains cost money.'

'Philip and me have been saving up our pocket money,' George said. 'We'll pay our own fares – yours as well, if you like.'

But it was not the cost or even the fear of travelling on one of those furious Puffing Billies which Taylor objected to – it was the fact that at the end of the journey he would get off the train in a different place to the one he'd started out from. He knew Northwich but he didn't know anywhere else, and after working hard all his life and raising six kids, he felt too old to go out breaking new ground.

'Dad ...' George began.

'Enough!' Taylor said, and this time he meant it. 'Go and boil some water for me shave.'

The boys rushed off, glad to do anything which would speed their father up.

It was a busy old life, Taylor reflected once his sons had

gone. Today there was the match and tomorrow the Adelaide Mine Brass Band was giving a concert in the park.

'It's becoming very popular, is that band,' he said aloud.

And not without reason. He'd been playing the trumpet in the band since he was little more than a lad, and he had to admit that he'd never heard them playing better than they were now.

Taylor picked up his bowl, carried it into the back yard and poured the dirty water down the drain.

The football season would be over soon, he thought, then they'd probably be on at him to captain the village cricket team again. Still, he didn't mind really.

He walked over to the rain tub and filled his bowl with fresh water. From the front room he heard tinkling music. Mary – practising on her new piano. And that night, no doubt, she'd have the whole family standing around it and singing songs like 'Home, Sweet Home' and 'Little Brown Jug'.

'Aye, it's a full life,' he told himself again.

From time to time it did cross his mind that all these interests he'd developed might be nothing more than a cover for the fact that he missed his eldest son, but he usually managed to brush the thought aside before it had done much damage. He'd done his best for Jack, and Jack had repaid him by an act of defiance. One day, perhaps, he might find it in his heart to forgive the lad – but that day was still a long way off.

'Have you ever seen a whole building move?' Old Gilbert Bowyer asked, lowering his copy of *The Northwich Guardian* and looking straight at Becky.

'Do you mean, like fall over?' Becky said.

'No,' Gilbert replied, his eyes twinkling. 'I mean like start in one place and end in another.'

Becky looked up and down the lane at the solid rows of terraced houses.

'You're making fun of me,' she said accusingly.

'Now would I do that?' Gilbert asked. 'Buildings *can* move, and according to the paper, one's being moved tomorrow.'

Becky put her hands on her hips in a fair imitation of Not-Stopping Bracegirdle.

'Pull the other leg — it's got bells on,' she said.

Old Gilbert laughed. 'You always were a Doubting Thomas,' he said. 'I'll tell you what. If your mam'll let you come to Northwich with me tomorrow, you can see for yourself.'

It was a sharp autumn morning when Becky and Old Gilbert set out for Northwich.

'Are they really going to move a building?' asked Becky, who still felt sure the whole excursion was an elaborate practical joke.

'They certainly are,' Old Gilbert assured her.

They reached the end of the lane and came to the mail coach road which led to Northwich. It was a raised road with a cinder surface, and as Becky walked along she could feel the cinders crunching under her feet. She looked to her left and saw a dozen salt mines with their winding gear and smoking chimneys. She looked to the right and beyond several more mines she could see Witton Flash, a small lake which was connected to the River Weaver. A steamer had just sailed up the Flash, and was beginning to load up with salt at one of the small docks.

'But why?' Becky asked.

'Why what?' Old Gilbert responded.

'Why are they moving the building?'

'You aren't half one for asking questions,' Old Gilbert told her.

'Mam says I'd mither a nest of rats,' Becky said — perhaps just a little proudly.

'They're moving the building because of the subsidence,' Bowyer said. 'Subsidence is Northwich's curse.'

'What's sub ... subsidence?' Becky asked.

It sounded a very important word — and it obviously was if it made people go to all the trouble of shifting things about.

'Subsidence,' Gilbert explained, 'means the ground giving way.'

'And why should it do that?'

'Look around you,' Gilbert told her.

Becky did, firstly straight ahead to the houses which made up the township of Dunkirk and then back to the smoking chimneys.

'What do you see?' Gilbert asked.

It seemed a silly question to Becky, but then she learned that grown-ups often asked silly questions, and it was wisest — in the long run — just to go along with them.

'I see salt works,' she said.

'And where does the salt come from?'

Another silly question.

'Out of the ground,' Becky said.

'And that must leave a hole, mustn't it?' Gilbert said patiently.

'Yes,' Becky agreed.

'And when the weight on top of the hole gets too much, the ground just gives way. It's happened on this road any number of times. Once, the crack was so big that the Warrington mail coach fell into it.'

Becky glanced down at her feet.

'Could it happen today?' she asked nervously.

Gilbert laughed. 'It's not likely,' he said, 'but it *could* happen any time. The ground's a honeycomb for miles around. But don't worry, Becky, if it *was* about to give way, we'd probably hear a lot of rumbling first.'

Somehow, Gilbert's assurances didn't seem very comforting.

They reached a pub called the Townshend Arms — but known locally as the Witch and Devil — on the outskirts of Dunkirk.

'You just sit there quietly,' Old Gilbert said, pointing to a bench just outside the front door, 'and I'll go and fetch us both a drink.'

Becky climbed onto the bench and thought about the treacherous ground which swallowed whole mail coaches. Nothing felt safe any more. She considered the bench she was sitting on, her feet not quite touching the floor. It seemed solid enough, but what was to stop it — and her — suddenly disappearing down a crack in the earth?

Old Gilbert reappeared with a pint of beer in one hand and a lemonade in the other.

'Do you see them ponds over there?' he asked as Becky sipped at her lemonade.

Becky looked in the direction he was pointing. There were several ponds, the smallest no bigger than a puddle, the largest about a quarter the size of Witton Flash.

'Yes, I see them,' she said.

'They didn't used to be there,' Old Gilbert told her. 'They're old salt mines which have flooded. I shouldn't be surprised if, one day, this whole area isn't under water.'

Becky tried to weigh being buried alive against drowning, and decided that neither prospect appealed to her.

They finished their drinks and set out again along the Dunkirk Road.

'Look at the iron bars fastened to those walls,' Gilbert said as they passed a row of terraced houses. 'They've been put up to hold the houses together, because part of the wall has started to slip.'

'Subsidence again,' Becky said, very proud to have mastered the word.

Becky had imagined the building they'd come to see moved would be a tiny house or perhaps a small shop — but this was immense. It was an inn, and it stood all alone on a patch of waste ground close to the river. It was three stories high — three whole stories! It was painted white, but running across its walls was a cross-hatch of black timbers.

Becky tried to picture a hundred men surrounding it, then all bending down at the same time and heaving the building off the ground. No! It was impossible — even with a thousand men.

'See all that timber?' Old Gilbert asked. 'Well that's what's holding the place up.'

'I don't follow you,' Becky said.

'Most houses have a foundation stone,' Gilbert explained. 'It's a sort of anchor for them, if you like. But quite a lot of buildings in Northwich aren't made like that. They're held together by a frame, a bit like the skeleton that's holding your body together.'

'I still don't see ...' Becky began.

'You will,' Old Gilbert assured her. 'Any minute now.'

A crowd was beginning to gather. There were shopkeepers in the their leather aprons, washerwomen with baskets of clothes under their arms, coachmen in full livery and a number of layabouts passing a single cigarette back and to between them.

'A good turn-out,' Gilbert commented. 'Still, it's not every day you see something like this.'

Four wagons pulled up, each with a number of workers in them. Most of the men seemed quite strong, Becky thought, but looking from them to the building she still couldn't imagine them lifting it.

From the backs of the wagons the workers began to unload big metal blocks with handles attached to them.

'What are they for?' Becky asked.

'I've no idea,' Old Gilbert said maddeningly.

The workmen placed pieces of their equipment all around the base of the hotel and then started to pump the handles up and down as if they were expecting to bring up water.

'See anything happening yet?' Gilbert asked.

'No,' Becky admitted.

'Just keep looking,' Gilbert told her.

For several minutes nothing happened. Becky's eyes began to water and the building she was staring at so intently seemed to be starting to wobble.

No! It really was wobbling! The inn was actually rising – very slowly – into the air.

'That's called jacking it up,' Gilbert said.

Inch by inch, the building rose until it was well over a foot off the ground.

'What they usually do when a place starts sinking is just jack it up and then build a new wall underneath,' Gilbert said. 'They've got so good at it that shops don't even need to be closed while the work's being done on them.'

'Really?' Becky said.

It sounded incredible to her, but after she'd seen an inn lifted off the ground she was prepared to believe anything.

'Really,' Old Gilbert assured her. 'Why, when they raised one of the other pubs a few years back, the customers carried on playing billiards the whole time.'

'So why don't they just build a wall under this one?'

'The ground the inn's on is sinking too fast for the normal methods to work,' Gilbert explained. 'They could build a new wall, but they'd only have to do the same thing again next year, and in the end you'd need to take a ladder with you if you wanted to go for a drink.'

Several new wagons arrived carrying what looked like big tree trunks.

'What are they for?' Becky asked.

'They're the rollers,' Gilbert explained.

'The rollers?'

'For rolling the building. You didn't think they were going to pick it up in their hands, did you?'

'Of course not!' Becky said disdainfully.

The workmen unloaded the heavy trunks and laid some under the hotel, some just in front of it. The drivers, meanwhile, had taken their horses from between the wagon shafts and re-harnessed them to hooks set in the front wall of the building.

Once all the rollers were in position the workmen who'd laid them stood at the sides of the inn with their hands pressed firmly against the walls.

'To steady it when it starts to move,' Gilbert said.

Finally, everything was ready.

'Go!' shouted the man who appeared to be in charge.

The drivers began to urge their horses to move, and slowly but surely the building trundled a few yards forward.

'Stop!' the foreman shouted.

Rollers which had been left behind were collected up and re-laid in front of the building.

'Go!' the foreman shouted.

Now that the hard labour had been done the workmen found that there was no end of volunteers from the crowd willing to help them steady the building, though the volunteers always seemed to melt away once it came time to move the rollers again.

Foot by foot the inn crept forward. By the end of an hour it had reached its new site, a hundred yards from the old one, and looked so much at home there that, even though she'd seen it for herself, Becky found it hard to believe the building had ever been anywhere else.

'Seen enough?' Gilbert asked.

'Yes,' Becky said, nodding happily.

'Right, then we'd better get down to the Bull Ring,' Gilbert told her.

'Why?' Becky wondered

'Because that's where Brooke's Confectioners is,' Gilbert replied. 'And I get really hungry watching other folk work.'

The old soldier splashed out on some cakes stuffed full of *real* cream, and they ate them slowly on the way home. They were wonderful cakes, so fresh and delicious that Becky sometimes forgot to look down at her feet to see if any new cracks had opened on the road to Marston.

That night she dreamed of buildings moving as fast as race horses, of mail coaches being swallowed up and of a huge flood engulfing the whole town. When Mary went in to check on her daughter, she distinctly heard her mumble 'subsidence'.

Now where's our Becky picked that mouthful up from? she wondered.

'We shouldn't really be here, you know,' Colleen O'Leary hissed to her best friend.

'Course we should. We're not doing any harm,' Becky

replied, parting a couple of branches and pushing her head cautiously forward.

From their hiding place in the bushes the two girls could see the whole of the gypsy encampment. There were five caravans in all – strange, exotic vehicles decorated even more elaborately than narrow boats. The horses which pulled them were tethered at the far edge of the clearing and gypsies themselves had gathered round an open fire, over which was suspended an iron pot.

Life was full of excitement, Becky thought. If there weren't buildings being moved from one place to another there were gypsies in the district, selling their clothes pegs and – according to Mrs Bracegirdle – stealing anything that wasn't actually nailed down.

'What're they cooking?' Colleen whispered.

'Don't know,' Becky replied.

One of the gypsy boys took a small spade and dug up the ground next to him.

'Dirt!' Colleen said. 'They're going to eat dirt!'

'Or maybe worms,' Becky said doubtfully.

The boy heaped the earth he had dug up, picked up a pewter jug and poured water over the mound.

'Mud soup,' Colleen giggled.

The gypsy mixed the mud until he was happy with its consistency, then reached for the sack next to him and took out three spiky balls, one after the other.

'What's he got?' Colleen asked.

'Hedgehogs!' Becky exclaimed.

The boy placed one of the creatures in the mud. He handled it gingerly at first, but once it had a coating of mud over its quills he began to roll it more vigorously. By the time he had completed his task it would have been difficult for anyone who didn't already know to guess exactly *what* was inside the muddy ball.

The boy held up his handiwork for one of the women to inspect, and when she nodded her approval he placed it at the edge of the fire.

'Let's get nearer,' Becky said.

'Don't be so daft!' Colleen hissed.

'But I want to see how they get them spikes off the hedgehogs,' Becky told her friend.

'If they catch you they won't let you go — ever,' Colleen said urgently.

'They won't catch us, not if we stay well in the bushes,' Becky assured her.

'Well, I'm not chancing it,' Colleen replied. 'So if you're going, you're going on your own.'

'All right, then,' Becky said. 'I *will* go on me own.'

She moved slowly — checking the ground for twigs before she put her foot down, gently brushing branches aside so as not to break them. It took her five minutes to reach the other edge of the clearing and by the time she settled down behind a new bush, her heart was beating furiously and she was trembling.

Despite her fear she was glad she'd taken the risk because, close to, the gypsies were far more exciting than they'd been at a distance. Becky's eyes greedily took in the details. The boy who'd making the hedgehog-balls was wearing a gold earring. Another boy — possibly the first one's brother — had a bright kerchief on his head. A girl — who couldn't have been older than Becky's sister Eunice — was smoking a clay pipe.

But it was the woman next to the fire who fascinated Becky the most. All the other women had on drab clothes which they had obviously either begged or stolen from clothes-lines, but she was wearing a long blue dress with stars, moons and circles all over it. She looked old — incredibly old, much older than even the most ancient person in the village. Her skin was the colour of the mahogany sideboard in which Becky's mother kept the best crockery. Her hands were as gnarled as the trunk of the old oak tree on the edge of the woods. Becky couldn't see her face, because the woman was shelling peas and her head was bent over the bowl.

The old woman suddenly looked up. Her eyes were almost yellow, and burned with the intensity of a bright fire. Her nose was very large and very hooked. Her mouth was wide, yet she seemed to have almost no lips. Tufts of grey hair grew from her pointed chin. All in all, it was a face of which nightmares are made.

'You can come out now, child,' she said in a voice which might have belonged to a frog rather than a person.

Becky felt the yellow eyes boring into her.

Me! she thought in a panic. She's talking to me!

'Yes, it is you I am calling to,' said the gypsy, as if she could read minds, 'just as by coming here, you have called to me.'

'Colleen!' Becky shouted. 'Colleen – help me!'

The old gypsy cackled. 'Colleen can't help you,' she said. 'You have gone too far down the road for anyone to help you. Take the last step, child. Come to me.'

Becky wanted to run away as fast as she could but her legs, against her will, took her to the very middle of the gypsy circle.

'I ... I wasn't doing anything wrong,' she stuttered.

Desperate for some sign of friendliness, she looked from gypsy to gypsy – from the boy with the earring to the one with the kerchief, from the girl with the clay pipe to the middle-aged woman sitting next to her. What she found drained away what little hope she had left – the Romanies' faces were as expressionless as a corpse's, as still as if they'd been made out of wax.

'They are no longer here. Now there is only the two of us,' said the one woman who Becky had not dared to gaze on.

Slowly and reluctantly, Becky turned her head until she was trapped by the bright yellow eyes.

'I was only curious,' she said, almost in tears, yet too frightened to cry.

'Curiosity killed the cat,' the old woman said. Putting down her bowl of peas she rose stiffly to her feet. 'Come with me, my little pussy.'

Wishing she had the will to resist – but knowing she hadn't – Becky followed the old woman across the clearing. The

Romany halted in front of one of the caravans and, without a word, pointed with her bony finger at the rickety steps which led up to the door.

Like a condemned man mounting the gallows, Becky climbed the steps.

The caravan had a rounded roof. There was a bed at the far end and a small let-down table closer to the door. Strong-smelling herbs hung like cobwebs for the ceiling and glass pots of strange-looking pastes and ointments squatted menacingly on a row of narrow shelves.

Standing hesitantly on the threshold, Becky felt the gypsy's cold breath on her neck.

'Do not fight your destiny, little pussy,' the old woman crooned.

Becky entered the caravan and sat down on a stool at the far side of the little table. She hadn't been told to do that, yet somehow she just *knew* that was what the Romany wanted her to do.

The gypsy followed Becky in and closed the door behind her. Now that the only light came from a tiny window, the caravan was suddenly as dark and mysterious as a cavern, as cramped and suffocating as a coffin.

The old woman slowly lowered herself into the chair opposite Becky.

'You have a special aura,' the gypsy said.

'I . . . don't know what you mean,' Becky stammered.

'I have lived long,' the old woman told her. 'I have travelled to the East, where my people – and their secrets – come from. And on my journey I learned from many wise men and women. Now I will pass on a little of that wisdom to you.'

'What do you mean?' Becky asked frightenedly.

'I will show you the future,' the old woman said. 'Those things yet to happen but which are destined – and so have already taken place.'

'I don't want my fortune told,' Becky said.

'You have no choice,' the gypsy replied. 'If there was

choice, you would not be here.' She held out a gnarled hand. 'Cross my palm with silver.'

Becky sighed with relief.

'I don't have any silver,' she said. 'Honestly, I don't.'

'Oh, but you do, my little pussy,' the gypsy told her.

And Becky realized that the old woman was right.

'I've got a silver rupee,' she admitted. 'Mr Bowyer gave it to me ages ago. But it's not for spending – it's my lucky rupee.'

The gypsy's yellowed eyes seemed to glow. 'An old man with a secret,' she croaked.

'What?'

'The man who gave you the coin. He is an old man with a secret. Give it to me, my little pussy. The Gypsy's Warning will serve you better than any good-luck charm.'

Becky slipped her hand down the side of her boot, took out the rupee and placed it in the gypsy's palm. The old woman's skin was dry, like dead leaves – cold, like an autumn frost.

'Look into the crystal,' the fortune teller said.

'What crystal?'

'The one in front of you.'

Becky looked down. A crystal ball dominated the centre of the small table – but she was sure it hadn't been there a second earlier, when she'd handed over her rupee.

As if it had a power of its own, the crystal ball began to glow, casting, as it did so, a silvery-blue sheen over the wooden walls.

'I have captured the moon,' the old woman said, 'and now it is my slave and must do my bidding.'

She bent her head and gazed into the crystal ball.

'I see pain and suffering,' she said. 'Suffering and pain – perhaps even unto death.'

'Will I die?' Becky asked, digging her fingernails into her palms to stop herself trembling.

'In time,' the gypsy replied. 'Yet this is the pain of a man. A man who is neither young nor old. A man who gave you life.'

'Dad!' Becky gasped.

'Time and tide sweep us forward,' the old woman said. 'I see a new force in your life – two men who will love you as much as they hate each other.'

'What about Dad?' Becky demanded. 'What's going to happen to him?'

'What has been revealed has been revealed,' the Romany said. 'For the rest, we can only wait.'

The crystal ball grew brighter – and brighter – until it filled the tiny caravan with a ghostly silver-blue glow and made everything as unreal as a dream, as alien as the moon.

'I see wealth beyond your wildest imaginings,' the gypsy continued, 'but beware – it will not be yours for long.'

She was no longer looking into the ball. Her head was rotating from side to side and her eyeballs had completely disappeared.

'Water,' she crooned softly. 'Rushing, furious water, sweeping away all in its path. And mud. Fountains of mud. The land will crumble, and tall towers will plunge to the earth as if struck down by the hands of the gods. And you can do nothing to stop it. Nothing! No mortal can.'

The old woman's head slumped forward.

'Are you . . . are you all right?' Becky asked.

The fortune teller made no answer. She was as still as the dead and seemed to have stopped breathing.

Becky forced herself to rise to her feet. Slowly she backed out of the caravan – feeling with her toe for the steps, holding the rough wooden walls for support – not taking her terrified eyes off the Romany for a second. Only when her feet finally touched the ground did she turn fearfully to face the other gypsies.

They had not moved! She would swear they had not moved an inch since she entered the caravan. They sat now, as they had then, staring with sightless eyes into the fire, their noses oblivious to the smell of burning hedgehog meat.

All she had to do was walk past them and she would be free. Yet though she was sure they were no threat, Becky could not summon up the strength to do it.

A loud wail of anguish came from within the fortune teller's caravan – a wail which would have chilled the blood of an exorcist.

Abandoning all caution, Becky made a furious dash past the camp-fire and towards the woods. The gypsies did not even look up.

She ran with all her might. Branches reached out malevolently and scratched her face. Brambles tugged at her stockings like the clutching fingers of the living dead. Yet she noticed nothing – not even the burning in her chest. Her only thought was to escape – to put as much distance between herself and the gypsy encampment as was humanly possible.

She had covered well over half a mile before she was forced to stop and catch her breath, and by then she was in sight of the Marston Old Mine. Looking up at the old familiar chimney, she felt a wave of relief wash over her whole body.

'Safe!' she gasped.

A slight breeze blew up, ruffling her hair and cooling her brow.

'Little Pussy,' said a soft voice in her ear.

Becky's stomach churned.

'Little Pussy,' the voice said again.

Becky looked around hysterically. In front of her she could see some of the workers from the mine – so far away they were almost matchstick figures. Behind her were the woods, completely still except for a gentle rustling of the leaves. To her right was Marston – comfortable, safe Marston. To her left was the canal embankment, on top of which a perfectly ordinary horse was towing a perfectly ordinary narrow boat. There was no one close to her – no one who could possibly be speaking to her now!

'Little Pussy,' the voice said for a third time. 'Can you hear me, Little Pussy?'

'Leave me alone,' Becky begged. 'Please leave me alone!'

'Soon,' the voice promised. 'Very soon. But there is something I must do first. My Guides are angry with me, Little Pussy. They say I was wrong to have taken your lucky charm from you and that if I am ever to know peace again, I must return it.'

'But how . . .?' Becky began.

Then she felt the familiar pressure of her lucky rupee against her ankle.

CHAPTER FIVE

As they walked up the humpbacked bridge past Worrell's Salt Works Ted Taylor could not fail to notice that Harry Atherton was dragging his feet, and when, as they reached the top, Atherton called for a rest, Taylor felt he had to say something.

'Are you quite sure you're fit enough to come back to work, Harry?' he asked.

Atherton coughed.

'Not much ch ... choice, is there?' he said bitterly. 'If you don't work, you don't get p ... paid, and I've got a family to keep, same as you have. Still, I'll admit I'd've been ha ... happier keeping to me bed this morning.'

'I'll bet you would,' Taylor said sincerely.

The two men gazed for a moment at the first rays of early-morning sunshine which were just finding their way between the spokes on the wheel at the top of the Adelaide's winding gear.

'If you don't work, you don't eat,' Ha-Ha Harry said quietly. 'It's a b ... bugger of a life, isn't it?'

Harry was right there, Taylor thought. And it wasn't just illness which could bring a family to the breadline, either. Slumps in trade were a bugger, too.

'One day they're screaming at us to mine all the salt we can, and the next they're telling us there's been a fall in demand and we're all to be laid off for a week,' he said aloud. 'How many days work d'you reckon we've lost already this year, Harry? Twenty?'

'About that,' Atherton agreed. 'D'you know what I think? I think, sod what's on the Order Books. If we're willing and ready to work, they should p ... pay us anyway – even when they don't want us down the mine.'

Ted Taylor laughed. 'And just who d'you think'd hand out money to you for doing nowt?'

'I dunno,' Atherton admitted. 'The government maybe.'

'Fat chance of that,' Taylor told him.

'Or the bosses,' Atherton pressed on, undeterred. 'It's the sweat from our brows, not their own, that's made 'em rich. The least they could do in return would be to see we've allus got some f . . . food on our tables.'

'Fat chance of that, an' all,' Taylor said. 'You don't get to be rich in the first place without being tight with your money.'

'Well, *somebody* should do something, any road,' Atherton persisted. 'It's not right that an honest working man should have to go to the Board of Guardians, cap in hand, and beg for whatever they see fit to give him.'

'It might not be right,' Taylor agreed, 'but that's the way of the world and it'll never change — not in our lifetimes, anyway.'

'It could,' Atherton mused, somewhat cheered up for having had his grouse. 'You never know.'

'Not if we live to see a hundred,' Taylor said.

'Oh, I'm planning to see at least that,' Atherton replied.

Taylor grinned. He could be a laugh, Harry, but sometimes he talked like a bloody idiot. Live to be a hundred? If he managed to last out half that long he'd be well ahead of the game.

As they approached the main gate of the mine they saw two young men waiting there. One of them was dressed like the rest of the workers in an old jacket, flat cap and collar and tie. The other, however, looked much smarter in his double-breasted jacket, top hat and cravat.

'Who the h . . . hell are them young sods?' Harry Atherton asked.

'They started here while you were off sick,' Ted Taylor said. 'They're Len Worrell's sons. He's already had them on the pans at his own works, and now he wants 'em to get experience of going down the mine.'

'So how c ... come we got landed with 'em?' Harry wondered.

'I dunno,' Ted admitted. 'Maybe Len's a friend of the gaffer's. Or maybe it's just a case of one boss scratching the back of another. Whatever the reason, they've been working with me for last fortnight.'

'And are they starting to shape up?' Atherton asked.

Taylor shrugged. 'The younger one, Michael, is willing enough, but the other, Richard, is hard work.'

'A bit thick, is he?' Atherton said.

'No, he's not thick,' Taylor replied. 'To be fair to him he seems quite clever. It's just that he thinks he knows it all already. And if there's a corner to be cut you can bet your last ha'penny young Master Richard will cut it.'

The older workers drew level with the younger men.

'Are we about ready, Taylor?' Richard Worrell asked.

'About ready,' Ted said gruffly.

He didn't like his surname being used by this whippersnapper. He'd always been 'Ted' to Richard Worrell's father. Yes, and Worrell had always been 'Len' to him — even after he'd made his money. Still, times changed, didn't they? People might talk about all this democracy, what with nearly every man having the vote now, but it seemed to Ted Taylor there was a lot less democracy down the pit than there used to be.

Len Worrell and the men like him might have been hard masters, he thought, but at least they didn't treat us as if we were dirt. *And* they were always willing to take the advice of workers who knew as much — or more — about the job as they did.

This new breed of manager was a different kettle of fish altogether. *They'd* not started working when they were hardly more than boys, picking up their education as they went along and ending up carving out little empires. No, it had all been too easy for this generation with their soft life and their fancy schools.

What could an ignorant bugger like Ted Taylor teach them? they asked themselves.

And the answer came back — sod all!

'What are we doing today, Mr Taylor?' Michael Worrell asked as they walked towards the shaft.

'Today, I think I'm going to let you do some blasting of your own,' Taylor told him.

'We've already done that,' Richard Worrell said churlishly.

'I know you have,' Ted Taylor told him, 'but only with me looking over your shoulders. Now you'll be doing it all on your own. So for God's sake remember everything I've told you about making sure the explosive's well packed down and ...'

'Yes, yes,' Richard Worrell said impatiently. 'Let's get it over with. The sooner we graduate, the happier I'll be.'

Graduate, eh? That'd be one of the words he'd learned at his fancy school, wouldn't it? Ted Taylor had no idea what it meant. *He'd* just be glad when he'd taught this lad all he knew and could get him out of the bloody mine.

'Your grandad was a cooper until he got sick,' Mary Taylor told her youngest daughter as they black-leaded the grate.

'What's a cooper, Mam?' Becky asked.

'He used to make them big wooden barrels you see on brewer's wagons. Very skilled work it was. Anyway, he started having these pains in his chest, you see ...'

Just the thought of her father's pains was enough to take Mary back in time to the damp kitchen of their old house in Leicester Street.

'You'll have to go and see the doctor,' Mary's mam had said.

'See the doctor?' her father gasped between fits of coughing. 'We can't afford that.'

'It's not a question of *can't*,' her mam replied firmly. 'We *have to* afford it.'

So they went, all three of them, to a surgery on Castle Street. The doctor, Mr Littler, was supposed to be the cheapest in town, and his waiting room was crammed with people, many of whom had hacking coughs just like Mary's father.

When their turn finally came the doctor told Mary's dad to take off his shirt and listened — briefly — to his chest.

'It's TB,' he announced.

'And what can we do about it?' Mary's mother asked.

'Do about it?' the doctor replied, as if surprised at the question. He looked Mary's mother up and down, taking in her shabby dress and worn clogs. 'I don't suppose you've got the money for a sanatorium in Scotland, have you?' he asked.

And he laughed! He actually laughed!

'No, we haven't got the money,' Mary's mother admitted, ashamed and humiliated by the confession of her obvious poverty.

'Then there's not much we *can* do,' the doctor said. 'We'll just have to let the disease run its course.'

Let the disease run its course! All that meant was that Mary and her mother were forced to watch her father gradually get worse.

'... he worked for as long as he could,' Mary told her daughter, 'but in the end he just had to give up, and we threw ourselves on the mercy of the Guardians.'

'The Guardians?' Becky said, seeing the tear in the corner of her mother's eye, but knowing instinctively that Mary would prefer her to pretend she hadn't noticed.

'The Guardians of the Poor Law,' Mary explained. 'The people who run the workhouse. You know where that is, don't you?'

'In Leftwich. Under the railway arches.'

'Yes, and a terrible place it is, too. Don't you ever end up there, Becky. Anything's better than that — even begging on the streets.'

'What made it terrible, Mam?' Becky asked.

'Well, for a start, they ran things according to something called "the principle of less eligibility".'

'I don't know what that means, Mam.'

'Neither did I at first — but I soon found out. It meant that they made sure that the paupers in the workhouse had a harder, more miserable life than even the poorest worker on the outside.'

'How wicked!' Becky exclaimed.

'I don't think they were trying to be wicked,' her mother said. 'It's just that the Board of Guardians had got this idea into its head that if they made things too easy, people would actually *want* to go into the workhouse.' She snorted contemptuously. 'As if anybody'd choose to break up their family unless they really had to.'

'What d'you mean, break up the family?' Becky asked.

'We were treated worse than criminals,' Mary said. 'We lived in what they called "dormitories" – long rooms full of beds. The men all lived in one dormitory and the woman and children lived in another.'

'But why?' Becky said.

'The principle of less eligibility again,' her mother told her. 'Oh, we were allowed to see each other – but not very often. And we were hardly ever let out of the place, even for a breath of fresh air – that would've made our lives too pleasant and encouraged more people to become paupers. By the time I went into service I'd almost forgotten what it was like to go for a walk or smell a flower.'

'How awful,' Becky said.

She tried to imagine herself in a workhouse – no family suppers in the cosy kitchen, no trips on Mr Hulse's narrow boat, no rambles around Forge Pool. How could anybody live like that?

'They were very close, my parents,' Mary Taylor said. 'And being separated from your gran killed your grandad faster than the TB would ever have done. She didn't last that long after him, either. I'd only been in service a couple of months when she passed on. Died of grief, poor soul. And not even a headstone to mark her pauper's grave.'

She was crying in earnest now. Becky reached out and stroked her mother's hair comfortingly.

'I'll never go back there,' Mary said through her tears. 'Never! I'll tell you something now,' she continued, almost in a whisper, 'and not even your dad knows this. I've been saving money – not a lot, but it all adds up – and putting it in the

Post Office Savings Bank. By the time your dad's too old to work, we should have enough so that we can manage to get by without being a drain on anybody else. That's all I want — just to be able to manage without having to go to the Board of Guardians again.'

Behind him, Ted Taylor could hear the clip-clop of horses' hooves and the clank of iron wheels running along the rails. Ahead of him he could see Richard Worrell in the last stages of fixing a charge to the wall of solid rock salt.

'Finished!' Richard called over his shoulder.

Hands on his hips, Ted Taylor turned so he was facing back down the mine.

'Blasting!' he shouted at the top of his voice.

And his word echoed through the long cavern, bouncing off the walls and roof — '. . . asting . . . asting'.

Taylor surveyed the scene. Everyone was clear.

'Right,' he called to Richard Worrell. 'Set the fuse and then get clear of the blasting area.'

Worrell lit the fuse and sprinted back to where Taylor was standing.

'There's no need to run,' Ted told him. 'Not if you've done it properly. A good explosives man should always leave himself time to get well away. And if he *really* knows what he's doing, he should be able to judge the explosion so the rock falls just where he wants it.'

'I know,' Richard Worrell replied, sounding bored. 'You must have told me a thousand times.'

'And I'll go on telling you until we're both blue in the face,' Ted Taylor said, starting — not for the first time — to get rattled. 'You can never be too careful with explosives.'

If young Worrell had made even a halfway decent job of it, the face should blow soon. Taylor put his fingers in his ears and waited.

Ten seconds passed . . . twenty . . . thirty.

After he estimated that two minutes had ticked by, Ted Taylor lowered his hands again.

'Buggered it up, haven't you?' he asked Richard.

Worrell did not look over-concerned. 'Perhaps the explosive was damp.'

'Damp!' Taylor echoed. 'It's as dry as the bloody desert down here.'

An amused smile flicked across Richard's lips. 'Know about deserts, do we? My, we *are* educated.'

For a moment Taylor was on the point of hitting him. Then, with an effort, he regained his self-control. If he *did* belt this cheeky young devil he would lose his job — no question — and as Harry Atherton had said earlier, you had to work if you'd got a family to feed.

'Right!' Ted said, striding angrily towards the rock face. 'Let's go and find out exactly what *kind* of pig's arse you've made of the job, shall we?'

But Richard Worrell made no effort to follow him.

People wondered, later, just what Ted Taylor had thought he was doing.

'He was one of the most experienced blasters in the mine,' they said to one another. 'He should have known — better than most — that you don't just walk up to an unexploded charge like that.'

Well, whatever had caused him to be so reckless they all agreed he'd paid a heavy price for it. He hadn't been more than ten yards from the rock face when there'd been a deafening explosion and huge chunks of salt crystal had shot through the dry air like cannon balls.

Mary Taylor had been preparing the hot-pot for over half an hour, and was just on the point of putting it in the oven when she heard the hammering on the back door.

'I won't be a minute,' she called over her shoulder.

But who could it be? she wondered. The men were all out at work at that hour. As for the women they usually just tapped lightly, then poked their heads round the door.

She slid the dish into the oven and closed the cast-iron door behind it. It was lovely and warm in there, she thought, and the hot-pot should be nicely simmering by the time Ted came home, tired and hungry, for his supper.

There was further hammering, more urgent this time. Mary wiped her hands on her apron and went to open the door.

Her heart sank when she saw who it was. Harry Atherton, who she knew to be one of her husband's ferriers, was standing on the doorstep, his eyes wild, his mouth flapping like a landed fish's.

'What's the matter?' Mary asked.

'There's b ... been an accident,' Atherton gasped.

'Ted! Is it my Ted?'

Atherton nodded helplessly. 'They're j ... just bringing him up, now. The g ... gaffer thought you should be there.'

'Is he ... is he ...?' Mary began, then found she could say no more.

Atherton looked awkwardly at the ground. 'He w ... wasn't when I left him,' he said. 'But he looked in a pretty bad way.'

In a pretty bad way? Oh, dear God, no!

There had been no room in the tub for Ted Taylor to lie down, and the makeshift stretcher to which he was strapped had had to be up-ended for the journey from the rock face. Once on the surface, however, willing hands soon returned the stretcher to its correct position.

A crowd had gathered round the winding house. At first, Mary found it impossible to get through, but once people realized that she was the injured man's wife – 'his widow', someone said! – a path was soon made for her.

Mary looked down at her husband. His face was ashen and he seemed to be finding breathing difficult. One of his legs was twisted at an unnatural angle.

'Hello, Mary, love,' he said weakly.

Well, at least he was conscious, his wife thought. That was something.

'Clear a way!' Mr Finch, the manager, shouted with authority.

The onlookers shuffled backwards and Ted Taylor's workmates carried his stretcher to a waiting wagon.

'Be careful with him,' Mary implored. 'For God's sake, be careful with him.'

'We've sent for the doctor, Mrs Taylor,' the manager told her. 'And don't worry – the company'll pay the bill.'

Don't worry! Mary Taylor thought. There was her husband, her big strong husband, lying helplessly on the back of a wagon, and she was supposed not to worry!

'Shall I go now, Mr Finch?' the wagon driver asked.

'Yes, but take it slow,' the manager said. 'We don't want him jogged about any more than we can help.' He turned to Mary. 'Do you want to go with him?'

Mary nodded and climbed up on the wagon beside her husband.

'Look at you!' she said, adopting a tone of mock severity though her heart was breaking. 'I just can't trust you out on your own, can I?'

Taylor smiled thinly. 'I've always been a bit of a mad bugger, haven't I?' he said with effort. 'But I've really overdone it this time.'

The horse started off at a gentle trot, and Taylor winced with pain.

'We'll soon have you home,' Mary said comfortingly, 'and the doctor'll patch you up good as new.'

If Taylor could have shaken his head he would have done. As it was he merely whispered, 'I'm a goner – and we both know it.'

'You're not!' his wife said fiercely. 'You're not! In three months it'll be as if this had never happened.'

But though she spoke the words she didn't believe them. Her husband might – with luck – pull through, but he would never be able to work down the mine again. And if he couldn't work as a miner, what could he do?

'We should do something to help Mr Taylor,' Michael Worrell said towards the end of dinner. 'Or if it's too late to help him, we should at least do something for his family.'

'Should we, now?' asked his father, reaching for the port. 'And what makes you say that?'

'Because what happened to him was all Richard's fault.'

Len Worrell turned to look at his elder son. Richard Worrell had been unnaturally pale at the start of the meal, but the large amounts of wine he had managed to knock back had done something to return the colour to his cheeks.

'Was it your fault, Richard?' Len asked.

'Was it hell!' Richard said, in a voice which was half angry and half defensive.

'You're not down the mine now,' his father said sternly, 'and I didn't send you to that fancy school to hear language like that across me own table.'

'I'm sorry, Father,' Richard said. 'I think I'm still in shock. That man Taylor nearly got me killed.'

'Did he?' Worrell said. 'And how do you work that out?'

'He never wanted us down the mine in the first place,' Richard explained. 'I heard him talking to his "mates" about having to waste his time dealing with toffee-nosed kids.'

His older brother sounded so plausible, Michael thought. Ted Taylor had complained to the other workers about having to train the Worrell boys – or, at least, Richard – and now Richard was using Taylor's dislike in his own defence because he knew, like all good liars, that the closer you keep to the truth the more convincing you appear.

'So he didn't take to you,' Len Worrell said. 'That's not the same as almost getting you killed, is it?'

'He couldn't be bothered to explain the job properly,' Richard ploughed on. 'At the very best, I think he wanted us to make fools of ourselves – and of you. At worst, I think he was hoping we'd get hurt, just because we've got more money than he has.'

Worrell nodded. 'There are people like that about,' he agreed, 'though I'd not have thought Ted Taylor was one of them.' He turned back to his younger son. 'You look as if you disagree with your brother, Michael,' he said.

'Mr Taylor may not have liked us very much, but he did his best to teach us all he knew,' Michael said. 'Richard didn't make a mistake because of what Mr Taylor told us – he made it because he was careless.'

Len Worrell munched thoughtfully on this new piece of information.

'Even if Richard was careless, is that any reason I should go playing Lord Bountiful to the whole of Ted Taylor's family?' he asked finally.

'I think so – yes,' his younger son replied.

'I like Ted – always have,' Worrell said. 'But it wasn't me who asked him to go down the mine in the first place, and it wasn't me who forced him to work with explosives instead of settling for being a ferrier and getting his hands dirty.'

'But ...' Michael said.

'I haven't finished,' Worrell told him.

'Sorry, Father,' Michael said, restraining himself only with effort.

'Suppose I do pay him off – a man who doesn't even work for me – I'll just be storing up trouble for myself, won't I?' Worrell continued.

'I don't see why,' Michael said.

'Then think about it,' his father urged him. 'If I give something to Ted Taylor, what's going to happen the next time a waller gets careless at my works and splashes himself with a bit of brine?'

'I expect he'll ...'

'I'll tell you what's going to happen. Instead of wiping the brine off with a bit of rag and carrying on working, he'll be straight up to the office demanding compensation, won't he? You must understand that if you get a reputation for being soft in my business, Michael, it won't be long before you're up in the bankruptcy courts.'

'Whatever it costs you, you have to do what's right,' Michael Worrell said stubbornly.

'Oh, I will,' his father agreed. 'I'll do what's right for me and mine.'

'No!' Michael said, banging the palm of his hand down on the table so hard that the wine glasses jangled together.

'You what?' asked his astounded father.

'Don't do it for me!' Michael shouted, his face as red with

rage as his brother's was with alcohol. 'Don't you dare do something dishonest and dishonourable and then say that you're doing it for me!'

'I'll not have this,' Worrell said, pointing his thick, strong index finger at his youngest son. 'You'll apologize. This minute.'

Michael stood up. 'I will *not* apologize.'

'Sit down, Michael,' Worrell said sternly.

'And I will not sit down,' Michael replied hotly. 'I won't share the same table with you a second longer.'

With that he turned and rushed towards the door.

Worrell stood up, sending his chair flying backwards.

'Come back here, you young bugger,' he bawled. 'Come back right now.'

Michael opened the door and dashed down the corridor, almost knocking the silver tray out of the hands of Chivers the butler.

For the first time in years Worrell was at a loss as to what to do next. He knew what his own father would have done in his place – chased the lad round the house and given him a leathering when he'd caught him. But his old dad hadn't been a gentleman like he was supposed to be.

Even if he did drop his carefully cultivated dignity and chase after the boy, was there any guarantee he'd catch him? And if he caught him, was he sure that Michael would stand passively while he received his thrashing? Five minutes earlier none of these thoughts would have occurred to Worrell, but five minutes earlier he'd never thought that Michael would openly defy him, either.

He was frightened of his own son, he realized. Not physically –though for all that Michael was only sixteen, he was a strapping boy and could probably stand up for himself quite well if he chose to fight back. No, it wasn't Michael's physical strength which intimidated him, it was the power of his previously hidden passion.

'Shall I clear away now, Sir?' Chivers asked.

Worrell glanced at his butler and in the split second before

Chivers had time to rearrange his features, caught the expression on his face.

I'm used to better than this, the expression said. I'm used to dealing with people with a little more class.

Showing me up in front of the servants, Worrell thought angrily. You young bastard, Michael.

Sod it! He *would* go after the boy, and when he found him he'd give him the beating of his life – even if the grooms had to hold Michael down while he did it.

'You can go, Chivers,' Richard Worrell said with an air of authority his father might have shown in front of his workers, but could never have achieved with his servants.

The butler, his tray only half full, wheeled smartly and left the room.

'What the hell ...?' Len Worrell asked as Chivers closed the door behind him.

'Don't do it, Father,' Richard advised.

'Don't do what?'

'Don't reduce all this to the level of a common brawl. If you want to get revenge on Michael for the way he's humiliated you in front of the servants, there are better ways to do it.'

Len Worrell sank back into his chair defeatedly.

Revenge? That wasn't what he wanted.

But what exactly *did* he want?

He wanted to be able to like Michael more.

He wanted to look at the boy without being reminded of Caroline, his wife – the woman who had given up her life to bring Michael into the world.

He wanted ... he wanted ...

If only Michael would make it a little easier for him, he thought. If only the boy would bend a little and try to see the world the way he did, as a place where weakness was always exploited – a place where one moment's carelessness could cost you your invention, the only thing you'd ever really been proud of.

Worrell sighed. Was Michael ever going to turn into the son he wanted him to be? Or was he going to have to hand the whole business over to Richard?

*

Trade was normally slack mid-week, but that night the New Inn was heaving.

It's Ted Taylor's accident that's brought them in, Paddy O'Leary thought as he pulled yet another pint.

Tragedy always took people like that.

'I need a drink,' they'd say.

To drown their sorrows? Maybe. But there was something else as well — something most of them wouldn't even admit to themselves.

'I feel right sorry for him,' they'd tell anybody prepared to listen, but even as they mourned for the victim they were celebrating on their own behalf and thinking, If it had to happen to somebody, thank God it didn't happen to me!

'You're getting too philosophical, O'Leary,' Paddy murmured under his breath. 'Must come of being Irish and running a pub.'

'And how's Mr Taylor, Mr O'Leary?' Not-Stopping Bracegirdle asked through the hatch between the bar and the best room.

'It's still touch and go from what I heard,' Paddy said sadly.

'Poor man,' Not-Stopping commiserated. 'They say they had to dig him out from under a mountain of rock — a real mountain of it.'

Not-Stopping withdrew her head from the hatch and returned to her cronies.

'Terrible thing to have happened,' Dottie Curzon said.

'Terrible,' Maggie Cross agreed.

'Mark my words, he'll not see the night out,' Not-Stopping Bracegirdle said, lowering her voice. 'And I'm not the only one as thinks so. I heard hammering when I was walking up the lane. And you know what that means, don't you?'

'No,' Ma Fitton said.

'You can be really dense sometimes,' Not-Stopping told her. 'It was Fred Emmett making the coffin. And you can be sure he won't be using his best walnut either — not for Ted. However many airs and graces Mary Taylor might try to put on, that family lives from hand to mouth just like the rest of us, and when he goes under it'll be in plain pine.'

'It's the children I feel sorry for,' Ma Fitton said. 'I brought them all into the world.'

'When she wasn't busy delivering royalty,' Not-Stopping mouthed at Dot and Maggie.

'Yes, every one of them,' Ma Fitton continued. 'Isn't there something we can do for them?'

'Like what?' Not-Stopping demanded.

'I don't really know,' Ma confessed. 'How about if we all chipped in a few coppers every week, just to help out?'

'This week. Yes, we could manage that,' Dottie Curzon said, not unkindly. 'Maybe even next week as well. But what about the week after that? There's nobody in this village can afford to keep on supporting charity cases. It's enough of a struggle keeping food on your own table.'

'It'll be the workhouse for them,' Not-Stopping Bracegirdle said with grim satisfaction. 'You mark my words. I'm never wrong.'

Ted Taylor's fever had begun almost as soon as the doctor had finished his examination, and as night set in his temperature continued to climb.

'He's burning up, Mam,' said Becky.

'It'll do him good to sweat it out,' Mary replied unconvincingly.

It was marvellous how her kids were rallying round, she thought – little Becky, standing by the bedside and mopping her father's brow till her small arms must have ached; her brother George, fetching the coal and guarding his mother from all the well-meaning neighbours who kept calling to see if there was anything they could do. Only Philip was not pulling his weight, but then Mary had long ago given up expecting miracles.

'You must be getting tired,' Mary said to her daughter as Becky's bedtime approached. 'Let me take over for a while.'

'I'm all right,' Becky answered, and her tone said that nothing – nothing – would make her give up her post by her father's side.

At around ten o'clock Taylor began to cough up blood.

'The doctor told us to expect that,' Mary said as she wiped up the spots with a clean rag. 'It's all part of getting better.'

But Becky was not to be comforted or fobbed off. 'Is he going to die, Mam?' she asked quietly.

Mary looked into her daughter's earnest young face and found she couldn't lie. 'I don't know,' she confessed. 'I just don't know.'

Towards midnight Taylor became delirious and began calling out for his mother and father, both long dead. It was terrible for Mary to see him like that, but even delirium was preferable to his condition two hours later, when his ramblings gave way to almost continuous gasps of pain.

'Don't let him die,' Mary prayed, kneeling at the foot of the bed. 'Please, please, don't let him die.'

Yet even as she pleaded for her husband's life she remembered the other times she had called on God's help — for her infant son Walter, who, if he'd lived would have been almost a man by now; for her daughter Clara, who could have been a perfect big sister for little Becky. God hadn't listened to her then — she could think of no reason why he should bother now.

CHAPTER SIX

Ted Taylor had a strong constitution and his ribs mended quickly. His left leg, however, which had caught the worst of the blast and been badly broken in three places, took longer to set and it was nearly two months before he could get out of bed and hobble round the house.

'You'll improve beyond this, Taylor,' the doctor told him, 'but you'll never be fit for really hard physical labour again. So if I were you, I'd start thinking about some other line of work.'

'Aye, I will,' Taylor said under his breath. 'But I can't make up me mind whether I want to be an accountant or a pox doctor like you.'

'Just remember to keep moving,' the medical man advised. 'Always keep moving – that's the trick.'

'Start thinking of some other line of work,' Taylor snorted once the doctor had left. 'What line of work? Mining's the only thing I know.'

'You're not too old to learn a new skill,' Mary said.

'No, but I'm too old to find anybody who'll want to teach me one,' her husband replied. 'Why should they bother training me when there's young lads – with maybe fifty years' work still in them – just ready to jump at the chance?'

Grasping the edge of the table with his powerful hands, Taylor pulled himself to his feet. Watching him, Mary thought her heart would break.

'Keep moving,' Taylor said bitterly. 'That's another thing that bloody quack told me to do. How the hell am I supposed to keep moving? If I didn't have the furniture to hold onto I'd fall flat on me arse.'

'I know, love,' his wife said.

'It's not me I'm worried about,' Taylor told her. 'It's you

and the kids. How am I ever going to be able to support me family again when I can't even support meself?'

'You just concentrate on getting better,' Mary said. 'We can put our minds to getting you a job when you're walking properly again.'

'But that could take months,' Taylor protested. 'What are we going to live on in the meantime?'

'Oh, we've still got our savings,' Mary said lightly.

And so they had — but those savings were growing smaller and smaller every day.

A week after Ted's first steps, Mary arrived home triumphantly bearing a pair of crutches.

'These'll be grand,' Taylor said, trying them out. 'Wherever did you get them from, lass?'

'A shop in Northwich,' Mary replied, looking away.

'I didn't know any shops in town sold crutches,' her husband replied. 'Which shop was it?'

There was no way out but to tell the truth.

'Sticky Sammy's,' Mary said shamefacedly.

'A pawn broker's!' Ted said. 'Some poor devil actually sold his crutches to a pawn broker.'

'Sammy didn't *want* to take them,' Mary said, 'but he told me the bloke was so desperate that he hadn't the heart to turn him down.'

'And now I've robbed him of them,' Taylor said in disgust.

'No, you haven't,' his wife said firmly. 'They've been in Sammy's window for over six months. If the owner could have afforded to redeem them, he'd have done it already. And where are they doing more good — stuck in a shop window gathering dust or stuck under your arms helping you to walk?'

'You're right,' Taylor agreed. 'But I won't need them for long, and when I've finished with them, we'll find the feller they belong to and give 'em back to him.'

If you've finished with them, Mary thought. If you've *ever* finished with them.

*

Ted was making great progress with his crutches. The first day he walked as far as Cross Street, the second all the way to the post office. By the end of the week he felt confident enough to tackle the steep climb up the humpbacked bridge and, for the first time in months, saw the Adelaide Mine.

Perhaps someone from the mine saw *him*, too, for it was the very night after this expedition that he received a note from Mr Finch, the manager. He read it out to Mary:

Dear Taylor,
It would appear that you are once again mobile. This being the case, I would appreciate it if you would report to the main office at three thirty on Thursday.

Yours faithfully,
J.L. Finch (Manager)

'What do you make of that, Mary?' Taylor said.

'What do *you* make of it?' his wife asked cautiously.

'Well, it's obvious, isn't it?' Taylor replied with enthusiasm. 'They want me to start work again.'

'You can't go back down the mine.'

'I know that,' Taylor said, 'and so do they. No, what they'll be wanting me for is some light work on the surface.'

A job on the surface? Mary thought. There were only two kinds of surface work — engineering and clerical — and Ted had neither the training for the first nor was enough of a scholar to cope with the second.

Where her husband saw hope in the letter she saw nothing but despair. They were calling him in to tell him he was sacked — and despite the fact that he was on crutches they hadn't even had the decency to say they'd send a cart for him.

She didn't tell Ted of her suspicion which was almost a certainty. It was another two days to his appointment and her husband was entitled to a short stay in a fool's paradise before he saw for himself the awful future which lay ahead of all of them.

*

Thursday came and Ted hobbled over to the Adelaide Mine. He'd not been further than the top of the bridge before, and the extra distance put an unexpected strain on him. He would have liked to stop and catch his breath, but there was no time.

'I've to be there at three thirty prompt, Mr Finch said,' he grunted as he made his way painfully down the bridge. 'And you can't keep a man like Mr Finch waiting.'

By the time he reached the mine Taylor's left leg ached and his armpits were burning.

'Can't let it show,' he told himself. 'Have to look as if I'm bloody near ready to run with the hounds.'

He raised his hand to knock on the door of the office anteroom. God, but that hurt!

'Come in,' said the severe voice of Mr Crabbit, Finch's chief clerk.

Taylor pushed the door open and shuffled inside. Crabbit gave him the briefest of glances, then returned to his work.

Taylor awkwardly removed his cap and stuffed it into his pocket.

'Mr Crabbit . . .' he began.

'One moment, please,' the clerk said sharply.

It was, in fact, a good five minutes before Crabbit lifted his head from his work again and said, 'Yes?'

'I'm here to see the gaffer,' Taylor explained.

'Here to see the *manager*, you mean,' the clerk corrected him, and then, though he'd seen Ted around the place any number of times over the years, he added, 'You must be Taylor then.'

'Yes,' Ted agreed. 'That's me.'

'Mr Finch is busy,' the clerk said. 'He asked me to tell you to wait.'

There was no chair on which to sit. Even if there had been, Taylor would not have dared take it – getting up again without help was still a problem for him, and he didn't want anybody in this office to see just how weak he still was.

The minutes ticked by . . . five . . . ten . . . fifteen. Taylor was beginning to feel feverish.

'Don't fall over!' he ordered himself. 'Don't bloody collapse now.'

Finally, after more than twenty minutes had passed, Mr Finch opened the door of his office and said, 'You can come in now, Taylor.'

The manager was not alone. Sitting behind the desk was a thin-featured, balding man wearing a pair of pince-nez spectacles.

'This is Mr Spratt,' Finch said, 'the company attorney.'

'How do you do, Sir?' Taylor said.

Spratt gave him an almost imperceptible nod and shuffled the documents in front of him.

'This accident,' he said. 'I take it you are not holding the company responsible for it.'

Taylor shifted uncomfortably on his crutches.

'Well, it was the company which told me to take them Worrell lads down the mine with me ...'

'But it was you, not the company, who decided when to let one of the young gentlemen, Mr Richard Worrell, set the charges,' Spratt said coldly. 'Isn't that correct?'

'Well, yes,' Taylor admitted.

'So, ultimately, the accident was caused as a result of a decision taken by you and no one else but you?'

'I suppose so,' Taylor agreed.

He wished he could sit down, if only for a second. And he would have given anything for a drink of water.

'The company has paid all your doctor's bills while you've been ill,' the attorney said.

'I know that, Sir.'

'The expense has not been inconsiderable.'

'I know that as well, Sir,' Taylor said, and then, because Spratt obviously expected more, he added, 'Thank you, Sir.'

'The company considers it has gone far beyond its obligations in your case,' the attorney continued. 'Should you seek to gain any additional redress through the courts, we will fight you – and we will win.'

'I wasn't planning to take the company to court,' Taylor said. 'All I want is a job.'

The attorney consulted one of the documents in front of him.

'According to the doctor's report, you are no longer suitable for heavy work,' he pointed out.

'There's other things I can do,' Taylor said.

He tried to catch Finch's eye, but the manager had turned away.

'It is our opinion that you would be best advised to seek alternative employment,' Spratt said.

'Does that mean I'm sacked?' Taylor asked disbelievingly. 'Just like that? Without a penny?'

'Not quite,' the attorney said, sliding another document across the desk so it was directly in front of Ted. 'This is a letter from Mr Leonard Worrell, the father of Mr Richard. He admits no liability on his son's part for your accident, but he is prepared to settle on you a certain sum of money provided you will sign a declaration to the effect that you will never reveal him to be the source of the payment.'

'How much?' Taylor asked dully.

'Twenty-five pounds,' Spratt told him.

Twenty-five pounds! So that was the price on a man losing his livelihood these days.

'Will you agree to sign such a declaration?' the attorney asked.

'I don't have much choice,' Taylor said. 'Do I, *Sir*?'

Len Worrell walked over to the book-lined wall and examined the titles on the spines of a few of the cracked leather volumes.

'Ovid, *Metamorphoses*,' he read aloud. 'Cicero, *De oratore*. It's all double-dutch to me.'

The study, with its atmosphere of ancient learning, made him feel uncomfortable and nervous. No! he thought. He'd been nervous long before the headmaster had invited him to wait there.

He took out his watch and looked at it.

'What's keeping you, lad?' he said to the empty room.

He hadn't spoken to Michael since his younger son's outburst at the dinner table.

'Tell Master Michael he's to take his meals in his room until he feels able to come to me and apologize for his behaviour,' Worrell had told the butler.

But even by the end of the school holidays Michael had not come to him, and had left by hired cab without so much as a farewell.

There was a knock on the door.

'Come in,' Worrell said.

The door opened and Michael took a few steps into the room. For a few seconds father and son gazed awkwardly at each other. Then Worrell broke the silence.

'By, but it's a grand place, this,' he said. 'Aristocratic, it is. The breeding ground of gentlemen. Who'd ever have thought that my sons would have ended up here?'

'I don't know, Father,' Michael confessed.

'Nobody!' Len Worrell said emphatically. 'Where I started out from, nobody would have thought it!'

He walked across the room so that he was closer to his son, then held out his arm to him. The two of them stiffly shook hands.

'I hear you're captain of the cricket team,' Worrell said.

'Just the House team,' Michael replied.

'Aye, well, that's not bad going, is it?' Worrell asked.

He began pacing the room as if he had something to say but couldn't quite bring himself to say it. Suddenly, halfway between the headmaster's huge oak desk and the window, he wheeled round.

'I've paid some compensation to Ted Taylor, just you like asked me to,' he said.

'But why?' Michael asked incredulously. 'I mean ... I'm very glad you have, but what made you change your mind?'

'You were never going to back down, were you?' Worrell said, answering his question with another one.

'I don't think I could have, even if I'd wanted to,' Michael admitted.

'Will you do something for me in return?' Worrell asked.

'If I can,' Michael said cautiously.

'If you can!' his father thundered, suddenly angry. 'It's always like that with you, isn't it? Never just "Yes, Father" or "No, Father". First you've got to see if it'll square with your precious cock-eyed principles.'

'I'm sorry, Father,' Michael said. 'It's just the way I am. What is it you want me to do?'

'Your brother's already part of the family business,' Worrell said, regaining a little of his control. 'When you've finished at this fancy school, I want you to promise me you'll join him there.'

Though he'd not yet told his father, Michael had very different plans. He had some talent in science, they'd told him at school, and while he'd gone along with Worrell's scheme of getting to know the salt industry, he had his sights set on becoming a doctor.

'Is it very important to you that I come in with you and Richard?' he asked.

'Yes, it is,' Worrell told him.

'Then I'll promise,' Michael said. 'But I'd like to know *why* it's important.'

'Because I want you to understand me,' his father replied. 'I want you to have to make the kinds of decisions I've had to make. Then perhaps you'll come to see that I'm not as big a bastard as you thought I was.'

'I never thought you were a bastard,' Michael protested.

'Maybe not,' his father conceded, 'but you don't like me very much, do you?'

'No,' Michael said. 'I don't like you very much. But that doesn't mean I don't love you.'

'You'd better get back to your lessons,' Worrell said gruffly. 'I'm paying a lot of money for this – I wouldn't like to see it wasted.'

'Yes,' Michael said sadly. 'It'd be a pity to waste it.'

From the window of the headmaster's study Worrell watched his son walk back across the quad. Michael was a fine young man by any standards, he thought – tall, good-looking, intelligent. So why was it that whenever they were together his main feeling towards his son was not pride, but guilt? And why – in God's name – when Michael had said he loved him, couldn't he have returned that love?

He looked down and saw one of the old, leather-bound book in his hands. He didn't remember picking it up. Nor did he remember tearing it in two, though he must have done. The headmaster wouldn't be too pleased, but the offer of a generous donation would soon fix him. Money could fix *anything*.

Mary Taylor carefully counted out the large bank notes her husband had just handed to her.

'. . . twenty-three, twenty-four, twenty-five.'

'All there, isn't it?' said Ted Taylor.

'Yes, it's all there,' she agreed.

Most people in Marston would think they'd died and gone to heaven if they had twenty-five pounds in their hands, Mary thought. But then for them, it would be nothing but a windfall – something to use to buy the little luxuries which could not be afforded from the normal wage packet. It wasn't a windfall for the Taylors. It was a final payment, probably the last money that Ted would ever earn.

'Why don't you go for a walk, love?' she suggested. 'You know the doctor said you should get plenty of exercise.'

'Aye,' Taylor agreed. 'Maybe I will.'

Mary waited until she was sure her husband was well out of the way, then went over to the sideboard and took a pencil and paper out of the drawer.

WEEKLY EXPENSES, she wrote in large capital letters.

Rent – three shillings and sixpence per week.

Bread – four and sevenpence.

Meat – two and fourpence.

Even if the family cut down on luxuries like tea (a shilling), sugar (one and tuppence) and fresh milk (one and eightpence), they couldn't possibly live on much under a pound a week. With the blood-money Len Worrell had paid them, and what was left of their savings, they had less than a year before they were completely destitute – less than a year before they would be knocking on the workhouse door.

Scenes from the bleak life of a pauper played themselves out in her mind's eye. Her living in one dormitory with Becky, Ted and the boys living in another. No family evenings around the piano. No walks in the country. Not even the remotest possibility of a day trip to the seaside.

She thought back to the magical day she'd visited Southport with Peggy, an old friend from her time in service. Ted had refused to go with them, of course – Northwich was as far as he ever intended to travel – but like the natural gentleman he was, he'd accompanied her as far as the railway station.

'Mind you're careful when you get there,' he'd warned her, as if he thought she were visiting Darkest Africa instead of Lancashire.

'And you mind you look after the kids while I'm away,' she'd said – as if she thought it, too.

It had been wonderful, that day in Southport. They'd walked along the prom and listened to the band in the park. She'd played croquet for the first and last time in her life, and laughed herself sick when she couldn't get the silly little ball through the stupid little hoop. There'd been outdoor dancing, too, though without her husband to partner her, she'd had to content herself with just watching others. Then Peggy had said she was feeling peckish and they'd gone and . . .

Mary jumped up from her chair and began to pace the kitchen.

That was it! she thought. That was it!

She found that she was trembling – as well she might. The idea which had just come to her was so audacious that it brought out goose-pimples all over her body.

'It's crazy!' she said aloud. 'Completely crazy.'

But was it any crazier than spending the rest of her life in the workhouse?

The back door opened and her husband hobbled into the kitchen.

'Ted!' she said excitedly, 'I've had an idea!'

'What sort of idea?' Taylor asked cautiously.

She was on the point of revealing her whole scheme when a tiny voice from deep inside her suddenly came to life.

Keep it to yourself, the voice urged. Ted'll say it's nothing but a mad gamble. He'll never let you do it!

Well, it *was* a gamble – and maybe even a mad one – Mary agreed. But even if the gamble failed they would lose nothing but a few additional months of freedom – months which would be poisoned, anyway, by thoughts of the misery to come.

'So what's this idea of yours, then?' Ted asked a little impatiently.

'It's nothing,' Mary assured him. 'Just a fancy of mine. Forget it.'

'You might as well tell me now you've brought it up,' her husband insisted.

'No, it was really daft,' Mary replied. She touched her brow. 'Maybe I'm a bit feverish.'

'Then you'd better go and lie down,' Ted advised.

She didn't want to lie down. She wanted to go to Northwich at that very moment – before her courage failed her.

'I think *I'll* have a walk,' she said, reaching up to the clothes hooks for her bonnet. 'Yes, I think the fresh air will do me good.'

'You've put that money somewhere safe, haven't you?' Taylor asked as she opened the back door.

'Of course I have,' Mary replied, clutching the bundle of notes more tightly in her hand.

It was shortly after midday, and things were very quiet in the New Inn. In fact, Paddy O'Leary thought, if you ruled out the pair of dray-men who were drinking for free after delivering several barrels of Greenall's Best Beer, the only customer was Ted Taylor. And even he had been nursing a half pint of ale for over an hour.

'Time I was going, Paddy,' Taylor said, and drained the last dregs from his glass.

Not that he was really in any hurry – there was little

enough he could do at home – but he didn't believe in taking up a pub's space when you weren't drinking, and another half would have been too much of a luxury.

What was up with Mary? he wondered as he opened the door. For the last three days, ever since she'd said she had an idea then refused to tell him what it was, she'd been acting very strangely.

He saw the horse and cart parked outside his house the moment he stepped into the street. Then he noticed that his front door was wide open.

'What the hell . . . ?' he wondered.

A large man with a shock of flaming red hair emerged from the parlour, staggering under the weight of the burden he was lifting. As he backed further down the path more of his load became visible.

'The piano!' Taylor gasped. 'He's taking Mary's piano – her pride and bloody joy.'

Taylor began to hobble up the lane. A second man, almost as big as his mate, had now emerged from the front room on the other end of the piano.

'What the hell's going on?' Taylor demanded.

The man on the front of the piano turned his head towards the angry cripple.

'Hang on a minute,' he said. 'I've got me hands full at the moment.'

The two removers heaved, and the piano was on the cart. The red-head straightened the piano a little, dusted himself down, and then turned to face Ted.

'Now, what's your problem?' he said.

'I asked you what the hell you think you're doing?' Ted said, growing more furious by the second.

'What's it got to do with you?'

'This is my house,' Ted said.

'And *this* is *my* piano,' the other man told him.

He held out a bill of sale for Ted to inspect. Mary's signature stood out clearly at the bottom of it.

*

Taylor made his way round the back and found Mary sitting in the kitchen. She had a bowl of water on her knee and was peeling brussels sprouts. It was obvious that she'd been crying.

'You shouldn't have sold the piano, love,' Ted said, his voice almost cracking. 'We're not that desperate yet.'

'We don't have the room for it any more,' Mary sniffed.

'Don't have the room for it?' Taylor asked. 'That's just plain daft. Now that Eunice and Jessie and ... and Jack ... have gone, we've got more room than we've had since we first got married.'

'That'll all change soon,' Mary said, trying to sound brisk and businesslike. 'When the fish and chip shop opens we'll be more crowded than we've ever been.'

'When the *what* opens!'

'The fish and chip shop,' Mary repeated.

'And what's that when it's at home?' Taylor asked.

'You know what chips are don't you?'

'Yes.'

'And fish?'

'Of course.'

'Well, that's what a fish and chip shop sells. I saw one in Southport once. They're all the rage in Lancashire.'

'Let me get this straight,' Taylor said slowly and carefully. 'You want to open one of these here fish and chip shops in our front parlour.'

'That's right,' his wife agreed.

'You must have gone bloody barmy,' Taylor said. 'This isn't Southport. It's not even Northwich. This is little Marston. There's no call for that sort of thing here.'

'I think there is,' Mary said firmly.

'Well, whether or not, we're not bloody opening one,' Taylor told her. 'I won't allow it.'

'You've no choice,' Mary told him, her voice quavering a little.

'No choice? Why not?'

'Because if we don't live off the shop, what will we live off?'

'We've still got most of the money Len Worr...' Taylor began. He stopped suddenly, as if struck by a thunderbolt.

'You've spent it, haven't you?' he demanded when he could finally find his voice again.

'You can't make fish and chips without a range,' Mary said.

'You've spent it,' Taylor said again, still unable to completely accept the fact. 'All of it? Isn't there even a bit left?'

'Just enough to buy coal for the range and fish and potatoes for next week,' Mary said.

During the whole of their married life Ted Taylor had never hit his wife, but he came close to it then.

'You've ruined us!' he shouted. 'You've completely bloody ruined us.'

'The money wouldn't have lasted for ever,' Mary reminded him. 'We were ruined already.'

Ted got to his feet and hobbled to the door.

'Where are you going?' Mary asked in alarm.

'Back to the pub,' Ted said. 'While I've still got a few coppers in my pocket, I might as well have a pint — because there'll be no more ale after this.'

'A fish and chip shop — it'll never work!' said Not-Stopping Bracegirdle, for once in agreement with Ted Taylor. 'You take my word for it, they're doomed from the start.'

'At least they're trying,' Dottie Curzon replied, taking a sip of her milk stout. 'At least they're putting up a fight.'

This sounded dangerously like a revolt, and Not-Stopping allowed her subjects no such luxury.

'Why should anybody buy cooked fish from a shop when they could just as easily make it in their own kitchen?' she demanded, fixing Dottie with her beady crow's eye.

'Well, I don't really know,' Dottie admitted.

'It might make a nice change,' Maggie Cross said disloyally.

'A nice change!' Not-Stopping scoffed. 'A nice change indeed! A rum kind of change, if you ask me.'

'Well I hope they make a go of it,' said Paddy O'Leary through the serving hatch.

Not-Stopping, who had not noticed him standing there, gave the landlord one of her biggest beaky smiles.

'Oh, so do I, Mr O'Leary,' she said. 'So do I.'

The cooking range arrived by train from Manchester on Friday and was picked up from the railway station by Hitchen's Carriers Ltd the next morning. By noon on Saturday it had arrived in Marston and was being unloaded by four of Mr Hitchen's workers.

'It weighs a ton, that thing,' Hitchen said as he watched his men manoeuvring it through the front door. 'What exactly is it, Missis?'

'It's a cooking range,' Mary explained. 'For making fish and chips.'

'Fish and chips,' the carter said with a grin. 'By, but you must really like 'em in your house if you need something that big to cook 'em in.'

'It won't just be for us,' Mary told him, wishing she sounded more confident. 'We're opening a shop.'

The carter scratched his head.

'A shop for selling fish and chips,' he mused. 'Sounds a rum idea to me.'

'That's what I've been telling you, Mary!' said Ted Taylor, who had been hanging around at the edge of the scene like an angel of doom. 'That's what I've been telling you all along.'

On Sunday Mary press-ganged her children into service.

'Some of the paint's got chipped off with all this moving about,' she said to George. 'Just go over it with a brush, will you? I'd like to have the place looking smart before we start serving customers.'

'Customers!' Ted Taylor snorted from the doorway.

Ignoring her husband, she turned to her younger son.

'Could you give all the windows a good polishing, Philip?' she asked.

'Aw, Mam,' Philip complained.

'It won't take you long,' his mother said encouragingly.

'And when you've finished that, you can tidy up the front garden a bit. I know folk'll be coming to buy fish and not to see our plants, but it doesn't cost much to look tidy, does it?'

'What can I do, Mam?' Becky asked.

Mary knelt down so her eyes were level with her daughter's.

'You and me are going to clean the range and the floor until the whole place is sparkling,' she said.

'And who's going to peel the five hundredweight of spuds you've got in the back yard?' Ted Taylor wondered.

'Me, Ted!' his wife said tartly. 'Me! Just as soon as I've finished my other jobs.'

'You'll never be ready on time,' Taylor said.

'I will,' Mary promised. 'If I have to stay up all night, I will.'

'Look,' Taylor said awkwardly, 'I don't approve of any of this — I don't want you to think that — but I'm doing nothing at the moment, so I might as well get them spuds peeled.'

'If you're sure ...' Mary began.

'If you want to talk me out of it ...'

'No, it's just that ...'

'Well, then, I'd better go round the back and ...'

Husband and wife finally stopped talking and smiled at one another — it was quite a while since they'd done that.

Early on Monday morning a cart belonging to Stanways the Fishmongers pulled up at the front.

'I don't normally make deliveries outside Northwich,' the driver said, 'but for such a big order as this it's worth going out of me way.' He looked at the boxes he'd just stacked in the corner. 'Do you really think you'll manage to sell all this fish, Missis?' he asked.

'Of course I do,' Mary said shakily.

'Well, you know your business better than what I do,' the fishmonger replied, giving his delivery one more dubious glance.

But that was the problem, wasn't it? Mary thought as she watched his horse trot away. She *didn't* know the business — she didn't know it at all.

*

At noon on Monday, Ted fired up the range.

'I still don't approve,' he told his wife, 'but lighting fires is men's work.'

So was erecting signs, apparently. Fred Emmett — coffin maker to just about everybody — had knocked together a large wooden fish, and it was Ted, not Mary, who struggled up the ladder to screw it to the wall.

'Looks good,' Taylor admitted when he'd climbed down again, 'but wouldn't it have been better just to have a sign saying "Fish and Chips"?'

'No,' Mary said. 'It'll make people curious, will that sign. It'll get them close enough to the shop for them to smell how delicious our fried fish really are. Still,' she continued, looking at the sign critically, 'I wish I'd got Mr Emmett to make me a bag of chips as well.'

At a quarter to five everything was ready and the parlour door — normally closed except for weddings and funerals — was thrown wide open. At five on the dot the steam hooter at Worrell's went off, signalling the end of another day's work.

The first group of workers to draw level with Taylor's stopped in the middle of the lane and looked up at the sign. Watching them through the window, Mary realized that her heart was galloping.

'Come on in, you buggers,' Ted Taylor said, softly but urgently. 'Come on in, for Christ's sake!'

The men stood in the street for perhaps a minute, pointing now to the shop, now to the New Inn. In the end, it was the pub they headed for.

'Never mind, lass,' Taylor said with false heartiness. 'There's plenty more fish in the sea.'

There were plenty more fish sitting out in the wash-house, too, Mary thought — that was the trouble.

'Perk up,' her husband told her. 'It's not often I make a joke, but when I do, I'd like it to be appreciated.'

Mary forced a weak laugh, though she had rarely felt more miserable in her life.

Other groups of workmen appeared. Some stopped to look at the sign, some walked straight past. None of them came into the shop.

Mary gripped the edge of her chopping table and bowed her head.

'You were right all along,' she said. 'Fish and chip shops might make money in a place like Southport, but they've no chance in a little village like Marston.'

Ted Taylor put his hand comfortingly on his wife's shoulder.

'It's your first day, love,' he said. 'You can't expect miracles on your first day.'

But if she couldn't sell her fish and chips when they were a novelty, when *would* she be able to sell them, Mary wondered.

'I heard you were opening a shop and I thought I'd come and see it for myself,' said a voice from the doorway.

Mary looked up hopefully, but her heart sank when she saw who was there – Archie Sutton, a waller famed for his boozing and, as a direct result of it, for having the biggest beer belly in Marston. If there was one man in the village who would always put ale before food, she thought, that man was Archie.

'Hello, Mr Sutton,' she said, trying her best to sound cheerful.

'A shop selling fish and chips,' Sutton mused. 'That is a funny idea. How much are you charging, Mrs Taylor?'

'A ha'penny for a bag of chips and a penny ha'penny for a fish in batter,' Mary told him. 'There's peas, too, if you want them. And the vinegar's free.'

Archie Sutton jingled some coins in his pocket.

'I was going to have a pint,' he said, 'but I have to admit, them fish and chips do smell good.' He slid tuppence onto the counter. 'Give us a helping of each.'

Mary selected the biggest fish and shovelled a generous ration of chips on to a waiting piece of newspaper.

'Be sure to tell your mates about us, won't you, Mr Sutton,' she said, as she twisted the newspaper into the shape of a bag.

'I will,' Archie Sutton promised. 'But I won't tell me missis

– and neither must you. She doesn't mind me spending me money on ale, but if she finds out I've been buying somebody else's cooking, she'll have me ball ... well, she won't be very pleased.'

There were perhaps another ten customers that day, and considerably more the next. As money ran short towards the end of the week, trade fell off a little, but on Saturday – pay day – customers were queuing up to get in.

'Well, it makes a change from cooking yourself, doesn't it?' Not-Stopping Bracegirdle said to Maggie Cross as they waited patiently in line. 'They've got a grand little business here, have the Taylors. It'll be a great success – you mark my words.'

With all the salt works being closed on Sunday, Mary and Ted had expected the day to be a quiet one, but they found they were more rushed off their feet than ever.

'I've not seen you before,' Ted Taylor said to a customer who had just tied up his whippet outside.

'No, you won't have,' the man agreed. 'I'm from Weaverham.'

'So what are you doing in Marston?' Taylor asked politely. 'Visiting relatives?'

'Nah,' the man replied. 'Got no time for relatives, me. I'm just taking the dog for a good long walk. Mind you, the reason I've come here rather than anywhere else is because of these,' he continued, holding up his bag of chips. 'Word's been getting round about Taylor's shop. Are you the gaffer?'

'Yes,' Ted Taylor said. 'Well,' he added in all fairness, 'it's more me wife's business, really.'

'Then why don't you tell her to sell meat pies?' the man asked. 'I mean, fish and chips are all very well, but people feel like a change now and again.'

'Maybe you're right,' Ted said, already beginning to calculate just what it would take for him to be able to expand into the meat pie business.

PART TWO
1882

CHAPTER SEVEN

The first people to learn of it did so from the fly posters which started to appear all over Northwich, but word of mouth travelled even faster than the speediest bill sticker and soon they were talking about it in every outlying village and hamlet.

'The circus is coming!' wide-eyed children and hardened rock-salt miners told each other excitedly.

'The circus is coming!' country curates informed common labourers with whom they would not normally have passed the time of day.

'The circus is coming!' well-bred ladies explained to washer-women they'd hardly even noticed before.

Yes, it was true! 'Lord' George Sanger's world-famous circus was actually going to visit their little town. There would be clowns and acrobats. There would be performing horses. There would be man-eating lions just like in the picture books. There would even be elephants.

'Have you ever seen an elephant?' Becky asked Gilbert Bowyer as she squatted beside his chair at the end of Ma Fitton's alley.

'Hundreds of them,' the old soldier told her.

'Really?' said Becky, who was never quite sure whether or not Old Gilbert was making fun of her.

'Really,' Gilbert assured her. 'They were all over India.'

'And what were they like?'

Gilbert thought about it for a while

'Big,' he said finally.

'Well, I know that,' Becky laughed, '*Everybody* knows that.'

'No, they don't,' Gilbert said seriously. 'I mean, it's easy to say "big", but you've no idea of just how *huge* "big" can be. The size of houses, some of them were. They lifted tree trunks as if they were nothing but twigs. And when they carried the rajah in a parade they were covered from head to foot in gorgeous silk cloth so expensive that the fanciest lady in Northwich couldn't even afford to have a blouse made of it.'

'Gosh!' Becky said, still not certain that she completely believed the old soldier.

'Some of them Indian princes used their elephants in battle, too,' Gilbert went on. 'Imagine it, Becky, standing there expecting to fight other men and suddenly finding yourself being charged by this vast grey beast which is trumpeting fit to chill your blood. We should have had a few of them jumbos in the Crimea – that would have scared the dickens out of them Russian farm boys.'

'I think it would have scared the dickens out of me,' Becky admitted. 'I hope Lord George's elephants are a bit quieter than that.'

'If you're going to the circus then you'll need a new dress,' Mary Taylor said as her daughter helped her with the mangling.

'But the circus is coming next Saturday,' Becky reminded her mother. 'You'll never have time to make me one by then.'

'Make you one?' Mary said, as if her daughter's statement had surprised her. 'I've no intention of making you one. I shall *buy* you one.'

Becky's mouth fell open. 'Buy me one!' she said. 'From a shop?'

'Of course from a shop,' her mother replied. 'You're not a salt-miner's daughter any more. Your dad was down in the last *Slater's Guide* as a "fried fish merchant", and if that doesn't mean he can afford to pay for a new dress, then I don't know what does.'

They went to Bratt and Evans'. Most of the drapers' shops in Northwich were pokey little places with everything piled up, but Bratt's was new and modern – full of wide-open spaces and dummies wearing all the latest dresses.

'How can I be of service, Madam?' asked a smartly dressed young assistant.

'I want a dress for my daughter here,' Mary said, and when the assistant had gone away to see what they had in stock she turned to Becky and whispered, ' "Madam", eh? Even *I've* gone up in the world.'

The first garment the woman returned with was a smock, much like the ones her mother had run up for her to wear to school.

'I don't think so,' Mary said, hardly giving it a glance. 'We're looking for something a little more grown-up.'

'Are we, Mam?' Becky asked, wondering how many more surprises her mother had up her sleeve.

'Of course we are,' Mary said. 'You've turned eleven now — that's quite the young woman. And you're big for your age. Just look in that glass.'

There was no full-length mirror at home, but there was in this shop, and it was something of a shock for Becky to see herself reflected in it. She'd already had evidence she was growing up, of course — the monthly discomfort which still took her by surprise, for example — but she hadn't realized she'd gone this far. Even in the childish dress she was wearing the image staring back at her from the mirror *was* that of a young woman, a young woman, furthermore, with long legs, a narrow waist and — slightly to her embarrassment — a fairly well developed bosom.

'Yes, and yours isn't the only head you'll turn,' said her mother, reading her mind.

Becky found that she was blushing.

'You even manage to do that prettily,' her mother said.

Mary Taylor shopped for clothes as if she'd been doing it all her life. This dress was too dowdy, she told the assistant with a superb air of authority, that one was too showy. She didn't like the cut of the frock the assistant was hopefully holding up now. Yes, that one was very pretty, but unfortunately it had a large bustle.

'You've got to be *really* grown up before you're allowed to wear something as ... well, as *feminine* ... as a bustle,' she confided to her daughter. 'Maybe you should even be married.'

It seemed to Becky that they had seen every dress in the shop at least twice before Mary finally settled on one with a high-stand collar, waterfall frill and knife-pleated tiered skirts.

'Shall I have the dress sent round, Madam?' asked the exhausted assistant.

'No, we'll take it with us,' Mary replied. 'How much have I to pay, please?'

Becky was horrified when she heard the cost.

'Can we afford it, Mam?' she whispered to Mary while the assistant was wrapping the extravagant frock in tissue paper.

'Of course we can afford it,' Mary said cheerfully. 'It just means selling a few more meat pies, that's all.' She laughed. 'And to think, not that long ago we were so poor that when I wanted crutches for your dad, I had to buy them from a pawn shop.'

They smuggled the dress into the house.

'Don't you want Dad to see it?' Becky asked.

'Oh, I want him to see it,' her mother told her, 'but not yet.'

All the way through her evening's work in the shop, Becky could think of nothing except the dress which was now safely hidden under her bed, but it was not until the plates had been cleaned away from their own supper that Mary said, 'Becky and me are going upstairs for a minute.'

Just putting the dress on wasn't enough, Mary explained to her daughter once they were safely on the right side of the bedroom door. Her hair had to be completely re-done, too, otherwise she'd only look silly.

'So sit down there and let me get to work on you,' Mary ordered.

Her skilful fingers worked rapidly on the plaits which Becky had worn since she was a very small child, and soon the hair fell free. Mary held it in her hands, assessing its weight and springiness.

'Yes,' she said thoughtfully. 'Yes, I think I know what to do with it.'

As her mother laboured at piling her hair up on her head, Becky looked into the mirror. Getting rid of the plaits had somehow transformed her, she thought, so that the face which stared back at her seemed almost to belong to a stranger.

She considered this new face critically. The hair was ash-blonde, like her mother's. The eyes were a deep blue. The nose was not small, but it had a gracious line which poor Colleen O'Leary's bulbous hooter sadly lacked. The lips were *quite* full and the mouth *quite* wide, though neither of them were displeasing. The chin was a gentle oval. On the whole, not a bad face at all, she decided.

'What are you doing up there?' Ted Taylor called from the foot of the stairs. 'You've been gone nearly half an hour.'

'Five more minutes,' Mary promised. 'Be patient. It'll be worth the wait.'

'What will?' Taylor wanted to know.

'You'll see,' Mary said enigmatically. 'Now get back in the kitchen and finish reading your paper.'

'I'll never understand women,' Taylor complained, as he often did after exchanges with his wife.

Once Mary had arranged her daughter's hair to her satisfaction she took some silk flowers from a drawer and began to weave them into her grand design. It had been an exaggeration to say they'd only be five minutes – but it certainly couldn't have been more than another half hour before the process was completed.

'Now creep down the stairs after me, then wait until I tell you to come in,' Mary said. 'And when you do come in, don't just walk. Glide! Float!'

As they descended the narrow stairs the mother deliberately clumped her feet loudly on each one and the daughter followed on tiptoe.

Signalling Becky to stay where she was, Mary entered the kitchen, almost – but not quite – shutting the door behind her.

'Are we finally to learn what all this is about?' Becky heard her father say.

'Of course, love,' his wife replied. 'My lords, ladies and gentlemen, may I present to you – Miss Rebecca Taylor.'

Becky wanted to turn round and run back up the stairs, but she hadn't the nerve. On the other hand she didn't feel brave enough to go into the kitchen, either. So she simply stayed where she was.

'Miss Rebecca Taylor,' Mary said, more insistently this time – and with perhaps just a touch of irritation.

Becky sighed. There was no point in trying to go against Mam, not once she'd got an idea in her head. Becky opened the door wider and did her best to float – or glide – into the kitchen.

Ted Taylor was sitting in his favourite chair by the fire, Philip and George were both at the table. All three of them looked at her in amazement.

'Well, turn round once or twice,' her mother said. 'Give them a proper look at it.'

Becky turned.

'So? What do you lot think of it?' Mary Taylor demanded.

'Our Becky looks smashing,' George said.

'Really smashing,' Philip agreed.

Ted Taylor said nothing. His mouth had fallen open and he had the dazed look of someone who's been told that a close friend has died.

'What do *you* think, Dad?' Becky asked anxiously.

Still Taylor seemed unable to speak.

'You do like it, don't you?' Mary said.

His wife's words got through to him where his daughter's had failed. He blinked as if he were just waking up.

'Oh, I . . . er . . . like it,' he said. 'It's lovely. Really lovely.'

'Then what's wrong?' Mary asked.

'Nothing,' Taylor protested. 'Honestly – nothing.'

'I know you, Ted Taylor,' his wife said accusingly. 'There's something on your mind. Tell us what it is.'

'Watching our Becky come through that door then,' Taylor said dreamily to his wife, 'why, it was like going back twenty years to the first time I saw you.'

'You're blinded by love,' his wife said, laughing. 'I admit I was pretty enough in them days – but our Becky's going to be beautiful.'

*

The circus's opening parade was to follow a route from the railway station to the Big Top, which was pitched on the waste ground next to the gas works. The streets of the town were hung with bunting and packed with virtually the whole population of the area.

'Well, I don't know where this Lord George's appeared before,' said a man standing close to Becky, 'but he'll not have got a warmer welcome than he's had from Northwich, wherever it was.'

They were standing outside Bratt and Evans'. Becky wasn't wearing the dress she'd bought in the store a few days earlier — that was to be saved for the actual performance — but instead had on her grey school smock.

'Are you excited?' her mother asked.

'Yes,' Becky said. 'Are you?'

'I suppose I am — a bit,' Mary Taylor admitted.

Everyone was excited. The entire crowd sizzled with excitement. The circus was the biggest thing which had ever happened to Northwich — and they all knew it.

From up Witton Street drifted the sound of a big bass drum being beaten furiously.

'They're coming!' Becky said, then wondered why she had almost whispered the words.

The elephants led the parade. They didn't look too intimidating at first, but as they got closer the spectators began to realize just how huge they were.

'I want to go home, Mam!' one terrified child near Becky screamed.

'I think I'm going to faint,' said a woman on the other side of her.

People tried to step back, but they were so tightly packed there was nowhere to step back to.

'Let's make a run for it,' Becky heard one lad whisper to another.

'What — and have them buggers chasing us,' his mate replied. 'I'd rather stay here and risk getting crushed.'

They're well trained, Becky told herself firmly. Very well trained.

The beasts lumbered on until they were level with Bratt's, until they were towering over the onlookers. Becky caught the hot smell of elephant flesh in her nostrils. It didn't half pong!

Despite her misgivings she was determined not to miss a thing, and so she forced herself to look up. Each elephant, she saw, had a small dark man in a turban riding on its back. One of them waved to her, and she waved back.

And then, without succeeding in trampling a single person, the elephants were gone – round the corner and heading for the gas works.

'That wasn't nothing,' said the lad who had suggested running away.

'Nothing!' his friend snorted. 'You were wetting yourself!'

'I was only having you on,' the first boy countered unconvincingly.

Well, *I* was a bit scared, Becky thought, and I don't mind admitting it.

Four clowns came next, two wearing papier-mâché heads of Mr Punch and two in oversized cocked hats which looked as if they might once have belonged to Napoleon. They ambled slowly along, occasionally tripping over their own feet, sometimes stopping to shake the hand of a grown-up or ruffle the hair of a small child.

The group which followed looked as if it didn't belong to a circus at all – though it was difficult to say exactly where it *did* belong. It consisted of three men and two women. They were all dressed in closely fitting vests and tights, and their short hair ended in plaits over their ears, almost as if they had horns. Strangest of all, they carried long ladders.

In front of Bratt and Evans' they stopped. The tallest of the men stood perfectly still, while the others raised the ladders, one each side of him. And then the man began to climb both ladders at once, one outstretched arm and one outstretched leg on each ladder.

'Bloody hell fire!' said the man who'd talked about giving the circus a warm welcome.

Higher and higher the acrobat climbed. The others had been

steadying the ladders at first, but now they stepped back, as if what he was doing was the easiest thing in the world. The big acrobat stopped when he was about twenty feet in the air, and the crowd breathed a sigh of relief.

I hope he can get down again without hurting himself, Becky thought.

But the acrobat had no intention of coming down. Far from it! As he stood there — spreadeagled and suspended above the street, the other two men each began to climb one of the ladders.

'Impossible,' gasped the warm-welcomer. 'It'll all come crashing down, any minute now.'

The two men reached the level of the third.

'They don't look like they're going to stop there, though,' Becky told her mother.

They didn't! Instead, they kept on climbing right past him, until they had reached the top rung where they sat down, perfectly at home.

'The girls will go up next,' Becky predicted.

'Don't talk soft,' Mary replied.

But even before she'd finished speaking the girls had begun to climb. When they reached the top the men leant backwards, and the girls stepped lightly from the ladder onto their chests.

'I don't believe it,' the warm-welcomer said. 'I'm seeing it, but I still don't believe it.'

The girls stepped back onto the ladders and made a calm descent. The men followed them and once all four had reached the street the big acrobat who had been holding the ladders apart climbed down too.

The spectators had hardly dared to breathe up to that point, but once the last foot was safely on the ground they burst into thunderous cheering. The acrobats bowed briefly, then picked up their ladders and walked on as if they were nothing more sensational than window cleaners.

What next? Becky asked herself. Whatever can they show us next?

The grand finale was the lions, in a wagon which had been

converted into an iron cage on wheels. They were magnificent creatures with flowing manes and sleepy eyes which seemed – very lazily – to be looking out for their next meal.

Becky shuddered when one of them yawned and revealed his huge white teeth. She wondered how their tamer, in his splendid scarlet uniform, could ever pluck up the courage to ride in their cage with them. She wouldn't have done it for anything.

'Well, now you've seen the parade, there's no point in going to the circus, is there?' Mary Taylor teased.

'Don't talk soft, Mam,' Becky said, returning the advice her mother had given her earlier.

'But you *have* to come to the circus, Dad!' Becky protested. 'You'd really enjoy it.'

'Maybe I would,' her father admitted, 'but pleasure's one thing, and business is quite another. There'll be a lot of folk hungry for a bit of food after the show, and if we close down, we'll miss 'em.'

Pleasure's one thing, and business is quite another, Mary Taylor thought, allowing herself a secret smile. Ever since he's become a fried-fish merchant, you'd think he was running Lipton's.

'We can't miss the circus, Dad,' Philip said.

'And who said anything about you missing it?' his father wanted to know. 'I'm giving me workers the night off. Me and your Mam'll manage.'

'But you're all to stick together once you're there,' Mary cautioned. 'And if there's any disagreements, well, George is the oldest, and you're to do what he says.'

'Aw, Mam, I don't want to go with them,' Philip complained. 'I've made plans to go with me mates.'

'What mates?' Mary asked suspiciously.

'Teddy Prince and Hubert Cross,' Philip said, quickly.

'I don't know ...' Mary began.

'They're good lads, both of 'em,' Ted Taylor interrupted. 'Let him go with them. George'll look after our Becky, won't you, George?'

Her husband would never have let Jack get away with anything like that, Mary thought, but he was too soft on the other two. It wouldn't harm George – he was turning into a fine young man with a good job on the railways – but she worried about what effect his father's softness would have on her youngest son. Still, it would probably be all right – both Teddy Prince and Hubert Cross were sensible boys from very respectable families.

'You don't mind going with our Becky, do you, George?' she asked.

'Of course not,' George replied. 'It'll be just like that first day when I took her to school, except that now she looks so much like a lady I won't mind if she walks by my side instead of keeping a few feet in front.'

He laughed and Becky laughed too.

'Why, thank you, kind sir,' she said, taking his arm and parading him around the kitchen.

The acrobats had been impressive enough in the street, but under the Big Top they left Becky breathless and trembling. How could they all balance on that thin wire so high above the ground? How ever had they learned to fly through the air like that when one slip could have stopped their lessons for ever?

The acrobats were not the only people to raise questions in Becky's mind. There was Mrs Sanger, too. When she stepped into the ring wearing Britannia's helmet and carrying a Union Jack shield, didn't she worry that instead of curling up docilely at her feet, the fierce man-eating lions would decide to be *woman*-eating lions?

And the clowns – did Lord George only employ people who were naturally clumsy, or was it all an act?

The circus lasted for nearly two hours, but to Becky it seemed to have finished almost before it began, and in no time at all she and George were standing outside the Big Top.

'Shall we go to the fairground?' George asked.

'I haven't got any money left,' Becky confessed.

'I have,' her big brother told her. 'Come on! I'll treat you.'

The fair had been erected close to the Big Top, and once she saw it Becky forgot all about the circus. What wonderful things the fairground people had brought with them. There was a huge merry-go-round on which elaborately carved hobby horses went round and round – ever faster. There were swing boats which rocked harder the more their passengers pulled on the ropes attached to their overhead axles. There were stalls selling all kinds of novelties which had never been seen in Northwich before, and other stalls where, with skill, you could win a prize.

For a few minutes they stood and watched the merry-go-round. Becky loved the spluttering steam engine which not only made the thing move but also found the puff – from somewhere – to pump out tunes on the mechanical organ.

'Fancy a ride?' George asked.

'No,' Becky replied.

'Too frightened?' her brother teased.

Well, yes, she was. Not of riding the hobby horse – she was sure that however fast it went, she could hold on – but frightened for her dress. It was the first shop-bought dress she'd ever had – and her mother was even prouder of it than she was.

'Then if you won't go for a ride, come and watch me win a coconut,' George said.

They marched over to the shy.

'Here's a lad who fancies his chances,' the barker called out loudly to passers-by. 'Three balls for a penny, sir.'

George took off his hat, then his jacket, and handed them both to Becky.

'Come and watch him throw,' the barker shouted, 'and then see if you can do better!'

George rolled up his sleeves, weighed the ball in his hand, and pitched it. It shot a good five inches over the top of the coconut.

'Show him how it should be done,' the barker encouraged one of the onlookers. 'Only three balls a penny.'

Becky saw the same look of determination and concentration

on her brother's face as when he'd announced his intention to be a soldier one day.

Now we'll see something, she thought.

George hurled a second ball. It fell short.

'Come on! Show him up!' the barker exhorted the growing crowd.

George bowled his third ball. It hit the coconut square in the middle. The nut rocked for a second, then fell to the floor. The people behind him cheered.

'Well done, young sir,' the barker said, handing over the coconut.

'Another penn'orth's, please,' George said.

'But you've already won a coconut,' the barker pointed out uneasily.

'I want one for me mam and one for me dad,' George told him.

'Save your money,' the barker said discouragingly. 'That was just a lucky shot.'

'Give the lad another go if he wants them,' a thick-set man in a greasy cap called out.

'What's the matter?' demanded a fat woman. 'Isn't his money good enough for you?'

Reluctantly the barker took the coin and handed over the balls. George had his eye in now, and two of the three balls succeeded in dislodging coconuts.

'He's the best bowler in the village cricket team,' Becky said proudly to the man running the stall.

'He wants to stick to cricket if you ask me,' the barker grumbled. 'Cost me a fortune, did them coconuts. Came all the way from Africa, so they did.'

They walked away from the stall carrying their prizes in triumph.

'I fancy a bite now,' George said. 'I've never tried coconut before.'

He smashed the smallest nut against a stone, took out his pocket-knife, cut out some of the white kernel and offered it to his sister.

Becky sniffed it, then shook her head. 'It smells bad.'

'That's how coconuts are supposed to smell,' George told her.

'How do you know, if you've never tried one before?' Becky asked.

Faced with a logic he had no idea how to argue against, George just shrugged his shoulders, said, 'Well, I'm going to eat some, anyway,' and popped it into his mouth.

It was less than a minute before he was clutching his stomach and regretting his recklessness.

'I've got to go!' he groaned.

'Go where?' Becky said.

'You know,' her brother replied embarrassedly. 'You stay here. I won't be long.'

He dropped his prizes on the ground and staggered off towards the piece of waste ground which lay beyond the fair.

Becky looked around her. The merry-go-round was doing such good business that there was even a queue for it. The coconut stall was doing a roaring trade too, with any number of likely lads attempting to repeat George's feat.

It came as a shock to see her brother Philip over by the hoop-la stall – a shock because though he'd said he was going to the fair with Teddy Prince and Hubert Cross, the boys he actually *was* with were complete strangers to Becky.

One of Philip's companions started talking to the stall-holder, and from the way both of them were waving their arms about Becky guessed they were arguing. Then, to her horror, Becky saw the second of Philip's new friends take advantage of the barker's distraction to reach across, grab one of the prizes and stuff it into his jacket. The theft was over in a blink, but Becky knew what she'd seen and began to walk determinedly towards the hoop-la stall.

She found her path suddenly blocked by three young men. From their battered bowler hats with tall crowns to their woollen mufflers and short-tailed check coats, they were dressed alike – as if wearing a uniform. They all carried canes, too, like real toffs. But they were not toffs – not at all. They were street-corner loafers, out looking for a bit of sport.

Becky tried to side-step them, but they fanned out. The one in the middle tipped his bowler hat to her.

'Harry Drew,' he said, and Becky knew instantly that he was lying about his name. 'Me and my friends were wondering if you'd like to go for a walk down by the river.'

'No ... no, thank you,' Becky stuttered.

'Come on,' the man who called himself Drew wheedled. 'A girl doesn't come here on her own unless she's willing to go for a walk down by the river.'

'I'm ... I'm not alone,' Becky said.

Hands on his hips, Drew made a comical display of looking all around him.

'Well, I don't see nobody with you,' he told her. 'Do you, lads?'

'Nobody,' a second loafer agreed. 'The little lady's all alone and looking for company.'

Forgetting Philip and his thieving friend for a moment, Becky turned round and walked quickly away.

'Bit of fun, that's what she's after,' said the voice of one of the loafers, closer to her than it should have been.

Glancing over her shoulder, she saw the three young men were following her. She searched around for a familiar face and saw only strangers. And even if she had come across someone she knew, would that person have dared take on three strong young men so obviously out for trouble?

Past the merry-go-round she rushed, past the coconut shy – and still the loafers were behind her, making their comments.

'Playing a bit hard to get, isn't she?'

'It's all show. Once we've got her down by the river she'll be friendly enough.'

In her blind panic Becky made a fatal error. Instead of staying in the fairground she kept on moving until she had left the bright lights of the stalls far behind her and was crossing a piece of waste ground in search of her big brother.

'George!' she called out. 'Where are you, George?'

Her only answer was silence.

What could she do? Where could she go? Becky's eyes fell

on a row of terraced houses in the distance. The nearest one must be at least a hundred yards away, she guessed, but once she had reached them — once she was under the glow of the street lamp — she was sure she would be safe. She started to run towards the houses. From behind came the sound of other pounding feet!

Faster and faster Becky ran. By the time she reached the edge of the row of houses she was gasping for breath, and had to hold onto the lamp post for support.

'Our pretty vixen is tiring — tally-ho!' called a voice from the darkness.

Looking back across the waste ground, Becky saw three black shapes coming closer to her every second.

'Help!' Becky screamed.

Desperately she looked around her.

The street was deserted.

All the houses were in darkness.

Of course! Everyone would be at the fair! Everyone except for her and the three young men set on mischief.

'Hide!' she told herself as she dashed up the street. 'Hide until they've gone away.'

An unlit alley loomed up ahead. Becky risked a glance over her shoulder and saw that the loafers had not yet reached the corner of the street. Without another thought she dove into the welcome darkness.

Halfway down the alley Becky stopped and crouched down against a back-yard wall. If she kept perfectly still they wouldn't be able to see her from the street, she thought. But was being invisible enough? Wouldn't the thumping of her heart betray her hiding place as surely as the beating of any drum?

There was a clattering of feet and a flash of check coat and bowler hat as the three loafers sprinted past the head of the alley. It would take them less than a minute to reach the end of the street, Becky calculated, and then they would have the choice of directions. Perhaps they would split up, one going to the left and the other two to the right. Or maybe they would all check both possible escape routes. Whatever they did it shouldn't take more than five minutes before they decided they'd lost her and went back to the fair. All she had to do was wait.

The alley smelled unpleasantly of rotting fish and cat piss. How long had she been squatting there? Becky wondered. Her calves ached as if she'd been there for hours, but she supposed it couldn't really have been more than a few minutes. She wished she'd had Jack's watch with her, so she could have seen what time it was. Then she realized that even if she had brought the watch, it was too dark to read it.

I'll count to fifty, very slowly, she told herself, and then I'll go. One butterfly ... two butterflies ... three butterflies ...

She had reached forty-two butterflies when a harsh, breathless voice said, 'Well, my pretty little vixen, you've been leading us all a merry dance, haven't you?'

Becky looked up in horror. The speaker was standing at the end of the alley. He was little more than a black shape, but she could see the outline of his tall-crowned bowler hat and the cane he was resting – almost like a rifle – on his shoulder.

Becky sprang to her feet and ran towards the other end of the alley. Two more bowler-hatted figures appeared in front of her, blocking her retreat. With a sob, she froze. The two men began to walk slowly towards her. At her back she could hear another set of approaching footsteps.

'You'll never be rich if you play so hard to get, my little tottie,' the man behind her said.

'Please, please, leave me alone,' Becky begged.

'I've got two and sixpence,' said one of the men in front of her. 'That should be enough for all three of us, shouldn't it?'

'I'm only eleven!' Becky protested.

'Eleven!' the loafer with two and sixpence scoffed. 'You're never eleven. I'd say you was at least sixteen. And even if you was that young, what we've got to show you won't be nothing new to you.'

A pair of hands grabbed Becky's arms from behind. She

tried to struggle, but the man's grip was too strong. The other two loafers drew level with Becky and her captor, and one of them ran the backs of his fingers up and down her cheek.

'Soft,' he crooned. 'Lovely and soft.'

'You know you'll enjoy it once we've got started,' the other one told her, 'and when it's all over, you'll be half a crown better off, won't you?'

Six hands – six guiding, fumbling, forcing hands – hustled Becky back up the alley and onto the street.

'Having a good time, Scum?' asked a new voice.

Becky felt the hands which held her tighten. She looked up and saw a tall young man in a top hat standing under the gas lamp. From his dress he was clearly a gentleman and, like the loiterers, he carried a stick.

The man who'd said his name was Drew released Becky and took a couple of steps towards the new arrival.

'Who are you calling Scum?' he demanded.

'The only reason I asked is that the young lady doesn't seem to be enjoying herself much,' the gentleman said coolly. 'Does she, Scum?'

Drew dropped his cane and raised his fists.

'I'm going to give you a bloody good thrashing,' he said.

'Are you really?' asked the gentleman, as if the whole incident was beginning to bore him.

Drew advanced like the street-fighter he was – both legs and both arms potentially lethal weapons. He was less than four feet away from his adversary when the gentleman's cane seemed to come apart, and a long metal blade flashed under the gas lamp.

'This is called a sword-stick,' the gentleman said, holding the tip of his blade inches from Drew's throat. 'It's razor sharp. Would you like to see what I can do with it?'

To turn and run would be to risk being stabbed in the back, and Drew knew it.

'We ... we don't want no trouble,' he said.

The gentleman suddenly lashed out with his foot, catching him in the groin. As Drew doubled up with pain his attacker swung his free arm and smashed his fist into the loafer's face. Drew's neck whipped back, his opponent kicked his legs from underneath him, and the fight was over.

The gentleman held out his weapon in front of him as if he were about to charge.

'Let her go,' he said to Becky's captors.

The other two loafers released their grips, backed away a few steps, then turned and ran.

'Come here,' her rescuer told Becky.

Slowly, unsurely, she did as she was told.

Drew was still lying groaning. The gentleman took hold of his lapels and lifted him a little off the ground.

'I think the young lady's entitled to an apology, don't you?' he asked.

'I'm sorry, Miss,' Drew mumbled through bloodied lips. 'We didn't mean no harm.'

The gentleman grunted his satisfaction and released his grip. Drew fell back to the pavement, his skull banging hard against the curbstone. To add to his discomfort, the gentleman kicked him in the ribs.

'And now,' Becky's rescuer said, 'I will escort you back to the fair.'

As they walked back across the waste ground Becky wondered what to make of the man who had saved her. He not only talked like a gentleman, he dressed as one too, in his corduroy jacket with its velvet collar and cuffs. He was quite young, she thought, not more than nineteen or twenty. And she had a funny feeling that she had seen him somewhere before.

They had reached the edge of the fairground.

'You should be safe enough from here,' the young man told her.

'Thank you very much for what you did, Sir,' Becky said.

'I enjoyed it,' he replied. 'It's fun to remind the riff-raff of their place once in a while.'

He turned to walk away.

'What's your name?' Becky called after him.

'My name? My name is Richard Worrell.'

Of course! From the salt works! *Now* Becky remembered where she'd seen him before. He was the grinning boy she had met on the way to her first day at school — the boy she'd always hoped to see again when she and Colleen had played hide and seek in the salt store. But if he was Richard Worrell, he was also the young man whose careless handling of explosives had almost killed her father. And now she was in his debt.

'Well goodnight, Becky Taylor,' Richard said.

Becky gasped. 'How did you know my name?'

'Oh, I've been following your progress for quite some time,' Richard replied. 'A number of years, in fact.'

He turned once more, and disappeared into the night.

As Richard Worrell walked back across the waste ground towards the Liberal Club he was feeling very pleased with himself. It was true that the search for a girl — preferably a young and innocent one like Becky — had been the very reason for his visit to the fairground. Yet he was glad he had resisted the urge with her, because he knew from experience that a girl was only really appealing to him until he had had her. A quick walk down by the river with Becky and he would have lost that special sense of anticipation which he had felt towards her since he'd been a boy.

No, better to wait — perhaps for months, perhaps, even, for years.

'The riper the fruit, the sweeter the taste,' he said to himself.

There *was* something very special about Becky. It would almost be a pity to deflower her — but then, it would be a pity not to.

CHAPTER EIGHT

'Will you carve, love?' Mary Taylor asked, placing the roast leg of lamb in front of her husband.

'What is it?' Ted Taylor asked suspiciously.

'What does it look like?' his wife countered.

'It looks like the biggest leg of lamb *I've* ever seen,' Taylor told her.

'Then that's what it must be,' Mary said. 'Are you going to carve, or what?'

Ted Taylor picked up the carving knife reluctantly, as if, by doing so, he was losing his last chance to send the meat back to the butcher's.

'I know Sunday dinner's special, like,' he said as he sliced into the tender meat, 'and I know that since we've had the chip shop we're a bit better off, but we've never gone so far as to have lamb before.'

'It wasn't expensive,' his wife told him.

'You're not telling me good English lamb like this comes cheap,' Taylor said, then he licked his lips and heaped several slices of meat onto his wife's plate.

'I never said it was cheap,' Mary pointed out. 'I said it wasn't expensive. And it isn't English. It comes from Australia.'

'Then you must have paid a fortune for it,' Taylor said, though he didn't stop slicing. 'It's bloody miles away, is Australia.'

'Aye, Dad,' George agreed. 'Even further than Manchester.'

'You cheeky young bugger,' Taylor said without rancour. 'What I mean is, if it's got to come all the way from the other side of the world, how can it be cheaper than our English lamb?'

'The butcher said it's because they kill it in Australia, *then* ship it over here,' Mary explained.

Taylor bent forward and sniffed the dish.

'I should have thought it'd've gone bad coming all that way,' he commented.

'They keep it cold,' Mary said. 'The butcher called it re-frigeration. It's the latest thing.'

'Whatever will they think of next?' Taylor asked. 'Just when they seem to have invented everything that ever could be invented, they come up with something new. Why, they'll be having trains that fly through the air before we know what's happening.'

It was agony for Becky to wait until everyone had been served before she could tuck into her own meal, but it was well worth it. The lamb was the tenderest and tastiest piece of meat she had ever eaten. And perhaps it was because of the lamb — because of this delicious new experience — that she forgot herself for a second and said. 'I wonder if this came from our Jack's farm.'

She realized her mistake as soon as the words were out of her mouth. The air in the cosy kitchen was suddenly as cold as it must have been on those re-frig-eration ships.

'What was that you said, Becky?' Ted Taylor demanded.

There was nothing for it but to tell the truth.

'Our ... our Jack,' Becky stuttered. 'He's given up the sea. He's working on one of them sheep farms in Australia now.'

Ted Taylor's face was almost black with rage.

'I want nothing to do with that disobedient young bugger,' he stormed. 'And I will not have him mentioned at this table! *Is that clear?*'

Becky felt the food turn to ashes in her mouth. She looked down at her plate and knew she could eat no more.

'Is that clear?' Taylor repeated.

'Yes, Dad,' Becky said meekly. 'Sorry, Dad.'

The Jupiter, pulled at a leisurely pace by Hereward, the Hulses' horse, glided its way along towards Burns Bridge. Mr Hulse was standing at the tiller and Mrs Hulse had disappeared into the tiny cabin to make a cup of tea for her guests. The guests themselves – Becky Taylor and Colleen O'Leary – were lying on the cabin roof and relaxing in the sunshine.

It was a *lovely* day, Becky thought. The sky was a deep, cloudless blue, the sun was smiling down kindly on them. And what better place to enjoy the day than on the roof of *The Jupiter*?

She looked around her. They had reached a part of the canal where the embankment ran high above the surrounding land. From her vantage point she could see Marston Old Mine, and beyond that Forge Pool and the Bluebell Wood. Everything seemed so peaceful – so perfect. Becky lay back on the roof and decided that she and Colleen were lucky to have friends like Mr and Mrs Hulse.

The sound of loud barking drifted past them on the breeze.

'Has Jip gone bird-nesting again, Mr Hulse?' Colleen asked.

'He has,' said the narrow-boat man. 'He should know by now he won't find any eggs at this time of year, but he's forever hopeful. I expect he'll be waiting for us at Marbury Bridge.'

'There he is!' Colleen said. 'Look, he's chasing something.'

Becky, who'd been on the point of falling asleep, opened her eyes again. Jip was in a field some distance from the steep embankment, and was running furiously.

'It'll be a rabbit he's after,' Mr Hulse said. 'You can put money on that.'

Jip suddenly stopped, sniffed the ground, then began to run around in circles. Whatever he'd been chasing he appeared to have lost it.

Becky closed her eyes again.

'Wake me up when we get to the bridge,' she told Colleen.

She had only just begun to doze off when a loud, angry rumbling brought her rudely back to consciousness.

'What's that, Mr Hulse?' she asked, sitting up.

'I don't know,' the old boatman said worriedly. 'I've never heard anything like it in me life.'

Becky looked up the canal, towards the source of the noise. A canal company repair boat, moored up ahead, was bobbing up and down helplessly in the middle of a large whirlpool.

A whirlpool!

On the canal?

'Can you see it, Mr Hulse?' Becky asked, beginning to panic.

'See what?' the old boatman asked.

Of course he couldn't see it! He was in the cockpit, she was on the roof. She had a much better view of the impending disaster than he did.

The repair boat began to move, sluggishly at first and then with greater vigour. Like a great, ugly crocodile it was actually beginning to slither its way onto the tow path.

Except that there wasn't a tow path to slither onto any more! The canal side had given way and an angry flood of water was rushing down the steep embankment.

'The canal's burst!' Becky shouted.

'Bloody hell fire!' Mr Hulse said.

The hole in the canal side was growing bigger by the second, until it was wider than Ollershaw Lane – much wider. The repair boat, riding on a cascade of water, was sucked out of the canal and went bumping down the embankment.

Something was happening to *The Jupiter*, too. Though Hereward continued to plod along the path at his usual pace, the boat had picked up speed and was almost overtaking him.

'Quick – take the tiller off me!' Mr Hulse called to Becky.

The girl scrambled off the cabin roof – scraping her knees as she went – and grabbed hold of the tiller. Mr Hulse leapt onto the bank and ran to his horse.

Hereward, though he didn't know exactly what was going on, had sensed that something was wrong, and looked nervous. Mr Hulse snatched hold of his bridle and began the awkward business of turning him around on the narrow tow path.

'Try and keep the boat steady,' Hulse yelled at Becky as *The Jupiter* sailed past the struggling man and horse. 'Just try and keep her steady.'

Becky gripped the tiller as hard as she could but *The Jupiter* seemed to have a mind of its own. Behind her she could see that Mr Hulse had turned Hereward so he was pointing back to Marston.

'Pull, you bugger!' the boatman urged. 'Pull!'

The horse flexed its huge muscles and began to pull.

The Jupiter slowed down. But it did not stop! Even a magnificent animal like Hereward was not strong enough to fight this current and the boat was still being dragged towards the hole.

'What's happening?' Mrs Hulse asked, opening the cabin doors and looking out.

'Canal's burst!' Becky gasped, tugging at the tiller.

'But it can't have!' Mrs Hulse protested.

'Harder!' Mr Hulse shouted from behind them. 'Pull harder, Hereward. For God's sake, pull harder!'

It was no good. With each second they were being drawn closer to the breach in the bank, and now the sound of the roaring water was filling their ears.

'I'm cutting Hereward free,' Mr Hulse shouted to his wife.

Mrs Hulse looked up the canal and then back to her husband.

'Not yet!' she screamed. 'Not until I've got my things.'

She disappeared into the cabin.

'Mrs Hulse, there's no time for that!' Becky protested.

'Won't be a second,' Mrs Hulse replied as she rummaged around her tiny home. 'Can't leave without my things.'

She re-emerged a second later with her most precious possessions — her decorated plates and her Measham tea pot — cradled in her apron.

'Get off the boat before it's too late, you kids!' she said.

Colleen scrambled down into the cockpit.

'You go first,' Becky said.

Colleen looked at the swirling water which lay between the boat and the bank — and she froze.

'Jump!' Becky coaxed. 'It's not far.'

'I can't,' Colleen said tearfully.

Becky took her hand.

'We'll do it together,' she promised. 'One, two, three — go!'

The two girls jumped. They landed heavily on the bank, lost their balance and sprawled forwards onto the cobblestones. Behind them they heard a thud and a clatter as Mrs Hulse followed them, her treasures still held in her apron.

Looking up, Becky saw the massive form of Hereward backing towards them. Every muscle in his thick hind legs bulged with effort, yet still he was being dragged to the breach.

'Roll, Collie!' Becky screamed. 'Roll!'

They rolled, and less than a second later Hereward's powerful hooves thudded heavily on the ground where they had been lying.

Mr Hulse had his boatman's knife in his hand and was doing his best both to calm the horse and to slice through the tow rope. It wasn't working — any of it. Hereward — his eyes wide, his nostrils twitching with fear — was making it almost impossible for Hulse to get a firm grip on the rope.

'Easy!' the boatman wheedled.

But the horse was not only being dragged backwards, he was also weaving a crazy sideways path of his own.

'If Hereward loses his footing now he'll never be able to get up again,' Becky thought. 'He'll be dragged right into the hole!'

She struggled to her feet and began to run towards the frightened horse.

'Keep away, Becky!' Mr Hulse shouted. 'It's too dangerous. Keep away!'

Becky drew level with the horse. She could smell his fear and hear the erratic breathing which was only partly the result of straining against the current. With one hand she reached up and grasped his bridle. With the other she began to stroke his nose.

'Don't worry, Hereward,' she crooned soothingly.

'This horse is going to go loopy in a minute,' Mr Hulse yelled at her. 'And if he kicks you, you're dead.'

'Easy, Hereward,' Becky said, ignoring the boatman. 'Easy – we'll soon have you free.'

Her words were beginning to have an effect. Though the horse was far from calm he seemed less frightened than a few moments earlier.

'Bloody rope,' Mr Hulse gasped as he continued to slice away at the tow line.

The roaring of the water was louder and louder in Becky's ears. They couldn't be far from the hole now.

'I'll give you some sugar later, Hereward,' Becky promised. 'A whole bagfull of it.'

Suddenly the horse sank to its knees.

'Hereward!' Becky called out in anguish. 'Get up! You have to get up!'

The animal rose groggily to its feet – and stood perfectly still.

The rope! Becky thought.

Mr Hulse had finally succeeded in cutting through the rope and it was the sudden release from the strain of pulling which had caused Hereward to lose his balance.

Becky turned to look at the *The Jupiter*. Now there was nothing to hold it back, it picked up speed as if it were nothing more than a leaf being washed along a gutter in a summer storm.

Jip appeared from nowhere, chasing after the narrow boat and barking furiously.

'Jip! Come back!' Becky screamed.

The Jupiter reached the breach, was sucked into it and disappeared from sight down the steep embankment. For a moment it seemed as if Jip would follow it, but he pulled up at the very edge of the chasm and contented himself with simply growling a final protest.

Becky became aware of Mr Hulse standing next to her. He looked very angry indeed.

'What the hell did you think you were doing?' he demanded.

'Hereward looked so frightened ...' Becky began.

'And so was I — when I saw *you* there. Didn't you know he could have killed you?'

'I didn't think about it,' Becky admitted. 'I just saw how upset Hereward was and ...'

'What could I have said to your mam and dad if Hereward had broken your stupid little neck?' Hulse wanted to know. 'You deserve a good leathering for not doing what you were told, don't you?'

'I suppose so,' Becky agreed.

The boatman's face softened and he put his hand on her shoulder.

'Thank you for saving me horse, Becky,' he said.

Becky and Old Gilbert Bowyer walked slowly along the tow path. The floodgates at Marbury Bridge had been closed and two stop-locks set up at Burns Bridge. Now the canal between the two bridges was completely empty.

Several narrow boats which had been far enough away from the breach to avoid being sucked into it — but not so far that they could get clear of the area — sat stranded at the bottom of the canal. A number of dead fish lay open-mouthed in the mud with other odd objects — a dead cat, some old boots, a battered copper kettle — next to them.

'The canal only burst because the land under the bank subsided,' Old Gilbert said. 'I'm surprised it hasn't happened before.'

They reached the point at which the tow path had fallen away. A cavern, at least sixty feet across and thirty-five deep, had been formed, and at the bottom of it were the repair boat and *The Jupiter*.

'Where's all the water gone?' Becky asked.

'Some of it will have found its way into Witton Brook and Marbury Brook,' Gilbert told her, 'but a lot more of it will have disappeared into the old mine workings. And what will it do once it's down there?'

'I don't know,' Becky said.

'The water'll start eating away at the rock-salt pillars holding up the mine roofs,' Gilbert replied. 'In time, when enough of the pillars have been dissolved, the roof'll collapse and more land will give way. It'll not happen overnight, but the subsidence that happened yesterday won't be the last — and I don't think it'll be the biggest, either!'

The idea of the ground suddenly giving way had bothered Becky ever since the day she and Old Gilbert had gone to see the building being moved in Northwich, and his latest pronouncements had done very little to reassure her. Still, it might never happen, and there were nearer, more pressing concerns to worry about. Like her dad, for instance. Ted Taylor had been very quiet of late — had almost withdrawn into himself — and no amount of questioning from his anxious wife would make him tell her what was wrong.

Yet what *could* be wrong, Becky wondered. It couldn't be his injuries that were bothering him. He still walked with a bit of a limp, but other than that there was no evidence of his accident.

Business?

The chip shop was doing well. True enough, the work wasn't easy, but she knew her father preferred it to going down the mine any day. And the family was certainly better off now that he was a fried-fish merchant.

It was all very mysterious — and if there was one thing Becky liked it was getting to the bottom of mysteries.

Her chance to start digging came one night when she and her father were alone in the shop. There'd been a rush of customers earlier but now there was a lull, and Taylor was twitching as if he'd rather be busy than left alone with his thoughts.

'Is your leg hurting you, Dad?' Becky asked artfully.

Taylor looked up and frowned.

'No,' he said. 'Why do you ask?'

'You were looking so miserable I thought you must have been in pain,' Becky replied, telling herself that was only a *white* lie, and anyway, she didn't know for certain that his leg *wasn't* hurting.

'I should have given up the brass band when I left the mine,' her father said, more to himself than to her. 'It's the Adelaide Mine's brass band. I should have jacked it in when I stopped being a miner.'

'But you're the best trumpet player they've ever had,' Becky pointed out. 'And you really enjoy it.'

'If I'd left then, they'd have had time to train a good replacement by now, and they wouldn't keep on at me,' Taylor said.

'Keep on at you?' Becky asked. 'On at you about what?'

'Give the range a bit of a rub-down, will you, love?' Taylor said, changing the subject. 'We don't want it looking mucky when the next lot of customers come in.'

It was Polly Atherton who finally provided Becky with the key to the puzzle of her father's behaviour. Polly was a fat girl with frizzy ginger hair and a talent for feeling superior. Her dad was the best miner in Marston and his racing pigeons flew faster than anybody else's. Her mother was the finest cook in the village. Her brother would be a famous prize fighter one day. She herself would marry into the aristocracy. And all this was completely, indisputably true – at least according to Polly.

It was no surprise to Becky, then, that when the two of them met in the lane, Polly should have something new to brag about.

'Most of the men are going on the trip by themselves,' she said without preamble. 'But *my* dad's taking the whole family. We're going to make a day out of it, like.'

'A day out?' Becky asked. 'Where are you going?'

'Hasn't your dad told you about it yet?' Polly said, implying from her tone that *her* dad had told the Atherton family almost before he knew himself.

'Told me about what?' Becky asked patiently, because, really, that was the only way to deal with Polly Atherton.

'The Adelaide Mine Band's entering this big competition at Belle Vue,' Polly explained. 'That's in Manchester. Of course, we've all been there before, but it'll make a nice change to go again.'

Now Becky understood. Much as he loved being in the band, Ted Taylor had never travelled beyond Northwich in his life, and had firmly announced his intention never to do so.

Well, she was sure her mam would love to go, and so would she. As for her dad, she remembered what he'd always said to her when she was little and refused to eat anything new – 'If you won't try it, how will you ever know whether you like it or not?'

Sorry, Dad, she thought, but I'm doing this for your own good.

If Philip was surprised when his sister volunteered to take his turn behind the counter of the shop, he didn't show it. After all, if Becky was fool enough to take on extra duties who was he to complain?

Becky was no fool – she knew exactly what she was doing. The shop was her father's kingdom. He felt safe and in control in the chippy, and he let his guard down there more than he did anywhere else. So what better place could there possibly be to launch her attack?

'I think you're quite right not to want to go to Manchester with the band,' she told Taylor as he dispatched a fresh batch of chipped potatoes into the bubbling fat.

'Do you, my love,' Ted replied, sounding surprised. 'Well, it's nice to know somebody's on my side.'

'Of course I'm on your side,' Becky said. 'It's only natural that at your age you should be frightened of going all that way.'

'I'm not frightened,' her father said gruffly. 'I just don't fancy going, that's all.'

The ploy had failed, but that didn't matter. Becky had another card up her sleeve.

'Why should you force yourself to go if you don't want to?' she asked reasonably. 'It'll be a waste of time anyway, won't it?'

'How d'you mean?'

'Well, round here, people think the Adelaide Mine Band is pretty good ...'

'And so they are.'

'. . . but that's only because there's no real competition. Put it up on a stage against a band that really knows its stuff, and the poor old Adelaide's going to look silly, isn't it?'

'There's nothing wrong with the Adelaide Band,' her father said grumpily.

Becky laughed. 'Oh come on, Dad. The Adelaide's bound to come in last at Belle Vue, and you know it. You're far better off keeping yourself well away from the shame and disgrace of it all.'

'You'll see who comes last,' Taylor said irritably. 'Yes, you'll see! Because I'm going to make sure you're sitting right there on the front row when we play.'

Becky quickly turned the other way, so that her father could not see the smile on her face.

The great Saturday came and the Adelaide Mine Brass Band set off for Manchester. The mine's management had been delighted that the band was entering such a prestigious competition, and no expense had been spared. A new set of uniforms had been purchased, and when they boarded the train at Northwich station, it was as second-class passengers – not third – that they travelled.

Despite being surrounded by his proud family Ted Taylor felt far from comfortable. The train seemed to whizz through the countryside, leaving fields and trees as nothing but a blur.

It didn't seem natural. It didn't seem safe.

Thousands of people travel this way every week, he told himself. Your own son works on the railways.

It *had* to be all right, however it felt – but he would still be glad when the great smoking monster pulled up in Manchester and he was standing on firm ground again.

Manchester was a revelation to Ted Taylor. He'd expected it to be like Northwich – only bigger. It wasn't. There were towering buildings in the city of a grandeur unknown in his own town.

The Free Trade Hall!

The Corn Exchange!

And a large round building they said was a library. Imagine having a library that big!

He began to see the point of the trams in Liverpool, too. Hadn't they got legs in Liverpool? he'd asked Jack scornfully. But if Liverpool was anything like as big as Manchester, then trams were a bloody necessity.

The size of the concert hall in Belle Vue overawed him — but not as much as the other bands did. He listened in amazement as the Black Dyke Mills Band played like angels. He looked with envy at the Leeds Railway Band, which was as smart and disciplined as any Guardsmen.

Our Becky was right, he thought miserably as his own band took the platform. We'll probably come last — and we'll be lucky to do that well.

They didn't come last — or even next to it. When the judges announced their decision, the Adelaide Mine Band had been placed fourth, almost within touching distance of the giants from Leeds and Black Dyke.

'And we'll do even b ... better next year,' Harry Atherton said enthusiastically.

'Not without more experience, we won't,' Ted Taylor told him. 'If we're to really improve we've got to have somebody to compete against. That band from Wigan was quite good, wasn't it? What do you think about challenging them — one on one?'

'You mean, ask them to come to N ... Northwich?' Atherton asked.

'Aye, we could do that,' Ted Taylor agreed. 'Or then again, we could go up to Wigan and fight them on their own ground. I'm not bothered which way we do it.'

There was a meat tea after the contest, and then it was time to go home again. It had been an exhausting day and most of the children — as well as many of the grown-ups — fell asleep on the train back.

Ted Taylor wasn't sleepy at all.

To think I've lived as long as I have and never been to Manchester before, he reflected to himself. Just over twenty miles it is, and I could never be bothered to get off me backside to go and see it. By, but I have been missing out.

Nor was that the only thing he had been missing out on, he suddenly realised.

'Are you asleep, love?' he asked his wife, whose head was resting on his shoulder.

'Mmm ...' Mary murmured softly.

'I said, are you asleep, Mary?' Taylor repeated.

It was the urgency in his voice which penetrated Mary's brain. She opened her eyes and looked up at her husband's troubled face.

'I didn't wake you, did I?' he asked.

'I was just resting my eyes,' his wife lied. 'Do you want to talk?'

'Yes,' Taylor said. 'I've been thinking. Do you remember when our Jack used to come back with all his tales about how wonderful Liverpool was, and I'd do nothing but ridicule him?'

'You weren't that bad,' Mary said.

'Yes I was,' Taylor told her. 'Yes I bloody was. Well this trip has been a real eye-opener for me. I'm starting to understand what he was on about now.'

'I'm glad,' Mary said.

'I've cut myself off from the boy for years,' Taylor continued. 'As if it was some terrible crime to want to travel. But if you're a young lad with nothing to tie you down, it's only natural you should want to get around a bit and visit new places, isn't it?'

'I suppose it is,' Mary said, as if the idea had only just occurred to her.

'Would you do something for me?' Taylor asked awkwardly.

'What?'

'I'm not much of a scholar, never was. But if I wanted to write a letter to our Jack in Australia, would you help me with it?'

'Of course I would,' Mary said, lifting her head and kissing him softly on the cheek.

Richard Worrell was watching the narrow boats being loaded when his father – leaning heavily on his stick – came up to him.

'That Horace Crimp's waiting for you in the office,' Len Worrell said with some distaste.

'Good,' Richard replied neutrally.

'I can't understand what ever possessed you to employ him as our lawyer,' Len Worrell complained. 'It's well known in Northwich that he's as bent as a fishing hook. Most of the other attorneys won't go near him.'

And that's precisely why I want him, Richard thought. No honest attorney would touch what I've got in mind with a barge-pole.

But aloud he said, 'Crimp may not have the best reputation in town, but he's the smartest legal mind within thirty miles of here and as long as I keep an eye on him he'll do an excellent job.'

Len Worrell shook his head. 'I'm still not happy with it.'

'If I'm going to run the business you have to let me do it my way,' Richard told his father.

'Aye,' Len Worrell admitted. 'I suppose you'll never learn if I don't let you make your own mistakes.'

But allowing his son to make his own mistakes was only part of the reason Len had given in so easily, Richard thought.

The other part – the major part – was that Len Worrell simply didn't have the strength to fight back any more. He was not a well man by any standards, and though he'd tried to hide it from his eldest son it was sometimes an effort for him to get up in the morning. He had pains in his chest, too – pains which often forced him to stop whatever he was doing and immediately sit down.

'I'll go and see what Crimp wants, then,' Richard said. 'Are you going to come with me?'

Len Worrell grimaced as a new wave of pain hit him. 'No,' he said through clenched teeth. 'I think I'll just stay here for a while.'

Richard looked anxiously at his father. He didn't want the old man to die. Not yet. Not until his brother Michael had finished his engineering degree at the University of London and joined the family business.

'How's work going?' Ted Taylor asked his youngest son over the family supper.

'It's all right,' Philip replied without much enthusiasm. 'Hey, Dad, did you see that Richard Worrell's got himself a new horse and trap?'

'Well, I hope he treats this horse better'n he treated the last one,' Taylor said sourly.

You'd like a horse and trap, wouldn't you, Philip? Becky thought. You'd really like to be riding up and down the lane looking down on everybody. The only problem is, you'll never be able to afford it.

She worried about her brother. Philip was clever — the cleverest of the lot of them in her opinion — but he was lazy, too. He wanted the good things in life — wanted them desperately — yet he was always looking for the easy way to obtain them. That was why, instead of taking an apprenticeship like Jack and George had done — or even trying to get an office job — he'd gone to work as a common waller at Worrell's.

'I'd like to have some money in my pocket,' he told his father when Taylor had tried to convince him to take a trade.

Well, it was certainly true that he was earning more than an apprentice, but when apprentices came out of their time they could command good money, and Philip would be stuck as a semi-skilled labourer for life.

'There were some soldiers on the station today,' George said.

'Were there now?' his father replied discouragingly.

But George's enthusiasm was not to be dampened by so light a sponge.

'They were home on leave,' he said. 'They're not much older than me, and they've already been everywhere. That's the great thing about the army. You get to travel all over the world, and it doesn't cost you anything.'

'Except maybe your life,' Taylor said, getting angry. 'I've told you before, you can take any job you like in Northwich, but I'm not having you ...'

'You've not told us about our Jack's letter yet,' Mary Taylor hastily interrupted.

'No, I haven't, have I?' Taylor said, calming down somewhat. He reached into his pocket, produced a couple of sheets of notepaper, laid them on the tablecloth and smoothed them out. 'He's working on a sheep farm, is our Jack.'

'Is that right, love?' Mary asked, although she, like the rest of the family, had been following Jack's progress all the time it had been a forbidden subject at the table.

'It's a big farm, an' all,' Taylor told them. 'Let's see what he says ... "The farm is huge, twelve hundred square miles in total – which makes it bigger than Cheshire ..."'

'One farm! Bigger than Cheshire!' Philip scoffed. 'Well, I just don't believe it.'

'Your brother may be headstrong,' Taylor said, with a dangerous edge to his voice, 'but he's no liar. If he says that's how big it is, that's how big it is.'

'Sorry, Dad,' Philip said, looking down at the tablecloth.

'Tell us what else he says,' Mary encouraged.

Taylor held the letter up to the light. As he re-read it, his lips moved.

'Well, let's see,' he continued. '"... The wages are very good. We sometimes earn up to ten shillings a day ..." Think of that – ten bob a day.'

Taylor glanced at his youngest son for signs of disbelief, but Philip had learned his lesson.

'And he doesn't even have to prepare his own food,' Ted told his family. 'Listen to this: "Me and the other men have hired a Chinese cook. His real name's something like Hau Fu, but he's got a pigtail, so most of the fellers just call him Nancy. He cooks us three meals a day, and we have meat at every one."'

'Meat three times a day!' Mary exclaimed. 'Good heavens above, the lad must be the size of a house by now!'

'And he gets through a quarter of a pound of tea a week *all by himself*.'

'I hope he's not working too hard,' Mary said a little fretfully.

'Oh, it isn't all work, not by a long chalk,' Taylor assured her. He glanced down at the letter again. '"The last time we sent some sheep to Melbourne, I went with them and saw a night-time football match," he says.'

This was too much for the chastened Philip.

'A night-time football match?' he said disbelievingly. 'However could they see to play?'

'Because they've got what they call "electric floodlights",' his father replied, more triumphant than annoyed. 'Jack says they make everything as light as day. Marvellous thing, that electricity. They're using it at football matches, they're lighting up shop windows in Manchester with it – we'll be having it in houses before you know what's happening.'

'Do you really think so, love?' Mary asked.

'Well, maybe not in the next few years,' Taylor admitted. 'But it won't be *that* long before they're selling it door to door, just like milk.'

Horace Crimp was sitting at the desk and probing his rotting teeth with an old toothpick.

You really are a repulsive little creature, Crimp, Richard thought, not for the first time.

Nor were Crimp's bad teeth the attorney's only unattractive feature. His frame was weedy, yet his rapidly balding head – as if to compensate – was huge.

Richard looked at that head now. Thick blue veins stood out prominently against Crimp's grey skin. But it was the brain inside the head which mattered – the sharp, devious, twisted, wonderful brain which Richard intended to use to the maximum.

'It's time you started looking for our buyer, Mr Crimp,' he said. 'I take it you're clear about exactly what kind of man we're looking for.'

'Very clear,' Crimp replied. He lifted up his toothpick and examined it against the light. 'But don't you think you're being a little premature, Sir? We have to give your brother at least two years in the business before we can carry out our plan.'

'I don't think I'm being premature at all,' Richard said. 'I may not be able to bury Michael yet – but there's no reason why I can't start digging his grave.'

'True,' Crimp agreed, nodding his big, ugly head.

PART THREE
1883–5

CHAPTER NINE

In the Football Association Cup of 1883 Blackburn Olympic triumphed over the Old Etonians. It was the first time a working-class side had won the Cup, and for George, who was now centre forward for the Northwich Vics, it seemed to offer great hope for the future.

'Great hope for the future? And how d'you work that out?' Ted Taylor asked his son.

'Isn't it obvious, Dad?' George replied excitedly.

Taylor took his cap off and scratched his head. 'Not to me. I'm a bit slow, you see, only being a fried-fish merchant. Why don't you explain it to me?'

'Ever since the Association was founded, the "gentlemen's teams" have had it all their own way,' George said, drowning his father's sarcasm with his own wave of enthusiasm. 'But things are finally starting to change. Football's moving towards being a professional game – Blackburn winning proves that – and soon there won't be any room for the amateur gentlemen. Are you following me?'

'Aye, so far,' Taylor admitted. 'As long as you don't use too many big words, I can probably keep up with you.'

'Up to now, the only thing us working-class lads have got in the way of pay has been they call "expenses" – train fares and the price of a bit of food. And the gentlemen haven't even been getting that.'

'Well, *they* don't bloody need it, do they?' Taylor asked.

'Exactly,' George continued. 'Now if football's going to become a professional game – and it's definitely heading that way – where are they going to get their players from? The gentlemen won't do it, for a start. They're far too busy running their estates and going to their fancy jobs in London to play football full time. So who *will* the players be?'

'Ordinary lads like yourself?' Taylor suggested.

'Yes,' George agreed. 'And if they *are* using ordinary lads, they're going to have to pay us a proper wage, aren't they?'

'Are you sure it'll happen like that?' his father asked dubiously.

'It's bound to,' George argued. 'Look, you only pay a few coppers to get into the match now. Would you mind paying double that if it meant seeing a much better class of football, played by fellers who'd been training for the game all week instead of wasting their time at some other job?'

'Probably not,' Taylor conceded.

'And if a tight-fisted old bugger like you will cough up, why shouldn't everybody else?' George asked.

'How old are you now?' his father asked.

'Eighteen, Dad.'

'Aye, well just remember,' Taylor said. 'As big as you are, and as old as you are, you're not too big or too old for a belting, you cheeky young sod.'

But he was smiling as he spoke. He'd almost lost one son by thwarting his ambitions and he did not want to run the risk of losing another. If George was not content to be a safe, steady railwayman, it was better – far better – that he should set his sights on being a professional footballer rather than yearning to join the army.

Taylor thought about his other kids. Jack was a sheep farmer eating meat three times a day. Eunice was engaged to a nice chap who was under-gardener at the big house where she was a maid. Jessie was walking out with a young man who worked behind the counter at the Co-operative Wholesale Society, but had the ambition – and the push – to become an assistant manager one day.

Even little Becky was fixed up.

'When Eunice and Jessie were old enough to start work we were too poor to do anything but send them into service,' Mary Taylor said when her youngest daughter turned thirteen, 'but we've got a bit more money now, and I'd like to see our Becky learn a trade.'

'Like what?' Ted had asked jocularly. 'I can't see our Becky as a boiler-maker.'

'She could do anything she put her mind to,' his wife told him. 'But I wasn't thinking so much of a boiler-maker as *dress* making. I've had a talk to Mrs Stanway at Clegg's Emporium, and she's more than willing to take our Becky on.'

And by all accounts Becky was making a good job of it. She'd already mastered one of them sewing machine things, and Mrs Stanway said she was the best apprentice the emporium had ever had.

It was only Philip who caused Taylor concern. The foreman was always complaining in the New Inn about him being late for work, and hardly doing a stroke when he did turn up. His gang couldn't like it much either, considering they were being paid on piece rates. Yes, Philip was a bit of a problem, but he'd probably settle down when he got a bit older.

He'll have to, won't he? Taylor told himself. He'll have no bloody choice!

Egypt, Egypt, Egypt! The newspapers were full of it. It was the main topic of discussion in every pub in the country. Even the women of Marston, who normally kept well away from politics, talked about it over their back-yard fences. And all because of 'Chinese' Gordon.

'He's the greatest living English hero, is General Gordon,' George told the family. 'He's seen action everywhere. The Crimea, China . . .'

'That'd be where he got his nickname from, would it?' Ted Taylor asked.

'That's right,' George agreed, his father's sarcasm going – as usual – over his head. 'And then, of course, he used to be the governor general of Egyptian Sudan. It was a dangerous place before he got there, but he soon tamed it. He almost stamped out slavery and he made it so safe that anybody could travel through the whole country armed with nothing but a walking stick.'

'Did you say he *used* to be in the Sudan?' Mary asked. 'I thought he was there now.'

'He is,' George replied. 'He went back after this feller called the Mahdi got all the tribes to revolt against the Egyptians.'

'But what's the Sudan got to do with us?' Ted Taylor asked.

'We've got troops in Egypt, guarding the Suez Canal,' George explained, 'and the Egyptian government asked old Gladstone if we'd use them to crush the revolt. Well, Gladstone said no, but what he would do was send Gordon into the Sudan to supervise the evacuation of the Egyptian garrisons.'

'Supervise the evacuation!' Mary Taylor said with a glance at her husband. 'You are using grand words these days. Would you mind telling us what it means?'

'Pull them out,' George said. 'Britain's talked Egypt into abandoning the Sudan.'

'But from what I read in the papers, Gordon's not pulling anybody out, is he?' Ted Taylor asked.

'Well, no,' George admitted. 'He's decided it's important to hold Khartoum and he's there now – under siege. He's asked the government to send some British troops to help him.'

'Seems to me it's not up to him to decide whether he goes or stays,' Ted said. 'But Gladstone'll not let him down. No, the Grand Old Man'll give him help if he really needs it.'

Not everyone shared George's admiration of Gordon.

'I served with him in the Crimea,' Gilbert Bowyer told Becky and George from his familiar stool at the end of Ma Fitton's alley.

'And what was he like?' George asked.

'Mad,' Gilbert replied. 'Completely off his head. Oh, I'm not saying he's not a good fighter – he's probably the most brilliant small-force commander alive – but what he isn't, is a good soldier.'

'How can you say that?' George demanded.

'Because a soldier obeys orders from his superiors, and the only person Chinese Gordon listens to is God – and then only so as he can contradict Him. The government doesn't want anything to do with the Sudan – we're only in Egypt at all

164

because of the Suez Canal – but Gordon's doing all he can to drag us in.'

'Do you think Gladstone will send British troops in to lift the siege of Khartoum?' George asked.

'He shouldn't,' Old Gilbert said. 'But in the end, he probably will.'

Michael Worrell stared across the desk, trying his best to read his brother Richard's face.

We're almost complete strangers, he thought.

Indeed, it had been years since they had seen much of each other. At school Richard had been two years above him – an almost unbridgeable gap – and then he'd left to join the business. Michael, for his part, had gone straight from school to the University of London, and even during the holidays his path had rarely crossed his brother's.

'So you're finally ready to come to work for us,' Richard said, breaking the silence.

He sounded friendly enough, Michael told himself, yet his mind couldn't help harking back to the day, over ten years earlier, when they'd had their last *real* talk.

'*You hate me, don't you?*' Michael had said after the brief fight which had ended with his brother straddling his chest.

'*Oh yes, I hate you, all right!*'

'*But why?*' Michael asked.

'*Who knows?*' Richard replied. '*Maybe I hate you because we're so different. Or perhaps it's just because you're so stupid. It really doesn't matter why, does it?*'

And then Richard had stood up and, giving Michael one last kick, walked away.

Could this be the same brother sitting across the desk from him and smiling affably? Michael wondered.

'So what do you see yourself doing, now you are here?' Richard asked. 'How would you feel about splitting the day-to-day running of the works between us – being part of one of those dual monarchies they taught us about in school?'

This didn't sound like Richard at all.

'*There's nothing so much fun as power,*' he'd once told his brother.

Was he now willing to give up some of that power — without even the show of a fight?

'Well?' Richard said, without even a hint of impatience in his voice. 'How does my idea strike you?'

'I'm an engineer,' Michael said carefully. 'What I'd really be interested in is expanding into chemicals, like Brunner Mond have done in Winnington.'

'A good idea,' Richard told him. 'But it's a little early to think of expanding. The first thing we have to do is consolidate what we've got. Do you know where I think you could be most useful to the business?'

'No,' Michael said suspiciously.

'In finding new markets for our salt,' Richard said. 'If we can once expand production, then we might have enough capital to put your plans into operation.'

And if I was out looking for new markets, I'd be well away from the works, Michael thought.

This was the Richard he knew.

'You don't trust me,' Richard said, reading his mind. 'I can understand that. I said some pretty rotten things to you when we were children, and I really am extremely sorry for that. But now we're both adults, couldn't we try to put the past behind us? Some day we're going to be partners whether we like it or not, and it would nice if we could get on. After all, we *are* brothers.'

'Yes,' Michael agreed. 'We *are* brothers.'

'And I really do think you'd be good at selling,' Richard continued. 'When you give people a delivery date, they'll believe you. And if you have to go to them later with an excuse for failing to meet it, they'll believe that, too.'

'Because I'll always mean what I say,' Michael said.

'And that, my dear little brother, is absolutely the best form of lying,' Richard said.

Michael was looking at him uncertainly.

Richard laughed. 'A joke, Michael,' he said. 'I was making a joke.'

Michael hesitated for a second, and then joined in with his laughter.

'Will you do the job I want you to do?' Richard asked. 'Will you at least try it for a while?'

'Yes,' Michael said.

Richard stood up.

'Then give me your hand on it,' he said.

They shook hands. And then something totally unexpected happened. Richard put one hand on his brother's back and then the other, and suddenly the two were hugging each other across the desk.

It was strange to have his brother's arms around him, Michael thought – strange and wonderful. For the first time in his life he felt as if he really belonged to a family.

'It's good to have you back, little brother,' Richard said. 'It really is.'

'It's good to *be* back,' Michael told him.

After Michael had gone Richard leaned back in his chair and, as his brother had done earlier, let his mind drift back to their last serious talk. He'd told Michael then that what he wanted was to be the sole master of Worrell's, and that had been a mistake because it was always a mistake to forewarn your enemy. Still, he was sure he'd now made up for his earlier foolishness. And how easy it had been, he thought. How *incredibly* easy. A slight quavering in his voice, a hint of moisture in his eyes – and Michael had been his.

He'd be doing his father a favour in destroying Michael, he told himself. Michael was so soft he'd soon run the business into the ground, and that would break the old man's heart. And what if he, himself, did get some satisfaction from ruining his brother? All work and no play made Richard a dull boy.

George Taylor and Harry Atherton stood in the corner of the Crown Hotel's public bar. The place was doing a roaring trade as players and spectators alike drank to Northwich's victory.

'You play . . . played well today, lad.' Ha-Ha Harry said. 'Bl . . . bloody well.'

'Thanks, Mr Atherton,' George replied. 'But I was a bit lucky, too.'

'Lucky be bu ... buggered,' Atherton said scornfully. 'There we were, two goals down, but did it put you off? Did it he ... hell as like! Bang — and we're only one behind. Bang — and we're equal. Bang — and we've won. It wa ... it was the bl ... bloody best game of the season, an' all.'

'I think it probably was,' George admitted. 'Especially for me.'

'You've earned a p ... pint, lad,' Atherton said. 'Hell, you've earned more than a pint. I'd buy you a bloody b ... barrel if I could afford it.'

'Let me buy the next one,' said a new voice in an accent which definitely wasn't local.

George and Harry Atherton turned to look at the speaker. He was a tall man wearing a double-breasted frock-coat and striped wool trousers which immediately placed him a cut above the Crown's usual customers.

'Do I know you?' George asked.

'No,' the man replied. 'But *I* know good football when I see it, and I'd like to show my appreciation. Anything wrong in that?'

'I suppose not,' George conceded.

The stranger went to the bar and returned with three pints and three whiskies.

'You wouldn't mind if I had a word alone with Mr Taylor, would you?' he asked Harry Atherton.

'T ... Ted's not here,' Atherton said. 'Oh, I see, you mean young George. What's it about?'

'I think that's rather between him and me, don't you?' the stranger asked coldly.

Atherton looked distinctly uncomfortable. 'Well, if you p ... put it like that ...' he began.

The stranger held out a sovereign. 'I'll tell you what,' he said, 'you go over there and finish your pint, then get another round in. We should have finished talking by then.'

Atherton stared at the coin for a moment, then took it.

168

'Aye, all r ... right,' he said, adding a slight slur to his usual stutter. 'I'll see you in a few minutes.'

'Is he a friend of yours?' the stranger asked as he watched Atherton's vaguely staggering progress back towards the bar.

'Not really,' George said. 'More a friend of me dad's.'

'I've no use for a man who can't hold his drink,' the stranger said. 'That's not your problem, is it?'

'No,' George replied. 'But why do you ask?'

'I'm a businessman,' the stranger said, 'Ryecroft's the name. Stan Ryecroft.'

'You're not from round here, are you, Mr Ryecroft?' George asked.

'No, not from round here,' Ryecroft admitted. 'Most of my investments are further up north.'

'I see,' George said, though he didn't really.

'I enjoy a good football match,' Ryecroft continued, 'but that's not why I'm talking to you now. There's going to be money made out of the game, and I want to be one of them that makes it. I'll be putting a team together next year, a really professional team, and I'd like you to play for it.'

'Where will it be based, like?' George asked.

'I haven't decided exactly where, yet,' Ryecroft said, 'but it'll be in one of the mill towns like Bolton or Oldham, because that's where people have got the brass to spend on a bit of entertainment.'

'I'm not sure I fancy moving to Lancashire,' George said. 'I mean, by the time I'd paid for my board and ...'

'I'll give you four pounds a week,' Ryecroft interrupted.

'Four pounds a week!' George exclaimed. 'But that's ...'

'A lot of money,' Ryecroft agreed. 'As much as I pay my senior clerks. But believe me, lad, if you're in my team, you'll bloody earn it. So, are you interested or not?'

'Of course I'm interested,' George told him.

'Here's my address,' Ryecroft said, handing him a thick visiting card. 'I'll be in touch in the new year. Don't go breaking your leg in the meantime, will you?' He glanced across at the bar, where Harry Atherton was just ordering the next round of drinks. 'I'm off,' he said. 'Tell your father's friend he can keep the change.'

The news from Khartoum was not good. At the start of the spring Gordon had had an army of well-disciplined Egyptian troops and adequate amounts of food, but as the summer dragged on supplies were beginning to run down and the general lost eight hundred soldiers — a tenth of his force — in a battle with the Mahdi's men on the very edge of the city itself. And still, despite all the clamouring in the press, the government did nothing about sending out a relief column.

'Gordon's still got a couple of steamers under his control,' Old Gilbert Bowyer said. 'If he wanted to get out himself, it wouldn't be difficult. But he won't — he's too bloody-minded for that. No, he'll stay on right to the bitter end.'

Finally, at the end of September, the government gave in to popular pressure and ordered a relief force of seven thousand men, under the command of Sir Garnet Wolseley, to set out from Cairo.

Crowds cheered openly in the streets.

'Now we'll see some action,' George said enthusiastically.

'Don't be so sure,' Old Gilbert cautioned. 'It's over twelve hundred miles from Cairo to Khartoum. Wolseley seems to think it'll be easy just to sail down the Nile — but it won't be. They haven't even got the boats built yet, and even when they have, they'll find they're on a treacherous river.'

Old Gilbert was right — as usual. The boats were not ready until the start of November, and even then progress was slow. There was no wind at first and the soldiers were forced to row against the strong currents until their hands were covered with blisters. Then they reached the cataracts — great roaring, bubbling stretches of water full of jagged outcrops of black basalt — and the boats had to be painstakingly unloaded at every one.

George, like the rest of the country, followed the column's progress avidly in the daily newspapers.

'They have to reach Khartoum before it's too late,' he said. 'They just have to.'

'That's one thing you learn in the Army,' Old Gilbert told him. 'There's no such thing as "have to"!'

Dusk had already fallen and what light there was came mainly from the village's three pubs and Ted Taylor's fish and chip shop. Michael Worrell's horse snorted as if appealing to his rider to turn back.

'Easy, Brutus,' Michael coaxed as he skilfully urged his mount on.

The horse didn't like being out after dark and if Michael hadn't needed some papers for an unexpected meeting in London the very next day, he would never have subjected the animal to this journey.

'We'll be back home before you know it,' Michael said reassuringly, and this time when Brutus snorted, it seemed to be with gratitude.

It was ironic that his brother should have spotted qualities in him he didn't even know he possessed himself, Michael thought. When Richard had suggested he take over the sales side of the business he'd never thought for a second he'd be any good at it, and had only agreed in the interests of the newly forged family peace. Yet Richard had been right, and he'd been wrong. Orders *had* increased, and some buyers had frankly confessed that they trusted Michael much more than most of the people they had to deal with.

They had reached the works entrance. Michael dismounted and tied his horse to the hitching post.

'Five minutes, Brutus,' he promised the animal. 'Ten at the most.'

It was an eerie experience walking through the works at night. The furnaces, which in a few hours would be blazing infernos, were now nothing more than vague black shapes, as squat and still as hunkering toads. The crane, used in the daytime to hoist up sacks of salt, stood silhouetted against the night sky like a gibbet. The whole building seemed to creak and groan, as if it had fallen into an uneasy sleep after its day's labours.

The office was at the back of the works, shielded from the lane by most of the other buildings. So it was not until he'd passed the boiler room that Michael got a clear view of it, and was so surprised that he almost stopped in his tracks.

A light was burning in the office window! At that time of night!

Richard? he asked himself. Richard – working late?

That wasn't like his older brother at all. Richard always appeared to put in a good day's work, but he jealously guarded the nights as his own.

Burglars, then?

Of course! The safe was in the office, with all the wages in it!

Michael thought of going for help, but quickly rejected the idea. For all he knew the burglary could be almost over, and he if left now the thieves would be long gone by the time he got back.

He groped around in the darkness for something he could use as a weapon.

Armed with a thick piece of wood, Michael crept up to the office door. He could hear talking inside, but was unable to make out the words or even decide how many people were speaking.

If there's only two of them, I can handle it, he thought. If there's three or more, I'm in trouble.

He placed his hand on the door knob. It was now or never. He turned the knob, kicked the door open, and sprang into the room.

There were two of them, one sitting each side of the desk, and it was difficult to say which of them was more surprised – Richard or his visitor.

'I thought you were burglars,' Michael said embarrassedly.

He looked down at the makeshift club in his hand, then turned and threw it into the yard.

'I must have given you a bit of a shock, coming in like that,' he said.

They were *still* in shock, especially the visitor, a young man who had an artist's sensitive face but was wearing the trousers and jacket of a common workman.

Why does the lad look familiar? Michael wondered.

Because he was a workman – one of theirs! And his name was ... was ... Taylor! Philip Taylor!

Now what the hell was Philip Taylor doing in the office at this time of night, holding a glass of Richard's best malt whisky in his hand?

Richard seemed to be coming out of shock quicker than his visitor.

'So ... er ... as I was telling you, Taylor,' he said, 'I've ... er ... been getting complaints about your work, and it's just not good enough.'

Philip Taylor seemed unable to speak.

'Did you hear me, Taylor?' Richard demanded.

Taylor made a massive effort to pull himself together.

'Er ... yes,' he said woodenly. 'I'm sorry, Mr Worrell. I promise you, it won't happen again.'

'It had better not,' Richard replied, sounding more natural now. 'All right. You can go.'

Philip Taylor sprang to his feet and rushed to the door as if he couldn't leave quickly enough.

'What was that all about?' Michael asked when he'd gone.

'Didn't you hear?' his brother countered. 'I was disciplining him for poor work.'

'Do you always ask people to sit down and make themselves at home before you start to discipline them?' Michael said. Then, glancing down at the whisky bottle and two glasses on the desk, he added, 'And do you always offer them a drink while you're telling them off?'

'I will do *whatever* is necessary to keep this works running,' his brother told him. 'And if that includes pouring my best whisky down the throat of some working-class lout, then so be it.'

'You're not making a lot of sense,' Michael said.

Richard smiled. 'I know I'm not,' he confessed, 'but I really *do* know what I'm doing in this case, and I'm just going to have to ask you to trust me. Will you do that?'

Richard had greeted him on his return from university like the long-lost brother he was — but had never felt before. Richard had given him a job which he both enjoyed and was good at.

'Of course I'll trust you,' Michael said.

'Thank you,' Richard replied. 'I really mean that. And one more thing, Michael. If you have the interests of the business as much at heart as I do, you'll forget everything you've just seen.'

The situation in Khartoum was becoming desperate, but news was still getting out.

'They're down to eating rats and boot leather,' George told Old Gilbert Bowyer.

'If Gordon had pulled out while he had the chance — as he was ordered to — that wouldn't have been necessary,' Gilbert pointed out.

But George, as usual, refused to have his enthusiasm dampened.

'Listen to this,' he said, reading from the newspaper. '"One evening, when bullets were spattering into the walls, Gordon sent for the leading merchant in Khartoum and insisted they both sit by the open window — under the largest lantern available. 'When God was portioning out fear,' he said, 'at last it came to my turn, and there was no fear left to give me. Go, tell the people of Khartoum that Gordon fears nothing.'"' What do you think of that?'

'I think that when the enemy missed, his own bloody troops should have shot him,' Gilbert said.

'You'll never understand, will you?' George asked.

'No,' Gilbert contradicted. '*You'll* never understand. Not until you've been under fire, like I have. Not until you've been responsible not only for your own life but also for the lives of the men serving with you. What right did Gordon have to take a risk like that, when everybody else was depending on him? No right in the world.'

Khartoum fell on the 22nd of January, 1885, just two days before the relief column reached the city. The Mahdi's troops had rushed to the palace, the papers said, where Gordon, wearing his best dress uniform, had been waiting for them on the steps. When speared in the chest, he calmly turned around and offered the tribesmen his back. He was quickly hacked to death and then decapitated. His body was thrown down a well, his head paraded around the fallen city.

All England was outraged. Crowds gathered in Downing Street to boo Gladstone. Once they'd called the Prime Minister the GOM — Grand Old Man. Now they reversed it and christened him the MOG — Murderer of Gordon.

Souvenir medals were struck, commemorative china jugs fired. There were even silk bookmarks which told the tale of the heroic struggle and the dastardly betrayal. The whole country was — for a while at least — Gordon-crazy.

'I've had another letter from our Jack,' Ted Taylor announced over supper.

'And what has he got to say for himself?' Mary asked.

'Like a bloody idiot, he's going to throw up that good job he's got himself, and try his hand at something else entirely.'

'Something else?' Mary said, trying her best to keep the alarm out of her voice 'What else?'

'Prospecting!' Taylor said with disgust. 'They've found silver at a place called Broken Hill in New South Wales and our Jack thinks he can just walk in and pick it up.'

Mary breathed a sigh of relief. There were a lot more dangerous jobs Jack could have chosen than prospecting.

'He must take after his dad,' she told her husband. 'Got mining in his blood.'

'Mining in his blood!' Taylor snorted. 'I don't know — sailor, farmer, miner — he wants to make up his mind what it is he wants to be.'

'He's still young,' Mary said. 'He's got plenty of time to settle down yet.'

'He might find silver and become a millionaire,' Becky pointed out.

'Aye, and pigs might fly,' her father said sourly.

'You got a letter today as well, didn't you?' Mary asked George.

'Yes,' George replied.

All eyes turned towards him, but George seemed unwilling to volunteer any more.

'Well?' his father said finally. 'Are you going to tell us what it was about or not?'

'It was from Mr Ryecroft,' George said flatly.

'The feller who was thinking of having his own football team?'

'Yes.'

Taylor sighed theatrically. 'You can be hard work sometimes, George,' he told his son. 'What did this feller Ryecroft have to say?'

It was the younger man's turn to sigh. 'It's all been fixed,' George said reluctantly. 'He's putting his team together now, and next season it'll be joining the Football Association'

'And he doesn't want you,' Mary said sympathetically. 'Oh, I am sorry, love.'

'He does want me,' replied George in a voice so low that the rest of the family had to strain to hear it.

'Then you're laughing, aren't you?' Taylor said. 'Four pounds a week at your age! Most men work all their lives and never earn anything like that.'

'Hush, Ted,' Mary said. 'What's wrong, George?'

'I'm not going,' her son told her.

'You're not going!' Taylor said. 'You'd rather stay on the railways? You want your bumps feeling. You're as mad as our Jack.'

'I'm not staying on the railways, either,' George said, quietly but firmly. 'I've finally made up me mind to join the army.'

'Because of Gordon?' his father demanded angrily. 'Then you're an even bigger bloody fool than I thought you were.'

'It was Gordon who gave me the final push,' George admitted, 'but he's not the main reason. I want adventure, Dad, and I can't get that just kicking a ball around. And I want to serve my Queen and Country.'

'Queen and Country!' Taylor echoed. 'Words! That's all they are – bloody words.'

'Will you give me your blessing, Dad?' George asked.

'Do you need it?' Taylor asked, still furious.

'Yes. Yes I do.'

For what seemed like hours, silence fell over the table. Taylor played with his stew while the rest of the family sat perfectly still, hardly daring to breathe. Finally, Taylor lifted his head.

'At least you were man enough to come right out and tell me what you were going to do,' he said.

'Does that mean I've got your approval, Dad?' George asked.

'It wasn't me approval you asked for a minute ago,' Taylor said. 'It was me blessing. I'm not a very educated man, but I know there's a difference between the two. I'll give the one, but I can never give you the other.'

'Thanks, Dad,' George said.

'You may thank me now,' Taylor said, 'but in years to come you'll probably be cursing my name for giving in so easily.'

There was nothing formally planned to mark George's Sunday-morning departure, yet when the day came people turned out and stood at their gates to watch him march down Ollershaw Lane with his parcel of clothes under his arm.

'It's free pints for you next time you're home on leave,' Paddy O'Leary shouted as the new soldier drew level with the New Inn.

'I'll hold you to that, Mr O'Leary,' George replied with a grin.

'With a bit of luck you'll get into some bloody good scraps in the army,' Cedric Rathbone said. 'I wish to God I was going with you.'

'They've no sense, that family,' Not-Stopping Bracegirdle told Dottie Curzon as George approached her gate. 'Not a one of them. Fancy him joining the army when he'd been offered ten pound a week just for playing football.'

'Yes, fancy,' Dottie Curzon agreed loyally.

George was almost level with them now.

'Good luck and God-speed,' Not-Stopping said, raising her voice well above its customary conspiratorial level. 'England needs more young men like you.'

'You've done it now, lad,' Old Gilbert Bowyer called out as George passed Ma Fitton's house.

'I have,' George agreed.

'Look after your mates,' Old Gilbert advised. 'Look after your mates, and they'll look after you.'

'I'll remember that,' George promised.

From their own gate what remained of the Taylor family followed George's progress down the street.

'You can tell he's done the right thing for himself just by the way he's walking,' Mary said.

'Maybe you can,' her husband grunted, 'and maybe you can't.'

'You're proud of him, aren't you?' Mary said, and though she phrased it as a question it was plain that she already knew the answer.

'Yes,' Taylor said. 'I probably wouldn't admit it to anybody but you, but I am proud of him.'

'The house used to be full of kids,' Mary mused wistfully. 'And now there's only our Philip and our Becky left.' She turned to her younger daughter, who was surreptitiously wiping a tear from her eye. 'And which of you will be the next to go, my little love?' she asked. 'Which one of you will be the next?'

CHAPTER TEN

The furnace had been shut down for the night, but though the brine was no longer steaming the air was still thick with the taste of salt. On a normal day the wallers who worked the pan would already have been long gone. But this was no normal day. The gang who worked the No. 3 Common Pan had a visitor, a young man who – despite his shabby coat and trousers – had been educated at Owen's College in Manchester.

There were six of them there to listen to what he had to say. Sitting on the edge of the pan was Cedric Rathbone, the gang boss, looking as wiry and ready for trouble as ever. Next to him was Ernie Bracegirdle, the worried expression on his face due – no doubt – more to the thought of going home to Not-Stopping than to attending this meeting. Tom Jennings – solid, stolid, middle-aged and dependable – was on Ernie's right. Archie Sutton, his huge beer belly spilling over the top of his trousers, was leaning against the wall, Brian O'Reilly – the fireman – was resting on his shovel, and Philip Taylor – the youngest member of the gang – was sitting on the handcart.

Cedric Rathbone handed round a packet of Players and everyone with the exception of the university man lit up.

'Right, let's get started,' Cedric said when all his gang was happily puffing away. 'Phil, you go and stand by that door and watch out for anybody coming.' He turned his attention to the visitor. 'You were going to talk about a union, Mr Donaldson,' he said. 'Now what I want to know is – why should we bother?'

Donaldson laughed. 'Why should you bother?' he asked. 'You put in fourteen hours a day and all you get for it is a shilling a ton — split between you. The brine rots through your clothes and clogs, but does the boss provide you with new ones? — does he hell as like.'

'That's true enough,' Tom Jennings agreed.

'When there's a slump in demand, you're laid off without pay,' Donaldson continued. 'If you're sick, you get nothing. If you have an accident, you get nothing. And finally, when you're too old to work any more, they kick you out — and you get nothing. Why should you bother, you say? How can you *not* bother?'

'Go on,' Cedric Rathbone said, starting to get interested.

'The owners are already talking about amalgamating ...'

'Amagelating? What's that when it's at home?' Archie Sutton asked.

'Forming one big company out of all the little ones,' Donaldson explained. 'And that'll only make your position worse.'

'How d'you mean?' Ernie Bracegirdle asked.

'If you have a row with Worrell's, you'll never get a job at one of the other works — because they'll be part of the same firm. By joining together the owners are developing clout. Isn't it about time you started doing the same yourselves?'

'And how would we go about doing that?' Cedric Rathbone asked.

'There's already a union for you ...' Donaldson said.

'The Brine Workers' Association,' Tom Jennings said.

'That's right, the Brine Workers' Association. But it doesn't operate in all the works, and besides, it's too narrow. What we're aiming at, in the end, is a union that includes the wallers, the lumpmen, the rock-salt miners, the alkali workers, the mechanics — everybody working in the salt industry.'

'What's the point of that?' Ernie Bracegirdle asked nervously.

'Unity is strength,' Donaldson said. ' "United We Stand, Divided We Fall." Once we've got one big union, we'll have the same bargaining power as the bosses.'

'They won't like that,' Cedric Rathbone said.

'Well, of course they won't like it,' Donaldson agreed. 'That's why it's best to tread cautiously at first.'

'Tread cautiously?' said Brian O'Reilly. 'How do you mean?'

'A union's like a person,' Donaldson explained. 'It needs care and nurturing if it's ever to become big and strong. Now, say I called a general meeting of all Worrell's workers, what would happen?'

'The gaffer'd do his best to bugger you up,' Brian O'Reilly said.

'Exactly,' Donaldson agreed. 'He'd try to strangle the infant union before it ever got out of its cradle. But if a few of you were able to recruit other members secretly, he wouldn't know anything about it until he was facing something as powerful as he is.'

'That's right,' Cedric Rathbone said thoughtfully.

'So will you help me?' Donaldson asked. 'Can I count on your support?'

'I don't know,' Ernie Bracegirdle said doubtfully. 'I've got enough trouble with me missis as it is. If she found out I was involved in anything like this my life wouldn't be worth living.'

Donaldson turned to Archie Sutton.

'Seems a lot of fuss about nothing,' Sutton said, rubbing his beer belly. 'As long as I've got enough money for the odd pint, I've no complaints.'

'What about you?' Donaldson asked Cedric Rathbone.

Had he known Cedric like the others did, there would have been no need to ask. The little man's body was tensed for action as it had been so often in so many pub back yards.

'Let's do it,' Rathbone said. 'Let's get a union and hit the buggers where it hurts — in the pocket.'

'And you?' Donaldson said, turning to Brian O'Reilly.

'Might as well give it a try,' the Irishman said. 'If it doesn't work out, I can always go back to cutting peat.'

'You don't think much about the workhouse when you're young,' Tom Jennings said reflectively, 'but by the time you get to my age it's starting to weigh a bit heavy on you. Would this union of yours do anything to keep fellers like me out of it?'

'We'd be pushing the bosses for pensions,' Donaldson said, 'and once we were big enough we could probably help out ourselves, too.'

'Then count me in,' Jennings said.

'And what about him?' Donaldson asked, glancing across at Philip.

'He's nothing but a slip of a lad,' Cedric Rathbone said. 'Best to leave him out of it.'

Across the road in the New Inn the talk was not of unions but of the O'Learys' silver wedding.

'The pub won't be open at all tomorrow,' Maggie Cross said. 'Mrs O'Leary's spending the whole day making Irish stew — pots and pots of it.'

'And when does she expect us to eat it?' Not-Stopping Bracegirdle demanded.

'After the show in the school,' Maggie Cross replied.

'The show in the school,' Not-Stopping snorted. 'Going to cost a fortune, that is. I know for a fact that renting the building alone is going to be ten shillings ...'

'But that does include the use of the oil lamps,' Dottie Curzon pointed out in all fairness.

'... and then there's the magic lanternist himself,' Not-Stopping continued as if her crony had not spoken. 'He's coming all the way from London, and that won't be cheap. If you ask me, the whole thing's a wicked waste of money.'

'So you won't be going to the show, then?' Dottie Curzon asked.

'Of course I'll be going,' Not-Stopping said tartly. 'The O'Learys'll notice if I don't, and it'll completely spoil the day for them. I mean, when you're celebrating your wedding anniversary, it's only natural you should want your friends around you.'

*

'That must be him,' Colleen said.

The man she was pointing to was standing by the guard's van of the London train and supervising the unloading of a number of boxes and crates. He was a wizened little man who reminded Becky of a monkey, and in his hand he carried a large double bass case.

The two girls walked to up where the lanternist was standing.

'Mr Armitage?' Colleen asked.

The little man smiled and looked even more like a monkey. Becky could just imagine him perched on an organ grinder's shoulder, holding out a tin cup.

'Yes, I'm Armitage,' the lanternist said. 'The bringer of magic to your parlour. The purveyor of the world's wonders to church halls the length and breadth of the country.'

His words seemed to throw Colleen into a confusion, and the speech of welcome she'd prepared went completely out of her mind.

'Colleen's Mr O'Leary's daughter,' Becky explained. 'We've brought a cart to take you to Marston.'

'A chariot for the messenger,' Armitage said. 'Excellent.'

Two porters were already loading Armitage's equipment onto a trolley. One of them reached across to take the double bass case, but the lanternist hugged it protectively to his chest.

'Nobody touches this but me,' he said. 'Nobody but me.'

'Was it very expensive?' Becky asked as she, Armitage and Colleen followed the porters to the waiting cart.

'Was what expensive?' the lanternist asked.

'Your instrument,' Becky replied, pointing to the case which Armitage was still clutching as if his life depended on it.

'My instru . . .? Oh, I see what you mean.'

Armitage glanced ahead to make sure the porters were out of earshot, then winked conspiratorially at Becky.

'It's not a big fiddle I'm carrying,' he confided. 'It's my lime-light.'

'Limelight? What's that?' Becky asked.

'My chemicals,' the lanternist explained. 'What I make the flame out of, to light up the pictures.'

The porters loaded the boxes, Colleen handed them the tip her father had sent, and the party was ready go.

The cart lurched forward and bumped its way over the cobblestones.

'Why are you carrying your chemicals in an instrument case?' Becky asked the lanternist.

'To fool the railway police,' the little man explained. 'If they'd known I'd got limelight on me, they'd never have let me on the train.'

The front wheel of the cart hit a rut in the road and the whole vehicle shook violently. 'But why should the railway police *want* to stop you taking your limelight on the train?' Becky asked.

'Ah well, there've been a few accidents, you see,' the little man said airily. 'Mainly through porters being too rough.'

'Rough?'

'Throwing the cylinders around or even dropping them. Very volatile stuff, limelight, but if you know what you're doing there's no chance of an explosion. Well, not much of one anyway.'

'Explosion!' Colleen said. 'Has anybody ever been hurt?'

The lanternist shrugged. 'A few people get killed every year,' he said, 'but not really enough to worry about. And the fires which come after the explosion aren't usually anything like as bad as the papers make them out to be.'

The cart hit another bump and thudded down heavily on its axle.

'Stop!' Becky shouted. 'Stop right now!'

The carter reined in his horses.

'Something wrong?' he asked.

'No, nothing,' Becky said, climbing down. 'I just thought I'd walk from here. I could use some exercise.'

'Me, too,' Colleen said, joining her friend by the side of the cart.

'The driver knows where to take you,' Becky told the lanternist.

'Right-oh!' the little man said cheerfully.

'We'll see you at the school,' Becky said, then turning to her friend she whispered, 'If he ever gets there, that is.'

Not only did the lanternist succeed in reaching the school in one piece, but by the time Becky and Colleen arrived he'd already set up his equipment and was in deep conversation with Philip.

'Why have you got two lanterns, one of them on top of the other?' Philip asked, with more curiosity and enthusiasm than Becky had ever seen him show before.

'This is what's called a *biunial* lantern,' explained the little man, clearly flattered by the boy's interest. 'If you haven't got one of these you can't do dissolving scenes.'

'What's a dissolving scene?' Philip said.

'You'll find out when you see the show,' the lanternist promised. 'Look, if you're going to be hanging around, I could use a hand. Would you like to learn how to do my special effects for me?'

'You bet!' Philip said.

Becky looked up at the clock and wondered how her brother happened to be free at that time of day.

'Shouldn't you be going back to work?' she asked him.

'Shouldn't you?' Philip replied unpleasantly.

'I worked last Saturday afternoon, so I've got a half day off,' Becky said.

'Yes, well so have I!' Philip countered.

Wallers, working as part of a gang on piece rates, didn't get half days off, Becky thought.

'Is anything wrong?' she asked worriedly.

'Stop fussing,' Philip told her. He turned back to the lanternist. 'Tell me exactly what you want me to do,' he said.

The gang were on the point of knocking off for the day when the foreman went up to them.

'You're wanted in the office,' he said. 'Right now.'

'All of us?' asked Ernie Bracegirdle nervously.

'No, not all of you,' the foreman replied. 'Just Rathbone, Jennings and O'Reilly.'

Cedric Rathbone and Tom Jennings exchanged a glance which said that after their meeting the previous evening, this could all be a coincidence – but they didn't think it was.

The three wallers were shown into the office by a big man with a prize-fighter's broken nose. A second bruiser was lounging by the window. Both men were strangers to the village.

Richard Worrell was sitting behind his desk and next to him was Horace Crimp, hard at work probing his rotting teeth with a toothpick.

'What's this all about, Mr Worrell?' Cedric Rathbone asked.

Worrell said nothing but Crimp slid three buff envelopes across the desk.

'This is your pay up to end of the day,' he told them. 'Take it and get out. You're sacked.'

'Sacked!' Tom Jennings said. 'What for?'

'Don't come the injured innocent with me,' Richard sneered. 'You don't like the conditions here. Well, you don't have to put up with them any more, do you?'

How the hell has he found out so quick? Cedric Rathbone wondered.

It was less than twenty-four hours since they'd had the meeting with that lad from the university, and Rathbone hadn't mentioned it to a soul. Maybe one of the others had talked, he thought. Maybe Brian or Tom had already started to recruit, and word had got back to Worrell.

'Nothing that happens in these works gets past me,' Richard continued. 'I know all about the fiddles and the lead-swinging, and I let some of it carry on – because it suits me. But I'm not having the place unionized. Not now. Not ever.'

'We've got a right to form a union if we want to!' Cedric Rathbone said hotly.

Richard chuckled. 'Right?' he asked. '*Might* is right – and

Might is on my side. I'll show you what I mean.' He turned to one of the thugs. 'Tell the other lads to come in, Ollie,' he said.

Ollie opened the door and whistled. Two more thugs appeared in the doorway, flanking Mr Donaldson, the union organizer. Flanking him — and holding him up.

The organizer looked in a bad way. There was a large dark bruise on his left cheek and both his eyes were puffed up. In the time since they had last met, he seemed to have lost several teeth.

Cedric Rathbone made a move toward Donaldson and found his path blocked by Ollie. For a second he contemplated slugging it out with the man, then he decided against it, because Tom Jennings and Brian O'Reilly were no fighters, and he didn't want them getting hurt.

Unclenching his fists, Rathbone turned back to Richard Worrell.

'You'll not get away with this!' he said angrily. 'I'll see you brought up before the law.'

'Will you now?' Richard asked interestedly.

'I would strongly advise you against making any defamatory statements against my client without witnesses to support your claim,' Horace Crimp told the wallers in general and Cedric Rathbone in particular.

'He's my witness,' Rathbone said, pointing at Donaldson. 'He's more than that. He's the living bloody proof.'

'And these are my witnesses,' Worrell said, indicating his thugs. 'Tell us what happened, Ollie.'

'This here feller was wandering around the works on his own,' Ollie said, grinning. 'Trespassing, as you might say. Well, works is a dangerous place if you don't know your way around. He fell over and hurt himself.'

Up to that point Richard seemed to have been enjoying himself enormously, but now the whole proceeding started to bore him.

'Take your friend *Mr* Donaldson and get out,' he told Cedric Rathbone. 'And if I ever catch you on my works again I'll arrange for you to have an accident too.'

*

'The bastard,' Cedric Rathbone said as the three sacked wallers and the union man made their way past the engine room. 'The complete and utter bastard.'

Mr Donaldson, who was being supported between Jennings and O'Reilly, groaned softly.

'They really gave you a working over, didn't they?' Tom Jennings said.

'Fists to the face, boots to the ribs and legs,' Donaldson said through clenched teeth. 'Not so hard they'd break any bones — they're too clever for that — but just enough so as it'd hurt like the devil.'

'We'll get you a drink,' Cedric Rathbone said. 'You'll feel a bit better once you've got some whisky inside you.'

But when they reached Ollershaw Lane they saw that the New Inn was in darkness.

'What the bloody hell's going on?' Cedric demanded.

'The magic lantern show,' Brian O'Reilly said, suddenly remembering. 'Everybody's over at the school. I was going to go meself.'

'Right,' Cedric said decisively. 'If the New Inn's closed we'll take our custom to the Red Lion.'

'If it's all the same to you, I'd rather just see Mr Donaldson somewhere comfortable, then go straight home,' Tom Jennings said.

'It's *not* all the same to me,' Cedric told him. 'First of all we have to find out who shopped us to the gaffer. After that, we have to deal with him. *Then* we can all go home.'

CHAPTER ELEVEN

Paddy O'Leary was wearing his best suit, and though he was pleased to see such a good turn-out, the large audience was obviously making him nervous.

'I'll keep me speech short,' he said.

'That'll be a nice change for you, Paddy,' somebody called out good-naturedly.

'I'll believe it when I see it,' another wit added.

O'Leary fiddled with his starched collar and wished he was back behind his bar.

'Me and Cathy have lived in this village most of our married life . . .' he continued.

'We've b . . . been together now for forty years,' Harry Atherton sang out.

'Twenty-five, in point of fact,' Paddy said.

'Just feels like forty!' another voice shouted.

'Give the lad a chance,' Ted Taylor pleaded. 'It can't be easy trying to address an ignorant load of buggers like you lot!'

'Thank you, Ted,' O'Leary said. 'Now, where was I?'

'You and your Cathy have lived in the village for most of your married life.'

'Yes, and all our children were born here, delivered by Ma Fitton, who, as you know . . .'

'Has delivered royalty,' the audience chanted.

'We all think of Marston as our home,' Paddy continued, finding the going easier now he'd got into his stride. 'You've always been good neighbours — all of you — and this is just our way of saying thank you. So, without more ado, put out the lamps and let the show begin.'

The room was immediately plunged into darkness and Paddy had to grope his way back to his seat on the front row.

'What you are about to see, ladies and gentlemen,' said the lanternist, 'is a programme which has thrilled the crowned heads of Europe.'

A picture of a thatched cottage appeared on the screen at the end of the room. There was snow on the ground, the trees were leafless and two heavily wrapped figures stood at the edge of a small bridge which ran across the stream in front of the cottage.

There were a few initial 'ohs!' but the scene soon lost its novelty. When all was said and done it was nothing but a picture, such as you might see in any book. If this was the show which had thrilled the crowned heads of Europe they must have been very easy to please.

And then, the audience realized that something wonderful was happening. Slowly but surely the snow was disappearing and the trees were growing leaves. The people, too, had somehow managed to cross the bridge and shed their winter clothes in favour of summer frocks.

'It's called a dissolving view,' whispered Philip, who seemed to have decided to be friends with his sister again. 'It's two different slides being shown on the same spot. That's why he needs two lanterns.'

After a few more dissolving views the lanternist announced that he would now show a story in pictures. 'A Bunch of Primroses' opened with the flowers being picked, followed their journey to the city and ended with the final purchaser presenting them to her dying daughter, who gazed on them as she breathed her last. When the series was over there was the sound of several women sniffling in the darkness.

'And now, another story,' the lanternist announced. 'This one is called "The Drunkard".'

'Down with d ... demon drink. Join the B ... Band of Hope,' called out a voice which could only have belonged to Ha-Ha Harry, and most of the men in the audience chuckled.

Paddy sat wrapped in a cloak of embarrassment while a number of coloured slides told the story of a man who squandered his money in a pub which was only slightly scruffier than the New Inn, and eventually ended his life in the gutter.

'Each photograph has to be painted by hand,' Philip whispered. 'It takes ages.'

'You seem to know a lot about it,' Becky said.

'I do,' her brother agreed. 'I've learned more this afternoon than I learned in the rest of my life put together.'

The drunkard finally realized the error of his ways, prayed to God for the strength to abandon the evil addiction, and in the last photograph was shown as a reformed man, surrounded by his happy family. The lanternist recited:

> Oh hear his call and hasten forth,
> To render what help you can,
> Remember when he struggles thus,
> He is a brother and a man.

Mopping his brow with his large check handkerchief, Paddy O'Leary hoped there were no more tales of temperance planned as part of the evening's entertainment.

The slide show was so popular that the three wallers and the injured union man had the back room of the Red Lion completely to themselves.

'Someone talked,' said Donaldson, speaking carefully through his bruised lips. 'Someone *has* to have talked.'

'I know that, but it wasn't me,' Cedric Rathbone said firmly. 'I didn't even tell me missis.'

'Me neither,' Tom Jennings said.

Brian O'Reilly nodded to confirm that he, too, had kept quiet.

'What about you, Mr Donaldson?' Cedric Rathbone asked the union organizer. 'Couldn't you have let something slip when they were working you over?'

'No,' Donaldson replied, shaking his head and then wincing to show he wished he hadn't.

'I wouldn't blame you if you had blabbed,' Rathbone said

sympathetically. 'There's not many men as can keep a secret when they're getting a damn good beating.'

'They didn't do this to me for information,' Donaldson said, running his finger carefully along his lip. 'When they started teaching me my lesson, as *they* called it, they'd already found out everything they wanted to know from someone else.'

'Ernie Bracegirdle?' Tom Jennings suggested.

'Definitely not,' Cedric Rathbone said. 'His missis might be the biggest gossip in Marston, but Ernie himself is one of the tightest-lipped men I've ever met. Wouldn't give you the time of day without thinking about it twice.'

'What about Archie, then?' Tom Jennings asked. 'You know how loud-mouthed he can be when he's had a few drinks.'

'He had a few last night,' Brian O'Reilly said. 'But I was with him all the time. I even helped him home and went round there this morning to make sure he got to work on time.'

'We've been overlooking the bleeding obvious, haven't we?' Cedric Rathbone said angrily. 'Who is it who never gets into trouble with the gaffer no matter how many times he's late for work? Who is it who goes missing for hours without anybody complaining? And who is it who didn't even bother to come back to the pan after the dinner break — because he knew exactly what was going to happen?'

'Phil Taylor!' Tom Jennings said.

'That's right,' Cedric Rathbone agreed. 'Phil-Bloody-Taylor!'

'Now let us leave the pyramids of Egypt behind us and travel to London — the hub of the Empire,' the lanternist said grandly.

The image of a large, crenellated building appeared. In the river in front of it, a paddle steamer was unloading scores of eager visitors.

'Lambeth Palace,' the lanternist announced. 'The home of His Reverence, the Bishop of London.'

Slides of the Houses of Parliament, Covent Garden and the Strand followed in rapid succession.

'Isn't it wonderful?' Philip asked his sister. 'Even Manchester's got nothing to compare with it.'

'And now for my grand finale,' the lanternist said, 'I am proud to present "The Charge of the Light Brigade".' He turned to Philip. 'Ready?' he asked in a whisper.

'Ready, Mr Armitage,' Philip said.

After the photographic slides of 'A Bunch of Primroses' and 'The Drunkard', the hand-painted picture of the Light Brigade came as an anti-climax and some of the spectators sighed with disappointment. But the sighs did not last for long – soon they had turned to gasps of amazement. The painted cavalry actually began to move – to gallop down the narrow valley towards the enemy's guns.

'Rackwork slides,' said Philip, who really *did* seem to know everything about magic lanterns.

No sooner had the audience come to terms with the fact that the impossible was occurring than something even more frightening happened.

The room was suddenly filled with the sounds of war – thundering hooves, cracking rifles, booming cannon. Women screamed. Children hid their heads in their mothers' laps. Strong men winced under the assault from the Russian guns. Philip, who was turning the handles on the boxes producing the noises, winked at his sister.

The Charge was finally over. The screen went blank and at the back of the room someone lit the oil lamps. The audience went wild, clapping, whistling and stamping their feet.

'And that, ladies and gentlemen, concludes our spectacle for this evening,' the lanternist said complacently.

'More!' people demanded. 'Give us some more.'

The lanternist made a show of looking at his pocket watch.

'I regret that if I am to catch the last train to London we must terminate the performance now.'

'G ... go back tomorrow,' Harry Atherton suggested.

'Would that I could,' the lanternist said regretfully. 'But

unfortunately I am contracted to give a show in Hammersmith tomorrow afternoon.'

He began to pack away his equipment, yet still the audience remained in their seats, hoping against hope that he would repent and at least show them 'A Bunch of Primroses' one more time. But it was not to be, and in the end even the optimistic spectators admitted defeat and made their way reluctantly to the exit.

Becky saw her parents waiting at the other end of the hall.

'Are we going, then?' she asked her brother.

Philip shook his head.

'I'm staying behind to help Mr Armitage load the wagon, and then I'm going as far as the railway station with him,' he said.

'You'll miss Mrs O'Leary's Irish stew,' Becky reminded him.

'I don't care about that,' Philip replied. 'Tell Mam not to expect me back until late.'

Talk of the slide show kept the Taylors occupied all the way back to the village, and they were still remembering magic moments when Ted Taylor saw the four figures silhouetted against his back gate and realized that something was badly wrong. Men didn't lounge around on street corners – not in Marston. Besides, there was something about the way they were standing which told him they were looking for trouble.

'Stay here,' he said to his wife and daughter.

'What's the matter?' Mary asked, alarm creeping into her voice.

'I don't know,' Taylor replied, walking towards the waiting men, 'but I'm about to find out.'

As he got closer the shapes lost their black anonymity and became people he knew, people he'd had a drink with now and again. Except, that was, for the young one – the one who looked like he'd been in the wars. Taylor had never seen him before.

But knowing 'em's not going to make it any easier, Ted told himself. Not with the mood they're in.

If there was to be a barney it would start with Cedric Rathbone — it always did — and so it was Rathbone that Ted chose to deal with first.

'Anything I can do for you, Cedric?' he asked mildly.

'We've no quarrel with you,' Rathbone replied. 'It's your Philip we've come to see.'

'So you think you've got a quarrel with our Philip, do you?' Ted asked.

'We know we have,' Brian O'Reilly said. 'The young bugger's just cost us our jobs.'

'Now how could a bit of a lad like our Philip do that?' Taylor wondered aloud.

He heard footsteps behind him and turned to see that Mary and Becky were coming towards them.

'I thought I told you to stay back,' he shouted.

'Oh, there's no need for that now,' said Mary in a sweet, reasonable voice which somehow managed to suggest that wild horses wouldn't drag her away. 'We're among friends here, aren't we, Mr Rathbone?'

Cedric Rathbone shuffled awkwardly and grunted something which may have been agreement — but probably wasn't.

Ted Taylor couldn't handle his wilful wife and these angry men at the same time, and he knew it. Putting first things first, he turned back to Rathbone.

'You were telling me how my lad cost you your jobs,' he said.

'He shopped us to the gaffer, that's how,' Rathbone told him.

Ted Taylor stiffened and his hands balled into fists.

'I'm not as fit I was before me accident,' he said angrily, 'but if you think I'm just going to stand by and let my lad be insulted ...'

'Take it easy, Mr Taylor,' the stranger with the battered face said. 'There's no need for that.'

'Isn't there?' Taylor demanded. 'That's easy for you to say — it's not your son who's being called a sneak. Who are you, anyway?'

'Roger Donaldson,' the stranger said. 'Look, Mr Taylor, can I tell you the whole story?'

'I think you'd better,' Taylor said.

Donaldson told his tale, from the meeting in the salt works to the moment in the Red Lion when the four of them had realized that Philip had to be the informer.

'Well, I don't believe it,' Taylor said flatly.

But Becky did. How typical of poor Philip — weak Philip, lazy Philip — to take the easy way out like that. He'd probably told himself he wasn't doing any real harm by acting as Worrell's spy. If he'd been there at that moment, he'd probably have said none of it was his fault — and most likely he'd have believed it, too.

Anyway, whether or not Philip was the spy didn't really matter, Becky told herself. These four fellers were convinced he was guilty, and men suddenly deprived of their livelihood weren't going to be very gentle with the bloke they thought had robbed them of it. If they found Philip they'd hurt him, and if Dad tried to stop them he'd only get hurt as well.

'Me purse!' Becky screamed.

'Your what?' her mother asked.

'I've left me purse in the school! And it's got all me wages in it.'

A look of comprehension came to Mary Taylor's face.

'You'd better run straight back and see if it's still there,' she said.

As Becky rushed away she could hear the argument still going on behind her —

'Are you going to tell us where your Philip is, Ted?'

'I am not.'

'Then we'll just have to wait here until he gets back.'

The biggest danger, Becky thought as she sprinted along the mineral line which led to Northwich station, was that she and Philip would somehow miss each other in the dark, and he'd walk, unknowingly, into the ambush which was waiting for him.

'How could you do it, Philip?' she gasped as she ran. 'How did you ever think you could get away with it?'

But that was Philip all over — always seeing the world the way he'd like it to be rather than the way it actually was.

The train was just steaming into the station as she arrived. Becky glanced frantically up and down the platform, then almost sobbed with relief when she saw Philip and the lanternist standing under a gas lamp next to the third-class waiting room.

'Philip! Philip!' she shouted, not slackening her pace even for a second.

Her startled brother stood rooted to the spot until Becky reached him and threw her arms around his neck.

'You scared the daylights out of me,' Philip said when she released him. 'Is something the matter?'

'Your ... your gang from the works,' Becky gasped, fighting for air. 'They're ... they're waiting for you outside our house.'

'How did they find out about it?' Philip asked sulkily. 'How did they know it was me?'

So it was all true, just as Becky had thought it must be!

'They've finished loading up the mail coach. The train'll be leaving in a minute or two,' Mr Armitage said to Philip.

'What are we going to do with you, Philip?' Becky said, ignoring the lanternist. 'You can't go back home — not right now, anyway. The state he's in, Mr Rathbone'll kill you, I swear he will — even if it means them swinging for you.'

'I was never planning to go home,' Philip said.

'What do you mean — never?' Becky asked, totally confused.

'I've found something I really like doing at last, and Mr Armitage says he could use the help, so I'm going to become a lanternist.'

'Oh, Philip!' Becky said.

But wasn't it for the best, after all? He *couldn't* go home, and wasn't the life of a lanternist — where wits mattered more than effort — the ideal one for her black sheep of a brother?

'It's time we were getting aboard,' Mr Armitage said.

Becky stood on tiptoe and kissed Philip on the cheek.

'Write to me,' she said, with far less hope than she'd had when she'd asked the same thing of Jack.

Philip picked up the double bass case containing the limelight and climbed onto the train.

'I'll miss you,' he said.

'And I'll miss you,' Becky told him.

The stationmaster waved his flag and blew his whistle. The engine snorted its willingness to go and the train began to slowly pull its way out of the station. Becky stood and watched until its lights had faded into the darkness and the sound of its puffing was no more than a distant rumble.

'Poor Philip,' she said softly as the tears ran down her cheeks. 'Now that you haven't got me and Mam, whoever's going to look after you?'

It was hard to say what had hurt Ted Taylor more — his youngest son's disappearance or the fact that Philip had betrayed his workmates. Whichever was the case, Philip's departure served to make Taylor turn more in on himself. He rarely ventured an opinion now, and even more rarely did he issue a decree across the supper table to what was left of his family.

Only one thing ever really seemed to cheer him up. A letter from Jack or George — propped up against the sauce bottle for him to read while he ate his supper — was a virtual guarantee that, for a few hours at least, Taylor would be in a good humour.

'Our George has written again,' he announced one evening.

'Has he, love?' Mary asked, though it was she herself who had put out the letter for him to see. 'And what's he got to say for himself this time?'

'He's in a place called Burma, now. Where's that, our Becky?'

'It's next to India, Dad.'

'Aye, I thought it was. Anyway, he's just taken it over on behalf of the Queen.'

'On his own, Dad?' Becky asked, knowing that she dared risk impishness for once.

Taylor grinned. 'I expect he had a few other fellers to help him,' he admitted. 'Anyway, he says it wasn't much of a war at all, but now the fighting's over they've got real trouble. What's left of the Burmese army is hiding in the jungle — that'd be like a big forest, wouldn't it, Becky?'

'Yes, Dad.'

'I thought so. Anyway, he says they've turned bandit, and it's a hell of a job knowing how to deal with them. They don't think like us, you see. George says they caught a dozen of them, and instead of shooting them all together they decided to execute them one at a time — as an example, like. Well, they shot the first one, and the others all started laughing, as if it was the funniest thing in the world. So then they shot another one, and the ten that were left thought that was even funnier. And they kept on laughing, until one by one they'd all been shot.' Taylor shook his head wonderingly. 'They're not British, are they?'

'I bet he can't wait to get out of there,' Mary said with a shudder.

'Oh, he says it's not such a bad country once you get used to it,' Taylor told her. 'He's in the regimental football team, you see, so he maybe has an easier time of it than some of the other lads.'

Jack wrote, too.

'Sounds like a rum place, that silver field,' Taylor commented. 'Jack says they live in huts made out of tree bark and there's armed thieves — bushrangers, he calls them — all the way from Broken Hill to Victoria — and I expect that's a good few miles. Still, there's whole families living at the diggings, so it can't be *that* bad, can it?'

'Is he planning to stay there much longer?' Mary asked.

'Just until he's saved up some money, then he'll be off again. He fancies West Africa next. Seems like the lad'll never settle down.'

Though Ted talked of his other sons with pride — and sometimes with incomprehension — Philip was never referred to. It was almost as if he'd wiped his youngest son completely from his mind.

But Becky knew he hadn't. Even if she'd failed to catch the looks of anguish which occasionally flashed across her father's face, she had proof that Philip's sin, if not Philip himself, still weighed heavily on Ted Taylor's shoulders. Why else would Cedric Rathbone's portion of fish and chips always turn out to be much bigger than anyone else's? Why else would her father often wrap a lovely fresh fish in newspaper, then tell Tom Jennings — in a voice everyone in the shop could hear — that the parcel contained a few scraps for his cat?

PART FOUR
1886

CHAPTER TWELVE

Though no one realized it at the time, the arrival of Septimus Quinn was to be a landmark in the history of Marston.

Quinn made his first appearance one late afternoon in the summer of 1886, at the reins of a pony and trap. He entered the village from the Northwich end, drove as far as Worrell's, then turned round and went back the way he had come. At the post office, he turned again and headed for a second time towards Worrell's.

What's he doing? Not-Stopping Bracegirdle wondered from behind her front parlour curtains.

What he *appeared* to be doing was to taking a very close look at the village, his eyes fixing first on this building and then on that. Twice more he passed Not-Stopping's window before, apparently satisfied, he tied his horse to the hitching post outside the New Inn.

No sooner had Quinn entered the pub than Not-Stopping was knocking urgently on Dottie Curzon's back door.

'I never have a drink during the day, as you well know ...' Not-Stopping began.

'Don't you?' Dottie asked, as if it was news to her.

'Well, not unless you count the odd nip of gin in me own kitchen,' Not-Stopping amended, 'but I could really murder a bottle of stout right now. Will you come with me?'

'Well, I don't know,' Dottie said hesitantly. 'I've still got the black-leading to do, and if my Norman found I was spending the housekeeping on afternoon drinking ...'

She trailed off and waited expectantly for her friend to come up with some counter-argument.

While Not-Stopping knew full well that Dottie could have been talked into it eventually – given time, she could be talked into *anything* — time was a luxury she didn't have, not if she was to get a proper look at the mysterious stranger.

'Keep your money, I'll treat you,' Not-Stopping said, forcing herself, in the interest of speed, to substitute bribery for persuasion.

All thoughts of black-leading quickly evaporated from Dottie's mind.

'I'll just take me apron off,' she said.

The one advantage of having to buy the drinks, Not-Stopping thought as she counted out her coppers, was that it was she, not Dottie, who got a good view of the stranger through the serving hatch.

He was around sixty years old, she guessed, but he had a powerful physique which many a younger man would have envied. His cheeks and nose bore the signs of heavy drinking, yet his eyes were as sharp and darting as those of a stoat on the prowl. He dressed like a gentleman, in a frock-coat with flared skirt, velvet collar and cuffs, but he managed to give the impression that he was unused to such finery — that prosperity had come to him rather late in life.

'He looks a really nasty piece of work to me,' Not-Stopping told Dottie when she got back to their table.

And for once, she was right.

'Will you have another whisky with me, landlord?' Septimus Quinn asked Paddy O'Leary.

'If I did, sir, that'd be the third you'd bought me,' Paddy reminded him.

'What of it?' Quinn asked.

He was a strange feller all right, O'Leary thought. He didn't look the friendly sort, yet he was being amiable enough. No, that wasn't quite true. The words themselves were amiable, but the way they were delivered turned them into a command — a command, furthermore, with menaces. Though he really didn't feel like it, Paddy O'Leary found he was pouring himself another whisky.

'Do you own this pub?' Quinn asked.

Paddy laughed self-deprecatingly. 'Chance'd be a fine thing,' he said. 'No, I'm just the tenant. The place belongs to the brewery.'

'And which brewery would that be?' Quinn said.

'Greenhall Whitley,' Paddy replied, wondering why the stranger's questions were making him feel so uneasy.

'Where's their head office?' Quinn asked.

'Warrington,' Paddy said, feeling more uncomfortable by the minute.

'Warrington,' Quinn repeated. He drained his whisky and turned towards the door. 'I'll be seeing you again, landlord,' he said.

Instead of returning to his pony and trap Quinn spent some time walking round the village, stopping now and again to examine a particular building more closely.

'As if he was thinking of buying the whole place, lock, stock and barrel,' Not-Stopping told her cronies later.

He called in at Cooke's Grocers, though it was clear to Sam Cooke that he was more interested in looking at the shop itself than he was in buying anything from it.

He paid a visit to Taylor's and ordered cod and chips.

'Is this your business?' he asked Ted.

'It is, sir,' Taylor said proudly.

But he could not help wondering why such a toff should be favouring the shop with his patronage.

'You own the house, do you?' Quinn asked.

'Well, no, the house is rented,' Taylor admitted.

'You can have a house without a business, but not the other way round,' Quinn said cryptically. 'I'll wish you good day.'

'Good day, sir,' replied a thoughtful Ted Taylor.

From the chip shop Quinn wandered up to the canal bank and watched the narrow boats loading. Some of them had *L. G. Worrell and Co.* painted on them, but others, like *Jupiter II*, bore the legend *The East Midland Canal Company* on their sides.

'The East Midland Canal Company,' Quinn repeated to himself.

He took a notebook from his coat pocket and wrote the name down.

The hooter in Worrell's screamed the end of the day's work. Quinn checked his watch. He'd wait for ten minutes, he decided, and then he'd get on with the main business of the day.

'He's late,' Richard Worrell said, glancing nervously at his pocket watch.

'Only a little,' Horace Crimp replied.

'Five minutes!' Worrell protested.

'You've been waiting for this for a long time,' Crimp pointed out. 'Will a few extra minutes really make a difference?'

No, Richard Worrell supposed, they probably wouldn't. It was just that after all the planning and scheming – after forcing himself to be pleasant to a brother he hated – he was eager to get the matter finally settled.

There was a heavy knock on the door.

'Come in!' Richard called out.

The door swung open and Septimus Quinn stepped into the office. Richard rose to his feet and walked around the desk to shake hands with his visitor.

'And this is Mr Crimp, my attorney,' he said as he offered Quinn a chair facing his own.

Quinn nodded to Crimp and sat down.

'I've been looking around your works,' he said.

'And what do you think?' Richard asked eagerly.

'It's got possibilities,' Quinn admitted.

'So we can do a deal?'

'Oh yes, we can definitely do a deal.'

Richard Worrell poured himself a glass of whisky and then, ignoring Crimp's expectant look, passed the bottle directly to Quinn, who gave himself a generous shot.

'If I had a good little business like this I'd never even

consider selling it,' Quinn said, 'So why should your old man?'

'Because he'll think he has no choice,' Richard replied. He slid a heavy accounting ledger across to Quinn. 'Get your book-keeper to look through this,' he said.

'A man with a book-keeper is a man who's put his fate in the hands of others,' Quinn said. 'I'll look over the figures myself. And just what will I find?'

'That we're on the verge of bankruptcy,' Richard told him.

'But you're not, are you?'

Richard passed Quinn a second ledger.

'These are the real figures,' he said. 'I think you'll find that business has never been better.'

'And if my assessment agrees with yours — what next?' Quinn asked.

'Tell him, Crimp,' Richard ordered.

The attorney shot him a look of extreme dislike. Richard failed to notice it — but Quinn didn't.

'You, Mr Quinn, will make Mr Leonard Worrell an offer for forty-nine per cent of the shares in the company,' Crimp said.

'Why only forty-nine per cent?' Quinn asked.

'Because I know my father,' Richard explained, 'and he'd rather go broke than hand control over to anyone else.' He turned to his lawyer. 'Tell him the rest, Crimp.'

'Before you buy the shares from Mr Leonard Worrell, you will already have signed a secret contract in which you will have agreed to sell just over half of them back to Mr Richard Worrell at a price considerably higher than you paid for them,' Crimp said.

'Leaving you a handsome profit for doing very little,' Richard pointed out.

'What do you get out of this?' Quinn asked.

'Twenty-six per cent of the shares,' Richard answered,

Quinn chuckled and took another sip of his whisky.

'I'll tell you what I think,' he said. 'I think your old man is going to leave half his shares to you, and the rest to your

207

brother. Now with things as they are, that'd mean you'd have joint control, but with the deal you're proposing, you'll end up as majority shareholder and Worrell's will be yours to do as you want with.'

Richard grinned.

'Yes, it will, won't it,' he agreed.

Septimus Quinn booked a private dining room at the Crown Hotel for his meeting.

'And give us the best of everything – whatever it costs,' he told the landlord. 'I want my guest to feel he's being treated like royalty.'

Quinn deliberately arrived early and was already waiting in the private room when the potential recipient of regal treatment stuck his head suspiciously round the door.

'I'm not sure this is quite proper, Mr Quinn,' he said.

Then why have you come, you hypocrite? Quinn thought.

But aloud he said, 'Not proper? What could possibly be *improper* about two gentlemen like us taking a meal together?'

'There's professional considerations,' the guest pointed out. 'A possible conflict of interest.'

'I invited you here for the pleasure of your company, not to talk about my business dealings with Richard Worrell,' Quinn told him, 'so why don't you just sit and enjoy the meal, Mr Crimp?'

It was an excellent meal, and Crimp's rotting teeth seemed to be no impediment to his enjoying it to the full. While the attorney did the lion's share of the eating and drinking, Septimus Quinn supplied most of the conversation, talking mainly about his web of business interests throughout the country.

It was not until the ruby port arrived that Quinn raised the subject of the salt works.

'You're wasting your time working for Richard Worrell,' he said. 'He was born to fail. Far better that you should devote your considerable talents to a man born to succeed, a man who could reward you as you deserve – a man like me.'

Crimp's eyes burned with greed, but he was not prepared to commit himself yet.

'You want to take over Worrell's, don't you?' he asked.

'I'm not a man to go for a little when I can have it all,' Quinn replied.

'But how?' Crimp wondered. 'Under the secret agreement you're going to sign with Richard Worrell you'll be legally obliged to sell over half the shares you've acquired straight back to him.'

'Unless ...' Quinn said.

Crimp thought about it.

'Unless I made such a hash of drawing up the document that it had no legal validity,' he said finally.

'Exactly,' Quinn agreed.

'But even so, you'll still have only forty-nine per cent of the shares,' Crimp pointed out. 'As long as he's alive Len Worrell will keep control, and once he's dead his sons, if they can patch up their differences, will always out-vote you.'

'There will be a second secret document,' Quinn told him. 'One in which Master Richard promises to sell me his remaining shares as soon as he inherits them.'

'He'd never sign it,' Horace Crimp protested.

'He'd have no choice,' Quinn said confidently. 'The papers in which I agree to sell some of my holding to Richard will have no legal validity, but what effect do you think they'd have if I showed them to his father?'

'He'd feel betrayed,' Crimp said.

'As indeed he would have been,' Quinn replied. 'And what action would he be likely to take as a result of this shocking discovery?'

'He'd ... he'd cut Richard off without a penny,' Crimp gasped.

'Of course he would,' Quinn agreed. 'So Master Richard will be faced with two choices – he can either agree to sell his inheritance to me and at least come away with some money, or he can refuse, in which case I go to his father and he gets nothing.'

'That's brilliant!' Crimp said, firmly nailing his colours to Quinn's mast. 'But Worrell's isn't the only thing which interests you in Marston, is it?'

'I knew you were smart,' Quinn told him. 'No, I'm not just after Worrell's. I want *everything*. I want to run what the Americans call "a company town". My salt will be carried by my boats. The workers will sleep in my houses. They'll spend their money in my pubs, my store, my fish and chip shop. Nearly every penny I pay out in wages will end up coming right back to me.'

Crimp shook his head doubtfully.

'I don't think you quite realize the trouble you're letting yourself in for,' he said. 'They're a stubborn, tight-knit lot, those Marstoners, and they'll fight you every inch of the way.'

'Then they'll have to fight from a distance,' Quinn said.

'I don't understand,' the attorney responded.

'More port, Mr Crimp?' Quinn asked, filling the other man's glass. 'You want to know why they'll have to fight from a distance? Because when I gain control of Worrell's I intend to sack nearly all the workers, and when I have completed my purchase of the houses I will evict all of my tenants. They can't stay in the village with no jobs and no roofs over their heads. Marstoners, as you call them, will simply cease to exist.'

'But ... but who'll run the works?' Crimp asked.

'There are thousands of Irishmen, living in poverty just across the water, who'd be glad of the chance to earn less and pay more out in rent than these villagers do,' Quinn told him. 'They'll run my works – and my pubs and shops. So if I was somebody like Paddy O'Leary or Ted Taylor, I'd already be putting my name down for the workhouse.'

Len Worrell, leaning heavily on a stick, made his way slowly around the grounds of Peak House. His elder son, Richard, walked by his side.

'Twenty years I've been running that salt works,' Worrell said mournfully. 'Twenty years – and it's always brought me in a good living. Look at this house. Look at the expensive education you both had. All that was paid for out of what I earned from the works.'

'I know, Father,' Richard said sympathetically.

'How could it happen?' Worrell asked. 'How could we suddenly find ourselves up to our necks in debt?'

'It's not my fault, Father,' Richard said. 'Since I took over we've been producing salt cheaper than we ever did before. You know that yourself – you've seen the figures.'

Worrell nodded. It was true what his son said – the works had never operated better. He felt a stab of pain in his chest, but tried not to show it.

'Take lots of rest,' the doctor had told him. 'And at all cost, avoid any excitement.'

But how could he keep calm when everything he had worked hard for all his life was falling to pieces? At the least – at the very least – he had to find out what had gone wrong.

'Why've we got in debt?' he asked, as a new wave of pain hit him.

'It's been on the selling side that we've lost out badly,' Richard said.

'And why's that?' Worrell demanded. 'Isn't our salt as good as it ever was?'

'Of course,' Richard agreed, 'but competition's got a lot fiercer since you retired. Besides, Michael isn't . . .'

'Michael isn't what?' Worrell wanted to know.

'Nothing,' Richard said hastily. 'Forget I ever spoke.'

Worrell stopped walking, turned stiffly towards his son and grabbed him by the shoulder.

'Michael isn't what?' he asked angrily.

'When he joined the business I thought he would make a good salesman,' Richard said awkwardly. 'And you agreed. Do you remember?'

'Yes, I remember,' Worrell replied, his rage growing by the second. 'I might be ill, but I've still got a few of me marbles left.'

'Well, I think we might have made a mistake,' Richard said, as if every word was being forced out against his will.

'Hasn't he been able to pick up any new customers?' Worrell asked.

'A few,' Richard admitted. 'But not really any big orders.'

Worrell squinted at his son through pain-filled eyes. Richard was trying to hide something from him, he was sure of it.

'What about the old customers?' he asked.

Richard shrugged helplessly. 'There may have been a perfectly good reason why some of them cancelled their orders with us,' he said. 'It probably didn't have anything to do with Michael at all.'

He should never had made Michael promise to come into the business, Len Worrell thought. If only he hadn't been so eager to make the boy see the world from his point of view. If only he hadn't nurtured the secret hope that once Michael was working for him, he might finally come to feel some affection for his younger son.

If only ... if only ...

He had made a tragic error of judgement and now he was paying for it, in his final years, by seeing everything he had worked for all his life turn to ashes.

'Tell me about the offer we've had from this feller Quinn,' he said, turning back to the path and taking a tentative step forward.

'It's not a brilliant offer,' Richard confessed, 'but it's probably the best we'll get, and at least with Quinn's money we should be able to keep our heads above water.'

'And I'd still have controlling interest, wouldn't I?' Worrell gasped. 'He wouldn't be able to take my company off me.'

'Of course not, Father,' Richard assured him.

The pain was making Len Worrell's head swim, and now he was starting to have serious trouble with his breathing.

'Go ahead and do what's necessary,' he said. 'I'm glad I've got at least one son who has the interest of Worrell's at heart.'

It was a worried group of men who sat over their pints in the New Inn a few weeks later.

'This f ... feller Quinn's already bought part of Worrell's,'

Harry Atherton said, 'and there's a rumour going round that he wants to buy the Ad ... Adelaide Mine, an' all. He seems to have money to burn.'

'He's been talking to the brewery about buying this pub,' Paddy O'Leary said gloomily. 'And if he does you can be sure there'll be a different face behind this counter next time you come in.'

'*If* we're still around to come in at all,' Ernie Bracegirdle pointed out. 'Our landlord's told us he's thinking of selling the house.'

'To Qu ... Quinn?' Ha-Ha Harry asked.

'He wouldn't say, but according to my missis it's definitely Quinn who's doing the buying. And the landlord's told us straight that if he *does* sell, we'd better start looking for alternative accommodation.'

'There is no alternative accommodation in Marston,' Ted Taylor said. 'Not unless somebody dies.'

'You think I don't know that?' Ernie Bracegirdle asked. 'It'll mean moving away. Me, who's been here all his life.'

'Narrow-boating's been in my family for three generations,' Wally Hulse said. 'But the company's made it plain that if their sale goes through, they won't be wanting me any more. And running a narrow boat's the only thing I know.'

Nowhere in the thick fog of gloom could they find even the tiniest spot of light.

'He wants to take my chip shop off me,' Ted Taylor muttered.

'He's after my grocery business,' Sam Cooke said.

'Isn't there anything we can do, Mr Bowyer?' Paddy O'Leary asked, turning to the wise old man sitting in the corner.

'The law's on his side,' Old Gilbert said, 'and you can't fight the law, can you?'

'I knew he was a b ... bad 'un the first time I set eyes on him,' Harry Atherton grumbled. 'Didn't you think the same, Gilbert?'

'As far as I know, I never *have* set eyes on him,' Old Gilbert said.

'Well, now's your chance,' Sam Cooke said, glancing out of the bow window. 'There he is, walking out of Worrell's as if he owned the place — which he almost does.'

Bowyer turned his head casually, almost out of politeness — and then he caught sight of the big man who had such grandiose plans for the village.

The effect on him was instantaneous — his face turned as white as the salt upon which Marston depended, his hands started to tremble uncontrollably and his breathing came in short, quick gasps.

'Are you all right, Mr Bowyer?' Paddy O'Leary asked anxiously.

'Give me a whisky,' Old Gilbert croaked. 'I'll be fine once I've had a whisky.'

'But what's the matter with you?' O'Leary persisted. 'What's upset you like this?'

'I think I've just seen the Devil,' Old Gilbert told him.

Richard Worrell sat at his desk with his head in his hands and an aura of despair hanging over him like a black cloud.

'How could I ever have allowed myself to become involved with Quinn?' he asked himself for the hundredth time. 'How could I ever have trusted a man like that?'

Well, he had trusted the man, and look where it had got him. Richard reached out, with a trembling hand, for the whisky bottle.

'You have a choice,' Quinn had said to him not fifteen minutes earlier. 'You either agree to sell me your shares, or I'll see to it your father finds out you're nothing but a little thief.'

What kind of choice was that?

'All I ever wanted was to be master of Worrell's,' Richard moaned to himself.

But that would never come to pass now. Once he'd signed over his shares to Quinn, even the brother he hated would own more of the place than he did.

'It's not fair!' he screamed at the empty office. 'It's just not fair!'

If only Quinn had never come into his life. If only he would go away now as if he had never existed.

Richard took a slug of his whisky. It stung his throat but brought him no mental relief.

Where could he go now that he had lost the works? What was he to do with the rest of his life?

'I might as well kill myself!' he sobbed.

Why not? he wondered. Apart from the night watchman, the works was deserted at that hour, and there were plenty of spars from which he could hang himself. Or he could throw himself into the canal – submerging his foolishness and failure for ever in the cold green water.

The idea of suicide disappeared as quickly as it had come. Suffering was part of life – he knew that – but it was usually possible, if you were clever enough and quick enough, to pass on your own suffering to someone else.

'And there has to be a way to do that here,' he told himself as he poured a fresh whisky. 'There has to be!'

It was closing time when Wally Hulse finally staggered out of the New Inn. He was not usually a heavy drinker, but that night he'd had a skinful.

'And why not?' he asked the stars belligerently.

If a man couldn't get drunk when he was about to lose his livelihood, the job he'd been born into, then when could he?

He tottered unsteadily around the side of Worrell's salt store, pausing once to relieve himself and once simply because the ground seemed to be rising up to meet him.

'It's the workhouse for you, Wally Hulse,' he told himself.

It would kill Emmie. The day the canal had burst its bank she'd risked her life to save her decorative plates and Measham tea pot, but they'd take her treasures off her in the workhouse.

They took *everything* off you in the workhouse.

'What about the horse?' he mumbled.

Would whoever took over *The Jupiter* from him know how to treat Hereward properly?

'And what about Jip?' he asked a clump of grass which had done its best to trip him up.

Jip had been a good little dog, retrieving rabbits and finding ducks' eggs whenever he could. Now he was old and fat, and nobody but the master he'd served faithfully all these years would have any use for him.

'I won't see you suffer, old pal,' Hulse promised. 'If I have to put you down, I'll make sure it's quick.'

More by luck than judgement, he reached the tow path. There was an almost full moon that night, and from where he was standing he could see his boat and the dark figure leaning against it.

'Can't wait to lay into me, eh, Emmie,' he said. 'Well, I suppose I deserve it.'

The figure moved, and Hulse realized his mistake. It wasn't his Emmie standing there — it was a man!

'Hey, what are you doing messing round my boat!' Hulse called out.

The man turned to look at him, then took off in a frantic dash up the tow path.

If the bugger had been bothering Emmie, he'd pay for it, Hulse thought. Drunk as he was, he set off in pursuit.

It was an unequal contest from the beginning. The man he was chasing had a head start and seemed to be younger and fitter, too. By the time Hulse was anything like close to *The Jupiter* he'd lost so much ground that the other man was already drawing level with Worrell's side entrance.

Hulse just had time to see his quarry slip through the small gate under the loading bay before his foot caught on a large cobblestone and he went sprawling on the tow path.

'Damn and blast!' he gasped.

It was as he was picking himself up again that he noticed the bundle floating in the canal. He thought at first that it was nothing more than a sack — perhaps containing a drowned dog — but then he realized it was too big for that.

And suddenly, he knew exactly what it was!

Back on his feet again, Hulse lurched the last few yards to

The Jupiter. By the time he reached the boat the bundle in the water was banging against its bow.

The cabin door opened and Emmie appeared. Hands on her hips, she looked her husband up and down.

'The state of you!' she said angrily. 'In all the years we've been married I don't think I've ever seen you ...'

'There's no time for that now, woman,' Hulse shouted, doing his best not to slur his words. 'Get me the hook.'

'The what?'

'The hook! The bloody boat hook!'

It was so rare for Wally to swear in her presence that Emmie Hulse knew something serious must have happened. Without another word she handed her husband the long pole with a hook on the end.

Grasping the edge of the cabin roof for support, Hulse reached over the water and attempted to hook the floating bundle. His first try merely succeeded in pushing it further away, but at his second try the hook secured a hold.

'It's not what it looks like, is it?' his wife said. 'I mean, it isn't ...'

'It is,' Hulse told her. 'It's some poor bugger who's gone and fallen into the canal.'

Little effort was required to pull the body through the water to the side of the boat, but getting it aboard would be another matter.

'Hold me round the middle,' Hulse instructed his wife, 'or I'll end up in the canal an' all.'

As he felt his wife's strong arms clasp him, Hulse reached over and grasped the body. Christ, it was a weight – he could tell that even before he started to lift. He struggled awkwardly until he had got his hands under the dead man's armpits, then heaved with all his might. Inch by exhausting inch he pulled the corpse aboard.

'Get the lantern,' he said as he laid the body out, as best he could, in the tiny cockpit.

Emmie disappeared into the cabin for a second and re-emerged again with the oil lamp. Its light cast an almost golden glow over the dead man's pale face.

'How long ago d'you think he drowned?' Emmie Hulse asked.

'He didn't drown at all,' Hulse said. 'Look at that.'

He was pointing at the left side of the corpse's head. The hair was matted with blood and the skull had been crushed inwards.

'He was dead before he ever went into the water,' Hulse said. 'And to think, not more than a couple of hours ago I saw him walking around as right as rain.'

'You know him!' Emmie Hulse gasped.

'Oh aye, I know him,' Wally agreed. 'His name's Quinn.'

CHAPTER THIRTEEN

Michael Worrell hardly recognized his brother when they met in the office the next morning. Richard's hair was a tangled mess, his eyes were bloodshot and his mouth was twitching compulsively.

'You look dreadful,' Michael said.

'So would you if you'd got as much on your mind as I have,' Richard replied self-pityingly. 'I've been up all night, worrying myself half to death.'

'Drinking yourself half to death as well, by the looks of it,' Michael said, glancing at the nearly empty whisky bottle by Richard's side. Then, relenting his harsh tone a little, he added, 'Do you want to tell me what the problem is?'

'It's Quinn.'

'What about him?'

'He's been murdered. His body *was* in the canal, but somebody's bound to have fished it out by now.'

'How do you know all this?' Michael asked.

Suddenly, realization hit him with the force of a sledgehammer.

'You killed him, didn't you?' he demanded.

Richard shook his head in violent denial.

'I ... I was drunk ...' he said.

'You're still drunk,' his brother told him.

'... I went out onto the tow path to see if the night air would clear my head. That's when I saw him. He was floating in the water. I thought he'd just drowned at first – but as I got closer, I could see ... could see ...'

'See what?'

'The left side of his head was all caved in. It was horrible, Michael.'

'You have to go to the police right away,' Michael said decisively.

'I ... I can't,' Richard replied. 'They'll think I did it.'

'Of course they won't,' Michael assured him. 'After all, Quinn was our partner.'

'That's the point,' Richard said, almost hysterically. 'I had a secret deal with him, and he was cheating me. He ... he was going to take the works off me.'

'Take the works off *you*?'

'I was going to tell you about it. Honestly I was,' Richard said. 'I did it for both of us. You do believe me, don't you?'

'No,' Michael said. 'I don't think I do.'

Richard looked wildly around the room, then reached for the whisky bottle. Michael clamped a firm hand down on Richard's wrist.

'Drink's not the answer,' he said.

'They'll hang me,' Richard cried. 'I don't want to die. Please don't let me die!'

Michael gazed into his brother's bloodshot eyes.

'Tell me again you didn't kill Quinn,' he said.

'I swear on my mother's grave I didn't,' Richard replied.

Michael released his brother's wrist.

'Then if you're innocent, we should be able to prove it – however black things look,' he said.

A small ray of hope appeared in the pools of despair which filled Richard's eyes.

'Thank you,' he sobbed. 'Thank you, thank you, thank you. If you can save me, you can have Worrell's, every lousy inch of it.'

There was a loud knock on the door.

'The police!' Richard screamed.

'Get a hold of yourself,' Michael ordered him.

'I can't ... I ... I'm terrified, Michael ... I ...'

'If it is the police, how do you think you're going to look to them now?' Michael demanded. 'Like an innocent person – or like the murderer of Septimus Quinn?'

'Get a hold on myself,' Richard said. 'A hold on myself.'

There was a second knock on the door. Richard looked desperately at the whisky bottle.

'Just one drink,' he pleaded. 'Just one little drink!'

'It'll only make things worse,' Michael said. He turned towards the door and called out, 'Come in!'

Bert Jenkins, the senior foreman, entered the room.

'Sorry to bother you, Sir, but there's a bit of a problem with Number Three Pan,' he said to Richard.

'I'll deal with it,' Michael told him.

'You?' the foreman asked.

'My brother's not feeling well,' Michael explained. 'Have his carriage brought round. And arrange for a driver – he's in no state to take the reins himself.'

The foreman looked questioningly at Richard and then back to Michael.

'What are you waiting for?' Michael asked. 'I've told you what to do, now go and bloody do it!'

The tone of Michael's words both surprised and chastened the foreman.

'Right, Sir,' he said 'Sorry, Sir.'

As Jenkins left the office Michael turned back to his brother.

'Now listen to me, Richard,' he said. 'You are *not* to talk to the driver on the way. And when you get home you're to have a hot bath and get a few hours' sleep. I want you back here by this afternoon at the latest.'

'This afternoon! I couldn't come back ... not this afternoon,' Richard protested.

'You have to!' Michael told him fiercely. 'What will the police think if one of Quinn's partners suddenly has a breakdown? Your only chance of avoiding suspicion is to act as normally as possible. Do you understand that? Do you remember everything I've told you?'

'Yes, Michael,' Richard said, as if he were a little boy addressing his stern father.

Inspector Capstick paced up and down the railway platform, his fury mounting with each step. *He* was the head of the

Northwich police, he told himself. The three sergeants and ten constables who made up the rest of the force answered to *him*. And the murder of Septimus Quinn had been committed on *his* patch.

There had been two other murders during the time Capstick had been in charge. In the first case, a drunken navvy had beaten his wife to death with a shovel. In the other, one man had killed another with a pocket-knife during a brawl outside the Volunteer Arms. On both occasions there had been a score of witnesses, and all the police had to do was arrest the guilty party.

The murder of Septimus Quinn was quite another matter. He was almost a stranger to the area, yet someone had hated him enough to stalk along the canal bank – stalk him and then cold-bloodedly kill him. And not with a weapon which had simply come to hand, like the shovel and the pocket-knife, but one which had been deliberately taken along for that specific purpose.

Here, then, was a crime with some meat on it. Here, then, was a crime worthy of investigation by a police inspector who was ambitious to get on in the world.

'But you're not going to get the chance, are you?' he asked himself angrily.

No, he wasn't going to get the chance, because the powers-that-be had decided that the case was too big for a simple provincial policeman like him to handle, and instead of giving him a week – or even a couple of days – to show them what he could do, they'd immediately called in the Metropolitan Police's Criminal Investigation Department.

The train steamed into the station, and only one passenger got off. He was a middle-sized man wearing a bowler hat and long double-breasted coat with a shoulder cape, a form of dress no longer in fashion – not even in Northwich. He had piggy eyes, a short blunt nose and a double chin. The only feature which looked out of place on his brutish face was his thin, sarcastic lips.

The local man walked up to the newcomer and held out his hand.

'Inspector Capstick,' he said.

'Barker,' the other man responded, his handshake somehow managing to make it clear that he had much better things to do with his time than spend it dealing with a local copper. 'Barker of the Chepstow Axe Murders.'

'I beg your pardon?' Capstick said.

'The Chepstow Axe Murders,' the man from London repeated impatiently. 'My most famous case. You must have heard of it?'

'I think I do remember something about it,' Capstick admitted uncertainly.

Barker sniffed the air and seemed to find it distasteful.

'I take it you've been ordered to give me everything I need,' he said.

'I have been asked to give you my full co-operation, yes,' Capstick replied.

He'd been more than willing to dislike the man who'd taken his case off him, but Barker was really making it *very* easy.

'I'll need your two best constables,' the Londoner said. 'I don't expect they'll be up to much, but beggars can't be choosers.'

'I'll assign you two men right away,' the Northwich police chief said through gritted teeth.

'And the room?' Barker demanded.

'I thought you'd want to be close to the scene of the crime,' Capstick said, 'so I've booked you in at the New Inn in Marston. It's not exactly luxury accommodation, but ...'

'Doesn't matter – I won't be there long,' Barker interrupted airily. 'I managed to solve the Chepstow Axe Murders in a week. This case shouldn't take more than two or three days.'

Inspector Barker stood at the crown of the humpbacked bridge and looked down on the village.

'There's nothing complicated about murder,' he told his two new assistants. 'Find out who's got a motive, and nine times out of ten you've also found the killer. Are you following me?'

'Yes, sir,' the constables said in unison.

'The murderer's down there, somewhere,' Barker continued. 'I want you to go from door to door, and there's only one question I want you to ask. Who had a reason to kill Septimus Quinn? Got that? Who had a reason to kill Septimus Quinn?'

'What about looking for evidence, Sir?' one of the constables asked.

'Evidence!' Barker repeated. 'We'll worry about finding evidence once we've worked out who did it.'

By nine o'clock that evening Barker was sitting at a corner table in the bar of the New Inn with his two constables who, though off duty, had been press-ganged into being his reluctant drinking companions.

On the whole his assistants had not done a bad job, he conceded. Despite the fact that most of the villagers had proved to be very tight-lipped, the constables had still managed to pick up enough tit-bits of information for him to fill half his notebook. The only problem was, he had far too many suspects.

He looked around the crowded bar.

They've all come to see me, he thought.

He didn't find the idea displeasing. He liked being the centre of attention. Besides, having all these people in one place at one time gave him the chance of employing one of his famous investigative short cuts.

He leaned across the table so that his head was almost touching those of his constables.

'I'm going to give a little speech in a minute or two,' he whispered. 'And while I'm giving it, I want you to study the faces of everybody in the bar for signs of guilt. Got that?'

The constables nodded and Barker swivelled around in his chair so he was facing the bar.

'Had he lived, Septimus Quinn would have bought this pub, wouldn't he, O'Leary?' he asked in a voice loud enough for everyone in the bar to hear.

The other drinkers had been talking quietly amongst themselves, but now they fell silent.

'Well?' Barker demanded. 'Wouldn't he?'

'There was that possibility, sir,' Paddy O'Leary said cagily.

'More than a possibility, from what I've heard,' Barker said. 'His death must have come as quite a relief to you. You must have wished him dead any number of times.'

'I've never wished anybody dead,' Paddy said, his face turning red.

Barker took out his notebook and swung round so that he was facing the other drinkers.

'Not that you're the only one with a motive for killing Quinn,' he said. He flipped the notebook open. 'There's a Samuel Cooke who was in danger of losing his grocery store, an Ernest Bracegirdle whose landlord was about to sell his house out from under him, a Walter Hulse, a narrow-boat man, who ...'

'You might be a big man in London,' an angry voice interrupted him, 'but when you're up here you want to be more careful about throwing accusations around.'

Barker looked directly at the speaker. 'And who might you be?' he asked.

'An Edward Taylor,' Ted told him. 'And if it'll make you happy, you can write that down in your book an' all.'

Barker smiled. 'Ah yes,' he said. 'The chip-shop owner. Don't worry, Taylor, you're already down in my book.'

The door opened and a new customer walked in. He was a youngish man – not more than twenty-six or twenty-seven – dressed in a conservative tweed suit. At the sight of him, Barker's look of complacent superiority changed to one of deep dislike.

'What are you doing here, Dr Doyle?' the policeman snarled.

'I'm on holiday,' the new arrival said mildly. 'Can't a man take a holiday when he wants to?'

'A holiday!' Barker said contemptuously. 'Now why would anybody in his right mind want to take a holiday in a dump like this?'

'The place is not without its interest,' Doyle replied. He

walked up to the bar. 'I'm looking for a room for a few days, landlord,' he said. 'Would you happen to have one free?'

'I'm sorry, sir,' Paddy said apologetically, 'but we only have one spare room, and the Inspector's taken that.'

It was the expression of malicious satisfaction on the policeman's face which stirred Ted Taylor into action.

'I could put you up at my place if you don't mind roughing it a bit, Doctor,' he said.

Doyle smiled. 'I'm sure your place would suit me admirably,' he said.

Mary Taylor went spare when her husband told her the news.

'A doctor!' she said. 'A medical man! Whatever will he think when he sees our house?'

'He said he wouldn't mind roughing it a bit,' said Taylor.

His remark had been intended to calm his wife down, but it had just the opposite effect.

'Roughing it?' Mary demanded. 'There's nothing rough about this house. We may be simple, but we've never been rough. I'm sure the doctor will be more than comfortable.'

Ted Taylor hid a smile and wondered why it was that even when he was trying to get round his wife, he only succeeded in doing so by accident.

Doyle did, in fact, seem quite comfortable in the Taylor house. More than that, he got on very well with the family — especially Becky, who was intrigued to know why the doctor should have chosen the village as the site for his holiday.

'You shouldn't go asking people personal things like that,' her mother scolded her when she put the question to Doyle over supper.

But Doyle only laughed.

'I don't mind answering,' he said. 'I have a medical practice in Southsea, but I'm also something of an amateur criminologist.'

'What's a criminologist?' Becky asked.

'Someone who studies crimes,' Doyle told her.

'So you've come here because of Mr Quinn's murder,' Becky said.

'Exactly,' Doyle agreed.

'But how did you find out about it? Was it in the papers?'

'It may well have been,' Doyle said. 'But I heard of it from quite another source.'

'Another source?' Becky prodded.

'I have an acquaintance in Southsea who was up at university with someone from this area,' Doyle said mysteriously. 'My Southsea acquaintance had obviously told his friend about my hobby, since shortly after the murder he telegraphed me and offered to pay all my expenses if I would come up here and investigate.'

'Who is this friend?' Becky asked. 'Will we have heard of him?'

'Becky!' her mother said sharply.

Doyle laughed again.

'Much as I applaud curiosity in a young woman,' he said, 'I'm afraid that in this case it must go unsatisfied because my client — fearing that his brother may be arrested for the crime — wishes to remain anonymous for the moment.'

'Well, I'll say this, you've more chance of finding out who did it than that feller Barker,' Ted Taylor said.

'Yes, the good Inspector does tend to be a little brutish in his approach,' Doyle agreed. 'But then criminal investigation is in its infancy in Britain. Now in France, they have a much better idea of how to go about things.'

'What are *you* going to do?' Becky asked.

'Hush, Becky,' her mother told her.

But Doyle took this question with the same good humour as before.

'I shall start at the beginning,' he said. 'Tomorrow morning, if the authorities will grant their permission, I intend to examine the body.'

'What the devil to you hope to gain from that, Sir?' Ted Taylor asked.

'Ah, you can learn a great deal from bodies,' Doyle told him.

*

When Richard Worrell heard the heavy knock on the office door he felt his bowels turn to water.

'Why did I let Michael force me to come into the office?' he asked himself in a panic. 'Why didn't I make a run for it while I still had the chance?'

There was a second knock, even louder and more insistent this time. Richard took a quick slug of whisky, then, as the door started to swing open, hastily stuffed the bottle in his desk drawer.

The man who walked into the room was wearing an old-fashioned double-breasted coat and was flanked by two police constables.

'Barker,' he said. 'The Chepstow Axe Murders. Didn't you hear me knocking, Sir?'

'Er ... yes ... I ...'

'Then why didn't you ask us to come in?' Barker wondered.

'I was ... er ... just putting some important papers away.'

Barker sniffed.

'Smells like a distillery in here,' he said. He looked around the office, then sat down, uninvited, in the chair opposite Richard's. 'You were a business partner of Septimus Quinn's, weren't you, Sir?' the Inspector asked.

'Yes,' Richard admitted, pressing his palms firmly down on the desk in the hope that would stop his hands from trembling.

'Have an argument, did you, Sir?' Barker asked.

'An argument?' Richard replied shakily. 'Whyever should you think that?'

'Talked to one of your foremen,' Barker said. He took his notebook out of his pocket and flipped it open. 'A man called Jenkins. He says that while he was waiting outside the door, the morning after the murder, he heard you shouting at your brother that Septimus Quinn had cheated you.'

'He ... he must have misunderstood,' Richard protested. 'Quinn and I had just concluded a very satisfactory deal. I was looking forward to working with him for a good number of years.'

'Don't believe you,' Barker said flatly.

'I beg your pardon!' Richard exclaimed, noticing – with a sinking feeling – that the Inspector had dropped the 'Sir' when addressing him.

'Don't believe you,' Barker repeated. 'We have a witness' – he consulted his notebook again – 'a Walter Hulse, who saw a young man matching your description on the canal bank – just before he noticed the body in the water. Was that young man you?'

'No!' Richard said.

'Strange,' Barker mused. 'Because your night watchman is prepared to swear that round about the same time, you used the door under the loading bay to gain access to the canal and were gone for no more than five minutes.'

'I ... I was on the canal bank,' Richard confessed. 'I remember now. I was worried and I was ... I was a little drunk. I thought the night air might clear my head.'

'And what exactly were you worried about?' Barker asked relentlessly. 'Business?'

'Yes,' Richard said, grasping at the straw Barker had thrown him. 'Yes, I was worried about business.'

The Inspector turned to face his constables.

'Am I losing my memory, or did I hear Mr Worrell say, not two minutes ago, that business was going very well?' he asked.

'That's what he said,' one of the constables replied.

Barker swung round to Richard again.

'Why don't you come clean, son,' he asked. 'I promise you, you'll feel much better for it.'

'I ... I ...' Richard gagged.

'I'll make it easy for you,' Barker promised. 'What I'll do, I'll tell you what I think happened, and every time I say something you agree with, all you have to do is nod. Is that fair?'

Though he didn't want to, Richard found that he was nodding his head.

'You had an argument with Quinn, probably in this very office,' Barker said soothingly. 'He left and you got drunk. Right?'

Richard nodded again.

'Now, you knew he'd gone for a walk along the canal,' Barker continued, 'so you went out to meet him. You had a weapon in your hand — we'll probably find it hidden somewhere around the works ...'

'No!' Richard croaked.

'Let me finish,' Barker said firmly. 'Quinn was standing on the bank — close to a narrow boat called *Jupiter II*. He was looking into the water. Maybe he was a bit drunk, too. You crept up behind him and tapped him on the shoulder. When he turned round, you hit him — bang!'

Barker slammed his hand down hard on the desk.

'It didn't happen ... I wasn't ...' Richard said feebly.

'Quinn's skull was crushed and he toppled into the canal,' Barker continued. 'You were just standing there, hoping he'd sink, when you heard this Walter Hulse call out to you. You ran back up the canal path and returned to the works through the same door you'd left by. Now isn't that how it happened?'

'I saw him floating in the canal, but I never touched him, I swear I didn't,' Richard said.

'First he says they didn't have an argument, then he remembers they did,' Barker told his constables. 'Next he claims he was never on the canal path, but a minute later he admits he was. And his latest story is that he never touched Septimus Quinn. How long do you think that particular tale will hold up?'

'Not long, Sir,' the constable on his left said.

'Not long,' Barker mused. 'Richard Leonard Worrell,' he continued, sounding suddenly formal, 'I am arresting you for the murder of Septimus Quinn. I would advise you to come quietly.'

Dr Doyle returned from Northwich looking well satisfied, and even the announcement that Richard Worrell had been arrested did not seem to spoil his good humour.

'Still, you must admit, Sir, that now the police have got their man your examining the body was pretty much a waste of time,' Ted Taylor said to the doctor over supper.

'Not at all,' Doyle replied. 'I learned a great deal from studying the mortal remains of the late Septimus Quinn.'

'Like what?' Becky asked.

'Well, for a start, Quinn was once a military man. Perhaps Inspector Barker knows that, too, though I would be surprised if the Inspector had also discovered that Quinn once visited Afghanistan, and was probably, at some time in his life, a prize-fighter.'

'How can you tell all that just from looking at a body?' Becky asked, fascinated.

'It's really no trick,' Doyle said. 'In fact, it's nothing more than elementary logic, though alas, however elementary the logic is, the police are sometimes rather lax about employing it.'

'How do you know he was a soldier?' Becky persisted.

'Oh that was easy,' Doyle said airily. 'He had a scar on his thigh which was consistent with a bullet wound. How else is a man likely to get shot but in the army?'

'The prize-fighting?' Becky asked, beginning to enjoy the game.

'Scarring again, especially around the knuckles and the eyes. I suppose it is possible he was nothing more than a street tough, but from the extent of his old injuries, I would put my money on his having been a professional fighter.'

'And his visit to Afghanistan?'

'That was the easiest thing of all to uncover. He had a tattoo on his right forearm, a very particular tattoo of the sort which is only displayed by members of the Pathan tribe. Where else could he have got it but in one of the bazaars of Kabul or Peshawar?'

'That's all very clever, Sir,' Ted Taylor admitted, his voice filled with admiration, 'but to get back to what I said before, isn't it a bit of a waste of time now that the murderer's been arrested?'

'On the contrary,' Doyle replied. 'The other thing which my examination of the body revealed is that Richard Worrell couldn't possibly be the murderer.'

CHAPTER FOURTEEN

'I need a guide,' Doyle said to Becky the following afternoon. 'Come with me and be my Watson.'

'Your what?' Becky asked.

'My Watson. He's a character in a detective novel I've been working on in the more-than-ample free time my medical practice affords me. But enough of that. My client is paying my expenses in order that I might investigate a murder, and that is what I should be doing now.'

'This client of yours,' Becky said. 'He wouldn't be called Michael Worrell by any chance, would he?'

'How do you know that?' Doyle asked sharply.

Becky grinned. 'You said your client was worried his brother was going to be arrested, and Richard Worrell has been. So it's – what-do-you-call-it – elementary, that your client is Michael Worrell.'

'I can see you will make a most promising pupil,' Doyle said. 'Now, if you wouldn't mind, I'd like to see the spot where Barker says Quinn was killed.'

'I shall want paying,' Becky told him.

'Of course,' Doyle agreed, reaching into his pocket.

'No, not with money,' Becky said hastily.

'Then with what?' Doyle wondered.

'You said last night that Richard Worrell couldn't possibly have killed Mr Quinn, but you wouldn't explain why,' Becky told him. 'If I'm going to help you, I'd like to know what's going on.'

Doyle chuckled. 'And as my Watson, it is right that you *should* know,' he agreed. 'Very well. Take me to the so-called scene of the crime and I will tell you about my findings on the way.'

Becky led Doyle up the Lane and around the side of the salt store.

'I'm told this Richard Worrell is a tall young man,' the doctor said, 'of about the same height as his supposed victim.'

'Yes, he is,' Becky agreed.

'Yet from the nature of the wound on Septimus Quinn's head, it was obvious to me that he was struck from below. So either Worrell was kneeling down when he delivered the blow – which you must admit seems unlikely – or the assailant was a much smaller man.'

They reached the point on the canal path where *Jupiter II* had been moored on the night of the murder.

'If we assume that Worrell is innocent,' Doyle said, 'then the killing could not have taken place on this spot.'

'What makes you say that?' Becky asked.

'It's quite simple, really,' Doyle told her. 'Tell me, Becky, why do the boatmen moor their craft to the bank?'

'Because the boats would drift away if they didn't,' Becky said.

'Exactly,' Doyle agreed. 'There is not a strong current on the canal, but there is a current of some sort, sufficient to carry a boat – or a body – along. Now in order for Septimus Quinn's corpse to have been found at this spot, one of two things must have happened. Either he was killed very shortly before he was discovered, or he was killed further up the canal. Now why is the latter case the more likely?'

Becky thought about it while Doyle watched her with obvious amusement in his eyes.

'If Richard Worrell didn't kill Mr Quinn,' she said finally, 'then somebody else did.'

'Obviously,' Doyle agreed.

'And if Mr Quinn had been killed just before Mr Hulse found him, then both Mr Hulse and Richard Worrell would have seen the murderer.'

'Excellent,' Doyle said, but before Becky had time to congratulate herself, he added, 'And what other clue do we have?'

'I don't know,' Becky admitted.

'It is conceivable that the murderer and his victim exchanged no words,' Doyle said. 'It is even possible that the blow to Quinn's head caused no more sound than a dull thud. But then Quinn fell backwards into the canal. He was a large man. When he hit the water he would have made a loud splash and ...'

'And Mrs Hulse would have heard it!' Becky said excitedly.

'*Jupiter II* was only ten feet from where the body was first spotted. Mrs Hulse would certainly have heard it,' Doyle agreed. 'Therefore, having established that Quinn was not killed here, let us see if we can discover just where he *did* meet his end.'

They walked up the canal towards Burns Bridge. Occasionally Doyle would stop to examine the tow path. Once or twice he actually knelt and looked at the ground through a magnifying glass.

'Pure clay would have been the ideal surface for our purpose,' he told Becky, 'but this mixture of clay and cobble-stones will serve us well enough.'

'Good enough for what?' Becky asked.

'For footprints. Most of the people who've walked along this path recently were wearing working boots or clogs, but not the man – and it could have been Quinn – whose steps we're following. He was wearing, I would guess, fashionable and expensive leather ankle boots. Note the pointed toe, my dear Watson. Note also the length of his strides, which tells us he must have been about Quinn's height.'

Near the bridge Doyle let out of whoop of triumph.

'This is where they met,' he said. 'See, Watson, the grass on the embankment has been recently flattened. That is the way the killer came, rather than along the tow path. Now why should he have done that?'

'A short cut?' Becky suggested.

'An admirable conclusion,' Doyle said. 'It would be much quicker to travel across country from the village than to follow the curve of the canal. However, it would also have been more uncomfortable. The murderer would have had to ford at least one stream, and would have a steep climb up the embankment at the end of his journey. So what does that tell us? Why should the murderer have chosen a more difficult route?'

'Because he was in a hurry?' Becky said tentatively.

'And why should he have been in a hurry?' Doyle asked.

'Because he wasn't waiting for Mr Quinn – he was trying to catch him up!'

'Admirable again!' Doyle told her. 'So, he does catch him up, and then what happens? Let us see what story the ground has to tell us.' The doctor got down on his hands and knees and sniffed around like a bloodhound. 'This is where they met, my dear Watson,' he said when he had reached a point at the very edge of the canal. 'Come and look.'

Becky squatted down beside him. There were clear imprints of two pairs of boots. One pair had pointed toes, like the footprints Doyle had been following since they'd left Marston. The other pair were rounder and wider.

'The sort of boots your ordinary working man might wear,' Doyle said. 'But they're not working boots, are they?'

'No,' Becky agreed.

'And how do we know that?'

'There's no marks from the hobnails.'

'Excellent,' Doyle said. 'We'll make a detective of you yet. So what we have here is the print made by a pair of best boots, the sort of boots a man might wear if, for example, he was respectable enough to dress up when he went to the New Inn for a drink. Now what else have you noticed?'

'They stood facing each other,' Becky said. 'They were probably talking.'

'Exactly. Inspector Barker, I'm told, has a theory that the murderer crept up behind Quinn. I already knew from the angle of the wound that that was rubbish, and this merely confirms it. They were facing each other, possibly talking as you say, and that was when the blow was struck.'

'How can you be sure of that?' Becky asked.

Doyle laughed. 'You are right to be sceptical, my dear Watson,' he said. 'Notice how deep an impression the heels of the pointed boots made in the clay at this particular point. Notice also that the edges of the prints are broken away. Now why should that be?'

'I don't know,' Becky confessed, really stumped this time.

'They are deeper because Quinn put all his weight on them just as he was about to topple backwards after the blow,' Doyle explained.

'Of course!' Becky said, cursing her own slow thinking.

Doyle stood up and dusted off his trousers.

'I think we've done enough for one day,' he continued. 'If I can beg a favour, don't tell anyone quite yet what we've discovered. Our keeping silent will mean that young Mr Worrell is forced to spend a little more time in the lock-up, but from what I've heard of him, the experience will do him nothing but good.'

Doyle's presence in the bar of the New Inn that night made Paddy O'Leary feel distinctly uneasy. It wasn't that the doctor was throwing around accusations as Inspector Barker had been. Far from it, he answered all enquiries about his investigation with a smile and polite nod of the head. Yet still, Paddy had an instinct that before the evening was over, Doyle would put him in an awkward position.

The moment came just as the pub was closing for the night. Doyle waited until the last customer was heading through the door, then rose from his seat and sidled over to the bar.

'I'd like to ask you one or two questions, if you don't mind, Mr O'Leary,' he said.

'Oh yes,' Paddy replied cautiously. 'What kind of questions?'

'I want to know exactly who was in the bar on the evening of the murder, and at what time they left,' he said.

Paddy hesitated.

'It's like this, Dr Doyle,' he said finally. 'From what I've seen of you, you're a good man. And the Taylors seem to have taken to you — which should be a strong enough recommendation for anybody. But still . . .'

'But still, you don't want to get any of your customers into trouble with the police,' Doyle supplied.

'That's it,' O'Leary agreed gratefully.

'Would you like to see the wrong man hang for the murder of Septimus Quinn?' Doyle asked.

'No,' O'Leary admitted. 'But I'm not sure I'd like to see the *right* man hang for it, either.'

'Neither am I,' Doyle told him. 'My task here is to get Richard Worrell out of gaol. Anything beyond that is simply to satisfy my own curiosity. I am no Inspector Barker. I may wish to see justice done, but for me justice does not necessarily involve an arrest. So could you please just give me the names of the customers and the times they left.'

Paddy O'Leary sighed. Doyle was a very hard man to turn down, the landlord thought.

'Well, let me see,' he said. 'Wally Hulse, the feller who actually found the body, was the last to leave. He was a bit the worse for drink, and he took some persuading to take himself back to his boat. Now before him — let me see — it must have been . . .'

Doyle spent most of the following morning down at the post office.

'Sent a lot of telegrams, didn't he?' Not-Stopping Bracegirdle asked after he'd finally left.

'Quite a lot,' agreed Mr Moores from behind the counter.

'Got a lot of replies, as well,' Not-Stopping observed.

'Yes,' Moores said neutrally.

'Nothing wrong at home, is there?' Not-Stopping asked, her voice oozing concern. 'I mean, his wife's not ill or anything, is she?'

'You know all telegrams are confidential, Mrs Bracegirdle,' Moores replied, more sternly this time.

'Of course they are,' Not-Stopping agreed. 'And quite right, too. Maybe all them telegrams were to do with his investigation. Maybe he was asking questions about somebody from the village.'

Moores' eye only twitched slightly, but for someone as sharp as Not-Stopping, that spoke volumes.

So Doyle had been interested in finding out about someone from Marston. But who?

In the late afternoon Doyle took a walk along the canal path in the company of Inspectors Barker and Capstick.

'The last time you interfered in one of my cases, Doctor, I had to let my man go,' Barker said morosely as they approached Burns Bridge.

'Well, he *was* innocent,' Doyle pointed out in his own defence.

'Maybe!' Barker admitted grudgingly. 'But if somebody had paid you to do it, *you'd* have tried to get the Chepstow Axe Murderer off.'

They reached the spot at which Septimus Quinn had met his end, and Doyle pointed out the footprints.

'How do we know they're Quinn's?' Barker asked bad-temperedly.

'I think you will find his dress boots fit them perfectly,' Doyle said. 'I think you will notice, too, as I did, that there is a considerable amount of clay, identical to the clay we see here, encrusted on his heels.'

'Some barge-horse could tread over these tomorrow,' Barker said. 'Then where would your evidence be?'

'Barge-horses usually walk further away from the canal,' Doyle told him. 'Besides, I have already taken plaster casts of the prints, which I would be glad to give you, should you require them.'

'What about the other set of prints?' Barker enquired belligerently. 'How do we know Worrell didn't make them?'

'Too small for his feet and not the kind of boots he wears,' Doyle replied.

'He could have squeezed into them to throw us off the track,' Barker countered.

'Even if that were true, he wouldn't have had time to commit the murder,' Doyle said. 'We're at least a mile from the works and we know from the night watchman that Worrell was only on the canal bank for five minutes.'

'He could have killed Quinn earlier,' Barker said.

'So could anyone else,' Doyle told him. 'Without witnesses to connect Worrell with the scene of the crime, you simply have no case.'

'You'll have to let him go,' said Inspector Capstick, making no effort to keep the delight out of his voice.

Barker picked up a loose cobblestone and threw it furiously into the canal.

'All right,' he agreed. 'All right – I'll let the bastard go!'

'I have spoken to Inspector Barker,' Doyle told the Taylor family at supper time, 'and he has agreed – though not, I might say, with very good grace – to release Richard Worrell.'

Ted Taylor dropped his fork.

'So young Worrell didn't kill Quinn after all?' he said.

'As I told you the other day, that would have been quite impossible,' Doyle replied.

'Hang on,' Taylor said. 'If Richard Worrell *didn't* do it, then who the hell did?'

'We shall probably never know that,' Doyle said blandly. 'Or, at any rate, *I* never shall. My short holiday is over, and I will be returning to Southsea tomorrow.'

The carriage had been booked in time to catch the early train, and it was still dark when it pulled up outside the Taylor house.

'Since you work in Northwich, my dear Watson,' Doyle said, 'would it not save your legs to ride with me as far as the station?'

'That's very kind of you,' Becky said.

'Not at all. I would appreciate the chance for one last conversation.'

Ted Taylor carried the doctor's bags out to the carriage, and Becky and Doyle climbed in.

'You didn't really believe me last night, did you?' Doyle asked as the carriage clattered down Ollershaw Lane.

'Pardon, Sir?' Becky replied.

Doyle chuckled. 'Come, come, my dear Watson,' he said. 'Don't play games with me.'

'I don't think you're the kind of man who'd go away without an answer,' Becky admitted.

'Quite right,' Doyle said delightedly. 'Quite right.'

'So who did kill Mr Quinn?'

'One step at a time,' Doyle cautioned her. 'I thought you would have learned that by now. When Septimus Quinn left Richard Worrell's office he went straight to the canal. We can't be sure whether he always intended to do that or whether he decided to take some exercise on the spur of the moment – but that doesn't matter. What *is* important is that the murderer didn't know Quinn was about to take a walk. And how can we be sure of that?'

'If he had known, he wouldn't have had to take the difficult short cut,' Becky said. 'He'd have been waiting in hiding further up the canal.'

'Correct,' Doyle said. 'Now how did the murderer find out about Quinn's plans?'

'He saw him,' Becky replied.

'Exactly,' Doyle agreed. 'But from *where*? Remember that the main entrance to Worrell's is quite close to the canal, and not many houses overlook the route Quinn took. Besides, people in Marston live in their kitchens, not their parlours – and from the kitchens, you don't have a view of the street.'

'The New Inn!' Becky gasped. 'The murderer had to have seen him from the New Inn!'

'Quite so,' Doyle agreed. 'And having concluded that, it is quite a simple matter to solve the rest of the puzzle, isn't it?' Doyle asked.

'Is it?' Becky replied.

'Of course. We know roughly how long it would have

taken Quinn to reach the point on the tow path where he met his – not undeserved – end, and we can estimate how long it would take his body to float down the canal until it reached *Jupiter II*. Thus we can establish his time of death with a fair degree of accuracy. From there, it was a simple enough matter to ask Mr O'Leary which of his customers left in time to commit the murder. Which is what I did – the night before last.'

'So you already knew, yesterday morning, who killed Mr Quinn,' Becky said.

'Indeed I did.'

'Then what was the point of all your telegrams?'

'No point at all,' Doyle admitted, 'save to see if they could satisfy my curiosity and confirm some of my theories.'

'And did they?' Becky asked.

'I didn't expect the exact replies I received,' Doyle told her. 'But I knew it would have to be *something* like that.'

'Something like what?' Becky wanted to know.

The carriage rumbled towards Dunkirk, passing chimneys which were just beginning to belch out smoke and miners who were trudging reluctantly to their day's toil. Becky looked at Doyle expectantly, but the doctor seemed to have said all he wanted to and was now perfectly content to sit in silence.

It was not until they were nearly at the station that Becky plucked up the courage to speak again.

'You still haven't told me who killed Mr Quinn,' she said.

'No, I haven't, have I,' Doyle agreed. 'But is there any need for me to? Should you wish to discover the truth for yourself, you have only to ask Mr O'Leary the same questions I did.'

'But why shouldn't you ...'

'Yet think carefully before taking so momentous a step, my dear Watson,' Doyle cautioned. 'Ask yourself first if you really do wish to know which of your friends or neighbours has taken a life, however unworthy that life may have been?'

Becky considered it for some time.

'No,' she said finally. 'I don't think I do.'

'A wise decision,' Doyle told her.

The carriage pulled up on the station forecourt and was immediately surrounded by porters eager to earn a tip from such a prosperous-looking gentleman. Doyle helped Becky down from the carriage, took her arm and led her into the station. The train was just pulling in.

'Goodbye, Dr Doyle,' Becky said.

'Goodbye, my dear Watson,' Doyle replied.

He boarded the train, then pulled down his carriage window.

'It has been a pleasure to meet you,' he said. 'You are a remarkable young woman, Becky Taylor, and if I were you I should not be too surprised if I eventually found a character not unlike myself playing at least a minor role in a successful work of detective fiction.'

I won't ask Mr O'Leary any questions, Becky told herself as the train pulled out of the station, yet I can't help wondering who did kill Septimus Quinn.

But she wouldn't find out – not for years.

For the next two weeks – to the ever-increasing pleasure of Inspector Capstick – the policeman from London continued to barge and bully his way around the village. Countless times Barker slung accusations at people who had stood to gain from the murder. On a number of occasions he dropped veiled hints that an arrest was imminent. But the truth of the matter was that with the loss of his prime suspect he had also lost all taste for the case. In the end he retired in graceless defeat and the village returned to the relative tranquillity it had known before the arrival of Septimus Quinn.

CHAPTER FIFTEEN

It was Becky's oldest sister Eunice and her under-gardener husband Charlie who presented Ted and Mary Taylor with their first grandchild – a little girl called Thelma.

'Isn't she champion, Grandad?' Mary asked her husband.

'Oh aye, she's bonny enough,' Taylor agreed.

Mary looked at her husband as if she were about to tell him off, then changed her mind and addressed the proud parents instead.

'She really is lovely,' she said. 'And I'm sure you'll have many more. Our Jessie's getting married, too, when Sid's promoted to deputy manager. It wouldn't surprise me if the house was soon full of grandkids.'

'It won't be long before our Becky's courting, an' all,' Eunice said teasingly.

'Get off with you,' Becky protested, feeling herself going red. 'I'm not interested in lads.'

But that wasn't quite true, she admitted to herself. In a way, she'd been interested in lads for as long as she could remember.

She thought back to her first journey to school – George, her bodyguard, tagging reluctantly some yards behind her – when she'd talked to Richard Worrell on the bridge and watched as Michael Worrell struggled to push the handcart. Wouldn't she have forgotten the incident long ago if, instead of Richard and Michael, they'd been Rachael and Margaret?

She recalled vividly the night of the circus when Richard Worrell had rescued her from the three hoodlums who had wanted to – well, she shivered even now at the thought of what they'd probably wanted to do to her.

'Come on, Becky, own up,' Eunice prodded. 'What's his name?'

'What's whose name?'

'The lad you're thinking about right now.'

'I'm not thinking about *any* lad,' Becky lied. 'I was just wondering what Mrs Stanway wants me to do with that new roll of cloth we've just got in.'

Richard had looked so dashing and sure of himself when he'd stood up to them three thugs, she thought. She hadn't liked it when he kicked the one who was lying on the ground, but she knew nothing about fighting and maybe all men did that.

'Geoff Bracegirdle,' Eunice guessed. 'She's got her heart set on Geoff Bracegirdle.'

'What! And have Not-Stopping for a mother-in-law?' Becky asked, trying to make a joke of the whole thing before it got too deep.

She caught sight of Richard Worrell quite often, when he was driving his carriage into the works or riding down the lane on his beautiful white horse. He cut a fine figure with his broad shoulders and muscular legs. He had a handsome face, too – jet-black hair, a wide brow, long thin nose and square chin. Becky wondered if he sometimes noticed her watching him from the chip-shop doorway.

She saw Michael Worrell, too, though not so regularly, because – according to village gossip – he travelled a lot. He was not quite his brother – his frame was not *quite* as solid, his hair not *quite* as black, his nose not *quite* as thin. Yet he was very attractive, too, perhaps because he looked the kind of man you could tell your deepest secrets to, knowing that he would guard them with his life.

'Bill Prince!' Eunice said. 'I bet he's the one!'

'He's nearly two years younger than me,' Becky said scornfully. 'And anyway, he's a drip.'

But Eunice was on the right lines, she thought. What was the point of thinking about Richard and Michael Worrell? They were gentlemen, and their world was a million miles from hers. When she did finally marry it would be to someone like Eunice's Charlie or Jessie's Sid – lads from her own class.

Still, you couldn't blame a girl for dreaming, could you?

*

'You didn't seem to be able to work up much enthusiasm for your granddaughter,' Mary said to her husband after the new parents had left for their cottage in the grounds of the Big House. 'What's the matter? Aren't you proud of her?'

'Oh, I'm proud of her,' Taylor replied, a little shamefacedly. 'It's just ... it's just I wish one of the boys was thinking of having children.'

'Maybe they are,' Mary said.

Taylor shook his head. 'Jack's all set on saving up to go to Africa. And what chance has George to meet girls — the sort of girls he could bring home, anyway?'

'You seem in a great hurry to rush your sons to the altar,' Mary said. 'That isn't anything to do with having grandchildren with the same name as you, is it?'

'Well,' Ted said awkwardly, 'I would like to see the family name carry on, like. Do you understand what I mean?'

'Of course I do, love,' Mary said with a smile. 'Taylor's such an uncommon name that you're afraid if your boys don't get married soon and start breeding like rabbits, it'll die out.'

Becky laughed when her mother told that story. For so many years, through all the trials and tribulations, Mam had kept up her spirits and maintained her sense of humour. Yet Becky worried about her. She had not had an easy life — straight from the workhouse into service, and then into marriage with six kids to worry about — and now she was approaching fifty, she was starting to show the strain. She was paler than she used to be, and sometimes, when she thought no one was looking, she would wince with pain. She didn't complain, of course — Mam never complained — but Becky sensed that there were days when the household chores and the work in the chip shop were getting to be too much for her.

'Please don't take Mam away from us,' she prayed to a God she had largely ignored since her Sunday school days. 'Please let us have her for just a few more years.'

*

The state of a parent's health was on Richard Worrell's mind, too. For a long time Len had been looking ill, and it had been years since he'd taken an active part in the business. Yet when there was an important decision to be taken, Len was the one who had to take it, because for anything that really mattered he was still master of Worrell's.

Richard consoled himself by thinking of the future, which, inevitably, also involved a review of the past.

He'd had three strokes of luck, he thought.

The first had been that someone – still unknown – had decided, when everything had looked its blackest, to murder Septimus Quinn.

The second was that his ever-gullible brother – who'd have stood to inherit the whole of his father's remaining shares if only he'd had the sense to do nothing to help – decided to bring in that amateur detective who had proved the police had arrested the wrong man.

And the third? The third had been delivered to him on a plate by an unlikely messenger – a small man with a bald head and bad teeth who had presented himself at the office just after Richard had been released from the lock-up.

'What are you doing here, Crimp?' Richard had asked coldly.

'I'm your attorney,' Crimp replied.

'No,' Richard said. 'You *were* my attorney. Or to be more accurate, I *thought* you were my attorney – but all the time you were working for Septimus Quinn.'

'Not all the time,' Crimp corrected him. 'Only from the point at which it became clear to me that I could get more out of him than I could out of you.'

'And now he's gone you've come crawling back, have you?' Richard asked.

'The king is dead, long live the king,' Crimp said shamelessly. 'But I haven't exactly come crawling. I've brought you a present.'

'A present? What kind of present?'

'Septimus Quinn has one surviving relative, a sister,' Crimp told him. 'It is she who will inherit his entire estate.'

'So what?' Richard demanded.

'As her attorney in the matter of her brother's holding in Worrell's, I felt it my duty to tell her of the secret agreement he signed with you,' Crimp said.

'But that agreement's not worth the paper it's written on,' Richard said.

'It is if she *thinks* it is,' Crimp said cryptically.

'If she thinks it is?'

'If I tell her that the agreement makes her legally obliged to sell the shares to you, she'll believe me. You have got the money to buy them, haven't you?'

Of course he had the money. In order to make Worrell's appear to be on the brink of bankruptcy, it had been necessary to syphon off a great deal of cash which was now hidden in a secret account at a Manchester bank.

'What's in it for you, Crimp?' Richard asked.

The attorney shrugged. 'The satisfaction of seeing a job well done,' he said. 'And perhaps a small reward for my labours – shall we say a hundred pounds now and a guarantee that you will continue to employ me as your attorney at a sum of not less than one hundred pounds per annum?'

'But can I trust you?' Richard wondered aloud.

Crimp smiled, revealing his row of rotten teeth.

'Mr Worrell,' he said, 'as long as you're winning, you can trust me with your life.'

The deal was struck – both with Crimp and Quinn's sister – and Richard became the owner of slightly more than a quarter of the shares in Worrell's – though no one in Marston but he and his attorney knew it. On his father's death he would receive another twenty-five per cent, and the works would be his to do with as he liked. How he longed for that day. And how it frustrated him to see his father, like the proverbial creaking gate, continue to hang on to life.

'Why doesn't he die?' Richard asked himself again and again. 'Why doesn't the old bugger just give up?'

It was a mild day in early summer, the sort of day when

people went for a long walk in the woods after work and then fancied a bag of chips to round off the evening. And even before that, there'd be workers knocking off from Worrell's and Adelaide Mine, eager to spend their coppers on a battered fish and mushy peas. Well, let them all come, Ted Taylor thought, looking down at the fat which was sizzling nicely in the fryer – he'd be ready for them.

'I'm just popping round the back to peel a few spuds,' Mary Taylor said weakly.

Ted lifted his eyes from the range and fixed them on his wife. She looked tired – very tired. Her face was paler than he ever remembered seeing it before and her eyes – once so alive – were as faded as an old pair of overalls.

'Are you feeling all right, love?' he asked worriedly.

Mary brushed a strand of limp hair to one side.

'I'm fine,' she said, forcing a smile.

Then why didn't she sound it?

'We'd better start thinking about taking you to see the doctor, hadn't we?' Taylor suggested.

'The doctor?' Mary replied with mock scorn. 'People only call the doctor when they're sick. All I need is a five-minute sit-down, and I'll get that while I'm peeling the spuds.'

'I'll peel the spuds,' Taylor told her.

'Well, if you're offering ...' Mary said gratefully.

In the doorway Ted stopped and glanced back at his wife. Caught unawares, Mary looked even worse.

'Are you sure about the doctor?' he asked.

'Of course I'm sure,' Mary replied unconvincingly. 'Now get on with your chip making. You know how bad-tempered them wallers from Worrell's can get if their penny-ha'penny's worth isn't ready the second they walk in through the shop door.'

Ted went through to the back yard where a sack of potatoes and an old dolly tub of water were waiting for him. After placing his stool in front of the tub he picked up his peeling knife and attacked a potato. As he worked he remembered the first time he'd done this particular job – the day the shop had opened to what he'd been convinced was certain failure – and a grin came to his face.

You were really kack-handed, weren't you? he thought as he skinned the potato with practised ease. Well, it's not the sort of job a man has the training for, is it?

The potato was peeled in the time it took that single thought to pass through his mind. As he dropped it into the tub of water with one hand Taylor was already reaching for a new spud with the other.

The kitchen door flew open with a crash, and Harry Atherton appeared in the doorway, as white as if he'd seen a ghost.

'What the bloody hell do you think you're doing inside my house, Harry?' Taylor asked.

'It's your m ... missis,' Atherton said.

'My missis?' Ted replied. 'What about her?'

'She's l ... lying on the chip shop fl ... floor,' Atherton told him. 'I c ... can't seem to make her h ... hear me.'

Ted sprang to his feet and, pushing the shocked Atherton roughly out of way, made a dash for the front room.

Mary was sprawled on the floor next to the range. She looked more like a discarded rag doll than the woman he'd been married to for nearly thirty years.

His heart pounding, Taylor knelt down and turned her over onto her back. Her face was chalk white and she felt cold to him – so cold.

'Mary, love,' Taylor sobbed. 'Are you all right, Mary love?'

'I d ... didn't touch her,' he heard Harry Atherton say behind him. 'Just as s ... soon as I saw her, I came st ... st ... straight out and told you.'

'I knew I should have got the doctor,' Taylor said. 'I told her she should have the doctor.'

'Shall I g ... go and get him now?' Atherton asked.

'What?' Taylor said, hardly able to think straight. 'The doctor? Yes – go and get him. And for God's sake, be quick!'

Atherton dodged around him and rushed out of the door. Taylor cradled his wife in his hands. She didn't seem to be breathing.

'I told you we should have got the doctor,' he said softly, 'but you never would listen, would you?'

'I should have done something long before now,' Ted Taylor said, poking miserably at the dying embers of the kitchen fire.

'You can't blame yourself, Dad,' Becky told him as she reached over to stroke his arm.

'Who else have I to blame?' Taylor asked, shrugging her off. 'I'm her husband. *I* should have known. *I* should have seen it coming.'

'We both should,' Becky agreed, 'but we didn't, and fretting about it now won't do any good.'

The heavy footfalls on the stairs told them that Dr Tripp was coming down. Father and daughter turned anxiously towards the doorway.

The doctor's face was a blank, as it always was whether the news he was delivering was good or bad.

'How is she?' Taylor asked.

'Exhausted,' Tripp said crisply. 'Anaemic. Possibly on the edge of a nervous collapse.'

'Can you ... can you give her anything?' Taylor said.

'I've already given her a tonic,' the doctor told him. 'What she needs now is plenty of rest and some proper nourishing food. I'll wager she lives off fish and chips, doesn't she?'

'Well, you know what it's like when we get busy,' Taylor said, abashed. 'We do so much cooking for other folk we don't have the time to ...'

'Liver,' the doctor interrupted. 'Liver and lots of red meat. A bottle of stout twice a day. Do you understand?'

'Yes, doctor.'

'And, of course, if you can afford it ...'

'Anything she needs, she shall have,' Taylor said. 'Is it expensive medicine or something?'

'What would really do her good is a change,' Tripp explained.

'You mean, like a holiday?'

'Exactly. Give her chance to breathe something other than

chip fat and chimney smoke. Take her to the seaside, for example.'

'Right,' Taylor said decisively, 'I'll do just that. People are going to have to learn to do without their fish and chips for a couple of weeks. We're going to Blackpool.'

It was during the second week of her parents' holiday that Becky herself took a day trip to Blackpool. Ted and Mary were waiting for her at the station. Mary seemed much improved and Ted had never looked better.

'I've been talking to some of the other guests in our digs,' Taylor told his daughter as they walked towards the promenade. 'There's people who come here every year, you know — whether the doctor tells them to or not.'

'And are you enjoying yourself, Dad?' Becky asked.

'Enjoying myself?' Taylor replied. 'Why, a man'd have to be a lunatic not to enjoy himself in Blackpool.'

'He's already had a word with the landlady about keeping us a room for next year,' Mary told her daughter in a stage whisper.

'Well, I thought I might as well — since your mother seemed to be enjoying it so much,' Taylor said awkwardly.

They reached the promenade, and for the first time in her life Becky saw the sea.

'It's so big,' she gasped. 'It goes on for ever!'

Her father laughed. 'All the way to America, anyway,' he said with the air of a man who, after nearly two weeks' exposure, found no difficulty in comprehending the ocean's vastness.

Green and cream trams, their poles attached to overhead cables, rattled along the prom at what seemed to Becky to be a furious rate.

'No horses, see!' Taylor said, as proud as if he'd invented the electric tram himself. 'Better than Manchester, this — isn't it?'

They climbed down the steps onto the beach — and new wonders unfolded. Huts on wheels, with advertisements for

Pears' Soap posted to their sides, were being winched in and out of the water.

'Bathing cabins,' Taylor explained. 'It's so anybody as wants to get into the sea can do it without any nosy-parkers watching. I've been trying to persuade your mother to hire one.'

'Get on with you,' Mary Taylor said, laughing. 'What business would I have going into the sea?'

'It's supposed to be good for you,' Taylor pointed out. 'A "restorative", I think they call it.'

'A restorative!' his wife mocked. 'As if the air itself wasn't doing me enough good, without dipping my whole body in the water.'

The air *did* feel wonderful, Becky thought. At home it was always smoky and tasted of cinders, but in Blackpool it was as clear as glass and had a salty tang to it which almost made her giddy.

They walked along the beach. Boys in dark suits and large caps were riding furiously on grey donkeys. Tweenies in floral hats had pulled their skirts up to their knees and were paddling in the sea.

On the horizon was a small armada of sailing boats.

'The Fleetwood shrimping boats,' said Ted, the acknowledged family expert on all things Blackpoolian.

They reached a barrow selling ice cream.

'Buy her one,' Mary Taylor said.

'I was just going to,' Taylor replied offendedly. He turned to the woman behind the barrow. 'Is it made with real cream?' he asked.

'Of course it is,' the vendor assured him.

'Only I don't want any of that sugar and starch rubbish,' Taylor explained. 'It's for me daughter, you see. She's come all the way from Marston.'

'That's nice,' the vendor said, though she obviously had no idea where Marston was.

The ice was cool and creamy to Becky's tongue, and, far too soon, she realized that she'd already eaten most of it.

'Let's go for a paddle,' she suggested when she'd finished savouring the last delicious blob of her treat.

'A paddle?' her father said. 'I couldn't do that.'

'You said you could never go to Manchester, either,' Becky reminded him. 'And you wouldn't be the only feller in the water. Just look around you.'

It was true enough. Quite a number of men, some wearing wide-brimmed hats and other with straw boaters, had shed their jackets — though not their waistcoats — rolled up their trousers and shirt sleeves, and were dipping their feet in the sea.

'Come on, love!' Mary Taylor urged. 'I will if you will.'

'Aye, all right,' Taylor agreed.

They sat down on the beach and stripped off their shoes and stockings. Keeping together — for safety's sake — they advanced cautiously on the water. The sand tickled Becky between the toes and the water which lapped around her ankles was both cold and refreshing.

'I don't know how anybody could ever leave this place,' she said, though she knew that in a few short hours she would have to go herself.

Taylor took out his pocket watch and examined it.

'Time we weren't here,' he said. 'It'd not do to keep the brass band waiting.'

Becky chuckled.

'What's so funny?' her father asked.

'You talk as if they couldn't start without you.' Becky said.

'Yes, I do, don't I?' Taylor replied mysteriously.

They dried their feet, put their shoes and socks back on, and returned to the prom.

'You take our Becky to the bandstand,' Taylor told his wife. 'I've just got to pop into the digs for a minute.'

Becky and her mother strolled along the promenade. A man who shared the same lodgings as the Taylors raised his bowler hat to Mary. A group of mill girls, their arms linked, walked past singing, *He was one of the early birds and I was one of the worms*.

The trams were the hardest thing for Becky to get used to. When the first few thundered by her, she jumped to the side before she could stop herself, but after several others had passed she managed to convince herself that they were probably safe – well, more or less anyway.

There was so much to see in Blackpool, she thought. As if the beach and the sea weren't enough for anybody, there were also shops selling all kinds of souvenirs, and gardens full to bursting with flowers the like of which had never been seen in Marston.

'One day,' she promised herself, 'one day I'll come back here and stay for a whole week.'

They reached the bandstand, a hexagonal, cast-iron structure set in the centre of one of the gardens. The bandsmen, resplendent in blue and gold uniforms, were already tuning up their instruments.

'They'll start with "Jerusalem",' Mary Taylor said as the two women took their seats. 'They always do.'

The bandmaster tapped his music stand.

'I hope he's not late,' Mary Taylor said anxiously.

'Hope *who's* not late, Mam?' Becky asked.

'No, here he is,' Mary said.

Becky turned her head in the direction her mother was looking and saw Ted Taylor hurrying along the prom. He was dressed in the same uniform as the men on the stand.

'What ...? How ...?' Becky asked. 'I mean, you've been here less than a fortnight.'

Mary laughed. 'The second day we were here one of the trumpeters got taken poorly,' she explained. 'And you know what your dad's like – he offered to take the feller's place like a shot.'

Taylor mounted the bandstand and sat in his place. The conductor raised his baton and – as Mary had predicted – the band embarked on their rendition of 'Jerusalem'.

Bliss, Becky thought. Perfect bliss.

She shut her eyes for a few moments to let both the music and the sea breeze waft over her, and when she opened them again she saw that her mother had fallen asleep.

'That's right, Mam, you have a good rest,' Becky said softly.

The band was now playing a piece by Bach which, Becky remembered, had always been one of her father's favourites. With only half her mind on the tune, Becky looked lazily around her at the bustling seaside scene.

An old woman with a wicker basket was selling flowers, another offered cockles and mussels. A photographer had set up his camera near the railings and was doing his best to persuade passers-by to have their pictures taken. Holiday-makers ambled between the flower beds, stopping occasionally to point with their canes at a particular bloom which had caught their fancy.

It was a shock to see the young man in the check jacket who was standing at the edge of the park with a leather satchel in his hand.

'It can't be!' Becky said, almost under her breath.

But it was! The passing of time had matured him, and he was more smartly turned out than Becky had ever seen him before – yet even so, there was no mistaking him.

Becky glanced nervously from one of her parents to the other. Her mother was still asleep and her father appeared completely absorbed in his music – but there was no telling how long either of them would stay like that.

Mary *might* wake up at any minute!

Ted *could* easily gaze around him – as she had done – once his trumpet solo was over!

The young man in the check jacket took an envelope from his satchel and gave it to a man in a top hat. The customer – for that was undoubtedly what he was – opened the envelope, rapidly examined the contents and then slipped the package furtively into the pocket of his frock-coat. Money changed hands and the top-hatted man walked away as if he couldn't put a distance between the two of them quickly enough.

Becky glanced anxiously back at her father. He was still concentrating on his music, but the piece was coming to an end. Any second now he would lower his trumpet and look around the park.

And then what would happen? Would he stay in his seat, too stunned to move? Or would he jump up and stride furiously across the park, unbuckling his belt as he went? Becky wasn't sure which of the two was worse.

She stood up and made her way hurriedly towards the young man. As chance would have it, he chose that moment to move on, and with a few long strides had left the park was heading along the prom. Becky gathered up her skirt and began to run, but her quarry was setting a brisk pace and it was not until he reached the bowling green that Becky drew level and was able to tap him on the shoulder.

He swung round guiltily, but the fear which filled his face at first was soon replaced by surprise – and then delight.

'Becky!' he said throwing his arms around her. 'What are you doing here?'

'What are *you* doing here?' Becky asked her youngest brother. 'Are you and Mr Armitage putting on a magic lantern show?'

'Oh, I don't work for Old Armi any more,' Philip said airily. 'I've got my own business now. A photographic studio – in London!'

'Then what *are* you doing in Blackpool?' Becky asked.

'Selling my work,' her brother told her. 'Views of the Strand and the Houses of Parliament. Folk are always a lot freer with their money when they're on holiday.'

'Mam and Dad are here,' Becky said. 'Will you come and see them?'

Philip looked uncomfortable. 'Better not,' he said. 'I'm not sure Dad has forgiven me for running away like that.'

Or for sneaking on Cedric Rathbone and his gang, Becky thought.

But she didn't say that. Philip had always been easily discouraged in the face of difficulties, and there was no point in letting him know just *how* difficult this particular situation was.

'Whatever you've done, Dad loves you and misses you,' she told her brother. 'He might take a bit of getting round, but won't it be worth it in the long run?'

'But I defied him, you see,' Philip said dubiously, 'and he's not a man to let that just slip by.'

'Jack defied him, too,' Becky pointed out. 'But he forgave Jack in the end, didn't he?'

'Jack was different,' Philip countered. 'First he was a sheep farmer and now he's a silver miner. Them's the kind of jobs me Dad can understand, but what I do . . .'

'You're a photographer with your own studio,' Becky said. 'In Dad's eyes, that'll be almost as good as being a doctor.'

'I'm not sure . . .' Philip began.

A man wearing a shabby double-breasted jacket sidled up to them.

'Are you the one that's selling the pictures?' he asked, with a mixture of nervousness and anticipation.

'Not now,' Philip hissed.

The man looked Becky lecherously up and down.

'Is she in them?' he asked hopefully.

'Bugger off, or I'll give you the thrashing of your life,' Philip told him.

'No need to be like that,' the would-be customer said.

'And when I say bugger off, I mean *now*,' Philip insisted.

The man hesitated for a second, then brushed an imaginary speck of dust from his shiny jacket and walked away with as much dignity as he could muster.

'Let me go and talk to Dad,' Becky said. 'Then, later on, we can all meet up and . . .'

But her brother was no longer listening to her. His face froze into an expression of horror and he was gazing into the middle distance.

Becky turned to look at what had upset him so, and saw two policemen walking towards them.

'Have you being doing something wrong?' she demanded.

'Of . . . of course not,' Philip stuttered. 'Look, Becky, I've got to go. I'm meeting some people.'

Becky grabbed hold of the leather satchel.

'Are you in trouble?' she asked. 'Because if you are, you'd better tell me now.'

'I'm in no trouble,' Philip said desperately, tugging at the satchel. 'It's just that I've made arrangements, see?'

As the policeman got closer, so Philip's agitation seemed to grow.

'Tell me about it, Philip!' Becky pleaded, struggling to retain a grip on the leather satchel.

'Nothing to tell,' Philip grunted.

With a final heave he managed to pull the satchel free.

'I'll always help you,' Becky said. 'You know that.'

Tucking the satchel under his arm, Philip turned and began to walk rapidly towards the pier.

'I'll write,' he called over his shoulder. 'This time, I promise I really will write.'

The policemen began to quicken their pace and when Philip broke into a run, they did too. The last Becky saw of them, they had just dodged in front of a tram and were disappearing down a narrow alley on the other side of the road.

'What have you done *now*, Philip?' Becky asked aloud.

And then she saw an envelope on the ground – an envelope like the ones in Philip's satchel.

It must have fallen out during the struggle, Becky thought.

She bent down, picked it up and opened it. Inside were a number of photographs. The one on top was, as Philip had claimed, a view of the Strand in London. It was a very good picture, so clear that she could read the advertisements for Fry's Cocoa and Coleman's Mustard on the horse-drawn omnibuses.

The photos underneath showed very different London sights. The first had been taken in a studio – perhaps Philip's studio. The background of a tree-lined avenue was obviously nothing but a painted screen, but the donkey and trap in the foreground were real enough.

And so were the young women!

There were three of them, one in the seat of the trap, a second leaning against the wheel and a third sitting on the donkey.

They were all completely naked!

Becky flicked quickly through the other pictures. One showed a girl who could not have been much older than she was herself, posed nude against a Grecian urn. Another was of a girl *considerably* younger than Becky who, though fully clothed, had her dress pulled down to reveal her bare shoulders.

Becky looked down at the beach. The women who swam in the sea wore costumes which covered them from head to foot, yet even so, modesty stopped them from emerging from their bathing huts until the huts had been winched well into the water.

What kind of girl was it, then, who would stand totally naked before the photographer, knowing that the pictures he took would eventually end up in the hot, sweaty hands of so many men?

And what kind of man would take the photographs and sell them to these eager, lecherous customers? Men like Philip, of course! Men like her poor, weak brother, who at that very moment was being chased by the police.

'Oh Philip!' Becky said, not for the first time. 'Oh Philip, whatever will become of you?'

PART FIVE
1887–9

CHAPTER SIXTEEN

It felt to Becky as if the years were flying by, slipping from between her fingers before she even had time to hold them up and examine them. It only seemed like days, for example, since Jack had woken her to say he was running away to sea. Yet she'd been little more than a baby then, and when Jack sent his first letter from West Africa, in the summer of 1887, she'd turned sixteen and could almost be called a woman.

'*This part of the world is known as the White Man's Grave,*' Jack wrote, '*and not without good reason. Mam, it would break your heart to see the graves of so many brave young Englishmen, who have perished in skirmishes with the natives or (more often) because of some barbarous tropical disease.*'

'I can't understand what possessed him to go there in the first place,' Mary said.

'I'm coming to that bit,' her husband told her.

'*It is an area rich in palm oil,*' Jack continued, '*and the demand for that product goes up year by year as more and more subjects of the Empire realize that soap is not a luxury, but a necessity.*'

Taylor laid the letter down.

'Our Jack's started talking very fancy since he's been abroad, hasn't he?' he said.

'That probably comes of rubbing shoulders with gentlemen,' Mary replied impatiently. 'What else does he have to say?'

'*Most of the trade is controlled by the Royal Niger Company,*' Taylor read, '*but the officials of that company are so afraid of catching the fever which is rife in the mangrove swamps that they refuse to go further than the settlements they have established at the mouths of the Oil Rivers. Thus, they are forced to buy through nigger middlemen, who they must pay a generous commis-*

sion. I, on the other hand, will buy my oil directly from the natives – and at a much cheaper price.'

'I don't like the sound of them swamps,' Mary said.

'Go on, Dad,' Becky urged.

'I've leased a steamer,' Jack went on, 'and have already sailed deep into the interior. What I've seen there would amaze you, Dad – even now, after you've been to Manchester! The Yoruba tribe near the coast have a remarkable civilization, but further up the river it's a very different story. Some of the natives are cannibals and their chiefs are said to drink nothing but human blood. Others have never seen a white man before, and fall at our feet, thinking we're gods (or perhaps devils).'

'The more you read, the less I like it,' Mary said.

'It's probably all right once you get used to it,' Ted told her. 'Shall I read you the rest?'

'I suppose you'd better,' Mary replied.

'I've hired a number of native workers to man the steamer and load the oil. I have also taken on three white men who are in charge of the cannon and will supervise the natives when I am occupied elsewhere. They're all sound men – at least, as sound as can be found out here – but I don't think I would turn my back on any one of them, even for a second.

'Soon, when my first cargo is on its way to Liverpool, I hope to be able to come and see you. Until then you are all in my prayers and in my thoughts.

'God bless you, Jack.'

Taylor laid the letter aside.

'Who would have thought, when he started out as lad on the packets, that he'd end up as captain of his own steamer by the time he was twenty-five?' he asked.

'Who would have thought, when he started out as a lad on the packets, that he'd end up working amongst godless heathens who eat each other?' Mary replied, trying to make light of her worries.

Ted laughed. 'Our Jack can handle himself, all right,' he said. 'Look how he's managed so far. And I'll tell you something else for nothing – before he's finished, he'll end up buying you that boarding house by the seaside you've got your eyes on.'

Another year passed by – another fleeting twelve months gone almost before it had arrived. Jack still could find no time to come home, not even for a brief stay, but George had written to say that now he was a noncommissioned officer.

'And what exactly does that mean?' Mary Taylor asked.

'Well ... er ... it means an officer who's not commissioned,' her husband explained.

'I'll tell you what it means,' Old Gilbert Bowyer said to Becky when she asked him the next day. 'It means he's a sergeant or – what's more likely – a corporal.'

'Is that good?' Becky wondered.

'It's the NCOs who run things,' Gilbert said. 'Oh, the officers are good at strutting around, and some of them are very brave when it comes to engaging the enemy, but without your NCOs there wouldn't be any army. And I should know – I was a sergeant myself.'

'You don't talk much about your time in the army, do you?' Becky asked.

Old Gilbert looked at her sharply.

'No, I don't, do I?' he said. 'Now tell me how things are going on in the dressmaking trade.'

Towards the end of the year the papers were filled with accounts of a series of grisly murders in London. The killer, who called himself Jack the Ripper, usually confined his attacks to prostitutes, and often partially disembowelled them.

'And you say West Africa's an uncivilized place,' Taylor told his wife.

As the attacks continued, so public interest grew. The Ripper and his atrocities became the main – often the sole – topic of conversation in the New Inn.

'Well if you ask me,' said Not-Stopping Bracegirdle – although no one had – 'If you ask me, they're getting no more than they deserve. Women like that! I blush even to think about them.'

'Maybe they're driven to it by desperation, Mrs Bracegirdle,' Ted Taylor said quietly. 'A few years back, after my accident, I know I'd have done anything I could to keep me and mine out of the workhouse.'

'Driven to it by desperation!' Not-Stopping snorted. 'What do you think, Mr O'Leary?'

'Well now,' Paddy said, scratching his head, 'it's my job to serve customers, not to get into arguments with them, isn't it? But if you pressed me, I'd have to say that I think Ted's right.'

'Typical men,' Not-Stopping, complained once she was safely back with her cronies. 'They'll stick up for each other no matter what.'

The spate of murders continued. The Ripper took to tormenting the authorities, but still the police had no clues.

'If that Inspector Barker has anything to do with it, then I'm not surprised they're getting nowhere,' Ted Taylor told his family over supper. 'They want to call in Dr Doyle – that's what they want to do. He'd soon get to the bottom of it.'

For no apparent reason the string of murders came to an abrupt end early in 1889. The sensational papers continued to speculate on the identity of the killer for a while, then public interest faded and the story was dropped. Yet the whole affair left an uneasy taste in the mouths of the inhabitants of Marston. London was a long way away, and the fact that the Ripper had never been caught was no real cause for concern in the north, but all the publicity had served to remind them that there had been a murderer in their own village – and he hadn't been caught, either.

It was shortly after Becky's eighteenth birthday that Mrs Stanway called her into the cramped office at the back of the emporium.

'I've got a special commission – a real lady,' she confided, 'and I want you to handle it.'

'But I'm not out of my time yet, Mrs Stanway,' Becky protested.

'Out of your time or not, you're the best worker I've got,' Mrs Stanway told her, 'and I'm putting you in sole charge.'

Becky had to stop herself from curtseying.

'Thank you, Mrs Stanway,' she said. 'And when will the lady be coming in for a fitting?'

The older woman laughed.

'When you're dealing with the gentry, they don't come to you,' she said. 'You go to them.'

'Of course,' Becky replied, feeling a mixture of confusion and embarrassment. 'And where does the lady live?'

'She *lives* somewhere in Hertfordshire, I believe,' Mrs Stanway said, 'but she's *staying* at Peak House.'

'Peak House!' Becky gasped. 'But ... but that's where the Worrells live!'

'That's right, she's some sort of cousin of theirs,' Mrs Stanway replied. 'But why are you taking on so, girl?' she laughed. 'Anyone seeing you now would think you knew the family well.'

'I do,' Becky said.

'What? You know one of the richest families in Northwich *well*?' Mrs Stanway said.

'Only by sight,' Becky confessed, growing more and more confused.

- The *sight* of Richard Worrell – with his broad shoulders and handsome face – driving his carriage into the works!
- The *sight* of Michael Worrell – who always looked so kind and understanding – riding up the lane!

'And I expect that is the way you will *continue* to know them,' Mrs Stanway asked, perhaps just a little severely. 'Don't you?'

'Y ... yes,' Becky stuttered.

Mrs Stanway was quite right, she told herself. When she'd visited Jessie and Eunice, had she ever seen any of The Family? Of course not. And it would be just the same at Peak House. She'd be admitted by the tradesmen's entrance and shown up the servants' stairs to the room in which the lady was waiting for her. She'd measure the lady up, and leave the same way.

Richard and Michael Worrell wouldn't even be aware she'd set foot inside their home!

'We'd better fix up a time when the lady can see me,' Becky said in a businesslike voice.

'I've already sent the boy round to ask when it will be convenient,' Mrs Stanway told her.

Becky took a deep breath. Everything she'd told herself had been quite true, she thought. She'd see less of Richard and Michael in their own house than she saw of them in the lane. Why then, she wondered, were her hands shaking so violently? Why then did the office, which had seemed quite cool before Mrs Stanway's announcement, now feel so unbearably hot?

The Honourable Hortense Sudley stood in front of the full-length mirror and examined herself critically. Her hips were not too wide, she decided. Her stomach had only a slight curve, she noticed as she turned to the side. And best of all, her breasts were as firm and pointed as they'd ever been – almost.

It was only her face, she was forced to admit, which was somewhat disappointing. She was not pretty, whatever angle she looked at herself from. If only her teeth had projected a little less, or her nose been not quite so blunt, she might have made a claim to being – at least – attractive, but as it was ...

Hortense was a very distant cousin of the Worrells on their late mother's side, but it had been a family link which, until recently, she'd been very reluctant to admit. Her twenty-seventh birthday had changed all that. Surrounded by all her old friends as she had been, she'd suddenly realized that she was the only one still unmarried and, reeling from the shock, had had to excuse herself for a full half hour.

That night, alone in her room, she composed a list of eligible men, and then ruthlessly crossed out those it would be unrealistic to aim for. Out went those too rich or noble to consider her. Out went those who were as poor as she, and who were looking to marriage as a way of reviving the family fortunes. Out, too, went the ones who had made it clear in the past that they would as soon not marry at all as tie the marriage knot with her.

It had been a long list when she started, but there were depressingly few names left when she had finished – and Richard Worrell was the best of a bad bunch.

At least she stood a good chance of being successful this time, she thought. She was older than Richard, but coming from a class in which dynasty and estate were the prime considerations, age differences were no great obstacle. Besides, old Mr Worrell, feeling the shadow of death hovering over him, was eager to see at least one of his sons marry someone with aristocratic connections, and for them as much as for her there was a very limited field to choose from.

It was Worrell himself who had suggested that she could use some new dresses.

'And don't worry about how much they cost, love,' he'd told her. 'I'll foot the bill.'

What a common, tradesman's way he had of talking, she thought. Foot the bill, indeed. Still, it was just as well that he'd made the offer, because there was no way Pater could have 'footed the bill' – not that year, anyway.

There was a soft knock on the door and her maid entered.

'Please, Miss, the dressmaker's here,' she said.

'Good,' Hortense replied, more than eager to spend some of Len Worrell's money. 'Tell her to come in.'

The dressmaker was not what she'd expected at all. For a start, she seemed very young. And from her awkward curtsey, it was obvious that she was not used to dealing with real ladies.

'What's your name, girl?' Hortense asked.

'Beck ... Rebecca, Miss,' the little dressmaker said.

Hortense made an impatient gesture with her hand.

'Not your Christian name,' she said. 'Your other name!'

'Taylor, Miss,' Becky said, blushing.

'Well, Taylor, I'm not sure you're what I'm looking for,'

Hortense told her. 'You don't look to me as if you have enough experience for the kind of work I had in mind.'

'Mrs Stanway says I'm her best worker, Miss,' Becky replied. She advanced uncertainly into the room. 'I've ... I've brought you some sketches of the latest styles. Would you like to see them?'

'I suppose there's no harm in looking now they're here,' Hortense conceded. 'Put them down on the table, Taylor.'

Becky laid out the pictures and her customer flicked through them.

'This looks pretty,' Hortense said, fixing on a dress with a draped bodice and knife-pleated skirt.

'The cut would suit you very well, Miss,' Becky said.

'Yes, it would,' Hortense agreed. 'But you really think *you* could make it for me?'

'Oh yes, Miss,' Becky said with conviction.

'Including all the embroidery on the bodice and skirt.'

'Well, it would take some time, Miss, but ...'

'I need it by Thursday,' Hortense said.

'That might be a bit difficult, Miss,' Becky replied. 'You see, all that embroidery has to be done ...'

'I am attending a ball on Thursday,' Hortense said. 'I simply *must* have it for then. Do you understand?'

'Yes, Miss,' Becky said.

'Very well,' Hortense continued. 'Now show me the rest of the drawings.'

The lady had chosen three more dresses, and seemed to need all of them almost as urgently as she needed the one for the ball.

Mrs Stanway will be very pleased with the order, Becky thought as the under-footman showed her to the servants' entrance.

But what a lot of work it would involve! How many night-time hours — working under a dull oil lamp at home — it would take to finish them on time.

Ladies like Miss Sudley never intended to make life difficult for ordinary folk, Becky told herself. It was just that, having been brought up to a life of luxury, they had no idea of the amount of effort which went into producing the things they so easily took for granted.

Deep in her own thoughts, she barely registered the sound of hoofs on the driveway, and was not really aware of either the horse or its rider until they came to a halt directly in front of her.

She looked up slowly, her eyes fixing first on the shining leather boot, moving from that to the muscled calf, the narrow waist, the broad chest and – finally – the handsome face.

Her heart was galloping, her breath coming short and fast. The confusion and embarrassment she'd experienced earlier in the day had been nothing to what she was suffering now. She had no idea of how to act or what to say – didn't even know, in fact, if she was required to say *anything* at all!

Should she greet Richard Worrell? Or should she say nothing and simply side-step his horse?

Help me! she appealed silently to the man on the horse. Tell me what I'm expected to do!

'It's Miss Rebecca Taylor, isn't it?' the horseman asked.

'Yes, Sir,' Becky mumbled.

She curtseyed – and the sketches under her arm spilled onto the driveway. As she bent down to gather them together again, she felt a hot breath on her cheek. Though she didn't dare look up, she knew that Richard Worrell had dismounted, and was crouching next to her.

'Do you remember the night at the circus, Becky?' he asked, handing her one of the sketches.

'Yes, sir,' Becky replied.

She remembered further back than even that – remembered the day she'd first seen him standing outside the salt store, laughing.

'How long ago was it – that night at the circus?' Richard Worrell asked.

'Seven years, Sir.'

They stood up so they were facing one another. The crown

of Becky's head did not even reach his chin, and because she felt silly staring at his chest, she looked up and gazed into his eyes.

'Seven years,' Worrell reflected. 'A long time to wait — but well worth it.'

'I don't understand, Sir,' Becky said.

Worrell climbed back onto his mount.

'Do you know your way around horses, Miss Taylor?' he asked.

Becky laughed.

'I knew an old cart-horse called Hereward,' she said. 'I helped save him from being sucked into a hole in the canal bank once.'

'I mean, do you ride?' Richard Worrell asked.

Ride? A working-class girl like her? Becky laughed again.

'What with making dresses and working in the chip shop, I never seemed to have the time,' she said.

'I'll teach you,' Richard Worrell told her.

'Don't talk daft,' Becky said. 'Oh, I'm ever so sorry, Sir. I didn't mean it to come out like that.'

'But I *did* mean it when I said I'd teach you to ride,' Richard Worrell insisted. 'Put down your drawings and hold out your arms.'

Almost in a dream Becky searched around for a small stone, placed it on top of the sketches and held out her arms as she'd been instructed. Worrell leant down and swept her into the air as if she weighed nothing, then planted her firmly on the horse in front of him.

They seemed to be so high off the ground. Becky clutched at the animal's mane for support.

'Take the reins,' Richard Worrell said.

'I can't . . . I . . .'

Worrell put his arms around her waist.

'Don't worry,' he said reassuringly. 'I won't let you fall.'

Becky gingerly took hold of the reins.

'Is this right?' she asked.

'Perfect,' Richard Worrell replied. 'Walk on, Caesar.'

The horse began to clip-clop its way forward. It was a strange sensation at first, being bounced up and down, but after a while Becky grew to enjoy it. And she liked the feel of Worrell's strong arms around her waist. Liked the touch of his thigh. Liked the way he smelled.

They trotted around the grounds of Peak House for a full half hour. Becky, wrapped up in the experience of her first horse ride and the close presence of Richard Worrell, noticed nobody else — but there were others who noticed her.

From his sickroom window Len Worrell watched the scene playing itself out below. A few years earlier he would have done more than watch — a few years earlier he would have stormed into the grounds and pulled that young fool Richard off his horse — but now his illness was so advanced that it was as much as he could do to sit on his commode without help.

'But I'm still a power to be reckoned with,' he said through teeth gritted against the pain and anger which filled his whole body.

His entire life had been devoted to one objective — seeing his family get on. He had done his bit by amassing a modest fortune and marrying well enough to be at least on the fringes of the aristocracy. Now it was up to his eldest son to build on the foundations he had laid.

What advantages the boy had had! *His* mother had been one of the Hertfordshire Sudleys, not a common washerwoman. When he opened *his* mouth to speak it was plain to everyone that he'd had an expensive education — unlike his father, who had started work at the age of twelve.

If he plays his cards right, it shouldn't be too hard for him to end up as *Sir* Richard, Len Worrell thought.

And Richard's son could do even better for himself. Though Worrell knew he would never last long enough to see it for himself, he could die happy if he thought there was at least some possibility that his grandson might one day be elevated to the peerage.

Yet none of that would happen — none of it — if Richard

refused to take the first step on the ladder, and the Sudley girl *was* the first step. He should be with her now, courting her, coaxing her towards matrimony. And what was he doing instead? Flirting with a little dressmaker – right under Hortense's nose.

His son and the girl rode past his window once more.

'I won't have it!' Len Worrell said, so loudly that his cry rapidly turned into a fit of coughing.

He *wouldn't* have it, he repeated silently as he struggled across to his bed and lay down. He was still the master of Worrell's. He still owned more than half the shares. He loved his elder son in a way he could never bring himself to feel for his younger one, but if Richard wouldn't do as he was told, he would leave all the shares to Michael.

'And you wouldn't like that, Richard, would you?' he rasped into his pillow. 'You wouldn't like that at all.'

Hortense Sudley's anger almost matched that of Len Worrell.

How dare Richard flaunt the girl like that? she asked herself. And how dare Taylor allow herself to be flaunted so?

She pulled on the bell-rope so hard that it almost came away in her hand.

The maid, when she arrived, looked a little flushed.

Because she's been having a good laugh? Hortense wondered.

Because she and the other servants, knowing full well why the lady from Hertfordshire was visiting Peak House, had found what was going on outside indescribably funny?

Hortense felt a wave of humiliation sweep over her, leaving behind it an even more intense rage than she had felt previously.

'You took your time getting here!' she screamed at the maid.

'I came as quick as I could, Miss,' the girl protested.

'Quickly,' Hortense said witheringly. 'The correct word is "quickly". And you didn't come anything like quickly enough. Perhaps I should suggest to your master that he employ servants who are a little more responsive to the needs of his house guests.'

'Sorry, Miss,' the maid mumbled.

'Oh, fetch me a pot of tea,' Hortense said exasperatedly. 'And try to bring it before it's completely cold.'

The maid left and Hortense went to the window again. Richard and the girl were still out there – she holding the reins, he holding *her*. And now their lesson – if that's what you wanted to call it – had progressed far enough for the horse to be cantering.

The girl looked so happy – God rot her.

'But she won't stay happy,' Hortense promised. 'Not if I have anything to do with it.'

She prayed that Taylor would fail to deliver the dresses on time.

And even if they are on time, Hortense thought, I'll find something wrong with them. Or *make* something wrong with them.

That little slut of a dressmaker would not go unpunished. She'd lose her job for certain, but if Hortense had her way that would be the least of the girl's troubles.

Michael Worrell had a strangely sinking feeling as he watched his brother and the girl trot around the grounds. He remembered the first time he'd seen Becky Taylor. She'd been nothing but a small child, yet even then she had seemed special – and even then it had been Richard who'd talked to her while his younger brother sweated and strained with the handcart.

The sound of Becky's laughter drifted in through the open window.

Escape! Michael urged her silently. Escape before you have time to find out what he's really like!

But what *was* Richard really like? he wondered. He had seen so many changes in his brother. The first Richard had been the hectoring, tormenting older brother of their childhood, the second a Richard who had said he wanted to bury their differences and make a new start. There had been the third

Richard, no longer strong and confident, but a quivering wreck who had begged his brother to save him from the rope.

And then a fourth, Michael said to himself.

The fourth Richard, the one who had been released from gaol, was closer to the child he had once been than the man Michael had come to know.

'You should have got it in writing, little brother,' he'd told Michael, a few days after the police had let him go.

'Got what in writing?' Michael asked.

'My promise to give you my shares in the works if you got me off the murder charge.'

'Do you think that's why I did it — so I could get my hands on the business?'

'Why else?'

'You're my brother.'

'And you,' Richard said with a sneer playing on his lips, 'are a bloody fool!'

Since then they'd hardly spoken, except to exchange necessary information on the running of Worrell's.

He's right, Michael thought. I *am* a bloody fool. Only a bloody fool would have trusted him in the first place. Only a bloody fool would have tried being honest and decent with him.

And yet there were worse things than being a fool, and he thanked God that he was himself, and not Richard.

Richard wasn't worthy of Becky Taylor. Richard wasn't worthy of any woman with even a speck of goodness in her.

'And he won't have her!' Michael said angrily.

'I've got to go,' Becky said, trying — and failing miserably — to keep the disappointment out of her voice.

'Got to go?' Richard Worrell repeated. 'Surely not yet?'

'They'll be missing me back at the shop.'

'Let them go hang themselves,' Richard replied irritably.

'That's easy for you to say, Sir,' Becky told him. 'You're your own boss — I'm not.'

Richard laughed. 'I suppose you're right,' he agreed.

He took the reins from her and wheeled the horse round. At the drive gate. he stopped, dismounted with elegant ease and held out his hands to help her down.

'Or I could take you all the way back to the shop, if you'd prefer it,' he said.

'I'd rather walk, if it's all the same to you, sir,' Becky replied, a little stiffly.

Richard grinned. 'Ashamed to be seen with me?' he asked.

'Of course not,' Becky protested.

It was not exactly shame she felt – more an uncertainty about whether what she'd been doing had been right or wrong.

Being so close to a man she hardly knew – touching his body at several points with hers – was probably perfectly acceptable and normal behaviour among what some people in Marston called their 'betters'. Certainly Richard Worrell acted as if it were. But it wouldn't be looked at that way by most of the people she knew, and she didn't want word getting back to her dad about how friendly she'd been with Richard.

Not yet, anyway!

Worrell helped her down from the horse and she savoured, for the last time, the feel of his firm, strong hands.

'Would you like to come riding with me again?' he asked.

Becky wanted to scream that of course she'd go riding with him – she'd go *anywhere* with him! Yet she held back. He was a gentleman and she was an apprentice dressmaker who had stopped believing in Cinderella long ago.

'Would you like to come riding with me again?' Richard Worrell repeated, more forcefully this time.

'I'm not sure, Sir,' Becky confessed.

'For God's sake, stop calling me Sir,' he told her. 'My name's Richard, as well you know. Promise me you'll come riding with me, Becky Taylor. You can borrow one of the horses from the stable – I'll choose a gentle one – and you'll pick it up in no time.'

'I don't know, Sir ... Richard,' Becky said. 'I'll ... I'll have to think about it.'

She turned away from him, gathered up her sketches and began to walk back towards the town. It could have been said, with some justification, that she was hurrying because she was late – but to anyone who did not know her circumstances she would have looked very much like a woman in flight.

Late that night Becky emerged from the emporium carrying a parcel under her arm. Her eyes ached, but she knew she would have to put in at least a couple of hours more on Miss Sudley's dress when she got home.

Looking up the street she saw a man standing under a gas light, as if he were waiting for someone. Even from a distance there seemed to be something vaguely familiar – and vaguely disturbing – about him.

For a moment Becky considered turning round and walking in the other direction. But she was very tired, and this *was* the quickest way home. Keeping her eyes firmly on the ground, she began to walk towards the lamp post.

The man remained silent until she drew level with him. Then he said, 'Good evening, Miss Taylor,' and Becky realized why he had looked familiar.

'Good evening, Mr Worrell,' she said.

It was only polite to stop, though Becky had no idea what she would do next.

'Are you waiting for somebody?' she asked.

'For you,' he replied.

'For me? Why would you do that?'

'To warn you about my brother,' he said.

'And why should you want to warn me about Richard?' Becky wondered.

Michael laughed bitterly. 'I see you're already calling him by his given name.'

'He asked me to,' Becky said defiantly.

'Half an hour with him, and you're already under his spell,' Michael told her. 'Be careful, Miss Taylor. He'll only use you – like he's used everyone else. And when he's finished with you, he'll discard you like a worn-out shoe.'

'What are you suggesting?' Becky demanded angrily. 'What kind of girl do you think I am?'

'A young one,' Michael replied. 'An innocent one. Just the kind who attract my brother.'

'Thank you for your warning, Sir,' Becky said with icy dignity, 'but even if what you've said were true, since I hardly know *Mr* Richard it was scarcely necessary.'

'Don't be a fool, Becky!' Michael said, his own anger growing by the second. 'Do you think you'd be the first virgin he's ever coaxed into his bed?'

'You go too far, Sir,' Becky told him.

Michael grabbed her by the shoulders and began to shake her.

'It's just a game to Richard,' he shouted. 'A challenge. Can't you see that? Don't you understand?'

'Let go of me!' Becky screamed.

The shaking stopped as suddenly as it had begun. Michael looked down at his arms as if they had somehow betrayed him, then let them fall.

'I'm sorry,' he said.

'I thought you were a gentleman!' Becky raged at him. 'Is *this* how gentlemen behave?'

'It's because I care,' Michael said. 'It's because I don't want to see you hurt.'

'I'm hurt now,' Becky said. 'And I shall be bruised in the morning.'

'Richard could harm you far more than that,' Michael said. 'Yes, and get pleasure from doing it.'

'You're a swine, and I hate you,' Becky said. 'Now will you get out of my sight – or do I have to call a bobby?'

'I'll go,' Michael said. 'I'm sorry I failed you, Becky.'

She watched him as he turned and walked back up the street. How could she ever have been attracted to that man? she wondered. Whatever could have convinced her that he was kind and understanding? Now, for the first time, she saw him for what he really was – a man burning with envy towards his handsomer brother, a man who would sneak behind his brother's back and plunge in the dagger.

CHAPTER SEVENTEEN

The jet-black horse was galloping at such a speed that its legs were almost a blur, yet still she could hear the pounding of another set of hoofs just behind her.

'Use your spurs!' Richard Worrell shouted. 'Dig them in hard! Make the brute give you every last inch.'

But Becky didn't use her spurs. Instead, she reined Midnight in, and allowed Richard to draw level with her.

'How long have I been teaching you to ride?' he asked.

'About two months,' Becky replied, noticing, as she did so, the look of annoyance on his handsome face.

'You're a natural horsewoman,' Richard said. 'I've rarely seen better. But you'll never get the best out of your animal until you learn to be firm. Horses are like men — you have to show them who's boss.'

'Do you hear that, Midnight?' Becky said to the horse. 'Mr Richard's very cross with you.'

'Mr Richard's not cross with the horse,' Worrell corrected her, 'but he is a *little* cross with you. Why didn't you use your spurs? You could have made the brute go faster, you know.'

'Yes,' Becky agreed. 'But only by hurting him.'

Richard laughed. 'You can be impossible, sometimes,' he said. 'I'll tell you what. Do you see that oak tree, over there in the distance?'

'The one that looks like a teapot.'

'Yes, that one. I'll race you to it.'

It was Becky's turn to laugh.

'What's the point?' she asked. 'You'll only beat me again.'

'I'll give you a bigger start this time,' Richard said. 'But not *much* more of one, mind, so you'd better get going now.'

Becky set off at a canter, but soon eased Midnight into a gallop.

It had been a strange few weeks, Becky thought as she and the horse thundered across the field.

'I want to teach you to ride,' Richard had said.

And that was exactly what he'd done. Every Sunday they met in the countryside, Becky walking to their meeting place, Richard riding one horse and leading another. And then they rode – nothing more and nothing less. Not even the most poisonous of gossips, not even Not-Stopping Bracegirdle herself, could have said – had she known their secret – that Richard had been anything but a perfect gentleman.

And yet ... and yet she did not feel quite at ease with him. His brother's warning, though she'd scorned it at the time, had planted the seed of doubt in her mind which had been growing ever since.

'He'll only use you,' Michael had said, 'like he's used everybody else.'

Then there was the other matter – employing Philip as his spy and sacking Cedric Rathbone and his mates just because they wanted to join a union. Did she really want to associate with a man who could behave as ruthlessly as that?

Besides, what did *he* want out of their friendship? What did he expect in return for these riding lessons?

She knew what they'd say in the village – 'He's after one thing, Becky. Keep your hand on your ha'penny when he's around.'

But if he'd wanted to try and take advantage of her, wouldn't he have done so by now?

'I'm catching you up, Becky,' Richard called from behind her and, turning her head, she could see that he was.

She urged Midnight on to greater effort, and the horse – who had grown to love his new rider over the previous few weeks – quickly responded.

Faster and faster they went – the oak tree looming larger with each second, the sound of the other horse's hoofbeats growing louder with every yard they covered.

Then it happened! Midnight caught a hoof in a rabbit hole and lost his footing! Almost before she knew what was going on, Becky was flying through the air — and then the ground came up to meet her and she hit it with a sickening thud.

The world refused to stay still. Trees, flowers, the sky itself, all whirled round at a furious pace in front of Becky's eyes. There were stars, too, dancing up and down, making her feel sick.

'Are you all right?' Richard Worrell asked in a voice which seemed very far away.

'Midnight!' Becky gasped. 'What about Midnight?'

'He's fine,' Richard assured her. 'He's over there, chomping grass as if nothing had happened.'

Becky turned her head to look at the black horse. He seemed to be bouncing up and down, but then so did the ground, so he was probably all right.

'I shouldn't try to get up for a minute or two,' Richard advised her.

'I ... I don't think I could even if I wanted to,' Becky told him.

The next few minutes seemed to pass so quickly that, looking back later, the whole thing seemed to Becky nothing but a blur. One second Richard was kneeling at her side, the next he was lying beside her with his arm on her shoulder — and then he was kissing her.

It was not a kiss like any she'd seen her parents — or anyone else in the village — exchange. It was a kiss which seemed to engulf her, to take her breath away.

His tongue was in her mouth, exploring, claiming and moving on. The thought was revolting — but the sensation was delicious. Instinctively Becky responded — discovering the soft skin of his cheeks as he had discovered hers, running the tip of her tongue along the edge of his strong, white teeth.

Richard's hands began to wander, first squeezing her waist, then stroking her ribs and finally coming to rest on her bosom. Sometimes she had dreamed guiltily of such a thing happening, but she had never known it would feel like this — so tingling, so exciting.

His hand went under her blouse — bare flesh touching bare

flesh — under her petticoat and onto the breast. Becky shivered with pleasure.

Don't you know what you're doing? a small voice screamed in her mind. Don't you know where all this is leading?

Though she longed for Richard's hand to stay where it was, she forced herself to pull away from him and sit up.

'What's the matter?' he asked testily.

'I'm ... I'm afraid,' Becky explained.

'Afraid? Of what?'

'I've never done anything like this before.'

'And a few weeks ago you'd never ridden a horse either, but that didn't stop you wanting to learn,' Richard said impatiently. 'Now let's forget all this silliness and get back to your first lesson.'

'I can't,' Becky said, starting to cry.

'Why can't you?' Richard demanded angrily. 'You've no right to lead a man on if you don't intend to go all the way.'

'I didn't mean to lead you on,' Becky sobbed.

'Well you did,' Richard said. 'And now I'm very disappointed with you.'

'I'm sorry, Richard,' Becky said, staring at the ground.

'It seems such a small thing to ask of you,' Richard complained.

'It's not a small thing,' Becky protested. 'Do you know what they say in the village about girls who let men do that to them?'

Richard stood up.

'Damn and blast you!' he said.

He strode furiously to his horse and was on the point of mounting it when he suddenly froze. For perhaps ten seconds he did not move. Then he turned round, walked back to where Becky was sitting shrouded in her misery, and knelt down.

'You're not like those girls you were just talking about,' he said softly. 'People only say bad things about them because they're prepared to do it with anybody. But I'm not just anybody. I love you, and I want you with me always.'

'Really?' Becky asked timidly.

'Of course,' Richard assured her. 'I think I've always loved you. That's why I fought my father to make him give your father compensation for his accident. I thought at the time I was doing it for him, but I wasn't – I was doing it for you.'

'You ... you got the money for my dad?' Becky said.

'Didn't you know?' Richard asked. 'Didn't you realize?'

'No,' Becky admitted.

So it was Richard who had saved the family from the workhouse. Richard who had rescued Mam from the nightmare which had haunted her since her childhood.

She wanted to show him both her gratitude and her love, yet when Richard reached out to touch her again, she felt herself tense.

Richard's face blazed with anger – but only for a second, and then he was smiling again.

'It's all been too sudden for you, hasn't it?' he said, standing up.

'I ... it's just that ...' Becky said.

'Don't worry about it,' Richard told her. 'It really doesn't matter.'

He held out his hand to help her to her feet.

'What do we do now?' Becky asked.

'When you've been thrown from a horse, the best thing to do is get back into the saddle as soon as possible,' Richard said.

Under Hortense's strict supervision the maid was preparing for the trip to Hertfordshire.

'Have I to pack this, Miss?' she asked, holding up the dress with the knife-pleated skirt and the embroidery.

'Oh yes,' Hortense replied.

It was a beautiful dress, so beautiful that she'd found herself unable to send it back to the emporium – even if that did mean the Taylor girl escaping her rightful punishment.

'And this, Miss?' the maid asked, holding up a gown with flared petticoats – another of Taylor's creations.

'That too.'

There was a knock on the door, and Richard entered.

'Did you have a good ride, my dear?' Hortense asked.

'Not as good as it might have been,' Richard said, smiling as if at a secret joke, 'but I have high hopes that next week's will be much more enjoyable.'

The maid held up a hat, and Hortense nodded.

'You're packing as if you were going away for ever,' Richard said reproachfully.

'I've been away from home a long time,' Hortense reminded him. 'My parents will expect me to spend at least a *few* weeks in Hertfordshire.'

'But then you'll be coming straight back here, won't you?' Richard asked.

'That will depend on whether or not I'm invited,' Hortense said playfully.

'My dear, you will always be welcome at Peak House, whoever is master of it,' Richard told her.

'You are the soul of generosity,' Hortense said.

'And any house in the country would consider itself graced by your presence,' Richard countered. 'And now, if you will excuse me, I must go and change for dinner.'

Richard withdrew with all the gracefulness of a true gentleman.

A great change had come over him since the day he had humiliated her with the Taylor girl, Hortense thought. Before that incident he had appeared to resent her presence, but now he deliberately sought out her company. It was true that he had not yet proposed marriage, but she had no doubt he would. And this journey to Hertfordshire, which she would once have seen in terms of a rout, was now more in the nature of a final victory parade.

'Are you taking this hat, too, Miss?' the maid asked.

'Yes,' Hortense said absently.

Soon, the servants would be calling her Madam instead of Miss, she thought. Soon she would be mistress of Peak House.

I've got a week, Becky thought after that Sunday meeting with Richard. A whole seven days.

Seven days in which to decide what to do the next time Richard asked her to give herself to him. What a long time that seemed on Sunday evening. Yet before she knew it, Monday had gone, then Tuesday, and she was no closer to making up her mind.

On the one hand, she told herself, she loved Richard and wanted to make love to him just as much as he wanted to make love to her.

On the other hand – and a very big hand it was – what if Michael was right, and once he'd had her, Richard discarded her like an old boot?

'They never respect you once they've had what they want,' people in the village said.

When she had told Jack, so many years earlier, to beware of fallen women, she'd had no idea what fallen women were. But she knew now, right enough. Fallen women tramped the cold, wet streets of Manchester, offering themselves to any man with a shilling in his pocket. Fallen women posed naked for pornographers like Philip. And what caused that fall in the first place, if not giving in to temptation?

She needed to talk to someone about Richard, what she felt for him and what he wanted of her. But *who* could she turn to? Who would offer her the advice she needed?

Not Mam. She knew what Mam would tell her to do – would *order* her to do – without even asking.

Not Colleen – for all that the Irish girl was her best friend, Colleen had even less experience than she did.

It's up to me, she told herself firmly. I'll have to choose, and if I choose wrongly I'll only have myself to blame.

It was Dottie Curzon who brought the news, early Wednesday evening, that Old Gilbert Bowyer was very ill and wanted to see Becky immediately.

'Did Ma Fitton say what it was about?' Becky asked as she hurriedly put on her bonnet.

'Ma's as much in the dark as you are,' Dottie told her, 'but he won't rest until he's talked to you.'

Ma Fitton was waiting at her back door when Becky arrived.

'How is he?' Becky asked.

'He's just a bit off colour,' Ma replied loudly, looking up at Old Gilbert's window. Then, lowering her voice, she added, 'If you ask me, he'll not last out the night.'

Ma showed Becky up to the old man's room. Gilbert was lying in bed. His face was drawn and his eyes had lost all their fire.

'I'm glad you came,' he wheezed. He turned his head weakly towards his landlady, who was hovering in the doorway. 'Thank you, Mrs Fitton,' he said with remarkable firmness. 'That will be all.'

Ma hesitated for a second, then stepped over the threshhold and closed the door behind her.

'How are you feeling, Mr Bowyer?' Becky asked.

'Old,' Bowyer told her. 'Old and tired. Pull up that chair, lass, and sit down beside me.'

Closer to, the old man looked even worse than from a distance. His skin was as dry as parchment and his chest rattled with even the slightest movement.

'When I've gone, I want you to write a letter for me,' he said.

'You mustn't talk like that, Mr Bowyer,' Becky told him.

'There's no point in talking any other way,' the old man replied. 'Now hush, I want to tell you a story.'

'You shouldn't be talking. The best thing for you is to get some rest,' Becky advised him.

'You been a proper little nosy-parker from the day you were born,' the old man said, ignoring her warning, 'and one of the things you've never been able to satisfy your curiosity about is my time in the army. Am I right, or am I wrong?'

'You're right,' Becky admitted, grinning despite herself.

'Well, now I'm going to tell you about it,' Old Gilbert continued. 'I've seen service just about everywhere, but I ended up as a sergeant in India. I loved it there. I even learned the language, and people said I spoke it so well you couldn't tell me from a native. I think it was because I knew the lingo that I ended up being assigned to work under a Political Officer. Samuel Quickly, his name was. I thought he was a decent sort at the time, but I was wrong – terribly wrong.'

Tears began to seep from the old man's eyes.

'If it's upsetting you, it might be better not to talk about it,' Becky said.

'I have to talk about it,' Old Gilbert replied. 'I've kept it secret all these years, but now, in my last moments, I've got to tell somebody.'

'Go on then,' Becky said gently.

'I'd been working for him about three years when he told me he had a special job for me. There'd been rumours of trouble brewing in Amritsar, he said, and he wanted me to go up there, disguised as a native, and see what I could find out. I knew it was a dangerous job, but if it was for my Queen and Country I was willing to take the risk. Anyway, I travelled up to Amritsar and took lodgings in the Indian quarter. I spent days walking round the bazaar and sitting in the tea shops. And do you know what I found out?'

'What?' Becky asked.

'There wasn't any hint of trouble – not a whiff of it. I sent a secret message back to Captain Quickly, telling him where I was and saying that I thought I was wasting my time. The morning after he got the message, I was arrested.'

'But why?' Becky said.

The old man tugged at his nightshirt until a portion of his scrawny chest was visible.

'Look at that,' he said.

On his torso, just below his right arm, were a series of purple dots which picked out a large letter D.

'They had this machine,' Old Gilbert said. 'Spikes one end and a pressure lever at the other. They dipped the spikes in Indian ink, then stamped the D on me. D for deserter.'

'But you hadn't deserted,' Becky said. 'You'd gone to Amritsar because that was what Captain Quickly had told you to do.'

'He denied ever issuing such an order. It turned out there was some money missing from the Political Fund. Quickly said I must have stolen it, and that would explain why I'd run away. I was court-martialled. There wasn't enough evidence to sentence me to the stockade, but the court decided I should be given a dishonourable discharge. Me — who'd risked my life any number of times in the service of the Queen.'

'What about the missing money?' Becky said. 'Captain Quickly was the one who stole it, wasn't he?'

'I could never prove it, but as God's my witness, I'm sure it was him,' Gilbert replied. 'And the Colonel must have suspected the same thing, because after my court martial he called me to his house. He thought I'd been badly done by, he said. He couldn't prevent my discharge — that would be undermining his officers — but he wanted to give me a pension. I've been living off it ever since. The old Colonel must have died years ago, but his relatives have kept on paying me. That's why I want you to write to them — to tell them I won't be needing the money any more.'

'Rest, now,' Becky said soothingly.

'I saw Captain Samuel Quickly once more after I'd left India,' Bowyer pressed on. 'He was a rich man by that time, and he'd changed his name, but I recognized him the moment I saw him striding out of Worrell's salt works, and I knew then I had to revenge myself for the disgrace he'd brought down on me.'

'*You* killed Septimus Quinn!' Becky said.

'I killed him,' Gilbert agreed. 'I cut across country and confronted him on the canal bank. He could see the hammer in my hand, but he just laughed at me. He thought I was too burned out to be a threat to him. Well, he was wrong, wasn't he?'

'Weren't you afraid you'd get caught?' Becky asked.

'I didn't care,' the old man told her. 'If I'd swung for murder, I'd have had no complaint. I was about to give myself up just after they'd arrested young Worrell, then that doctor came and told me it wouldn't be necessary.'

'Dr Doyle, you mean?'

Old Gilbert chuckled drily.

'That's the man,' he said. 'He had the whole story, right back to my days in India. He said he couldn't condone what I'd done, but he certainly wasn't going to turn me in.'

'Yes, that sounds like him,' Becky agreed.

'So I escaped the rope,' Gilbert told her, 'and any punishment I get now will be doled out by a much higher authority than the Lord Chief Justice.' He closed his eyes. 'We've had some good times together, haven't we, Becky?' he asked. 'Remember that day we went to Northwich to see the building being moved, and how we ate cream cakes on the way back?'

'Yes, I remember,' Becky said, fighting back the tears.

'I think I'd like to sleep now,' the old man said. 'You shan't see me alive again, Becky, so I want to thank you now for being my friend these last few years.'

'Don't talk daft,' Becky said awkwardly. 'The pleasure's been all mine.'

'I wish I'd met you – or somebody like you – when I was a young man,' Gilbert said. 'If I'd known you then, everything might have turned out different.'

He coughed and Becky saw a fleck of blood appear on his nightshirt.

'Mr Bowyer . . .' she said.

'Enough talking,' Old Gilbert told her. 'Bugger off now – before I start yowling like a baby.'

Ma Fitton – 'Midwife to Royalty' – proved to be as skilful in her diagnosis of old age as she'd been in her handling of deliveries. When she took his breakfast tray up to him the next morning, Old Gilbert was lying still, his eyes closed and a look of perfect peace and contentment on his old face.

It was a warm day, but Len Worrell, sitting on a chair in the conservatory, was shrouded in scarves and rugs. Before him stood his eldest son.

Like a guilty schoolboy summoned by the headmaster, Richard thought, not without amusement.

'Not more than a few months ago, I caught you parading that chit of a Taylor girl around the grounds on your horse,' Len Worrell said. 'And what did I tell you after she'd gone?'

'You do realize I'm several years past my majority, do you not, Father?' Richard replied indifferently.

'What did I tell you?' Len Worrell repeated.

Richard shrugged. 'You mumbled something about me never seeing her again,' he said.

'And now what do I find out?' his father demanded. 'Every Sunday since then, you've been riding out to the woods to meet her in secret! Explain yourself, Richard!'

'It had to be Sundays,' Richard said. 'Like most members of her class, she works nearly all day Saturday.'

'Listen to me . . .' Len Worrell began.

'No!' Richard said, leaning over his chair. 'You listen to me for once, *old man*. I've been to bed with so many women, I've lost count. I had my first when I was thirteen – she was the sister of a school friend who'd invited me home for the half-term holiday. Since then there must have been hundreds – more of my friends' sisters and cousins, then shop girls from Manchester and mill girls from Bolton. I've had prostitutes, too – sometimes two or three of them at a time.'

'Why are you telling me all this?' Len Worrell asked with a tremble in his voice.

'Because I *can*,' Richard replied. 'Because now you're old and feeble, I can say what I like and there's *nothing* you can do about it!'

'I could cut you out of my will,' Len Worrell threatened.

Richard laughed. 'What – and give the works to Michael, the man who almost bankrupted us? You wouldn't do that, Father. You care far too much about Worrell's to ever do that.' He stepped away from the chair, and smiled. 'Ask me about all those girls, Father. Ask me if I enjoyed them?'

'You hate me, don't you?' Len Worrell said in amazement. 'For God's sake, why? What have I ever done to you?'

'You've lorded it over me for far too long. That's what you've done,' Richard replied. 'Well, now my time is finally coming. So ask me about the girls, Father. Ask me if I enjoyed them.'

'Did ... did you enjoy them?' Worrell said fearfully.

'The chase is always interesting enough,' Richard replied, 'and for a few minutes after it's over I'm perfectly satisfied. But then there's this great feeling of emptiness — of loneliness — that smothers me like a heavy blanket.'

In less than a minute Len Worrell had read both anger and contempt in his son's eyes, but now there was a new look — of a lost little boy searching desperately for someone to love.

'Becky is different from all the others,' Richard continued dreamily. 'I've always known that. Why else do you think I've been holding back all these years?'

'All these years?' Len Worrell said. 'Do you mean this has been planned all along?'

But his son was not listening to him — was not listening to anything but the voice of his own thoughts.

'I've been like a miser, hoarding my treasure while it grew,' Richard said. 'Like a gardener waiting for the fruit to fully ripen before I picked it. Becky is mine. She's always been mine. And now she's finally ready, nothing — and nobody — is going to keep us apart.'

'The thought of Michael running Worrell's frightens me,' Len Worrell confessed, 'and though I didn't know it until just now, the idea of crossing you scares me even more. But if you marry that girl, I swear everything I own will go to your brother. Don't do it. Don't end up saddled with some salt-worker's daughter.'

'Ted Taylor is a businessman, not a salt worker,' Richard said, his eyes still glazed. 'You should know that better than anyone — you gave him the money to get him started.'

'And I wish I'd never let Michael talk me into it,' Len Worrell said bitterly. 'Without my help he'd have been in the workhouse now, and that damned daughter of his would have been a scullion in some house far away from here.'

'You would rather I married Hortense Sudley than Becky Taylor?' Richard asked, suddenly coming out of his trance.

'Yes, you bloody idiot!' Len Worrell said, his exasperation temporarily overriding his fear. 'Of course I'd rather you married Hortense Sudley.'

'Hortense is very plain and rather old,' Richard mused.

'And Becky Taylor is young and beautiful,' Len Worrell said. 'But Hortense is an aristocrat. She could open doors which are closed to you now. Please, Richard, if not for my sake then for your own, don't let your heart rule your head.'

'You misunderstand me, Father,' Richard said, a smile playing on his lips. 'It is because she's old and plain that Hortense is such a good marriage prospect.'

'What do you mean?' Worrell asked.

'She may tell herself she's making a good match, but really she'll have very low expectations of her marriage,' Richard explained. 'If she were young and beautiful – like Becky – she'd demand constant attention. Being what she is, she'll be forced to settle for a husband who will merely give her respectability and occasionally visit her bed for the purpose of procreation. And if she does sometimes suspect that her husband is getting his pleasure elsewhere – well, she'll not be such a fool as to enquire into it any further.'

'Are you saying that you're willing to marry her after all?' Len Worrell asked.

'Well of course I'm willing to marry her,' Richard said. 'You surely didn't think it was ever my intention to become the husband of a shopkeeper's daughter, did you?'

CHAPTER EIGHTEEN

There were butterflies in Becky's stomach as she approached the tree where she always met Richard. She had lain awake the night before, wrestling with her problem, but she still had no idea what she would do or say if Richard wanted to make love to her.

If he wants to make love to you? she thought, angry at herself. Don't talk like a fool, girl! Of course he's going to want to make love to you.

She saw the heart the moment she reached the tree. It had been carved into the bark at her eye level. There was an arrow through it, and it contained two sets of initials — RW and BT. It hadn't been there the previous Sunday.

'Richard Worrell and Becky Taylor,' she said softly to herself.

The sound of a whinnying horse made her turn her head, and she saw Richard in the distance, riding Caesar and leading Midnight behind him.

How magnificent Richard looked sitting astride that powerful animal, she thought to herself.

How handsome!

How strong!

The closer he came, the faster she felt her heart beat. He was Sir Galahad, Robin Hood, William Tell — all the heroes she had read about in her childhood storybooks rolled into one.

Normally, Richard would lead Midnight up to where she waiting and hand her the reins, but today he dismounted and tethered the two horses to the tree.

'Aren't we going to go riding?' Becky asked.

'Not yet,' Richard replied. 'First, I have a surprise for you.'

He reached around to the blind side of his horse and — with a flourish — produced a square wicker basket.

'What's that?' Becky asked.

'This, my dear girl,' said Richard grandly, 'is a Fortnum and Mason's hamper.'

'And what's a Fortnum and Mason's hamper?'

'You'll soon see,' Richard promised. 'Sit down on the grass and all will be revealed.'

Becky sat and Richard placed the hamper in front of her.

'Open it,' he said.

Gingerly, as if she expected live snakes to spring out of it, Becky undid the toggle and lifted the lid.

'It's food,' she said.

'Not *just* food,' Worrell replied. 'The richest, most expensive food you're ever likely to have tasted. I thought we might have a picnic.'

Becky clapped her hands delightedly.

'That's a wonderful idea,' she said.

They laid the tablecloth on the grass and unpacked the feast. There were cheeses which smelled unlike any Becky had ever known before. There was glazed ham, turkey legs, and a kind of meat paste Richard said was called pâté. And to wash it all down there was champagne, a drink Becky had only heard about from music-hall songs.

They sat under the warm afternoon sun and worked their way through the wonderful picnic. At first Becky was put off by some of the more exotic offerings, but she forced herself to try them all and found everything delicious. She liked even the champagne — especially the way the bubbles tickled her nose.

Only when they reached the caviar did she look questioningly across at Richard.

'It's really nothing but fish eggs,' he told her, and though he kept a straight face Becky was sure he was making fun of her, and ate some of it anyway.

Richard had promised food the like of which she'd never tasted before, and the contents of the hamper had lived up to that promise. Yet it was not so much the food itself which had given her the warm, contented feeling in the pit of her stomach as the fact that they had eaten it *together*. She felt like a newly-wed who was not just sharing a meal with her husband but who also knew that everything in life – the troubles as well as happiness – would be shared between them from now on.

The picnic was finally over. Becky lay back in the grass and closed her eyes. Tiny insects buzzed busily close to her ear and the sun cast its gentle warmth on her face. She heard Richard stand up but she did not move, not even when he walked towards her – not even when he knelt down beside her.

'What would you do if I kissed you now, little Becky?' he asked softly. 'Would you run and hide? Or would you give yourself to me as I'd like to give myself to you?'

He was not talking about just kissing – and they both knew it.

'Did you mean what you said last Sunday?' Becky asked, surprised to find that she was slightly slurring her words.

'What I said last Sunday?'

'About wanting me to be with you always.'

'Of course I meant it.'

Becky opened her eyes and looked deep into his.

'If you were to kiss me now,' she said slowly and carefully, 'I wouldn't run and hide. If you kissed me, I'd give myself to you as you'd like to give yourself to me.'

He kissed her passionately and lingeringly and she did not resist him. She made no effort to fight him off when his hand found her breast, nor when it burrowed under her skirt. And as he was mounting her, she made no move save for the slightest quiver of anticipation. Even when he entered her, only the softest of moans indicated how much it had hurt.

Lying by Becky's side, Richard Worrell congratulated himself. He had planned it all – carving the heart in the tree, feeding Becky exotic dishes, plying her with just a little too much champagne – and it had worked, just as he'd known it would.

Their love-making had been just as he'd always known it

would be, too. He'd had some experience of deflowering virgins – sometimes he'd even paid for the pleasure in one of Liverpool's more exclusive brothels – and this virgin, he could tell, had enjoyed it.

And more to the point – much more to the point – so had he. Becky had taken to love-making as naturally as she'd taken to horse riding, and this time, when it was all over, there was none of the feeling of emptiness he'd known in the past.

Worrell stood up.

'I'll have to be going,' he said. 'I'm expected back at the house.'

Becky turned to face him.

'When will I see you again?' she asked.

The question took him by surprise.

'Why, next Sunday, of course,' he said. 'Here – under this tree.'

As Sunday meeting followed Sunday meeting, Becky found herself growing increasingly uncertain and confused.

She was sure – for most of the time, at least – that Richard loved her as she loved him. And what he did to her – and taught her to do to him – gave her more physical pleasure than she would ever have thought possible.

Yet she yearned for something beyond the merely physical. She wanted to recapture the feeling of sharing – of being a part of each other's lives – which she'd experienced during their picnic. She longed for Richard to open up to her, to tell his dreams and fears. And most of all, she wished they didn't have to meet in secret – wished they could parade their love for each other openly.

Richard did not seem to share her wishes.

'That's quite impossible at the moment,' he said firmly when she suggested that they should attend a dance in Marston School.

'Are you ashamed to be seen with me?' Becky asked, tears welling up in her eyes.

Richard laughed. 'Ashamed of you? What a silly little thing you are! Who could possibly be ashamed of you?'

'Then why can't we go to the dance?'

'Because word would get back to my father.'

'So we must go like this until your father dies,' Becky said gloomily.

'Of course not,' Richard assured her. 'Father will come to accept you in the end, but he will not be rushed into it. Don't worry, little Becky. I have a plan and slowly but surely I am wearing him down.'

But just how *long* would it take to wear down Len Worrell? Becky wondered. How much longer must their love exist in this half light, where it could never grow to its full glory – where it might, through lack of sunshine, even wither and die?

Patter . . .

Patter, patter . . .

Patter, patter, patter . . .

At first, Becky thought the insistent noise was nothing more than the sound of rain on her bedroom window. But raindrops were usually more regular than that. And did the rain, even during a storm, ever sound so heavy?

Patter, patter, patter.

Hating whoever or whatever was causing the disturbance, Becky dragged herself from her warm bed and went over to the window.

Patter, patter, patter.

Pebbles – that's what it was! Someone was throwing pebbles up to attract her attention.

She looked down into the lane. There *was* someone standing below her window – a fairly tall man, as far as she could tell.

She lifted the window sash and the cold night air engulfed her, almost taking her breath away.

'Becky?' the man in the lane hissed. 'Is that you, Becky?'

She tried to recognize the voice, but in his attempt to avoid waking anyone else, the man had effectively disguised it.

'Who are you?' she asked, adopting the same sort of stage whisper as the pebble-thrower.

Richard — come to beg her to elope with him?

George — back from the North-West Frontier?

'It's me — Philip!'

It would be, wouldn't it? If anything unexpected or inconvenient happened, you could almost bet that Philip would be behind it.

'Hang on,' Becky said, 'I'll come down and let you in.'

She pulled on her coat over her nightdress, slipped her bare feet into shoes, and crept down the stairs. Philip was waiting for her on the back doorstep. He was shivering, but Becky didn't think that had much to do with the cold.

'Come inside quick,' she whispered. 'And for God's sake try not to wake up Mam and Dad.'

The kitchen fire had been backed up with slack for the night, but by prodding it vigorously with the poker, Becky soon managed to produce a few cheery flames.

'Would you like a cup of tea?' she asked her brother.

'You don't happen to have a drop of whisky about, do you?' Philip asked shakily.

'You know Dad never allows spirits in the house,' Becky reminded him. 'And how long have you been drinking the hard stuff?'

'I don't, really,' Philip said unconvincingly. 'Well — you know — just now and again.'

'Now and again!' Becky snorted. 'Do you want tea or not?'

'Please.'

The kettle was already full of water. Becky slid the hob over the open fire and turned back to look at her brother.

Philip was a mess. His face was drawn and his eyes looked like two pools of blood.

How old was he now? Becky wondered. Twenty? If she hadn't known, she'd have given him at least ten years on top of that.

His clothes were in even worse shape than he was. The fashionable jacket with shaped panel seams and the check wool trousers must once — probably quite recently — have looked very smart, but now they were only suitable for a tramp.

'What's the trouble this time?' Becky asked.

'Trouble?' Philip replied, as if he had no idea what his sister was talking about.

Becky sighed. 'You look bloody awful and from the state your clothes are in, I'd say you've been sleeping rough. You come home in the middle of the night, and it's me — not Mam or Dad — you wake up. Are you trying to tell me you're *not* in trouble?'

'The bobbies are after me,' Philip confessed.

'Why? What have you done?'

'Nothing. It's a misunderstanding, that's all.'

Becky shook her head sadly.

'I know what you do for a living, Philip,' she said. 'I've seen what you were selling in Blackpool that time.'

Philip blushed.

'My studio was in the back of a greengrocer's shop,' he said. 'I didn't think the police knew about it, but somebody must have tipped them off. They raided the place last Friday, and took everything. If I hadn't been out at the time they'd've had me, too.'

'And you've been on the run ever since?'

Philip nodded tiredly.

'I got a lift with a carter as far as Edgware — that's a little village outside London. Then I jumped on a goods train, but the guard threw me off. I've walked most of the way. I've had nothing to eat but the bits of bread I've scrounged from cottage doors and the odd turnip I've stolen from the fields.'

'Would you like some food now?' Becky asked.

'I'm too exhausted to eat,' Philip replied.

'Then get upstairs,' his sister told him. 'You can have my bed.'

'But what about you? What will you do?'

'I'll stay down here so I can break the good news to Dad as soon as he gets up,' Becky said.

Ted Taylor hit the roof.

'He can bugger off, that's what he can do,' he thundered at

his wife and daughter, 'because I want nothing more to do with him.'

'You can't just send him away, Dad,' Becky protested. 'When all's said and done, he is your son.'

'He's no son of mine,' Taylor said. 'Selling mucky pictures for a living! It's disgusting!'

'He *is* your son,' Mary Taylor said quietly, 'and however much you rant and rave now, you know that when push comes to shove, you won't be able to bring yourself to turn him out.'

'Aye, I suppose you're right,' Taylor admitted. 'So what are we going to do about him?'

'He can't stay on the run for ever,' Mary said. 'We'll stick by him – that's what family's for – but he's done wrong, and he's going to have to take his punishment like a man.'

That was the problem, wasn't it? Becky thought. Poor, weak Philip had never taken anything like a man. And it was all very well for her mother to talk about sticking by him, but how could they give him the support he needed when he was locked up in a jail so far from home that his family could rarely – if ever – visit him?

'He's sleeping now,' she said to her parents. 'It wouldn't do any harm to let him stay like that a bit longer, would it?'

'I suppose not,' Ted Taylor said.

'And once he's awake he doesn't have to give himself up to the police right away, does he?'

'No, a few hours wouldn't make that much difference,' Taylor agreed.

'Then don't do anything until I get back from work,' his daughter said.

Taylor's eyes narrowed. 'You're planning something, our Becky, aren't you? Just what are you up to now?'

'I'll tell you later,' Becky promised. 'What I've got in mind might not do any good – but it certainly can't do any harm.'

Inspector Capstick was a big man anyway, and sitting behind his large oak desk, he looked even more intimidating.

'What can I do for you, Miss ...?'

'Taylor,' Becky told him. 'Becky Taylor.'

Capstick frowned.

'Now why does that name seem familiar?' he asked. 'Never been in trouble with the police have you?'

'No sir,' Becky assured him. 'Never.'

Capstick's frown suddenly melted away and was quickly replaced by a beaming smile.

'Becky Taylor,' he said. 'You're the girl that Dr Doyle told me about, aren't you? The one who helped him with his investigation?'

'That's right,' Becky admitted.

'By, but the pair of you made a monkey of that stuck-up copper from London, didn't you just,' he said with obvious pleasure. 'Now why was it you came to see me?'

'I've got a question,' Becky said slowly and carefully. 'Suppose somebody had committed a crime in London, but got caught somewhere else. Where would he go to prison – here, or in London?'

The frown was back.

'First you talk about somebody being arrested "somewhere else", and then you ask me if he'd go to prison *here*,' he said. 'Do you have knowledge of some criminal hiding in this area, Miss Taylor? Because if you do, you'd better tell me – or you'll be in serious trouble yourself.'

He was no fool, Becky thought. It would be pointless to try and lie to him.

'It's my brother Philip I'm talking about,' she admitted.

'Where is he?'

'At our house.'

'And what's he supposed to have done?'

Becky reached into her bag and pulled out the envelope of photographs which she had kept – though never looked at – since Philip had dropped them in Blackpool. She slid it across to Capstick.

As the Inspector examined the pictures, his eyebrows shot up.

'Do you know what you've just given me?' he asked.

'Yes, sir,' Becky replied, blushing as she spoke.

'I can't say for sure — it depends on the judge — but he could get a couple of years for trafficking in muck like this,' Capstick said, placing the envelope carefully in his desk drawer.

'But would he have to serve it in London, or in Manchester?' Becky persisted. 'You see, if it was Manchester, we could visit him regularly, and that might make it a bit easier for him.'

'Normally, we'd send him back to London,' Capstick said.

'But you could keep him here if you wanted to?'

'I could make a case out for it, I suppose,' Capstick admitted reluctantly, 'but it'd be a lot of extra work for us.'

'We'd be very grateful,' Becky told him.

As Capstick hesitated, Becky felt her hopes soar, but then she read his final decision on his face, and they plummeted to earth again.

'It's like this, Miss Taylor,' he said. 'I really wish I could do something for you, especially after you were so much assistance to Dr Doyle and all that. But quite honestly we have more than enough work here as it is, even without me getting into a paper fight with the Metropolitan Police.'

Becky had only one card left to play, and frightened as she was to use it, she knew she had no choice.

'If you can arrange to have Philip serve his sentence in Manchester,' she said, 'I'll help you do something that stuck-up copper from London couldn't do.'

'What exactly do you mean by that?' Capstick asked.

Becky took a deep breath.

'I'll tell you how to find out who killed Septimus Quinn,' she said.

Inspector Capstick's solution of a murder which had defeated the best brains of Scotland Yard was loudly trumpeted in *The Northwich Guardian*:

Using only the same evidence as was available to the Metropolitan Police, Inspector Capstick was able to deduce that the crime was, in fact, an act of revenge committed by the late Gilbert Bowyer. Thanks to the Inspector, the cloud of suspicion and mistrust, which has for so long hovered over the village of Marston, has finally been lifted. Had there been policemen of the calibre of Inspector Capstick in the metropolis, we have no doubt that the identity of Jack the Ripper would long since have been uncovered.

The London newspapers must have taken up the story, too. What else would explain the letter Becky received with the South Kensington postmark?

'*My dear Watson,*' it said, '*Knowing you as I do, I can only assume you had a good reason for giving the game away!*'

There was no signature but for the initials A.C.D.

Inspector Capstick was not to stay in the town much longer. A man of his calibre was obviously wasted in Northwich and he transferred – with promotion – to the Liverpool Police. Before he went, however, he decided that it was probably possible, after all, for Philip Taylor to be tried in Cheshire for a crime he had committed in London.

Philip's crime was little more than a folly of youth, his lawyer argued at the trial. The boy was truly repentant, as was evidenced by the fact that he had voluntarily given himself up. Could the court, when passing judgement, perhaps temper justice with a little mercy?

The court could. Philip was sentenced to only eighteen months' imprisonment, to be served in Strangeways Gaol, Manchester, a short train ride from his parents' home.

If only I could deal with my own problems as well as I seem to handle everybody else's, Becky thought.

'It says in the paper that the Worrell lad's getting married,' Ted Taylor said, folding up his copy of *The Northwich Guardian* and placing it neatly at the edge of the table.

'Michael Worrell's getting married?' Becky said, surprised that Richard hadn't mentioned so important a family event to her.

'Not Michael,' Taylor said. 'The other one. The young bugger who nearly blew me up.'

'Richard!' Becky gasped.

'Aye, that's right — Richard.'

It couldn't be true! Not after all they'd been to each other! Not after all the things he'd promised her!

Becky grabbed for the newspaper.

'Is anything the matter, love?' her mother asked worriedly.

'What page is it on?' Becky said — almost screamed — at her father.

'The next-to-back one,' Taylor said. 'Right beside Births, Marriages and Deaths.'

The print seemed to be swimming and Becky had to force her eyes to focus on it.

Let it all be a big mistake, she prayed silently. Let Dad have read it wrong.

There it was — *The Engagement is announced between Mr Richard Leonard Worrell of Peak House and Miss Hortense Charlotte Sudley of Drumlin Lodge, Hertfordshire.*

Becky's hands clenched into fists and the paper crumpled in her hands.

'Here, steady on lass. I've not finished reading that paper yet,' Ted Taylor said.

For the first time in her life Becky rose from the table without asking permission, and headed for the door.

'Becky . . .' her mother said.

'Not now, Mam,' Becky choked. 'I can't . . . I can't talk about it now.'

'At least put your coat on,' her mother called after her as she ran across the yard.

Richard Worrell was alone in his office poring over ledgers. When he looked up, his face showed annoyance that anyone should have dared to enter without knocking. Then he saw who was standing there, and his expression changed to one of delight.

'I was going to come and tell you the good news later,' he said.

'Good news?' Becky gasped. 'What good news?'

'I've finally got my father to agree to accept you,' Richard said smugly. 'I told you it was only a matter of time, didn't I?'

Becky felt a wave of relief wash over her. So it had been a mistake, after all! One of the names had been printed wrongly. The paper should either have said that Mr *Michael* Worrell was marrying Miss Hortense Sudley – or that Mr Richard Worrell was marrying *Miss Rebecca Taylor*.

'We can start looking for a house for you as soon as I'm married,' Richard continued.

Looking for a house for *her*? As soon as *he* was married?

'I don't understand,' Becky said.

'You surely didn't think I'd expect you to go on living in your parents' hovel, did you?' Richard asked. 'I can afford much better than that.'

'I . . . I . . .' Becky began.

Then words failed her.

'I spelled it out very clearly to Father,' Richard said. 'I told him, "If I'm to marry Hortense to please you, then in return my mistress must have nothing but the best." '

'Your mistress?' Becky shrieked. 'Your mistress!'

'Does the term offend you?' Richard asked. 'Then let's phrase it another way. Let's say you'll be a woman of independent means, and I shall be the generous gentleman friend who visits you occasionally.'

'I won't do it!' Becky said, almost sobbing now. 'I won't!'

Richard frowned. 'Come, come, there's no point in being so hasty,' he told her. 'Consider what I'm offering you – a house of your own, a standard of life you could never otherwise hope to aspire to . . .'

'I won't be your whore!' Becky screamed. 'I'd rather starve in the gutter first.'

Finally, she had got through to him. Finally, she had burst his bubble of complacency.

'I love you,' he said. 'You're like no other woman I've ever met.'

'Then marry me,' Becky pleaded. 'Share your life with me.'

'My father would disinherit me if I did that,' Richard said, 'and then *neither* of us would be able to live in luxury.'

'Do you think I give a damn about living in luxury as long as we can be together?' Becky demanded.

'Sit down, Becky,' Richard Worrell said soothingly. 'Give yourself a few seconds to think things over and I'm sure you'll see that marriage between the two of us would be quite impossible.'

'If you really loved me, nothing would be impossible,' Becky told him. 'But you don't love me, do you? You love what we do together under the oak tree.'

'Isn't that the same thing?' Richard asked, sounding genuinely puzzled.

'No, it isn't,' Becky said sadly. 'Goodbye, Richard.'

She turned her back on him and headed towards the door.

'Don't walk out on me, Becky,' Worrell threatened.

She grasped the handle and turned it.

'I want you – and if I can't have you, nobody will,' Worrell shouted from behind her.

She pulled, and the door swung open.

'If I can't have you, I'll destroy you,' Richard screamed.

'You've already done that,' Becky said as she stepped out into the night.

It was a chilly evening, but the cold in the air could not match the frozen numbness that Becky felt inside her.

She knew she should go home – but she couldn't bring herself to. Home meant her parents, with questioning, reproachful looks in their eyes. Home meant confession, because of the scene earlier, there was nothing she could do but tell them all. Home meant shame, home meant humiliation, and she couldn't face that – so instead she walked.

Down the lane she went to the railway crossing where she had once waited for the boiled sweets the fireman would throw at her as the huge locomotive steamed furiously past.

Along the cart road she trudged, to the spot at which there had once been a romany encampment and a gypsy with strange golden eyes had told her fortune.

She wandered up the canal towards Burns Bridge, stopping occasionally to revive memories of earlier days. Here, the bank had collapsed and *The Jupiter* had been sucked out of the water. Here, she and Dr Doyle had examined the ground for signs of the struggle between Old Gilbert Bowyer and Septimus Quinn.

Finally sheer exhaustion brought her to a halt under Marston Bridge. There were usually a few narrow boats moored there, ready to load up with Worrell's salt the first thing in the morning. Tonight there were none, and she was all alone. She wondered if that was a sign.

She looked down at the gently lapping water. When she'd been a child, her mother had warned her that if she went near the canal, Nellie Green-Teeth would get her. Nellie Green-Teeth didn't exist — she knew that now. But there were real enough monsters in the world without inventing any more.

They were not like Nellie, these real monsters. They didn't have to look frightening — they could be as beautiful as Greek gods — yet there was always a hideous ugliness squatting inside them. And sometimes, rather than slay their victims themselves, they just took away from them everything which made life worth living.

'I've had some good times,' Becky whispered softly to herself. 'It was worth being born for.'

She shivered as she realized she'd just pronounced her own epitaph. Well, why shouldn't she? She'd just lost the man she loved. Worse — she'd found that the man she loved had never existed.

And now she was a fallen woman. No decent man would marry her, and even if she found one who would, she could never accept — that wouldn't be fair on him.

So what — when all was said and done — was so bad about throwing herself into the canal? Why not let the water slowly engulf her and black out her misery? Death was nothing but a long, long sleep — and she was very tired indeed.

'Would it help you to talk about it?' a kindly voice asked.

She turned and saw Michael Worrell standing next to her.

PART SIX
1890–91

CHAPTER NINETEEN

The summer of 1890 was mild and dry, ideal weather for following the latest craze – bicycling.

It was the recent technological advances which had made the sport so suddenly popular. The old penny-farthings of the seventies had been awkward, dangerous things, but the new cycles were low-built and chain driven. They were more comfortable, too, for since the invention of the pneumatic tyre a couple of years earlier, cyclists no longer had to bounce along on solid metal wheels.

Bicycling was a sport which embraced both sexes and all classes, and cycling clubs sprang up all over the Northwich area. Every Sunday groups of carefree young people could be seen happily cycling along roads which, since the spread of the railway, had been almost unused.

Becky Taylor owned a bicycle – or rather she *should* own it when she had paid off the balance of her debt to Michael Worrell.

Michael had tried to give her the machine as a gift, but she was having none of that.

'Why not?' he'd asked.

'It's nothing against you personally, Michael,' she'd explained. 'I just don't want to be under an obligation to *anybody* in your family.'

'You wouldn't be under any obligation.'

'That's not how I see it.'

Michael hadn't argued any further. Instead he'd just smiled and said, 'When they handed out stubbornness, you must have sneaked back into the queue for a second helping.'

That made her laugh. In fact, Michael seemed to be the only person who *could* make her laugh any more.

'But if you can bring yourself to see the gift in the spirit it was intended,' Michael continued, 'I hope you won't let your pride stop you taking it.'

Life is very strange, Becky often thought to herself as she and Michael cycled through the countryside, along with the rest of the Norwich Cycling Club.

Richard Worrell had brought her a horse and taught her how to ride it and Michael had done the same with a bicycle. Yet in all other ways her relationships with the two brothers had been very different.

Richard had had her up on his horse — with his arms around her — only seconds after they met in the driveway of Peak House. If Michael touched her — and he rarely did — it was either to help her dismount from her bicycle or because he had accidentally brushed against her.

Richard had never talked much to her, either, whereas Michael never seemed to stop. His life at university; his theories on how Worrell's should be run; his interest in history, art and politics — all these were grist to Michael's conversational mill.

'Why don't you tell me to shut up now and again?' he asked her once, after he'd been talking for over half an hour.

'I enjoy listening to you,' she replied.

It was true. His enthusiasm was infectious, and though many of the things he spoke about were far beyond the range of her experience he had an ability to make them seem both real and exciting.

'I've only really been nosy about the village before,' she told him, 'but you're making me nosy about everything.'

He was a good listener, too, and seemed to enjoy her tales of Jack's adventures on the Oil Rivers or George's on the North-West Frontier.

'But I still don't understand what's going on with you two,' Ted Taylor complained after Becky had returned from one of the NCC expeditions.

'Nothing's going on,' Becky assured him. 'Michael's a friend, that's all.'

'Rum sort of friendship if you ask me,' Ted replied, 'but I suppose you're better off with him than that other bugger.'

Neither Ted nor Mary had discussed with Becky what had happened between her and Richard Worrell. But they knew all right – she had heard them arguing about it in the privacy of their bedroom.

- 'Don't push it, Ted. The girl's suffered enough.'
- 'I'm her father. I can't just let it pass.'
- 'So what are you going to do? March up to Peak House and horsewhip him You'd be in the lock-up before you knew what had hit you. Or is it our Becky you're planning to punish? Going to turn her out on the streets, are you? That'll do a lot to make her more virtuous, won't it?'
- 'Of course I'm not planning to turn her out, Mary love. She may have done wrong, but she's me daughter. I just wish ... I just wish there was something I could do about the whole mess.'
- 'Well, there isn't! Life's unfair, and if you haven't learned that by now – well, all I can say is, you bloody well should have.'

Only once before in her life had Becky heard them argue like that – the day Mary announced she'd used the compensation to buy chip-shop equipment – and it weighed heavily on the daughter that she should have been the cause of such disagreement between her parents. If she had been a Catholic she was sure she would have joined a convent. As it was, she used cycling to fill those spaces in her mind which she would rather have not occupied with thoughts of the past.

In the Worrell home there was no such reticence about discussing what had gone on between Richard and Becky.

'You do realize your brother *had* her, don't you?' Len Worrell demanded of his younger son.

'Yes, I realize that,' Michael replied quietly. 'I can see the pain on her face almost every time I look at her.'

'At least Richard didn't spend all his time following her

around on one of them infernal bicycles,' Len Worrell said. 'At least he was sensible enough to want to put things on a business footing.'

'And she wouldn't have it, would she?' Michael asked triumphantly. 'She never wants to see him again after what he said to her.'

'Be that as it may, I'm not having *you* getting involved with this girl,' his father said, coughing heavily. 'I've not much longer for this world, but before I go I want to see you and your brother properly settled. Richard'll be getting married to Hortense soon, and we should be looking round for a match for you. A proper match, mind – or you kiss your inheritance goodbye.'

Richard added nothing to the debate. Why should he, he asked himself, when both his father and brother were doing such a good job of driving the wedge between them even without his help?

'Where shall we go today?' Michael asked.

'Overton Hill?' Becky suggested.

'But that must be fifteen miles,' Michael said.

'Well, if you don't feel up to it ...' Becky replied with a smile.

Michael laughed. 'If you can manage it, then so can I.'

These expeditions as a pair – rather than as just two of a group – had started when summer had turned to autumn and the cycling club had begun to meet less regularly. Over the course of the next few weeks the rides had become a habit and, like most habits, grew as familiar and comforting as old slippers.

The routine never varied. They would take it in turns to select a destination and then set off towards it. They rarely spoke while they were pedalling their machines, but on the way back home they would stop at a tea shop or public house, and while they were eating and drinking they would say whatever came into their minds.

But we won't be doing that today, Michael thought.

If Becky had noticed the unfamiliar box strapped to the back of his cycle, she hadn't mentioned it. He was glad of that because though he didn't want to lie to her, neither did he wish to spoil the surprise he intended to spring on her later. And want a grand surprise it was. A picnic! They had never had a picnic before – she was bound to love it.

It was perfect picnic weather, he thought as they rode along. Although it was mid October, the air had a balmy quality which would make eating al fresco delightful. He couldn't wait to see Becky's face when he opened his hamper.

The last stretch of the journey, climbing the hill itself, was hard work, but the reward of reaching the top was well worth the effort. Behind them spread the Cheshire Plain. In front of them stretched the River Mersey. Becky laid her bicycle on the ground and took in the view.

'Look at that,' she said, pointing to a steam packet making its way down the river. 'My brother Jack used to work on one of them.'

'And now he owns one,' Michael said.

Becky grinned. 'What do you think his name is – Worrell?' she asked. 'He doesn't own it, it's only *rented*. Still, with a little bit of luck who knows what might happen one day?'

For half an hour or so they wandered happily over the hill, stopping at this point or that to admire the view, but rarely speaking. Finally, they returned to the spot where they left their bicycles.

'Well, if we're going to have time to eat anything on the way back, we'd better start out now,' Becky said.

'No need for that,' Michael replied grandly. He walked over to his machine and unstrapped the package from the back. Pulling away its protective covering, he held it up for Becky's inspection. 'This,' he told her, 'is a Fortnum and Mason's hamper.'

Becky gazed with horror at the wickerwork basket.

There'll be a glazed ham inside, she thought. And caviar. And that champagne which tickles your nose when you drink it.

Of all the nightmares of the past which could have come to haunt her, this was the worst — the very worst. Though her body was still on the hill, her soul had already made the journey back to the secret place under the oak tree — to the afternoon she had freely given herself to a man she thought had loved her.

Without even realizing it she was beginning to back away from the brother of the man who now filled her mind.

'What's the matter, Becky?' Michael asked worriedly.

Almost in a trance, Becky picked up her cycle and mounted it.

'Where are you going?' Michael asked. 'Wait for me.'

She didn't want to wait for him. She wanted to be far away from him — as far away as she could possibly be.

The road began to follow the slope of the hill almost immediately. Under normal circumstances Becky would have cautiously free-wheeled down it, but now she pumped the pedals with all her might.

'Be careful!' Michael called. 'You're going too fast!'

But for Becky there was no such thing as too fast.

At the first bend her cycle wobbled dangerously but she just managed to pull round it. She risked a glance over her shoulder and saw that Michael had got on his own machine and was following. Becky hit the pedals with new urgency.

It was on the third bend that she made a real error of judgement. In a desperate attempt to correct a violent skid, she slammed on her brakes too hard, the cycle bucked — and suddenly she was flying through the air.

She landed badly on the grass verge, jarring her spine and sending shock waves through her whole body. For a few seconds — perhaps even longer — everything went black.

When she came too again she was aware of someone bending over her.

'Are you all right?' a fuzzy voice asked.

'What about Midnight!' Becky gasped. 'Is Midnight hurt?'

'Midnight?' the voice said wonderingly. 'What are you talking about?'

'The horse,' Becky groaned.

'Our horse, Midnight? Is that who you mean? What's he got to do with anything?'

Michael! It was Michael bending over her, his big hands touching her shoulders.

But where would those hands stray next? Onto her breasts? Under her skirt?

The nightmare was to be replayed in its full horror – and she simply did not have enough strength to fight against it.

'Becky!' Michael said. 'Can you hear me, Becky?'

'Yes,' she replied weakly.

'Don't you ever do that again,' he said, shaking her. 'Don't you ever frighten me like that again. Do you understand?'

Her eyes were beginning to focus on his face now. She had never seen him look so angry. Then, suddenly, that anger drained away, and in its place was the sensitive, understanding expression which, so often in the past – before her days with Richard – had made her want to hug him.

'Will you marry me, Becky?' he asked softly.

She was suffering from concussion, she told herself. Yes, that must be it – because Michael couldn't possibly have said what she thought she'd just heard.

'Will you marry me, Becky?' Michael repeated. 'Please!'

She was still groggy from the fall and this only served to make things worse.

'How can you be so cruel as to joke with me like that?' she cried.

'It's no joke,' he assured her.

'But you know all about me ... about me and Richard.'

'That doesn't matter,' he said.

'It *has* to matter,' she insisted.

'Do you think you're the only girl my brother's ever seduced?' Michael asked. 'And do you think any of the others will have any scruples about getting married?'

'I'm not one of the others,' Becky said.

'I know you're not,' Michael replied. 'Maybe that's why I love you as much as I do.'

Her head still ached, and it was so difficult to think — so difficult to put her hazy thoughts into words.

'You say you love me,' she told him, 'but I'm not sure I love you. I'm not sure that I'll ever be able to love anyone again.'

'Do you at least like me?' he asked.

'You know I do.'

'And you have some respect for me, don't you?'

'Respect for you?' Becky asked. 'You're kind and understanding, but you're strong and principled as well. You saved my life the night I was about to throw myself in the canal. I don't think there's anybody I respect more.'

'Then that's enough for me. Please say you'll marry me, Becky.'

It was insane — completely insane — but just as she would not have had the strength to fight him off if he had decided to take advantage of her, so now she could not summon the will to resist him on this.

'Yes. I'll marry you, Michael,' she said. 'If you're sure that's what you really want.'

By rights the meeting should have taken place in the front room, but the Taylors' parlour was a chip shop, and so it was in the kitchen that they went through the ritual.

It was difficult to say which of them felt more awkward. Ted Taylor was embarrassed at entertaining Michael Worrell in surroundings much more humble than his guest was used to. Michael, for his part, knew that Ted had no reason to love the Worrells.

'Sit down by the fire, lad,' Ted said. 'I mean, sit down by the fire, *Sir*.'

'I think "lad" will do me well enough,' Michael replied. 'And if you don't mind *Sir* I'd prefer to stand.'

Ted Taylor nodded, grateful that one of them, at least, had kept his head enough to maintain the correct form.

'So what can I do for you, Mr Worrell?' he asked.

'I have come to ask for your daughter's hand in marriage,' Michael said formally.

Ted looked round the simple room in which he'd spent so much of his married life.

'This is where I should ask you if you'll be able to keep her in the luxury to which she's become accustomed, isn't it?' he said. 'Only there doesn't seem much point in that, does there?'

'There's a lot of point,' Michael told him. 'When my father learns I intend to marry Becky, he'll probably cut me off without a penny.'

'Thinks she's not good enough for you, does he?' Taylor said, suddenly angry. 'Is that it?'

'Yes, that's it,' Michael agreed. 'That's what he thinks.'

'And what do you think?' Taylor demanded.

'I think *I'm* not good enough for *her*,' Michael said. 'I'm not sure anybody is. But I'm the one she's agreed to marry.'

'And how would you support her if your father cuts you off?' Taylor wondered.

'The same way any man supports his wife,' Michael said. 'By working. I know as much about salt as any man in the area – a good bit more than some. It's in my blood. I'll soon get a job as manager at one of the works.'

'Suppose there's no vacancy for managers,' Taylor said, 'what will you do then?'

'Whatever I have to,' Michael replied firmly. 'Work as a waller, if need be. But I promise you one thing – Becky'll never starve.'

'You may say that now,' Taylor told him, 'but you've no idea what it's like to be really poor – no idea at all.'

Becky and her mother had been banished from the house while the men had their discussion, and to avoid fuelling the speculations of the village busybodies, had gone for a walk along the canal.

'Do you love him?' Mary asked Becky.

'Yes, Mam.'

'You've never lied to me before,' Mary told her daughter severely. 'Don't start now.'

'I admire him tremendously,' Becky said.

'And ...?'

'And he'll be a good father, if we ever have any children.'

'And ...?'

'He loves me, Mam. He really does. I couldn't turn him down.'

'I hope you know what you're doing,' Mary Taylor said seriously.

'I do want to marry him, Mam,' Becky said. 'Honestly I do.'

'Well, then, we'd better hope your Dad gives his permission,' Mary said. She looked up at the setting sun. 'It's time we were getting back.'

They walked back along the canal in silence, each wrapped up in her own thoughts. Even in their own back yard they still said nothing. Until Ted Taylor had made his decision, there *was* nothing more to say.

Mary lifted her hand and knocked on her own back door.

'Come in,' Ted Taylor called out.

Hesitantly Becky and her mother entered the kitchen. Ted and Michael stood by the fireplace facing each other, their elbows on the mantelpiece, serious expressions on their faces.

Becky tried to speak, and found she couldn't. She sensed that her mother was experiencing the same difficulty, too.

'You pair took your time, didn't you?' Ted said.

'We thought you'd have a lot to talk about,' Mary said.

'Aye, we did,' Taylor agreed. 'And now we're going for a pint.'

'Look who's there,' said Not-Stopping Bracegirdle, bobbing up so she could see through the hatch. 'Ted Taylor and that Worrell lad, having a drink together as bold as you please. I wonder what that's all about.'

'He's been seeing a lot of their Becky – cycling and that,' Dottie Curzon said. 'Maybe he's going to marry her.'

'Marry her!' Not-Stopping scoffed. 'I've never heard anything so daft in me life. You're losing your marbles, you are, Dottie.'

'I think Dottie might be right,' Maggie Cross said.

Not-Stopping drained her glass.

'Do you?' she asked. 'Do you indeed? Well, we'll soon see, won't we?' She got from her chair and stuck her head through the hatch. 'Another of the same when you're ready, Mr O'Leary,' she called out. 'And how are you tonight, Mr Taylor?'

'I'm fine,' Ted told her. 'And in case you're wondering, Mrs Bracegirdle, I've just brought me future son-in-law out for a pint. You've no objections, have you?'

'Oh, no objections, Mr Taylor,' Not-Stopping assured him. 'None at all.' She paid for her drink and bobbed down onto her seat again. 'Told you that's what it was,' she said triumphantly.

It's perfect, Richard said to himself as he entered his father's bedroom. Len Worrell was lying in bed. His nightshirt seemed to envelop him, and the skin hung slack on his shrunken body.

'Michael's having the banns read,' Richard said gleefully.

'He's what?' the old man rasped angrily.

'He's having the banns read. He's going to marry Becky Taylor three weeks from Sunday.'

'Then he'll not get a penny from me,' Len Worrell said. 'What's the name of that attorney you use nowadays?'

'Crimp. Horace Crimp.'

'Have him draw me up a new will saying you're my only heir. Tell him I want it for three weeks on Sunday.'

'He can have it ready by tomorrow,' Richard said.

The old man shook his head weakly.

'I'll not sign it until I'm sure Michael's let me down,' he said. 'I'll not sign it until he's really wed.'

'Father . . .' Richard started to protest.

The old man was suddenly attacked by a coughing fit. His emaciated body shook and shook under fresh assaults, until it seemed he was actually being torn apart by it.

'Medicine,' Worrell gasped.

'What medicine?' Richard asked.

'Bottle ... on the table ... quick ...'

It was a green bottle, and it stood next to the hair brushes which the invalid had had neither the energy nor the enthusiasm to use for weeks.

Richard unscrewed the bottle, poured out some of the purple liquid onto a spoon and held the spoon to the old man's lips.

The coughing began to subside almost immediately.

'That stuff's the only thing that's keeping me alive,' Len Worrell wheezed.

'About the new will ...' Richard said.

'I'm not signing till after the wedding,' Worrell replied.

'You could be dead by then,' Richard told him.

The sick man examined his son through watery eyes.

'You're a callous young bugger, aren't you?' he said. 'Ambitious, too. I thought I was hard but – by God – I'm nothing next to you.'

'I'm only thinking of the works,' Richard said, making little effort to sound sincere.

'You're only thinking of yourself,' Worrell spat. 'Well, you're going to have to take the chance that I don't die before the wedding, because I want to give your brother *his* chance to obey me. Bugger off now – I'm getting so I can't stand the sight of you.'

It would be all right, Richard thought as he let himself out of the sickroom. The old man wouldn't die before that bloody fool Michael married Becky. Len would hang on for weeks after that – maybe even months. But eventually he'd have to snuff it, and when he did he would leave his remaining shares in Worrell's to his eldest son.

'Finally,' Richard sighed, 'after all these years the works will be mine – and only mine.'

What power and influence that would give him. First, he'd kick Michael out, then he'd put pressure on all the other owners in the area to make sure that none of them gave him work. So what would Michael do then? He might persuade himself for a while that he could manage with a lowly job –

working as a waller or behind the counter of his new father-in-law's chip shop — but that couldn't last.

Michael was a gentleman, fit only to do gentleman's work, and eventually he must realize it. And when he did, he'd have no alternative but to come cap in hand and beg his brother for his old job back.

And I'll give it to him, Richard thought.

Oh, yes — but he'd make it quite clear to Becky that one of the conditions attached to Michael's reinstatement was that she would make herself available to him whenever he felt the urge.

And she wouldn't have any choice but to agree, either.

CHAPTER TWENTY

People in Marston went into debt to put on a good funeral, but weddings, by and large, were not considered important enough to merit any real extravagance.

'Still, I think I'll put on a bit of a do for our Becky's wedding,' Mary Taylor decided. 'After all, she is marrying a gentleman . . .'

'A soon-to-be *unemployed* gentleman,' Ted Taylor pointed out.

'. . . and it'll give Michael a chance to meet a few of his new relatives, won't it?'

'I bet he can hardly wait,' Ted said — but not loudly enough for his wife to hear.

On the morning of the wedding Mary rose at dawn, and by the time her daughter and husband had woken up she already had the pies in the oven and was struggling to turn the chip shop back into the front parlour it had once been.

Eunice and Jessie arrived just after nine. Jessie was dispatched upstairs to help her younger sister get ready, while Eunice was appointed her mothers' chief assistant.

'Our Becky'll be wearing a proper wedding dress, you know,' Mary confided to her eldest daughter as they heaved the cooking range against the wall and covered it with a cloth. 'Michael insisted on that. Paid for it himself, the lad did.'

Eunice sniffed. 'It's a bit of a rum thing to lash out like that when you're about to lose your job.' she said. 'It's a bit of a rum thing getting married at all, when there'll soon be no money coming in. Just how *does* Michael expect to support our Becky?'

'He'll find a way,' Mary said, wondering if she should go

and check on the pies in the oven. 'He'll not let her down — not that feller.'

Ted Taylor appeared in the doorway. He was wearing his best suit — and didn't look the least bit comfortable in it.

'Is there anything I can do?' he asked.

'Yes,' Mary said cheerfully. 'You can keep from under foot. Men are no good at getting things ready for weddings — never were, and never will be.'

Taylor shuffled uncertainly back into the kitchen.

'What's Dad's opinion of Michael?' Eunice asked, once her father was out of earshot.

'Must be quite high, mustn't it?' Mary replied. 'Otherwise he'd never be letting the lad marry his daughter.'

She had begun scrubbing down the paintwork, but now she stopped and looked up at her eldest daughter.

'I'll tell you something, our Eunice,' she said. 'Michael might be quiet — but that doesn't mean he's wet.'

'I never said he was wet,' Eunice protested.

'No, but that's what you were thinking,' her mother said reprovingly. 'He's a dark horse, is Michael, and Becky did just right when she said "yes" to him. D'you know, I wouldn't be surprised if in the end she doesn't turn out to have been the most sensible of the lot of you.'

Upstairs in her bedroom, Becky was feeling far from sensible.

What have I got myself into now? she wondered.

Michael was kind and loving. He deserved a woman who would return his love and instead here was one who, even if she didn't mean to, would probably end up hurting him.

'Hold still, our Becky,' mumbled Jessie, her mouth full of pins. 'I don't know how you ever expect me to do a proper job if you keep thrutching like that.'

'Sorry,' Becky said absently.

'Now listen,' her sister continued, lowering her voice. 'About tonight. He'll want to play with your thingy-me-jigs — they all do. But you mustn't let him. And when he starts the other business, try to think of something to take your mind off it.

When Charlie does it to me, I usually add up the Co-op bill, and it's over before I know it.'

Poor big sister, Becky, thought. You don't know what you're missing.

She hadn't wanted to take her mind off it — not when she'd been doing it with Richard. And as for his playing with her thingy-me-jigs — oh God, she'd loved that.

But it wouldn't be Richard who'd be making love to her in future. It wouldn't be *his* hands which were reaching eagerly for her breasts. Michael wasn't Richard, and never would be. Maybe she'd have to resort to adding up the Co-op bill after all.

'And once you've got a bun in the oven, you're best not letting him come near you at all,' Jessie counselled. 'There's drawbacks to carrying — the aches and the being sick — but at least it means you're spared the other thing for a few months.'

'I heard a joke about that,' Becky said, partly to shut her sister up and partly to stop herself thinking. 'The first time the Queen and Prince Albert did it, he rolls off her and she's really quiet. "Vot's the matter, my dear?" he asks. "Do the working classes do this?" she says to him. "Vell, yes," he says. "There should be a law against it!" the Queen goes, disapproving like. "A law against it? But vy?" Albert asks. "Because it's much too good for *them*," she tells him.'

Jessie giggled so much she almost swallowed her pins.

'Fancy my little sister telling me a joke like that,' she said. 'You are awful. And imagine that fat old woman doing it with *anybody*! Gives me a funny feeling just thinking about it.'

Imagine me and Michael doing it, Becky thought. Why, why did I ever say yes?

There was the sound of horses' hoofs clip-clopping up the Lane. Jessie rushed over to the window.

'Oh God,' she said, 'the carriage is here already, and we're not half finished. Come on, our Becky. You're going to have to help me or you'll never be ready.'

Though the smell of stale frying fat still hung in the air, the room finally looked more like the front parlour it had once been than the chip shop it had become.

'But why are the curtains drawn?' Becky asked.

'That's your mother's doing,' Ted Taylor said. 'It's supposed to bring you good luck.'

'Good luck?' Becky mused. 'From drawing the curtains? That's a new one on me. And how long's Mam been superstitious, anyway?'

'It's come over her lately,' Ted replied, opening the front door. 'Are you about ready to go?'

The moment Becky stepped across the threshold she understood the real reason the curtains had been drawn. Her mother, who knew her better than she knew herself, must have realized that if she'd seen what was waiting outside any earlier, wild horses wouldn't have dragged her from the house!

Becky gazed with horror at the sea of faces beyond the waiting carriage. The whole of Marston had turned out to see her. She tried to back into the front parlour, but her father had anticipated that, and was blocking her way.

'Help me, Dad!' she pleaded, taking Taylor's arm and digging her fingers into it.

'You'll be all right,' he assured her. 'All you've got to do is climb into the carriage and you'll be away.'

'Will you come with me?' Becky asked.

'I will not,' her father told her. 'This is your day. I'll walk behind you, like everybody else.'

'But I don't want to be alone,' Becky protested.

'You won't be alone,' her father told her with a twinkle in his eye. 'You'll have the coachman for company.'

'But I want my family by me,' Becky persisted.

'Aye, well you'll have to have what you get,' her father replied. 'Now look lively, or you'll be late for your own wedding.'

As she stepped into the lane, the crowd cheered and Becky wished she was dead. She looked across at all the smiling faces – Mr O'Leary, the Hulses, Ma Fitton, countless others who all blurred together – and she felt very unworthy of the good wishes they were heaping on her.

327

'Get going then, lass,' Ted Taylor urged her.

Becky climbed into the open coach. The driver's broad back was to her, but she thought he reminded her of someone.

'Ready, Miss?' he asked.

His voice seemed familiar, too.

'Ready,' Becky said.

The coachman jerked on the reins and the horses set off at the gentle pace suitable for the occasion. Up the bridge they went, over the crown and down the other side towards the Adelaide Mine, the National School – and the church!

Becky wondered how much you could hurt yourself jumping out of a moving coach.

'No need to be nervous, Miss,' the coachman said over his shoulder. 'You're in good hands.'

'I'm not nervous about that,' Becky replied. 'It's just that I ...'

She *did* know the coachman. Though she hadn't seen him for years, Becky instantly recognized the strong, tanned face which was grinning at her. Mindless of either her dress or her safety, she stood up and threw her arms around the coachman's shoulders.

'Go easy,' he said, 'or you'll have us turning over.'

'Oh Jack,' Becky cried. 'My dear, dear, wonderful brother. When did you get back?'

'Docked in Liverpool last night,' Jack said. 'For a while there, I thought I was going to miss the chance of surprising you.'

'Tell me all about it,' Becky said. 'Tell me everything you've been doing.'

Jack chuckled. 'This is your day,' he said. 'You don't want to go talking about me.'

'But I do,' Becky insisted. '*Anything* to take my mind off the church and what's going to happen there.'

'All right,' Jack agreed. 'I told you about the Royal Niger Company, didn't I?'

'Yes.'

'Well, they started charging the independent traders fees for using the Oil Rivers.'

'Why does the government allow them to do that?'

'The government doesn't,' Jack said, 'but London's a long way from Akassa, and it's the Royal Niger Company that's the law out there. What they're doing, you see, is to levy such high fees that they'll eventually drive us out of business.'

'That's unfair,' Becky said.

'Isn't it?' Jack agreed. 'That's why I hardly ever pay them.'

'But how can you avoid it?'

'By working the tributaries they don't patrol. By shutting off the engines when I get near one of their trading posts and drifting past under cover of darkness. There's lots of tricks, if you know 'em. Mind you, the Company's been getting even nastier recently.'

'How?'

'There was this agent from Liverpool – nice feller he was, we shared a few pegs of palm wine. Anyway, he was operating on what the Company claimed was its territory, so the bosses had him beaten up, and then blockaded the town which had had the nerve to trade with him.'

'It all seems very dangerous,' Becky said worriedly.

'Not if you know what you're doing,' her brother told her. 'And I do. The Company's got guns, but so have I. And the men it employs aren't as tough as they think they are. They wouldn't have lasted ten minutes in an Australian silver field.'

'I still think you should . . .' Becky began.

'Here we are, then,' Jack interrupted.

Tearing her eyes away from her brother's face, Becky was shocked to see that what he had said was true. While she'd been listening to his tales of the Oil Rivers, they passed the Adelaide Mine and the National School, and now the carriage was standing right outside the church.

Becky's gaze moved quickly from the open door – through which the sound of organ music was gently wafting – to the Adelaide Mine Prize Brass Band, which was already lined up against the church wall, ready to play for her when she came out of the church again as Mrs Michael Worrell.

As Mrs Michael Worrell.

Suddenly she felt like a hunted animal, trapped between the congregation already waiting in the church and the villagers who had followed behind the carriage.

'By, but you gave them horses some stick, our Jack,' she heard her father say from outside the coach. 'It took me all me wind to keep up with you. Are you right, our Becky?'

'Yes Dad,' Becky said as he opened the carriage door. 'At least, I'm as right as I'll ever will be.'

Richard Worrell knocked on his father's door, but entered without waiting to be invited. The old man looked neither any better nor any worse than he had done every day for the last few weeks, Richard thought.

No, he was wrong! Examining the sick man from closer to, he could see that there had been a change – there was more determination in his eyes than he'd shown for years.

And what were the company's ledgers doing on his side table? Whoever'd been responsible for that wouldn't be in a job much longer.

Richard took out his watch and made a show of looking at it.

'They should be married by now,' he said. 'Not that I expect you'll sign the will until you've got half a dozen witness to swear they've actually seen it for themselves.'

'You're wrong there, I've already done it,' said the old man.

With a shaky hand he reached across to the table, picked up a thick piece of paper and offered it to his son. Richard snatched the precious document from his father's hand and walked over to the window. Here it was at last – the will which gave him sole control of Worrell's.

'*I, Leonard George Worrell,*' the old man had written in his wavering, invalid's hand, '*being of sound mind, do hereby make the following bequests:*

To my son, Michael, I bequeath all my remaining shares in Worrell and Company ...'.

To my son, *Michael?*

'You've made a mistake, you old fool,' Richard said angrily.

'You've written Michael where you should have written Richard.'

'It's no mistake,' Worrell told him. 'I've been going through the books. I should have done it years ago. I used to do the accounts myself back when I was starting out, and I'll admit I learned to pull a few fast ones – but nothing like this.'

'Accounting's got more difficult since your day,' Richard protested.

'Remember when you said we were broke and the only way out was to sell shares to Septimus Quinn?' Worrell continued. 'We weren't broke at all, were we?'

'No,' Richard admitted, because it was pointless to pretend any longer.

'So, you were milking money out of the company,' the old man said. 'And what did you do with it? Buy back the shares from Quinn?'

'From his sister,' Richard said.

'So you already own part of the company?'

'That's right.'

'Well, you won't get the rest. It's all going to your brother.'

'I'll fight you,' Richard said angrily. 'I'll fight you right up to the highest court in the land.'

'No, you won't,' his father chuckled throatily. 'Because there's no way you can do that without the truth coming out – and if that happens you'll go to gaol for embezzlement.'

Richard quickly checked through the will. The form looked legal enough – the old man had obviously copied it from the one Horace Crimp had drawn up – but it hadn't been witnessed yet.

'This *is* the only copy of the will, isn't it, Father?' he asked.

'Yes,' the old man admitted, 'but if you destroy it I'll write another one. And another after that. If it's the last thing I do, I'll see that Michael gets what's rightfully his.'

I've lost it all, Richard told himself despairingly. Lost it all – at the very last minute!

Despair gave way to a blind rage so powerful that it seemed

to engulf him. Almost without willing it, he strode furiously across the room to the sick man's bed.

'Richard ... please ... don't ...' Len Worrell said as he cowered against his pillow.

Richard grabbed his father by the nightshirt and began to shake him with all his might.

'You old bastard,' he hissed as he roughly pulled the invalid first this way and then that. 'You rotten, stinking old bastard ...'

'Can't breathe properly ...' Len Worrell gasped.

'... you filthy bag of dirt, you upstart lower-class swine ...'

A coughing fit – as bad a one as Worrell had ever had – did a little to restore his son's sanity. Richard let go of his father and allowed him to fall back on to the bed.

'Medicine ...' the old man gasped between coughs.

'Didn't you tell me once that this medicine was the only thing keeping you alive?' Richard asked, *much* calmer now.

'Get it ...' the old man choked. '... Please ...'

'Of course I'll get your medicine for you, Father,' Richard said solicitously. 'As long as you promise to change your will again – this time in my favour.'

'... Yes ... yes ... anything ...'

'You say that now, beloved Papa,' Richard told him. 'But how do I know you really mean it?'

'... Mean it ...' the old man spluttered.

With an almost superhuman effort he dragged his racked body across the bed to the bedside table. The tips of his fingers were almost touching the medicine bottle when his son reached over and moved it just a few more inches away.

'I don't think I believe you, Father,' Richard said conversationally. 'I don't think I believe you at all.'

A gurgling sound, as loud a geyser on the point of eruption, forced its way from Worrell's throat. The old man fell back on the bed, his eyes wide with both fear and pleading.

'Try to rob me of my inheritance, would you?' Richard said savagely. 'Well, it's too late now.'

The gurgling grew louder and louder, so that it seemed to

fill the whole room. Then it was gone, and there was only silence.

Richard bent over and, with Len Worrell's lifeless eyes staring up at him, felt the pulse in his father's neck.

Nothing!

Good!

Richard walked over to the bell-pull, pocketing the will as he went. He was almost on the point of ringing for the maid when he remembered that the ledgers which proved his embezzlement were still on open view.

'And that will never do,' he said lightly to himself.

When the maid opened the door the first thing she saw was Richard Worrell, kneeling at his father's side and holding one of the old man's hands in both of his.

'Is he . . . ?' the maid asked.

'It was very sudden,' Richard said with tears in his eyes. 'And do you know what his last words were?'

'No, Sir,' the girl replied.

'He said – and remember I'm quoting him exactly here – he said, "I could have lived another ten years if your brother hadn't broken my heart by marrying that Taylor girl."'

'Oh, the poor Master! What a thing to have on your mind in your last moments,' the maid said. 'Just wait till I tell the rest of the . . .' She stopped suddenly, and flushed. 'I'm sorry, Sir,' she continued shakily. 'I didn't mean I was going to . . .'

'That's all right,' Richard said kindly. 'I know you're upset. Go and get someone to call the doctor, will you?'

The girl turned and fled from the room. Richard reached into his pocket and took out Len Worrell's new will.

What were his chances of getting away with changing the name 'Michael' to 'Richard'? he wondered. Not very high, he decided. Besides, he didn't need to take the risk. With only the half his father's shares he'd been left in the old will, he would still have control of the company.

He took the new will across to the fireplace and held it over the bright flames. The paper caught immediately, but not until everything but the corner he was holding had been reduced to ashes did he release it and let it fly up the chimney.

He glanced back at his father's bed, under which he'd hidden the ledgers.

It wouldn't do any harm to burn them too, he thought.

'You may kiss the bride,' the Vicar said.

Michael turned towards his new wife.

It's our first kiss! Becky realized in a panic. We're married – and we've never even kissed!

She remembered the hundreds – the thousands – of kisses which his brother had showered on her. And with that memory came the shameful – humiliating – knowledge that though she no longer loved Richard, he still had the power to excite her. Worse yet, there was still at least a small part of her which wished it was Richard's mouth, not Michael's, which was searching for hers.

It was a tentative kiss, little more than a gentle brushing.

Is *that* because of Richard? Becky wondered.

Could Michael taste his brother on her lips – even now? Would they ever be able to exorcise Richard – or would he always be there, an invisible presence lying between them?

The Vicar led them into the vestry, the bride signed away her right to be Becky Taylor, and it was all over.

They stepped outside into the pale autumn sunshine and stood in a semi-formal pose while the Adelaide Mine Prize Brass Band serenaded them with a brief selection from Gilbert and Sullivan.

'Isn't she dressed lovely,' Ma Fitton said to her companions standing by the churchyard wall.

Not-Stopping Bracegirdle subjected the bride's costume – a long, flowing, white dress and a broad white hat with feathers spilling over its rim – to a critical examination.

'People should cut their coats according to their cloth,' she pronounced. 'They say he'll scarcely have two ha'pennies to rub together now that his father's disinherited him, and there he goes splashing out on all that silk and lace.'

'Still, it is nice to *look* nice, isn't it,' Dottie Curzon said. 'Especially on your wedding day.'

'It's nothing but pride and vanity,' Not-Stopping told her. 'And pride comes before a fall. You mark my words — I'm never wrong.'

The band reached the end of its melody. Michael thanked them, then took his wife's hand and led her towards the carriage. It was not until they passed through the lych-gate that he noticed the family butler, discreetly signalling to him.

'Is there a problem, Chivers?' he asked.

'I've been instructed by Mr Richard to ask you to come back to the house right away, Sir,' the butler said.

'Is it my father?' Michael asked, alarmed.

'I'm afraid so, Sir,' Chivers said gravely. 'He passed away just over an hour ago.'

'So his father's dead, is he?' Becky heard one of the Adelaide bandsmen say to the man next to him. 'Well, that's buggered up their big night for a start, hasn't it?'

The carriage bounced its way along the road to Dunkirk. Michael Worrell, sitting next to his new wife, turned his head away and was as silent as the grave into which his father would soon be laid to rest.

Poor Michael! Becky thought, and gripped his forearm with her hand.

They'd passed the Witch and Devil and Becky felt her husband suddenly shudder.

'Don't try to hide your feelings,' she said soothingly. 'It's usually better just to get it all off your chest.'

Michael turned to face her and there were tears in his eyes.

'My father was a hard man,' he said. 'A very hard man. I don't think he ever loved me. I don't think he even really knew me.'

'Go on,' Becky said, stroking his hand. 'Let it all out.'

'I don't think I knew him, either,' Michael continued. 'We were connected by an accident of birth, but we were never more than two strangers living under the same roof.'

'That happens,' Becky said sympathetically. 'And more often than you'd imagine.'

'And yet I miss him,' Michael told her. 'He's only been dead for an hour, and I miss him already.'

'He was your dad, when all's said and done,' Becky agreed.

Michael lapsed into silence again. Becky wondered whether she should try to keep him talking. No, she decided, it was probably best to leave him alone – even though that set her free to wander reluctantly through her own emotional jungle.

She thought back to what she'd heard the bandsman say just as they were leaving the church.

'So his father's dead, is he? Well, that's buggered up their big night for a start, hasn't it?'

Yes, Becky agreed silently. That's buggered our big night, all right.

Weighed down by his grief, there was little chance that Michael would come to her that night, little chance that he would make love to her – as his brother had done so many times before.

And she was not sure whether she was sorry or relieved.

CHAPTER TWENTY-ONE

Michael Worrell sat at one side of the desk. Richard Worrell — looking very proprietary and flanked on his right by Horace Crimp — sat at the other.

'You're very lucky Father died when he did, you know,' Richard said. 'Had he lived any longer he would undoubtedly have cut you out of his will.'

'Have you no respect for the dead?' Michael asked angrily. 'We've only just buried the man, for God's sake!'

'Yes, and a very nice funeral it was,' Richard said. 'Very touching. But life goes on, doesn't it? Now, would you like me to tell you a second reason why you're lucky?'

Michael stood up.

'I'm not going to listen to any more of this,' he told his older brother.

He was almost at the door when Richard said, 'The second reason you're lucky is that I'm about to make you a comparatively rich man by buying all your shares off you.'

Michael whirled round.

'Buy my shares?' he asked. 'Is that some kind of joke?'

'No joke,' Richard said, almost lazily.

'Do you really think I'd give up my right to have a say in how Worrell's is run?' Michael demanded. 'And what can make you imagine, even for a second, that I'd leave the fate of the company, and all the people who work in it, to your mercy?'

Richard laughed. 'Too late, Michael, always too late,' he said. 'With or without your shares, you will have no say in running the company. The best you can hope for from your holdings is a dividend. That is, if the company pays one — and I may decide it doesn't.'

'*You* may decide!' Michael said. 'What right have you to decide?'

'Every right in the world,' Richard told him. 'I am the majority share holder.'

'The Quinn Estate has more shares than anyone else,' Michael said. 'Even together, we only just out-vote it.'

'Wrong again,' Richard chuckled. He picked up a wad of share certificates from the desk and waved them in the air. 'These *did* belong to the Quinn Estate, but now they're mine.'

Michael strode rapidly across the room and snatched the certificates away from his brother.

'Oh, they're genuine enough,' Richard said as Michael started to examine them.

'How did you get your hands on them?' Michael demanded.

'I bought them.'

'Using what as money?'

'That's really no concern of yours, is it?' Richard asked. 'But if it will make you feel any happier, let us just say I made some lucky bets at the races.'

'You stole it!' Michael said, realizing that there could be no other explanation. 'You stole it from the company.'

'Isn't what my brother said libel, Mr Crimp?' Richard asked.

'Slander, sir,' Horace Crimp replied. 'For it to be libel, he would have to write it down.'

'Slander, then,' Richard agreed. 'You see, my dear brother, even if what you say were true, you'd never be able to prove it.'

'The books ...'

'Father burnt the books just before he died. We found the remains of several ledgers in his fireplace — totally indecipherable.'

'Why should Father have burned the books?' Michael asked grimly.

'There you have me,' Richard said. 'From a letter which has recently come into my possession, I know that he ordered the book-keeper to take all the ledgers to him last week. From

338

questioning the servants, I know that the books were still in his room an hour before he died. But what made him burn them some time in that last sixty minutes of his life? Who can say? Who can ever hope to fathom the mind of a dying man?'

It hadn't been a dying man but very much a live one who had burned the books, Michael thought. Yet what was the point in saying that now? He could no more prove that Richard had destroyed the evidence than he could prove that there had been evidence to destroy in the first place.

'I could plough all the profit we make back into the business,' Richard continued, 'so that you'd never see a penny of income from them. I, on the other hand, would meanwhile be living high on the fat salary I'd voted myself. Sell me the shares, Michael. You really don't have any other choice.'

His brother might be morally in the wrong, Michael thought, but his logic was irrefutably right.

'How much are you offering me?' he asked.

Richard reached into his drawer, took out a cheque and handed it to his brother.

'This much,' he said.

Michael read the figure on the cheque. It seemed fair — almost generous.

'We need to discuss how you'll pay for my share of the house and grounds, too,' he said. 'Assuming you still want to live there.'

'You don't understand,' Richard told him. 'With this one cheque, I am buying you out of my life. With this one cheque, I get the works, the house and the grounds — everything. This is all you get, Michael — there won't be any more.'

'There's a heat out on the Oil Rivers the like of which you've never known,' Jack said. 'A sticky heat, so that you never feel clean even when you've just doused yourself in water. Sometimes you find yourself praying for a breeze — only when it finally comes you're sorry you ever asked for it, because it just seems to make things worse.'

'And are there clockadiles in the river, Uncle Jack?' asked Thelma, Eunice's eldest.

'Hundreds of them,' Jack told her.

'What are they like?'

'Great big slimy things. Man-eaters. Sometimes, in the dead of night, they come crawling and slithering up the bank and right into the village. Then you have to watch out because they'll have you,' – he clapped his hands together – 'as quickly as that.'

Thelma shuddered.

'Be careful you don't frighten her too much,' Becky warned.

But Thelma appeared to be quite enjoying being frightened – just as her Auntie Becky had done at her age.

'Have you ever seen one yourself, Uncle Jack?' she asked.

'All the time,' he told her. 'They lie in the river, just like logs. Sometimes the natives think they *are* logs and swim up to them. And, my goodness, that's the last you see of that particular nigger.'

'I mean, have you ever seen one close to,' Thelma persisted.

'I should say I have,' Jack replied. 'I even shot one once.'

'You're just making up stories now,' Becky protested.

'I'll swear I'm not,' her brother replied. 'There was one big brute which was terrorizing this village I was trading with. He liked babies especially, did this old croc – carried off two piccaninnies in just one week. Anyway, the villagers asked me to help them, and I was glad to oblige. So one night I tethered this goat on the edge of the village and hid behind some bushes. It was about midnight when he came slithering along. He never took his eyes off the goat for a second, and you could see his mouth was fair watering at the thought of clamping his choppers round it. Anyway, I waited until he was no more than a few yards away from me, then I shot him – right between the eyes.'

'You'd killed him!' Thelma said, wide-eyed.

'That's what I thought at first,' Jack told her, 'but I hadn't. He just kept on coming, only now he was looking angry – and it was me, not the goat, that he was heading for.'

'What did you do?' Becky asked.

'I thought of making a run for it,' Jack admitted, 'but I wasn't all that sure which of us could move faster. So I just stayed where I was and kept pumping bullets into him.'

'But you managed to kill him in the end, didn't you?' Becky asked breathlessly.

Jack laughed. 'No,' he said. 'The old bugger ate me! Of course I managed to kill him – or I wouldn't be here to tell the tale. But it was a close thing. He couldn't have been more than a couple of feet from me when he finally dropped, and by then his head looked like a colander. And although I didn't know it at the time, there was worse yet to come.'

'What could be worse than facing a crocodile?' Becky wondered.

'Eating one,' Jack said.

'I beg your pardon.'

'Well, you see, the niggers went wild when they saw what I'd done. Singing and dancing all over the place, they were. Then somebody brought out a big jar of palm wine. Well, I had to stop and have a drink, didn't I?'

'Of course you did,' Becky replied. 'It would have been rude not to – even for a teetotaller like you.'

'Exactly,' Jack grinned. 'Anyway, I couldn't see it going on, but while I was drinking with some of them, the others were skinning the croc and roasting the meat over a fire. I noticed there was a funny smell in the air, but I had no idea what they were actually doing until the chief's daughter came up to me with this wooden platter of cooked croc.'

'You didn't eat it, did you, Uncle Jack?' Thelma asked, pulling a long, disgusted face.

'I wasn't going to,' Jack confessed, 'but then the chief explained to me this was the heart and that by eating it, the croc's strength would pass into me.'

'You didn't believe that yourself, did you?' Becky said.

'Well, of course not,' Jack replied. 'But it was a great honour to be given the heart, you see, so I couldn't refuse.'

'And what did it taste like?' Thelma wanted to know.

'Like old boots dipped in cow dung,' Jack told her.

Mary, who had been dollying in the wash-house, now appeared at the kitchen door.

'Better give you a quick scrub before your mother comes to pick you up,' she told her granddaughter.

'Uncle Jack ate a whole clockadile's heart, Nana,' Thelma said.

'Did he now?' her grandmother replied. 'That is nice. But if I don't get you washed soon your mam'll play merry hell with me. So you'd better look sharp, hadn't you, young lady?'

Thelma rose reluctantly to her feet and followed her grandmother to the wash-house.

'Was that true?' Becky asked her brother.

'Was what true?'

'About the crocodile.'

'Well of course it was true! You don't think your brother — Honest Jack — would ever lie to you, do you?'

'The Oil Rivers seems to be a very dangerous place,' Becky mused.

'They're all right if you're careful,' Jack said.

'But you're not careful, are you?' his sister demanded. 'You do mad things like going after crocodiles. Why risk your life like that when you don't have to, Jack?'

'Listen, there's good and bad among the niggers like there is with anybody else,' her brother said, 'but on the whole, a friendlier bunch of people you couldn't hope to meet. And yet the way some of the other merchants treat them almost makes me ashamed of being white. So if I can help them out occasionally, like killing a croc that's eating their babies, then I'm glad to do it.'

'When do you go back?' Becky asked.

'Day after tomorrow.'

'Does it have to be so soon?'

'The steamer's not making any money while it's tied up,' Jack said, 'and there's only one feller I'd trust to take it up-river — and that's me.'

'But you will try not to take too many risks when you go back, won't you?' Becky urged.

'You'll never change, will you, our Becky?' Jack asked with a smile. 'Always fretting about how everybody else in the family is getting on. Well, you're married now, and your first obligation is to mither the life out of that husband of yours. Where is he, by the way?'

'I don't know,' Becky admitted.

They'd spoken briefly during his father's funeral, but other than that she hadn't seen him since the wedding carriage had dropped him off outside Peak House three days earlier.

'You go back to your parents' home,' he'd told her. 'I'll come for you when I've got all this cleared up.'

'I'm your wife,' she protested. 'My place is by your side.'

'I don't want you involved in any of this,' he said firmly.

Involved in *this* or involved *with* Richard? she'd wondered. But like the obedient wife she'd so recently promised to be, she'd gone back to her parents' house to wait on his pleasure.

'Speak of the devil,' Jack said, bumping her back to the present.

Becky looked up and saw her husband standing in the back yard and signalling her.

'Why doesn't he come straight in?' Jack asked. 'It's not as if he has to wait for an invitation – he's family now.'

'I don't think he *wants* to come in,' Becky said worriedly.

She stood up, took off her pinny and joined her husband in the yard.

'Let's go for a walk,' Michael said. 'We've a lot to talk about.'

Their walk took them up the cart road. From the urgency of the way he had spoken in the back yard, Becky had expected her husband to tell her what was on his mind immediately, yet he chose to be silent and she was reluctant to push him.

Past the Marston Old Mine they went, along the track leading to the squat cottages which housed the mine workers. They came to a halt at Burns Bridge and stood looking back down the canal at the village of Marston and the smoking chimneys which dominated it – Worrell's chimneys.

'I've just sold out my entire holdings in the company to my brother,' Michael said suddenly. 'And not just the company. The house, the stables, it's all his — lock, stock and barrel.'

Because of her? Becky wondered, her eyes still fixed on the chimneys. Because the less *he* was involved in Worrell's, the less *she'd* get to see of Richard?

She switched her gaze from the village to her husband.

'Am I to be told why?' she asked.

'Of course,' Michael replied. 'I did it because I had no choice. For years Richard has been scheming to force me out — and now he's finally succeeded.'

Richard wouldn't have given in so easily, Becky thought. Richard would have fought back to the bitter bloody end.

'You think Richard frightens me, don't you?' Michael demanded.

She'd angered him, she saw. For only the second time in their relationship, she'd really angered him. And she'd never meant to. It wasn't his fault Richard had beaten him. Michael could never be like his brother — and in many ways she was glad of it.

'Isn't that what you think?' Michael asked, his rage growing by the second.

'He scares *me*,' Becky admitted, avoiding his questions.

And not the least because, if he came to her now, she was not sure she could resist him.

'I've been fighting Richard for most of my life,' Michael told her, 'and usually the odds have been weighed against me. But my biggest fear has never been that I'll lose — it's been that I'll win by becoming another Richard, by learning to fight dirtily, as he does.'

Yes, Becky thought, Richard did fight dirtily. Even when he'd been her knight errant, the day of the circus, he'd been armed with a sword stick and the young thug had had nothing but his bare hands to defend himself with. Yet did that make Richard a coward — or merely clever? She didn't know.

'I could have spent hours — days — arguing with him,' Michael said, 'but the result would have been exactly the same.

I saw right from the start that this battle was lost and I'd be far better conserving my strength for next time.'

Becky prised a small stone from the mortar on the parapet and threw it into the canal. She watched as it made a series of ever-widening circles. And then the water was smooth again, as if the pebble had never been.

'What do you mean — next time?' she asked her husband. 'Richard has complete control of Worrell's now — you said so yourself. How can there possibly be a next time?'

'I want to go into business on my own,' Michael said fiercely. 'I want to set up in direct competition with my brother.'

'You mean, you want to get even with him for what he's done to you,' Becky said.

'By God — yes!' Michael agreed. 'But there's a lot more to it than that. Do you know what Richard sees when he looks at the world?'

'Tell me,' Becky said quietly.

'He sees nothing but greed and brutishness.'

'And what do you see?' Becky asked.

'I can see some of the same — I'd be a fool not to. But I can also find patches of hope and decency. And that's something to build on. I want to prove that brutishness only comes from brutality. I want to run a factory full of people who are treated like human beings.'

Becky looked at her husband in amazement. She'd thought she'd got to know him well during all the bicycle rides they'd taken together, but now she was coming to see that she hadn't even scratched the surface.

'Do you understand what I'm saying?' Michael asked.

'You want to know who's been living a lie — you or your brother,' Becky said.

Michael nodded. 'Yes, that's what I want.'

'And what if it's you?'

'If it's me, then Richard will go on being more and more successful, and we'll end up penniless,' Michael told her.

'Are you sure you're doing the right thing?' Becky asked.

'As sure as I am that I love you,' Michael replied.

Becky turned away from him. She wished that when Michael said he loved her, she could tell him that she loved him in return. But it wouldn't be true – and she had too much respect for him to lie.

She felt Michael's hand on her shoulder, turning her to face him once more.

'I won't pretend that opening a business is the only choice we have,' her husband said. 'Richard may have cheated me out of most of my inheritance, but even with the money we've got left, we could probably manage to live in modest comfort for a good few years. And if that's what will make you happy, then that's what we'll do.'

'What you're saying is, we don't have to work if we don't want to,' Becky said.

'Exactly.'

Becky remembered her one real holiday – her day trip to Blackpool. How the air had tasted! How the sand had felt between her toes when she'd paddled in the sea! God, she'd adored it! And what her husband was offering her now was the prospect of a future which was nothing but *one long holiday*. Even the idea of it was enough to make her feel giddy.

Yet would that sort of life really suit Michael? Could he ever be really happy, weighed down by the knowledge that he'd fled from the field of battle and left Richard the victor by default.

'Well, what's it to be?' Michael asked.

'You mean, it really is my choice?'

'It really is your choice.'

Becky prised another pebble free, threw it into the canal and watched it sink – soon without trace – as the previous one had done.

You only get one shot at life, she thought. One shot, and then – like that pebble – it's as if you'd never been. So make the best out of it, girl!

'Do you need more time to think it over?' Michael asked.

'No,' Becky said. 'I've already made up mind. I've never

had the chance of being a boss's wife before, and I think I'd like to give it a try.'

Michael flung his arms around her and hugged her to him.

'You're a wonder,' he said. 'A real wonder.'

'Get away with you,' Becky replied, embarrassed by his praise.

'A real wonder,' he repeated.

It felt good to be in his arms. He was a strong man, she thought as his muscles pressed hard against her, as strong as Richard. She wondered why she had never realized that before – why she had always seen Richard as physically powerful, yet never observed the same quality in his brother. Perhaps it was simply because in everything he did, Richard seemed to flaunt his strength, while with Michael there was always a sense of holding back.

'Mam'll have supper on the table soon,' she said, 'so we'd better be heading back.'

Michael released his grip on her.

'Yes, we'd better be heading back,' he agreed. 'It'd never do to get on the bad side of my mother-in-law only three days after the wedding.'

After living in a grand house all his life, it must have been strange for Michael to spend the evening in a humble terraced cottage, Becky thought. Yet he seemed to take to it naturally – chatting with Jack about life on the Oil Rivers, complimenting Mam on the pie she'd made in his honour, helping Dad in the shop as if the fish and chip business really interested him.

But now the evening was over, and they were making their way up the narrow stairs which led to Becky's bedroom.

How should I behave? Becky wondered in a panic. What does he expect from me?

What he *should* have been expecting was a blushing bride, new to the ways of love – but they were both all too well aware that Becky was anything but.

How she wished that the stairs to her bedroom went on for ever, that instead of getting there in just a few seconds, they could keep on climbing – climbing all night long.

347

They reached the door. Becky pushed it open and led Michael into her bedroom.

'Well, this is it,' she said awkwardly as she placed the oil lamp on her bedside table.

'We'll start looking for a house of our own in the morning,' Michael promised.

'Good,' Becky said.

But all the time she was thinking, *Tell me what you want me to be, Michael. Tell me, and I'll do my best to be it.*

'Where shall I put my clothes?' Michael asked.

'Use the chair,' Becky told him.

He shed his jacket and draped it over the chair.

Richard would have undressed me first, she thought. *Richard wouldn't have been able to hold himself back.*

Damn Richard! Damn Richard to hell!

Michael took off his waistcoat, and then his tie. Becky stood as still as a statue.

'Would you feel more comfortable if I turned out the light before you undressed?' Michael asked.

'Yes ... No ... I don't know.'

What do you want me to say, Michael!

Michael reached across, turned the wheel on the oil lamp, and blacked out the room.

They took off their clothes in complete darkness, and — apart from their breathing and the rustling of the fabric — in complete silence. Then Becky heard the bed creak as Michael got into it, and, after pulling her nightdress over her head, she groped her way across the room to join him.

He had brought no nightshirt, and as she slipped into the bed beside him she realized that he was completely naked.

What should she do now? Becky wondered. If it had been Richard in bed with her she would have taken him in her arms, run her fingers over his hard muscles, kissed his neck ...

But it was Michael, not Richard. Michael, the husband she was learning more about every day, yet who she still hardly knew.

What would *he* feel if she did to him what she'd done to

348

Richard? Wouldn't it be as good as saying: *See what I can do! Your brother taught me this!*

She felt her body tense until she was as stiff as a board.

'We can't change the past by pretending it never happened,' Michael said softly.

'I don't know what you mean,' Becky replied, her panic and confusion multiplying with every breath she took.

'Everything that's happened to us has been a part of making us what we are,' Michael said. 'And my brother is a part of what happened to you.'

'I know,' Becky said helplessly. 'But I didn't think . . .'

'No — don't think,' Michael told her. 'It's you I fell in love with — not some idea of what I'd *like* you to be. So, for God's sake, Becky, be yourself — *whatever* that is!'

She was no longer sure she had a self — couldn't work out how she would have acted without the shadow of Richard hanging over them.

'I've waited a long time for you, Becky, and I can wait a little longer if I have to,' Michael said soothingly. 'If you just want to go to sleep, that's all right.'

'No,' Becky said. 'I don't just want to go to sleep.'

She reached over and ran her fingers over shoulder muscles which were just as hard — just as powerful — as Richard's had ever been.

'Make love to me, Michael,' she said.

CHAPTER TWENTY-TWO

Becky and Michael walked hand in hand along the road to Dunkirk. It was a crisp day in early December. Hoar frost clung to the few miserable clumps of grass which had sprouted on the barren land, and the puddles which lay between these clumps were covered with a thin layer of ice. Several sparrows sat hunched on telegraph poles, ruffling their feathers against the cold, but a robin red-breast circled the area just once, and then flew off in search of more rewarding pastures.

'I remember the first time I came across here,' Becky said. 'It was with Old Gilbert Bowyer.'

'Gilbert Bowyer!' Michael exclaimed. 'But he was the murderer!'

'Gilbert wasn't a murderer,' Becky said. 'He was just a sweet old man who happened to kill someone who'd treated him very badly.'

'Even so, I'm not sure that I like the idea that you once went walking with him,' Michael told her.

Becky laughed.

'Anyway,' she continued, 'we went to see this house being moved in Northwich. And on the way there he told me about a crack appearing in this road which was so big that the mail coach fell into it. He wasn't just spinning me a line, was he?'

'No, that really happened,' Michael said.

'Well, it scared me so much that I kept expecting new cracks to appear. And I must have looked worried, because Old Gilbert bought me some cream cakes on the way back — to take my mind off it, I think.'

'I'll buy you some cakes when we've seen the mine,' Michael promised.

Becky laughed again. 'Go on with you,' she said. 'I'm a

married lady now. What would I be wanting with cream cakes?'

'Please yourself,' Michael replied with mock indifference.

'I suppose just *one* might be quite nice,' Becky conceded.

A hooter sounded in the distance, and looking in its general direction, Becky saw a steam boat moored next to one of the salt works on the edge of Witton Flashes.

'Does that mean it's loaded with salt and ready to go?' Becky asked.

'Yes,' Michael replied. 'Half an hour from now it'll be on the River Weaver, and before the day's out it should be docking in Liverpool.'

Liverpool, Becky thought, the gateway to the wider world – the gateway through which her dear, dear brother Jack had passed only a fortnight earlier. She wished he'd never gone, but she supposed that just as Michael felt compelled to set up in business on his own, so Jack had had to follow what was driving him on, too.

'Is the mine you're interested in near the Flashes?' Becky asked.

'No,' Michael said. 'It's on the other side of the road.'

Becky turned to her left and surveyed the scene. It was a desolate view. There were no trees, only half a dozen small salt mines, whose tall chimneys belched out smoke and towered like giants over the squat brick buildings which huddled round them.

Between the salt mines were water-filled craters – rock-pits, they were called locally. Some of them were quite small, but others occupied at least an acre. These, too, had once been working salt mines, but Nature had caused them to collapse and reclaimed them for herself.

It was a landscape from hell, Becky thought, and wondered which of these infernal structures her husband had selected as the foundation stone of his business empire.

'It's over there,' Michael said, pointing in the distance to the one mine which was not pouring out filth into the atmosphere.

They climbed down the embankment and made their way

over the rough ground. The closer they got to the mine the more Becky could see of it. And the more she could see – the more depressed she became.

The brickwork on the chimney was crumbling and weeds grew from the cracks in the mortar. Some bird, probably a crow, had built a nest at the top of the stack, but from the state of the nest it was plain that even this black scavenger had long since abandoned the mine.

Nor were the rest of the buildings in any better shape. The glass in the workshop windows was broken, slates were missing from the roofs and much of the timber work seemed to have been plundered for firewood. Even the engine which hauled the tubs up and down the shaft had rusted.

'Well,' Michael said, 'what do you think?'

What did she think?

She was shocked!

She was dismayed!

'It looks ... er ... a little run-down,' she said.

'It's always much cheaper to buy a business which has gone to pot rather than to try and take over one which is making a steady profit,' Michael told her.

It should be more than just cheaper, Becky thought. The owner should be giving it away – and glad to get it off his hands even at that price! Did Michael really think he could make a go of this place?

'When was the mine last worked?' Becky asked. 'I'd say ten years ago, at least.'

'Oh, at least,' Michael readily agreed. 'In fact, I think it's closer to twelve years ago that the place was flooded.'

So the mine wasn't just unworked, it was probably unworkable. Better and better! Becky was glad that she still had her skills as a dressmaker to keep food coming to the table.

'You're planning to pump it dry, are you?' she asked.

'Eventually,' Michael said, 'but not, I hope, for a long time yet.'

So what did he expect his miners to do – work under water? Becky gazed into her husband's eyes. He seemed rational enough, but could anyone contemplating – with such obvious relish – the prospect of opening Britain's first underwater mine, really have all his marbles?

'I don't want you to rush into anything, my dear,' she said gently. 'Perhaps we should go away for a few weeks. You'll see things more clearly when you've had a rest.'

'But I don't need a rest,' Michael protested. 'And anyway, what particular part of my thinking do you consider unclear?'

'Well, for a start,' Becky said carefully, 'if the water could have been pumped out and the mine worked again, why didn't the owners do it themselves?'

For a moment, Michael was stunned, then he threw back his head and laughed loudly.

'Pumping out water!' he said, unable to contain his amusement. 'You're looking at the whole thing upside down. What you're seeing is a flooded rock salt mine, isn't it?'

'And what do you see?' Becky asked.

'I see a huge reservoir of brine!' Michael answered.

Of course! Becky thought. Michael didn't know that much about mining, but there wasn't a great deal you could teach him about brine extraction.

'You're very clever, aren't you?' she said admiringly.

'I'm going to do more than just make the salt myself,' Michael told her.

'More? How can you do more?'

'I've been talking to the owners of some of the smaller works around Marston and Wincham,' Michael explained. 'They're very worried that their brine reserves are dropping. And what's the point of having the pans and all the other equipment if you haven't got the basic raw material?'

'That's true enough,' Becky agreed.

'So they have two choices. They can either close down their works and build new ones closer to fresh supplies of brine – or they can have the brine come to them.'

'I don't understand,' Becky said.

'Pipelines,' Michael said. 'I could pump the brine they need from here to their works, they'd do the extraction and we'd split the profits.'

And to think that only a few moments earlier she'd been convinced he was losing his mind!

'You've already decided to buy, haven't you?' Becky said.

'Not yet. First, I've got to talk to that chap there,' Michael said, pointing to a round man in a heavy tweed suit who was just emerging from behind one of the buildings. 'But if his report is favourable, I very well might.'

The round man reached them and held out a podgy hand to Michael.

'This is Mr Brock,' Michael said. 'He's a geologist.'

The round man raised his hat to Becky.

'I've completed my survey, Mr Worrell,' he said.

'And what are your conclusions?' Michael asked.

'As you probably know there are two types of mines in this area,' the geologist said. 'The first type, the top-rock mines, are located about forty yards below the surface, in a bed of salt which is usually about twenty-five yards thick. Below the top-rock mines is a layer of clay, approximately ten yards deep, and then we come to the bottom-rock mines. Which means, if you think about it, Mr Worrell, that of the first one hundred and fifteen yards below the surface, fifty have been hollowed out.'

'Go on,' Michael said.

'None of this matters as long as there are salt pillars to hold up the roofs,' Brock continued. 'But when a mine gets flooded, the water will eat those pillars away. Once that happens, of course, the thin salt crust in the mine's roof is no longer able to support the superincumbent earth above, and thus, the ground subsides.'

'And some of the mines are interconnected,' Michael said thoughtfully, 'so what affects one will inevitably affect the others.'

'Exactly,' Brock agreed.

'But what are the chances of that happening in the near future?' Michael asked.

'It is always difficult to be absolutely accurate in matters of this nature,' Brock told him. 'After all, we geologists work

354

with time scales of hundreds of thousands of years, but if you pushed me I would estimate that the ground in this area should be relatively stable for at least the next fifteen or twenty years.'

'Which is easily long enough to justify the investment,' Michael said. 'It looks like we're back in the salt business, Becky.'

Michael had more questions for the geologist, questions which soon became so technical that Becky was quite out of her depth.

'I think I'll go for a walk,' she told her husband.

'I'm sorry,' Michael said. 'This must be very boring for you.'

'It is,' Becky admitted, grinning. 'But I'd like to have a walk round, anyway. After all, this will soon be your kingdom, and *somebody* has to decide where to hang the lace curtains.'

Michael laughed and kissed her on the forehead.

'We won't be much longer,' he promised.

Becky wandered among the ramshackle buildings, trying her best to estimate what it would take to restore them to working order. It seemed a formidable task – but she was sure that Michael was up to it.

Going beyond the works she crossed a stretch of rough ground, walked past several rock-pits and eventually came to a halt at Wincham Brook.

As she looked down into the water she saw an autumn leaf, helplessly caught in the current, being dragged – whether it liked it or not – towards Witton Flash and from there to the River Weaver and the mighty Mersey.

Making love with Richard had been a little like being a leaf, she thought – though she hadn't realized it at the time. His passion was a raging torrent which picked you up and swept you along to manage as best you could.

That was not Michael's way at all. Michael was passionate, there was no doubting that, yet he also seemed to be more in control than his brother – aware of not only where *he* was going, but also of the fact that he was taking her with him. It was hard to put it into words — and she felt daft even trying — but when she made love with Michael, it was like they were two streams of equal force which had converged and were flowing on much stronger and more forcefully because they were together.

Becky turned towards the derelict works and saw Michael was waving that it was time to go. Smiling to herself, she began to walk back to where her husband was waiting for her.

When Chivers came into the library to inform him that his expected visitor had arrived, Richard Worrell was in the last stages of making arrangements for his trip.

'Tell him to wait outside,' Richard snapped. 'I'll ring when I'm ready to see him.'

He was not in the best of moods — and with good reason. Hortense had flatly insisted that they should be married in her family home rather than at his.

'The Berkshire Sudleys would travel to Hertfordshire for the wedding,' she'd told him, 'but you couldn't really expect them to come up here, now could you?'

He supposed not, but he still did not like her attitude. Once they were married, once she'd presented him with a son and heir, then he'd show her that he was just as much master of Peak House as he was of Worrell's Salt Works. He'd take a horse-whip to her if need be — although he suspected she might rather enjoy that.

The idea of horse-whips naturally turned his mind to the party he'd arranged for himself in his favourite Liverpool brothel. What a send-off that would be! What a spectacular farewell to bachelorhood!

Not that he intended to change his habits much once he was married, he thought. Being unfaithful to his wife had always been part of his plan. But the plan had also included Becky Taylor — Becky *Worrell* — and for the moment that didn't look possible.

'But *only* for the moment,' he said aloud.

Michael could have taken the money he got from his share

of the works and gone away. If he had done, then both he and Becky would have been beyond his older brother's power. Yet the fool had decided to stay instead, thus giving Richard another chance both to destroy him and to get his hands on Becky once more.

Richard Worrell pulled at the bell-cord and his visitor was ushered in. He was a small, round man who, despite his university education, looked very uneasy when surrounded by the opulence of the library.

'Well, have you done it?' Richard demanded, not bothering to invite the other man to sit down.

'I gave your brother a verbal report less than an hour ago,' the visitor replied.

'What exactly did you tell him?'

'What we agreed. That in my professional opinion there should be no trouble for the next fifteen or twenty years.'

'Whereas, your *real* professional opinion is . . .?'

'That everything's hanging by a thread, and that thread could snap at any time.'

'And what did my brother say to that?'

'He said he was back in the salt business.'

Richard chuckled. 'Why, so he is,' he said, 'but hopefully not for long.'

He waved his hand in a gesture of dismissal.

'My money, sir,' Brock said feebly.

'Go and see Horace Crimp,' Richard told him. 'He's the one who handles my bribery and corruption.'

Bad weather prevented much being done to Michael's new purchase during January and February, but by the middle of March work was well under way. Roofs were being restored and windows and doors replaced. The nest had been cleaned from the top of the chimney stack and the brickwork repaired.

'I'm keeping the section in front of the office for a garden,' Michael told his wife.

'A garden!' Becky said. 'In the middle of this wasteland?'

'It's precisely because it's a wasteland that I'm having the garden made,' her husband told her. 'I've been talking to the chap who makes Sunlight Soap in Warrington. Bill Lever, his name is. He thinks that workers perform better when their surroundings are pleasant. He says that when he can afford it, he's going to build a complete model town for his workers to live in.'

'And is that your plan, too?' Becky teased. 'Worrelltown?'

'Not quite,' Michael laughed. 'But a few flowers don't cost much, and they're good business sense.'

'Oh, I'm sure they are,' Becky mocked him. 'Very good business sense.'

Cedric Rathbone, Tom Jennings and Brian O'Reilly stood in front of Michael's new desk in Michael's newly completed office.

'There are seats behind you, if you want them,' Michael said.

'That's very kind of you, Mr Wo ...' Brian O'Reilly began.

'We'd prefer to stand,' Cedric Rathbone cut in. 'What's all this about? Why are we here?'

'My brother sacked you for union activity, didn't he?' Michael said. 'What have you been doing since?'

'Casual work, mostly,' Tom Jennings said.

'It's all we can get, Sir,' Brian O'Reilly added candidly. 'Since Mr Richard's put the word out about us, none of the other salt companies are willing to risk taking us on.'

'Bastard!' Cedric Rathbone muttered to himself.

'What if I offered you a job?' Michael asked.

'Offer us a job!' Rathbone snorted.

'Why not?' Michael asked mildly.

'We may have lost our jobs over the union,' Cedric Rathbone said, 'but I still think it's a good thing – the more so since I've found out what it's like to be without work most of the time. If you took us on, I couldn't guarantee we wouldn't try to get unionized again.'

'I admire your honesty,' Michael told him. 'You join the

union if you want to, but I promise you, you'll find conditions here will already be better than the ones your union is agitating for.'

'What's the catch?' Cedric Rathbone asked suspiciously.

'If I treat you fairly I expect to be treated fairly in return,' Michael said. 'No swinging the lead, no fiddles. An honest day's work for an honest day's pay.'

'Sounds right to me,' Tom Jennings said.

'It'd be an honour to work for you, Sir,' Brian O'Reilly said.

'There's one more thing,' Michael cautioned them. 'Philip Taylor's coming out of gaol next month – and I'm going to offer him a job.'

'That little sod!' Cedric Rathbone said. 'Well, I'll not work with the bugger, for one.'

'That's up to you,' Michael told him. 'You all got a rough deal from my brother, but if you're asking me to make a choice between you and a member of my wife's family, then I'm going to have to choose family every time.'

Tom Jennings saw Cedric Rathbone's wiry body tense as he'd seen it tense so many times in the past when there was about to be trouble.

'Easy, lad,' Jennings said.

'He spied on us,' Rathbone said tightly. 'We took him in as one of our own, and he spied on us.'

'I'm not excusing him,' Michael said, 'and I'm not offering him a soft option. He's got a past to work off, and if he does take a job with me he'll start right at the bottom.'

'Start right at the bottom!' Rathbone said belligerently. 'And how long will he stay there?'

'It'll be the same for him as it'll be for the rest of you,' Michael said. 'He'll stay where he is until he's proved he deserves better.'

'I don't believe that!' Rathbone snorted.

'Let's get this straight right now,' Michael said. 'I've no intention of running my works like my brother runs his – as if it were some kind of penal colony – but I'm still going to be the gaffer. And that means you take my word and trust my judgement — or there'll be no place for you here.'

'Come on, Cedric,' Tom Jennings urged.

'Give it a try,' Brian O'Reilly pleaded.

Cedric Rathbone's body relaxed.

'Aye well, he was only a slip of a lad back then,' he said. 'I suppose we could give him one chance to show he's changed. But only one, mind.'

'One chance is all most of us get,' Michael said, glancing out of the window at his still-uncompleted works.

Becky looked up at the tall imposing gates, and shivered. Any minute now the small door in the base of the left-hand gate would swing open and her brother Philip — ex-company spy, ex-pornographer — would step out into the cold morning air.

She'd thought she would never survive her first visit to the prison, shortly after Philip had begun his sentence. The grim-faced expressions of the prison officers had chilled her to the bone and the look of desperation on the faces of some of the convicts had torn at her heart. She'd felt as if the high walls were closing in on her, as if bars were being built around her soul.

She'd been to see her brother several times since then, and though it had become a little easier to bear she had never been able to completely overcome the sensation of total hopelessness she'd experienced on that initial visit.

'I'd rather starve to death in freedom than be well fed in such a place as that,' she told herself over and over again.

Yet strangely enough, the prison had not affected Philip as badly as she'd feared it would. True, he had the unnatural pallor of a man denied the sunlight, but the place in no way seemed to have broken his spirit. If anything, it had given him confidence.

The small gate swung open, and suddenly Philip was standing there. Becky rushed over to him and flung her arms around his neck.

'It's good to have you back,' she sobbed. 'I've got a cab standing at the corner and we'll have you home in no time.'

Philip broke free of her embrace and looked around him.

'Where's everybody else?' he asked petulantly.

'This isn't exactly a victory parade, you know,' Becky told him, then, relenting, she added, 'I said I wanted to come alone. There's something I wanted to talk to you about.'

'Talk to me about?' Philip asked as they climbed into the waiting cab.

'Yes,' Becky said. 'But first of all, tell me about yourself. How are you feeling?'

Philip shrugged.

'All right,' he said. 'The nick's not such a bad place once you've learned the rules.'

'But aren't they very strict?' Becky asked, surprised at her weak brother's easy acceptance of the prison regime.

'I'm not talking Standing Orders,' Philip told her, almost contemptuously. 'I mean the real rules – the ones made by the men who actually run the pokey.'

'I don't quite follow you,' Becky said.

'You wouldn't,' her brother agreed. 'You'd have to have been in here to understand. Now, what was it you wanted to talk about that was so important you kept Mam and Dad away?'

'Michael wants to offer you a job,' Becky said.

'What sort of job?' Philip asked suspiciously.

'As a waller.'

'A waller! What sort of a job is that?'

'The sort of job you're qualified for,' Becky told him.

'But I'm a photographer,' Philip protested. 'I'm planning to set up my own studio.'

'Using what as money?' Becky asked.

Philip looked uncomfortable.

'I thought you and your rich husband would give it to me,' he said. 'Well, lend it to me till I get on me feet, anyway.'

'We can't,' Becky said.

'You mean, you won't!'

'I mean we can't,' Becky repeated. 'All the money's gone into the business. We're living in a terraced house not much different from Mam and Dad's, and even then, Michael's worrying about how we're going to pay the rent if the works doesn't open soon.'

'Huh!' Philip said in disbelief. 'Well, if you won't help me, I'll find somebody else who will. There must be loads of people who want to invest in a photographer's.'

'Things have changed while you've been in prison,' Becky warned him. 'Some American feller called Eastman has invented a new kind of camera – the Kodak, its name is. It's small, and anybody can use it. I think you'll find a lot of people who would have been your customers a few years ago are now taking their own pictures.'

Philip fell silent and did not speak again until they had reached the railway station. Then, as if a bright side to the whole situation had occurred to him, he suddenly appeared to perk up.

'Is Michael planning to produce just common salt, or will he be making fine as well?' he asked innocently.

'Why do you want to know?' Becky asked.

'Just taking an interest in the business,' Philip replied.

What could be the harm in telling him?

'He'll be making both common and fine,' Becky said.

'And where will he be sending the blocks, like?'

'Wherever there's a demand.'

'But some of it will be going abroad, won't it?'

'Yes,' Becky agreed. 'Some of it probably will be going abroad.'

'All right, then,' Philip said magnanimously. 'I'll give working for your husband a try.'

During the train journey to Northwich Becky found herself worrying about whether or not she had done the right thing.

On the one hand she had been right to argue that Philip had little choice but to accept the job – and as long as he was working for Michael, she could at least keep an eye on him.

On the other hand her first loyalty was to her husband now, and she was not sure it was such a good idea to bring someone like Philip into his business.

CHAPTER TWENTY-THREE

Becky walked some distance away from the works, then turned and looked round.

It's hard to believe that only a few months ago all them buildings were derelict, she thought.

Now the recently re-slated roofs glimmered in the bright sunshine and the freshly painted woodwork stood out from the newly pointed walls. Only the central chimney – which, for some reason, Michael had had shrouded in a green canvas – was hidden from her inspection.

The works would never be a beautiful place, she decided, not even with the flower garden – now in full bloom – in front of the office. But at least it no longer resembled a factory in hell, as it had when she'd first set her eyes on it.

A great deal had happened in the family since the beginning of the year, she thought. For a start, there was a chance they'd finally get a visit from her brother George.

'*The regiment's being transferred to Egypt,*' he had written in his last letter, '*and there's talk of us having some home leave before we take up our new posting. It'll be smashing to be with you all after so long.*'

Smashing, Becky agreed. Really smashing. All the family – apart from Jack – back together for once.

Even Philip looked as if he'd be there. She'd worried a lot about him in his first couple of weeks out of prison. She knew him of old, and he had a wanderlust which might grip him again at any time. Now her worries looked as if they'd been unfounded. He seemed to have settled down, and while it couldn't be said that he was burning with enthusiasm to work for Michael, he at least appeared reconciled to the idea.

Becky caught sight of a tall man wearing a new, knee-length

frock-coat, who was walking up and down in front of the works.

Michael – making a final close inspection of his little empire before the opening ceremony.

She turned around and her gaze fell on one of the rock pools. It was only a tiny one – scarcely more than a puddle – yet she was sure it hadn't been there the last time she'd passed this way.

But it must have been, she told herself.

After all, hadn't that geologist – Mr Brock, wasn't it? – assured them that there was no danger of subsidence in that area for another fifteen years?

Becky's stomach rumbled out a demand for food. She wasn't surprised. Mam had always insisted the children eat a big breakfast –eggs and bacon when they could afford it, plenty of bread and marg when they couldn't – and her body had got used to that. Yet for the past two or three mornings she'd felt too nauseous to eat any food at all – and once she'd actually been sick.

I must be run down, she thought.

That would also explain why her hair, which was normally so springy, had suddenly become lank and lifeless.

Her stomach complained again.

'After the ceremony,' she promised it. 'After the ceremony, there'll be loads to eat.'

Talking of which, if she didn't get back to the works soon she'd miss the whole thing and Michael would be angry with her.

She picked her way carefully across the rough ground, wondering as she went just why her husband had been so mysterious about the green canvas which shrouded the chimney.

She found Michael standing next to the smaller of the two marquees he'd had pitched. A number of carriages had already arrived and several others were just pulling up.

'Did we really need to make such a big show of it?' she asked.

'It's good business sense,' Michael told her. 'It'll make an impression on the owners of the other works, and if the day ever comes when their own brine runs out and they need to buy it from someone else, they'll remember my name and come to me.'

Ted Taylor wandered up to them, looking splendid in his Adelaide Mine Prize Brass Band uniform.

'The band's ready when you are, Sir,' he said.

'I'm back to being "Sir", am I?' Michael asked good-naturedly.

'When you're in my kitchen, drinking my tea, then you're Michael to me,' Taylor said with a broad smile, 'but when you're paying my band to play for your grand opening, then you're "Sir". That's the way it has to be – right, lad?'

'I suppose so,' Michael said with a grin.

'And as for you, Madam,' Taylor said, winking heavily at his daughter, 'your Mam was wondering if, when you've finished taking tea with the Mayor, you could find the time to slip into the other tent, where us lesser mortals will be having *our* tea.'

'I'll be there,' Becky promised.

As Ted Taylor went to rejoin his band, Michael consulted his watch.

'About another ten minutes,' he said. 'Are you nervous?'

'My stomach's full of butterflies,' Becky said.

Of course! That was why she hadn't been able to eat! That was the reason she'd been sick! She'd been nervous about the Grand Opening!

Well, thank heavens it was nothing more serious than that.

Philip Taylor had taken advantage of the fact that everyone else's attention was focused on the front of the works to slip his visitor in around the back.

'This is where we'll do it, Mr Leech,' he said when they'd reached the first of the fine pans. 'See them wooden tubs over there? That's what we'll use.'

Caspar Leech was a big man with a broken nose and piggy

eyes, and the frown which now filled his craggy face did nothing to improve his appearance.

'You're sure these blocks of salt are solid?' he demanded. 'You're sure there's no danger of the buggers falling apart before they get where they're going?'

'Trust me, Mr Leech,' Philip said earnestly – and not a little fearfully. 'I've been around salt all me life and I tell you, this'll work.'

'It'd better,' Leech told him. 'You're in the big time now, and you know what that means, don't you?'

'That I'll make a lot of money?' Philip asked hopefully.

Leech moved like lightning. One second he was standing some feet from Philip, the next one of his hands had Philip by the scruff of the neck and the other was waving an opened cut-throat razor in the young man's face.

'It means you'll be handling a lot of *my* money,' he snarled, 'or anyway things that are *worth* a lot of my money. It means that if you make a mistake I'll be badly out of pocket. And what will happen to you then?'

'You'll k ... kill me,' Philip stuttered.

'Yes – and it won't be that quick,' Leech said grimly. 'Next time you see one of your pals from Strangeways, ask him about Batty Pringle. Not very bright, old Batty. Thought he could double-cross me and get away with it. Well, they were fishing bits of him out of the canal for weeks. Am I getting through to you, lad?'

'Yes,' Philip said, half choked. 'Yes, I understand, Mr Leech.'

From in the distance came the sound of the Adelaide Mine Prize Brass Band striking up. Leech released his grip on Philip's neck and neatly pocketed his razor.

'You'd better get back before you're missed,' he said. 'And remember what I told you about not letting me down. I don't take excuses – I take it out of your hide instead.'

It was worth the risk, Philip told himself as he made his way back to the festivities. With all that money involved, it was well worth the risk.

*

Becky saw Cedric Rathbone walking towards where they were waiting. He was wearing his Sunday suit and looked more like a small businessman than a waller in a salt works.

'You asked me to tell you when the Mayor got here, Sir,' Rathbone said to Michael. 'His coach is just coming up now.'

Becky and Michael went to greet the Mayor and his Corporation, then led them onto the platform which had been constructed near the base of the central chimney stack.

From her elevated position Becky looked down on the scene. There were two enclosures. The first was for those people important enough to merit being entertained in the same marquee as the Mayor, yet not of sufficient eminence to share the platform with him. The second was for anyone else who had felt like responding to the blanket invitation Michael had issued to everyone in the area.

The second enclosure was full to bursting, and Becky recognized most of the faces in it.

'They've come because of you,' Michael whispered, seeing where his wife's gaze was falling.

'They've come because in my village you never turn down a free tea,' Becky replied.

But secretly, she was pleased.

Michael signalled that the band should stop playing once they reached the end of the tune, and when they did the Mayor stood up and turned to face his audience.

'It is always a great pleasure for me to open a new enterprise,' he said, 'especially when that enterprise is concerned with salt – the life-blood of our town ...'

Becky found herself fascinated by his chain of office. She supposed that from a ceremonial point of view it was impressive, but it was the sheer weight of the thing which really interested her.

It must be like having a big sack of bricks strung around your neck, she thought.

'... brought up in a salt family,' the Mayor droned on. 'Many of you will remember his father, the late Len Worrell ...'

If he leant forward just a little more, the chain would take over and pull him to the floor, Becky thought. For a second she felt the urge to reach forward and give the chain a tiny tug — just to test if her theory was right — but then she managed to banish the imp inside her and assume the expression of the respectable wife of a respectable businessman.

'. . . and so, without further ado, I declare this new salt works well and truly open,' the Mayor said.

Cedric Rathbone, who had been standing discreetly at the edge of the platform, now stepped forward and handed the Mayor the end of a rope. The Mayor pulled on it, and slowly, with a curious kind of grace, the canvas which covered the central chimney stack began to fall away.

There was loud applause from both the enclosures. But Becky did not clap. Instead, she stared with horror at the words which were written in bright white paint on the chimney:

M & R WORRELL & CO. LTD.

Michael had talked of being free of Richard. He'd told her he wanted to compete with his brother, to find out finally which of them was right. And what had he done instead? Gone into partnership with the last man in the world he should have had anything to do with!

'How could you do it?' she hissed angrily into her husband's ear.

'How could I do what?' Michael responded, sounding genuinely puzzled.

'How could you go into business with Richard?' Becky demanded.

'I haven't!' Michael protested.

'Then why is his name up there on the chimney?' Becky demanded.

'It isn't,' Michael replied.

The clapping had died down. The Mayor and his Corporation were looking at them curiously and even a few people in the enclosures had noticed that something was not quite right on the platform. But Becky didn't care what anyone else thought – she was furious with Michael and she didn't care at all!

'Not his name on the chimney!' she said. 'Come off it! I wasn't born yesterday. How many other "R Worrell's" are there in Northwich?'

It infuriated her even more that Michael was smiling as if he were really enjoying himself.

'How many other "R Worrell's" are there?' he asked. 'Why don't you think about it for a second – *Rebecca*.'

The people on the platform were looking distinctly uncomfortable and there were uneasy whispers below.

'Is it me!' Becky said incredulously. 'Does that "R" up there on the chimney belong to me?'

'As you said yourself, how many other "R Worrell's" are there in Northwich?' Michael asked her.

Oblivious to both the civic dignitaries sitting next to her and the crowd of villagers standing in the enclosure, Becky threw her arms around her husband's neck.

'I'm sorry I doubted you,' she said through her tears. 'I promise I'll never do it again.'

Though most of the people watching had no idea what was going on, they knew a good scene when they saw one, and as Becky hugged her husband, the clapping broke out again.

It had been a good do, everybody agreed later, a really good do.

'I th ... thought them sandwiches and cakes would never stop coming,' Harry Atherton said.

'And you got exactly the same food whether you were in the posh tent or eating with the rest of us,' Paddy O'Leary pointed out.

'You can believe that, if you like,' Not-Stopping Bracegirdle told her cronies in the best room, 'but if you ask me, the ham in them sandwiches we were served had never come off no pig.'

'Then where did it come from?' Dottie Curzon asked.

'Now how would I know?' Not-Stopping demanded. 'Probably off one of them foreign animals. A yak or summat.'

'Tasted like real ham to me,' Maggie Cross said.

'The number of times you've had real ham on your table, you wouldn't recognize it if it grunted at you,' Not-Stopping said sourly. 'And didn't that Becky Taylor-as-was make an exhibition of herself, throwing herself all over her husband like that.'

'I thought it was sweet,' Ma Fitton told her. 'It looked to me like she was really fond of him.'

'Really fond of him,' Not-Stopping scoffed. 'Course, I'd expect you to stick up for her, what with you having brought her into the world — as well as half the Royal Family.'

Whatever anyone else thought about it, for Becky the day of the grand opening of the works had simply been the happiest one in her whole life.

Richard Worrell had once linked their names in a heart on the bark of an oak tree — Michael had linked them on a factory chimney. Not one person in a hundred would have said Michael was the more romantic of the two.

But I know better, Becky thought.

Richard had used the heart as nothing more than a part of his cynical seduction of her. Michael, by his action, had said that it was not just his bed he wanted her to share, nor even just his home — he wanted her to be a partner in his whole life.

He had told her many times that he loved her, but she had never realized the depth of that love before. She hoped she was up to such a heavy responsibility.

CHAPTER TWENTY-FOUR

Richard Worrell padded along the corridor, a candle in his hand to light his way. The floor felt cold against his bare feet and the night breeze blew in through an open window, ruffling the folds in his nightshirt. He hated these long walks to his wife's bedroom, but better that — far better — than that she should have a room any closer to his.

Though he had never intended to be monogamous, he had — in the beginning — been prepared to gain at least part of his sexual satisfaction from his relations with his plain wife.

After all, he'd told himself, she may be ugly but her body's not bad — and you don't look at the mantelpiece when you're poking the fire.

Nothing like that had ever been part of Hortense's plan. Though she relished shows of affection in public, and welcomed a peck on the cheek in private, what went on in the bedroom was something to be endured, rather than enjoyed.

Whatever he did, he could not arouse her! Though he was sure he'd managed to excite every other woman he had ever gone to bed with, including the ones he had paid for, he could not arouse his own wife — and he would never forgive her for that.

It's like trying to make love to a corpse, he thought.

Worse! A corpse shows no disgust. A corpse does not emanate loathing for the act and — by extension — loathing for the person who is forcing that act upon it.

Richard pushed thoughts of what lay ahead of him to one side and turned his mind to other matters.

It had been two months since the Grand Opening of his brother's works. He'd read about the opening in *The Northwich Guardian* — the brass band, the Mayor and Corporation, the 'sumptuous feast provided for one and all' – with ever-growing fury.

According to the report the geologist had given him, the whole spectacle should never have been possible! The land was hanging by a thread, Brock had told him – a thread which could break at any moment. Long before Michael had had time to swank before the entire town, his shiny new works should have disappeared into a great, gaping hole in the ground.

And what had happened instead? Michael was not only producing salt for himself but was pumping brine to several other companies in the area. He had, in fact, taken the first step on the road to becoming a wealthy man.

And the further he travels down that road, the safer he is, Richard thought angrily.

A wealthy Michael would be harder to destroy. A wealthy Michael was better able to protect Becky. As long as M.&R-.Worrell and Co. was a success, Richard would be denied the two things he wanted most in the world.

He had finally reached his wife's door. He hesitated for a moment, then knocked, and entered.

Hortense was sitting up in bed, doing her needlework. She had curling papers in her hair and some kind of white cream on her face. She rarely did much to make herself attractive for their nocturnal meetings, but this was extreme, even for her.

'Yes,' she said, not even looking up from her work.

'It's Thursday,' Richard said.

'So it is,' his wife agreed.

'I always come and visit you on Thursday night,' Richard continued, forcing himself to infuse his voice with charm.

Hortense looked up and he could see the dislike in her eyes.

'Do you really wish to do it to me tonight?' she asked.

'Of course,' Richard lied.

'Why?' Hortense asked.

'Because I desire you,' Richard told her.

'Because you want me pregnant,' Hortense replied.

'That's part of it,' Richard agreed.

'Well I am pregnant,' Hortense replied, 'but if you still

want to have me for myself — because you desire me, as you say — you're welcome to join me between the sheets.'

Richard found himself instinctively backing away.

'It's probably not wise in your condition,' he mumbled.

'There'll be no more Thursday-night visits, will there?' Hortense asked. 'At least, not until you decide it's time to breed again?'

'No,' Richard admitted. 'No, there won't.'

'You wanted me because you desired me,' Hortense said mockingly. 'What do you think I am? One of your whores?'

Richard fled down the corridor, his wife's scornful laughter snapping at his heels.

As she sat at the dressing table brushing her long blonde hair, Becky looked around her at the new bedroom. She was sure it was nothing like as splendid as Michael's old room in Peak House, but compared to the one they'd shared in the first few months of their marriage, it was luxury indeed.

To be perfectly honest, the whole of this house overwhelmed her. It just seemed to go on for ever — breakfast room, reception rooms, a study for Michael, a conservatory, five bedrooms ...

There was even a servants' quarters — though, as yet, the only servant they had was a little scullery maid.

'Are you sure we can afford it?' she'd asked Michael when he'd first showed it to her.

'This is only the beginning,' he told her. 'When the business is really established, we'll be able to afford a much grander house than this — *and it won't be rented.*'

But Becky wasn't sure she wanted a grander house than this. She'd already gone far beyond her wildest imaginings. A home with a conservatory — she'd never have believed that possible a few years earlier! She couldn't wait to show it to her Mam.

Her gaze fell on her husband. Michael was lying in bed, his eyes shut tight.

'Are you asleep?' she asked.

'Nearly,' he confessed.

'Please stay awake,' she said. 'Just until I come to bed.'

'All right,' he promised.

There was something she had to tell him — something really important.

'I should have told him a long time ago,' she rebuked herself.

Yet it had been so hard to choose the right moment. First, he had been working like a trojan to get the business on its feet. Then, he spent so much time searching around for a suitable house — 'A palace for my princess' he'd called it. And possibly now — when he was so exhausted that, for once, he seemed to have no interest in making love — wasn't the right moment either. But she just couldn't keep her news to herself any longer.

Becky laid down her brushes on the dressing table and slipped into bed beside her husband.

Michael rolled over and put his arm around her.

'Are you still awake?' she asked earnestly.

'Yes,' he replied. 'I said I would be.'

'I've got something to tell you, Michael,' Becky said.

'Hmm.'

'I said, I've got something to tell you.'

'So tell me.'

'I'm going to have a baby,' she said.

'Good,' Michael responded.

Good? Was that all he had to say?

'Aren't you pleased?' she asked.

'Of course I'm pleased,' Michael mumbled. 'Very pleased. Now goodnight, Becky.'

'Goodnight, Michael,' she said dully.

Becky rolled over onto her side, feeling utterly miserable and rejected. She was giving him the greatest gift she ever could, and he was 'very pleased'. As she lay there, she felt tears rolling down her cheeks and landing with a 'plop' on her pillow.

Michael stirred uneasily in his sleep.

'Very pleased,' he muttered.

Then – suddenly – he was sitting bolt upright.

'You're having *what*?' he demanded.

'A baby,' Becky said. 'Your baby.'

'Are you sure?' Michael asked.

'I'm sure,' Becky told him. 'It won't be long before you should be able to see for yourself.'

Michael flung his arms around her and hugged her tightly to him. Then, as if fearing for the baby, he released his grip and contented himself with gently kissing her neck.

'My wonderful Becky,' he said. 'My wonderful, wonderful Becky.'

That night, for the first time since her childhood, Becky dreamed of the gypsy with the yellow eyes.

They were back in the caravan with its strange herbs and perfumes, she on one side of the tiny table, the gypsy on the other – and a glowing crystal ball between them.

'*I see pain and suffering,*' the gypsy crooned lazily. '*Perhaps even unto death.*'

'*For me?*' the dreaming Becky asked in a voice that she now hardly recognized as her own.

'*This is the pain of a man,*' the gypsy told her. '*A man who gave you life.*'

And not long after that, Dad had the accident which almost killed him.

'*I see a new force in your life,*' the gypsy continued relentlessly, '*two men who will love you as much as they hate each other.*'

'But Richard doesn't love me,' Becky mumbled in her sleep. 'Richard never loved me.'

'*I see wealth beyond your wildest imaginings,*' the old Romany told her, '*but it will not be yours for long . . . not be yours for long.*'

'Tell me what's going to happen!' Becky pleaded. 'I'm expecting a baby! I have to know what's going to happen!'

The dream-gypsy was no longer looking into the crystal ball. Now, her head was rotating from side to side, and her yellow eyeballs had completely disappeared.

*'Water. Rushing, furious water, sweeping away all in its path.
And mud. Fountains of mud. The land will crumble, and tall
towers will plunge to the earth as if struck down by the hands of
the gods. And you can do nothing to stop it. Nothing! No mortal
can.'*

The gypsy glowed as brilliantly as her crystal ball. Then she
began to fade – but slowly, so that it was almost impossible to
notice it happening. One second she was solid, the next she
was translucent. Now her outline was sharp, now fuzzy.

And then she was gone altogether, leaving Becky staring at
a blank bedroom wall.

Becky leapt out of bed and rushed over to the chest of
drawers. When her noise finally woke her husband several
minutes later, she was still searching frantically for the lucky
silver rupee that Old Gilbert Bowyer had given to her so long
ago.

How quickly time passes, Becky thought as she sat in the
conservatory looking out onto her modest garden.

Spring had seemed to turn into summer so rapidly, and
summer – almost before she'd noticed it – had glided gently
into early autumn. Now it was michaelmas daisies, not dog
roses, which thrived on the waste ground around Dunkirk.
Now the birds, instead of basking lazily in her sun-warmed
garden, flocked frantically in preparation for their epic journey
south.

The maid entered with a glass of lemonade.

'Will that be all, Ma'am?' she asked.

'Yes, thank you, Daisy,' Becky replied, thinking as she
spoke, Imagine *me* having a maid.

At first Becky had found it difficult to be the mistress of a
household – and she was still not doing everything as it should
have been done according to the Gospel of Mrs Beeton.

She should, for example, have addressed her maid as 'Fletcher',
but she just couldn't bring herself to use a surname to a girl only
slightly younger than she was. Heavens above, it was hard enough
to accept the fact that Daisy insisted on calling her her 'Ma'am'!

Yet for all her lack of experience and informality, Becky didn't find she had the same trouble with servants as did the ladies she'd sometimes overhear talking when she went for a fitting in Bratt and Evans' dress emporium.

'You have to watch them every minute of the day,' one of the ladies would inevitably complain.

'No other choice,' a second would agree. 'You just can't trust them otherwise.'

Becky *did* trust her servants. She liked them, too, and they seemed to like her in return. She knew that was not the way it was supposed to be, but she didn't really see what she could do about it.

As she sipped at her lemonade Becky thought about the baby growing inside her. Some days it would lie so quietly that, but for the swelling of her stomach, it was hard to believe it was there at all. On other days, however, it would kick furiously, as if impatient to begin the business of living.

Well, if freedom was what the baby was clamouring for, it would soon get its wish. Some time round about Guy Fawkes Night, when all the children of Marston were working fever-ishly to make sure that their bonfire was the biggest and best in the area, Becky would give birth to her daughter. And she was sure it *would* be a daughter – as sure as she'd ever been of anything in all her life.

Yes, Becky thought, her life was full and rich. Her days were occupied with the house and the works, her nights filled with gentle love-making and deep, dreamless sleep.

It was small wonder, then, that she soon forgot about the gypsy's warning.

Becky was already well into the seventh month of her preg-nancy when the visitor from Liverpool – like an Angel of Death – paid his call.

'His name's Harris, Ma'am,' Daisy told her. 'He won't say why he's come, but he says it's urgent. He looks right agitated, an' all.'

'Then you'd better show him in immediately,' Becky said worriedly.

Harris was a tall man wearing a long overcape. And Sally had been right – he did look agitated.

'Will you take a seat, Mr Harris?' Becky asked.

'No thank you, Ma'am,' Harris replied, twisting his top hat nervously between strong, short fingers.

'You told the maid you had an urgent message.'

'Yes, Ma'am.' Harris hesitated. 'Well, it's not exactly so much urgent as it's something I thought you should hear as soon as possible – if you see what I mean.'

Becky had no idea what he meant. But she did know instinctively that whatever it was he was about to tell her, she wasn't going to like it.

She took a deep breath.

'Go on,' she said bravely.

'I'm a wholesale merchant in a small sort of way,' Harris told her. 'I have a lot of dealings with trade from the West African coast and ...'

'Jack!' Becky interrupted him. 'You've got a message from Jack!'

'He said if anything happened I should come to you rather than his mother,' Harris said awkwardly.

'If anything happened! What *has* happened?'

'The Royal Niger Company's been making it more and more difficult for the independent traders,' Harris said, looking at the carpet rather than at Becky. 'So what Jack's been doing is taking *The Discovery* – that's the name of his steamer, Ma'am ...'

'I know,' Becky said.

'... taking it even further up the Oil Rivers than he normally would. Anyway, on his last trip he was planning to go up almost as far as Jebba – that's on the River Niger.'

'He *was* planning to go as far as Jebba?' Becky asked, feeling as cold as if she'd plunged head-first into icy water.

'For all we know he might actually have got that far. But what he *didn't* do was return to Bonny at the time he was expected. Well, our agents there didn't worry at first. Anything can happen once you're up-river – vines can snarl up the propeller good and proper, the natives don't always turn up when they've promised to ...'

'For God's sake, get on with it!' Becky told him.

'This is very difficult for me, Ma'am,' Harris said, keeping his eyes fixed firmly on the floor. 'Please let me tell it my own way.'

Becky took another deep breath.

'All right, Mr Harris,' she said. 'Tell it your own way.'

'There's no what-you-might-call rescue services on the Rivers, but our agent in Bonny asked the next steamer which was heading that way to keep an eye out for any sign of *The Discovery*.'

'And did they see anything?'

'They did, Ma'am,' Harris said heavily. 'But it wasn't good news, not by any manner of means. Just past the junction with the River Benue, they found something floating in the river. It was one of *The Discovery*'s lifebelts.'

'Is that all?' Becky asked, determined to know the worst.

'No, Ma'am. There was also some polished driftwood which could have come from the steamer and a ... a copper kettle with the *The Discovery*'s name engraved on it.'

Becky thought back to the day Septimus Quinn had met his end and toppled over backwards into the canal.

'Bodies!' she said. 'Did they find any bodies?'

'No, Ma'am,' Harris replied. 'But then they wouldn't, would they?'

'I don't follow you,' Becky said. 'They found the lifebelts, didn't they? And dead bodies always float just as well as pieces of wood.'

'Well, yes, that's true,' Harris admitted. 'But on the Oil Rivers, they wouldn't be floating for long, you see.'

'Why not?' Becky demanded.

'It's the er ... crocodiles,' Harris said reluctantly. 'The river's thick with them, and they'll have a body stripped down to the bone before it's had the chance to float a hundred yards.'

'Oh God!' Becky gasped. 'Is there ... is there any chance that though *The Discovery* went down, her crew were saved?'

Harris twisted the brim of his hat again.

'There's *always* a chance,' Harris replied. 'But if you'd been out there like I have, Ma'am — if you'd seen for yourself what it's like — you'd know there's no point in getting your hopes up.'

Ted Taylor sat, ashen-faced, in his favourite armchair by the fire.

'Well, I'll not believe it,' he said.

'You have to, Dad,' Becky told him, doing her best to fight back her tears.

'It couldn't happen — not to our Jack,' Taylor insisted.

He turned to his wife, who was perched on the arm of his chair and had taken hold of his hand.

'It just couldn't happen, could it, Mary?' he asked pathetically. 'Not when we love him so much.'

'I've loved all my children, but it didn't stop two of them dying when they were no more than babies,' Mary Taylor said dully. 'These things happen whether we want them to or not, and we just have to accept them.'

'Well I won't,' Taylor said stubbornly.

'You've no choice,' his wife said gently. 'None of us have.'

And Becky knew her mother was right, though in her heart she felt just as her father did. How could Jack — who had given her his watch one cold morning before he ran away to sea, who had disguised himself as a coachman to drive her to her wedding — really be dead? Yet Mr Harris had told her not to get her hopes up — and Mr Harris should know.

It was five days after the Liverpudlian had brought the tragic news that Michael dropped his bombshell.

'I've decided to put Cedric Rathbone in temporary charge of the works,' he told his wife as they sat quietly together in their sitting room.

'Cedric Rathbone!' Becky exclaimed. 'But you can't do that!'

'Why can't I?' Michael asked.

'Because he's not on your side,' Becky told him. 'Cedric Rathbone's a union man — through and through.'

'He's his own man more than he is the union's,' Michael corrected her. 'He's a fighter, too. And things being the way they are, if I'm going to leave anybody in charge, it should be somebody who knows how to stick up for himself.'

'But ...' Becky protested.

'Besides,' Michael said, winking at her, 'Cedric Rathbone's going to find he's not got much time for union activity once he's got a business to run, isn't he?'

For all that Michael seemed to be making sense, there was something about his words which didn't quite add up, Becky thought.

And then she realized what it was! The Michael she'd come to know since her marriage wasn't a man to hand control of his works over to *anybody* — not without a very compelling reason.

But what could that compelling reason possibly be?

'So you leave Cedric Rathbone in charge,' she said. 'And what will *you* do then? Take up fishing?'

'I shall do what I'm best at,' Michael told her. 'I shall find new customers and open up fresh markets.'

'But we've already got all the business we can handle,' Becky pointed out.

'Only for the moment,' Michael countered. 'We must look to the future. That's why I'm planning to make my first trip within the next few days.'

'And where do you intend to go?' Becky asked. 'London?'

'No, not London,' Michael replied. 'This time I thought I'd strike out further afield — maybe take a trip abroad.'

This wasn't Michael talking, Becky thought. He sounded too vague, too casual — and he was never vague or casual where business was concerned. He was hiding something from her — and she was determined to find out what it was.

'So you thought you might go abroad,' Becky said. 'Abroad's a big place. Do you have any particular place in mind?'

'Paris,' Michael told her. 'Possibly Berlin and Prague, too.'

Why was he lying to her? Why?

'If you go all that way, the chances are you won't be here when the baby's born,' Becky said.

'I know that,' Michael replied.

An expression of pain and regret crossed his face, and Becky was sure that this, at least, was genuine.

'We've always been honest with each other,' Becky said, feeling tears prickling her eyes. 'Why won't you tell me the truth now?'

Michael turned away from her, but not before she had a chance to see the look of hesitation and uncertainty on his face. What had happened to him? This was not the man she had married at all.

'Tell me the truth,' Becky begged. 'Please tell me the truth.'

Michael turned to face her once more.

'I didn't want to deceive you,' he said, 'but I didn't want you worrying so close to the end of your pregnancy, either.'

'Didn't want to worry me about what?' Becky asked.

'The area I intend to visit is supposed to be somewhat dangerous,' Michael said. 'I'm sure the stories you've heard about it have been greatly exaggerated, but I still thought it best not to let you know where I was going. I should have realized I could never fool you.'

'The stories *I've* heard?' Becky said. 'Where exactly *are* you going?'

'West Africa,' Michael told her.

'West Africa!' Becky exclaimed.

And suddenly she saw it all.

'You're going to look for Jack, aren't you?' she demanded.

'Of course not,' Michael said firmly. 'I'm going on business. But,' he conceded, 'I may take the opportunity while I'm there to travel a little way up that river — what's it called, the Niger? — and see if I can find out anything about your brother.'

'I won't let you do it,' Becky said.

'You can't stop me,' Michael told her.

He smiled, and at last she had *her* Michael back with her.

'When you made your marriage vows, you promised to obey me, didn't you?' he asked.

'Yes,' Becky admitted.

'Very well, then. I order you to allow me to go to West Africa.'

'As long as I can go with you,' Becky replied.

Michael looked at his wife's distended stomach and shook his head.

'I hope to get back before the baby's born,' he said, 'but there's no guarantee that I will. And from what I've heard, the Oil Rivers are no place for any white woman, let alone one who's about to give birth.'

There was no point in arguing with him, she realized. He might speak softly, he might be willing to give way to her on most things, but there were some points on which the Devil himself wouldn't make Michael Worrell back down – and this was one of them.

Becky rose heavily from her chair, walked over to her husband's, and put her hands on his shoulders.

'You're very, very good, Michael,' she said sincerely.

'Nonsense,' Michael replied, looking up at her. 'I've been planning this for some time. It's good business sense.'

Good business sense again!

Becky hugged her husband to her.

'I love you, Michael,' she said.

She had never told him that before – never even thought it to herself. But the moment the words were out of her mouth, she knew they were completely, deeply true.

CHAPTER TWENTY-FIVE

Becky looked up at the work's central chimney. Only a few months earlier, at the Grand Opening, it had pointed straight up the sky, but now there was a definite list to it. More worrying still, the list seemed to be getting worse with each week that went by.

'It can't be more than three or four days since the last time I looked at it,' she told Cedric Rathbone, 'but I can notice a definite difference even in that time.'

'If it did fall down – and I'm not saying it will – we'd get a team of brickies in and have a new one up before you had time to miss it,' Rathbone reassured her.

'It's not the chimney falling down that bothers me,' Becky confessed. 'I'm more concerned about *what's making it* fall down?'

'It's just a bit of subsidence,' Rathbone said airily. 'Get a lot of it round here. It isn't anything to break into a sweat over.'

But Becky wasn't convinced. She remembered walking to Dunkirk with Old Gilbert Bowyer and listening to his tales of the disaster to come. The ground below Dunkirk was honey-combed with abandoned mines, he'd told her – absolutely honeycombed.

Yet hadn't that geologist Michael had hired assured them that there was no danger of a major groundshift for at least fifteen years?

She wished that Michael was by her side at that moment, so she could confide her fears in him. But Michael had been gone for weeks, and from his last letter it looked as if there was little possibility of his imminent return.

'*There is still a great deal of business to do,*' he'd written, '*and given the great distances involved, it would be foolish not to*

*try and conclude it while I am here, rather than be forced to make
another trip later.'*

She didn't believe a word of — not for a second. It was not
business which was detaining her husband — it was Jack.
Michael would not leave Africa until he had positive proof that
her brother was dead.

She loved him for his kindness to her family, but she
couldn't help wishing that he was back at her side, reassuring
her that the works would be fine.

And the baby, too! she thought.

It was due to be born in less than a week, and she was
terrified something would go wrong.

'There's nothing to worry about all, Mrs Worrell,' Dr
Maitland had told her. 'It should be a perfectly normal birth.'

He was supposed to be the best doctor in Northwich —
certainly he was the most expensive — but Becky would have
had more confidence in his words if he hadn't looked away
from her as he'd uttered them.

Come home soon, Michael! Becky prayed silently. I need
someone to hold my hand — and nobody but you will do.

Philip Taylor, unaware that his sister was on the premises,
picked up a skimmer and scooped some brine out of the fine
pan. This was a promotion, Cedric Rathbone had told him,
recognition of the fact that he'd worked so hard as a waller on
the common pan. And Philip had nodded gratefully, thinking
only that now he had been transferred to a place where blocks
of salt were made, he would have a chance to put his master
plan into practice.

'If you work hard at this job, too, there's the possibility of
going even further,' Rathbone had promised him.

What a fool you are, Cedric! Philip thought as he poured
the brine into a waiting elm tub.

Did Rathbone really think that he, Philip Taylor — photographer and friend of important men in the Manchester underworld
—could ever satisfy his ambitions with a job in a salt works?

Philip checked around him to make sure he was not being

observed, then went quickly over to the corner where he'd placed an old sack earlier in the morning. He opened the sack and took out a package which was double wrapped in flannel and oilcloth. With another furtive glance over his shoulder, he walked back to the elm tubs.

This was the best scheme for making money he'd ever come up with, he thought. The idea had come to him in a flash, as he sat beside Becky on the journey back from Strangeways Gaol – and despite its simplicity it really was brilliant.

Philip placed the carefully wrapped package in a half-full tub, then quickly covered it with a fresh scoop of brine. Satisfied with his work, he knelt down and made a chalk cross near the base of the tub.

Later, when the salt had started to crystallize, he would make a cross in the top of the block, too. It would be a small one, hardly noticeable unless you were looking for it – but the people who were expecting delivery *would* be looking.

He wondered how Caspar Leech and his gang had ever managed without him. How dangerous it must have been before to transport jewels stolen from Manchester or Liverpool to London, where they could be fenced in relative safety. And if they were to be shipped abroad – as they sometimes were – the risk was doubled. But there was no danger now, not with his master plan. Railway police and customs officers examined all kinds of packages for stolen goods, but who would ever think of breaking open a block of salt to see if anything was hidden inside? Who would even think to hide something there in the first place?

Only me, he told himself happily. Only clever Philip Taylor.

Pregnancy makes some women – like Becky – look even more beautiful, Richard thought.

But it hadn't done much for Hortense, who was now also in her final month. He looked at his wife across the breakfast table. Where Becky's skin seemed to glow with health, Hortense's was sallower than ever, and while Becky carried her child with grace, Hortense wobbled like a balloon on the point of bursting.

And the larger Hortense grew, the more she sniped at him. She was about to do it now – he could read it in her face.

'You're thinking about her, aren't you?' Hortense demanded.

'Thinking about whom?' Richard asked.

'You know very well,' his wife sneered. 'The little dressmaker. My dear sister-in-law.'

'I assure you ...' Richard began.

'She should be giving birth quite soon, shouldn't she?' Hortense interrupted.

'I really don't know,' Richard replied neutrally. 'I haven't seen her for some time.'

'Don't lie to me,' his wife told him. 'I've seen the way you moon around, hoping to catch a glance of her. You've been infatuated with her ever since the day you paraded her around the grounds on your horse.'

'You'll never forgive either of us for what happened that day, will you?' Richard asked.

'On the contrary,' Hortense replied. 'I'm a good Christian – I'll forgive anyone once they've been sufficiently punished. But she hasn't been punished yet. In fact, I'd say she'd got rather more than she deserved out of life. Wouldn't you agree?'

'More than she deserved?' Richard asked, rising to the bait even though he knew he shouldn't. 'In what way?'

'Well, Michael does seem to be doing rather well, doesn't he? I've heard it said around Northwich that before long M. & R. Worrell will be a much more successful business than L.G.Worrell and Co. ever was – or ever will be.'

'That's not true,' Richard growled.

'If you say so,' Hortense replied blandly. 'I wouldn't know. *My* family has had no experience in trade.'

If she'd devote half as much time to trying to be a good wife as she put into needling him, she might just be tolerable, Richard thought. As it was, she'd done all he wanted of her and now he could but hope that she'd die in childbirth.

'I'm giving you fair warning,' Hortense said. 'I will tolerate your other whores – but I'll kill you before I'll see you have anything else to do with the little dressmaker.'

After a grilling like this, he'd earned a treat, Richard decided. He would go to one of the rougher brothels in Liverpool that night and hire a prostitute who didn't mind being whipped. But that would only make him feel better for a short time. Long-term satisfaction would never come until Michael had been completely destroyed.

As her carriage rattled along the road to Dunkirk, Becky felt a twinge which could almost have been a contraction, and realized that however worried she was about the leaning chimney, this was probably the last visit she'd be able to make to the works before the baby was born.

She looked across at the bleak landscape – the rock-pits, the smoking factory chimneys, Wincham Brook wending it way towards Witton Flash. It wasn't a pretty sight, she thought, not for the first time. Yet she had grown strangely attached to it. The works was more than just a source of income – it was a symbol of both Michael's determination to be useful and his willingness to share his life with her.

The carriage pulled up on the forecourt in front of the office, and, as usual, Cedric Rathbone was waiting to welcome her as she stepped down.

'How's the chimney, Mr Rathbone?' Becky asked.

Rathbone grinned back at her as if it were a standing joke – which it almost was.

'Chimney's fine, Mrs Worrell,' he said. 'And we're pumping out more brine now than we ever were.'

Becky looked up at the central stack.

'It doesn't look fine to me,' she said. 'In fact it seems to have slipped at least another coup ...'

She was cut off by a sudden loud noise which was not quite like anything she'd ever heard before. She looked around her – at the works, at the wasteland, at the chimneys of the other factories which surrounded the works. Everything seemed perfectly normal.

No it didn't – not when you knew where to look!

Becky's gaze fixed on the nearest rock-pit, which was separated from the works by Wincham Brook. Its surface was usually completely calm. Yet though there was no wind, the rock-pit was far from calm – in fact, it was bubbling as furiously as a cauldron on the boil!

Becky felt another of those twinges which could not quite be called a contraction.

'I want to go and have a closer look, Mr Rathbone,' she said. 'Will you take my arm?'

Rathbone led her carefully over the rough ground to the edge of the brook. The rumbling sound had grown louder and the bubbles on the surface of the rock-pit were so fierce that they kept exploding into fountains several feet high.

'Why is that happening, Mr Rathbone?' Becky asked worriedly. 'What does it mean?'

'I don't know,' Rathbone admitted. 'Unless water's got into one of the old mines and is pushing air out of it.'

Of course! Becky thought. It must be a bit like drowning – when water rushes into your lungs and forces the air out of your mouth. But in this case, the 'mouth' of the old mine was the rock-pit.

Something new was happening! The ground around the edges of the rock-pit was erupting, and dark brown mud volcanoes – taller than a man – were spurting up all along the bank.

'It'll settle down, Mrs Worrell,' Cedric Rathbone said reassuringly. 'As soon as all the air's been forced out, it's bound to settle down.'

But Becky wasn't listening. Though her body still stood next to Cedric Rathbone's, her mind had travelled back to that day, years earlier, when the canal bank had burst near Burns Bridge.

She remembered Hereward, pulling with all his mighty strength against the current, yet still being dragged towards the breach in the bank. She could see *The Jupiter* being carried along as if it weighed no more than a cigarette packet, then being flung effortlessly into the deep hole which had opened below the embankment.

Subsidence wasn't a thing to be treated lightly, she thought. Subsidence wouldn't necessarily go away – just because you wanted it to.

'Pull some of the men off the pans and send them out to look at the other rock-pits,' she told Cedric Rathbone. 'I want to know if they're all in as bad a state as this one.'

'If we take men off the shift, it'll mean a drop in production,' Rathbone said dubiously.

'Not as much as if the whole of the works falls in,' Becky replied.

'I don't think . . .' Rathbone began.

'I didn't ask you to think,' Becky said fiercely. 'I've told you what to do – now bloody well do it!'

Hortense Worrell groaned with pain. She'd thought the discomfort of making the baby had been bad enough, but that had been nothing compared to this.

Never again! she promised herself as she bit down on the clean piece of rope her maid had brought her. Never again!

'It shouldn't be long now, Mrs Worrell,' said Dr Maitland, returning his watch to his waistcoat pocket.

Hortense looked up at the grey-haired man with loathing. It was easy for him to talk, wasn't it? Easy for them all to talk. *They* didn't have to go through this.

'Actually, it should be a fairly easy birth,' the doctor continued. 'It's your sister-in-law I'm more worried about. It looks on the surface to be a fairly normal pregnancy, but I'm told that there's a family history of complications.'

'To hell with my sister-in-law!' Hortense gasped.

'Well, really!' Dr Maitland said, in his tut-tutting voice.

From the corner of her eye Hortense saw the maid mouthing at him that Becky Worrell was not a subject which was discussed in this house – unless, of course, the mistress decided to raise it herself.

'Where's Richard?' Hortense demanded. 'He's responsible for all this! Is he waiting outside?'

An embarrassed silence fell over the room.

'I said, is he waiting outside?' Hortense persisted.

'No, Madam,' the maid admitted.

'Then where is he?'

'He heard that there was some trouble over in Dunkirk,' the maid said awkwardly, 'and he's gone to see it for himself.'

All the rock-pits in the Dunkirk area were bubbling as fiercely as the one close to the works. Worse yet — cracks had appeared in the ground around some of them and the scream of the air being forced through these new fissures was enough to chill the blood.

It could all fall down, Becky thought, looking at the buildings into which her husband had put all his hopes. It could all fall down any second. Oh God, Michael, I wish you were here.

Brian O'Reilly came rushing into the yard.

'Ashcroft's mine is flooding,' he said, fighting for breath.

'Flooding?' Cedric Rathbone asked. 'How in damnation can that be happening? Ashcroft's isn't anywhere near any of the rock-pits.'

'They say the water's coming in from the abandoned mine next to it,' O'Reilly explained. 'But God alone knows how it got in there.'

The whole area's a honeycomb, a voice screamed in Becky's head. *A honeycomb! A honeycomb! A honeycomb!*

She looked around the works — her eyes travelling from the expensive pumping machinery to the pans, from the pans to the furnaces. If the ground gave way now, they would lose everything. There had to be something she could do!

'Close down the pans,' she told Cedric Rathbone.

'I beg your pardon, Mrs Worrell,' Rathbone said, obviously astonished.

Becky winced as another twinge hit her.

'Close down the pans,' she said again. 'And as soon as you can, start taking them to pieces — them and everything else in the works we can move away from here to somewhere safer.'

'Why should we do that?' Rathbone asked.

'Because that way, we'll at least rescue something if the ground subsides.'

'But what if it doesn't give way at all?' Rathbone asked. 'It's easy enough to take buildings down, but it's a lot more difficult – and a lot more expensive – to put them up again.'

'I just feel in my guts it's going to go,' Becky said.

And that was not the only thing she was feeling in her guts at that moment!

Rathbone hesitated for a moment, then shook his head.

'I couldn't possibly do anything of that kind without your husband's say-so,' he said firmly.

'If he was here, he'd tell you the same thing,' Becky said, praying that she was right – praying that what was going on inside her hadn't warped her judgement.

'You may be right,' Rathbone agreed, 'but he left me in charge, and I can't take the responsibility for it myself.'

Becky searched around desperately for some argument she could use to sway him. Her eye fell on the central chimney, leaning more than ever.

'Do you see the name up there?' she asked.

'Yes, Mrs Worrell.'

'That "R" is me. This is my works. So do as I say – or I'll get somebody else who will.'

Only an hour earlier Wincham Brook had been a quiet stream no more than twenty feet wide and two feet deep – but the new crack in the ground had changed all that.

It appeared around noon, a gash running from one bank of the brook to the other. At first it seemed to Becky to be no different to any of the other crevices which had opened up that morning. Then it began to grow, and what had started as little more than a hairline fracture rapidly became a yawning chasm.

Instead of flowing on to Witton Flash, the brook began to pour down this new hole, and as the crevice got even wider, it began to suck in water from further upstream.

Just like when the canal bank burst, Becky thought miserably as she watched the stream rushing backwards to fill the new opening in the earth.

Faster and faster the water went. It tore up the banks of the brook. It ripped out the bottom. Soon, the raging, frothing torrent had turned dark brown from the thousands of tons of mud it carried, but even that tremendous weight didn't slow it down.

Nothing could quell its fury. Nothing could withstand its power. The brook was forty feet wide now – four times what it had once been.

When will it end? Becky asked herself. When will it ever end?

And what would happen to the millions of gallons of water which were pouring down the hole? Where would they go once they had filled the honeycomb of underground workings?

Becky tore her eyes from the horror in front of her to look at the work going on behind. She'd had trouble making Cedric Rathbone accept her, but now that he had, he'd thrown himself into the task with all the energy and determination that had won him a score of pub brawls against men almost twice his size.

Not everything in the works could be saved, Becky thought. Whatever they did, the brick shells would be doomed if the ground gave way – but at least the timbering, the roofing and the pans might be preserved.

Time was what they needed. And time was the one thing they didn't have. Rathbone's men were working at a feverish pace, but Nature was feverish, too – and so much more powerful.

A fresh roar made Becky turn round again. The ground around the nearest rock-pit had given way and the water from the pit was rushing furiously down the newly created slope towards the crevice which had opened up across Wincham Brook.

Richard Worrell dug his spurs deep into the flesh of his frightened horse.

'Keep going, you bugger!' he ordered the animal.

Caesar cried out in pain, but not even his fear of Richard was enough to force him on any further.

'Damn and blast you!' Richard screamed as he dismounted.

He dragged the horse to the edge of the raised road and tied it to a telegraph pole which was shaking dangerously. Maybe the horse, the pole — and even the road — would no longer be there when he got back, Richard thought, but at that moment he couldn't have cared less.

He made his way on foot down the embankment towards his brother's works. The ground beneath his feet trembled, and even from a distance the roar of Wincham Brook was terrifying. Yet he did not hesitate, even for a second, because ahead of him he could see Michael's workers dismantling the factory — and that wouldn't do at all.

He had reached the edge of the works. Two men, holding a heavy pump between them, were staggering towards him.

'Who's in charge here?' Richard shouted.

'Cedric Rathbone,' one of the men screamed back.

Cedric Rathbone! That was a stroke of bad luck, Richard thought. Of all the people in the world who had reason to dislike him, Rathbone probably ranked near the top. Still, it would be easier handling Rathbone than it would have been dealing with Michael.

Rathbone was standing near one of the common pans, shouting out frantic instructions to three groups of workers at once. Richard walked up to him and tapped him on the shoulder.

Rathbone swung round, irritated at being disturbed, but when he saw who was standing there, his irritation rapidly changed to anger.

'What are you doing here, you bastard?' he demanded.

'I'm here to help,' Richard replied.

Rathbone's aggression drained away and he even managed to look a little shamefaced.

'Aye, well, every extra pair of hands helps,' he said. 'Go straight over to the main pumping station and ...'

'I'm not here to help my brother,' Richard cut in. 'I'm here to help you.'

Rathbone turned away for a second to issue fresh orders, then gave Richard his full attention again.

'Help me? How do you mean?' he asked.

'I don't think it's safe for you and your men to be working here,' Richard told him.

Rathbone swung around to examine the scene. The brook was still rushing furiously. The chimney stack was listing even more than it had been the last time he looked. But there did not seem to be any immediate danger.

'We should be all right for at least another half hour,' he told Richard Worrell.

'I disagree,' Richard said. 'I think you should pull your workers out now. And if you did, there'd be something in it for you.'

Rathbone's muscles tensed, and for a second Richard thought the foreman was about to lash out at him.

Then Rathbone smiled craftily and said, 'How much?'

What would be a fortune to a man like this? Richard wondered.

Twenty-five pounds! The same amount that Michael had persuaded his father to pay Ted Taylor.

'I'll give you fifty pounds,' he said.

'Not a chance!' Rathbone replied.

He'd obviously underestimated his man, Richard thought. Rathbone knew what a strong bargaining position he was in, and was exploiting it to the full.

'Seventy-five pounds,' Richard said.

'No,' Rathbone told him.

'Then how much *do* you want?' Richard demanded. 'A hundred? A hundred and twenty-five?'

'So you'd pay me a hundred and twenty-five pounds to see this place go under, would you?' Rathbone asked.

'Yes,' Richard agreed. 'But that's my final offer. Don't start getting too greedy, Rathbone.'

'I just wanted to see how high you'd go,' Cedric Rathbone

said. 'Let me tell you something, *Mr* Worrell. As rich as you are, you don't have enough money to buy me. Now get the hell out of here before I break your worthless bloody neck.'

Becky felt her whole body shudder violently.

Oh God, the baby! she thought. Not now. Not now.

And then she shook again and realized that the motion did not come from her own body – from the tiny life inside her demanding to come out – but from the earth beneath her feet!

In a panic, Becky stepped – practically ran – backwards. The ground directly in front of her began to slip, almost lazily, towards the crack across Wincham Brook – and at the very spot on which she'd been standing, a crater slowly began to open, as if the earth, tired from its exertions, was gently yawning.

Becky looked around her in despair. A second crater had formed less than ten yards away, and a third was opening up even closer to the works.

The air, already thick with the smell of smoke, now became almost unbearable as stinking gases, imprisoned underground for so long, rushed through this new opening in the earth's crust.

Becky gagged. She had to get away from there, she thought – had to leave before the foul gases overcame her and she passed out.

Suddenly there was a new rumbling sound – even louder and angrier than the ones which had preceded it. And it was closer to the works than any of the others, too! Though every move she made brought her fresh discomfort, Becky struggled towards the source of the furious roar.

It's coming from the brine shaft, she told herself. The roar's coming from the brine shaft.

Yet how could it be? The men had dismantled the pump over an hour earlier and battened down the top of the shaft itself with a heavy wooden cover.

Then where is the noise coming from? Becky wondered. Think – this is important!

But it was so hard to think when your head was pounding. When you were burning hot one moment and freezing cold the next. When sometimes the ground really did move, but at others it was only your eyes playing tricks on you ...

The rumbling swelled and swelled, more demanding – more insistent – with every second. Becky clamped her hands over her ears, but still the terrifying noise would not go away.

The heavy wooden cover on the brine shaft began to bulge outwards, but the sound of its creaking protest was lost in the general cacophony.

'No!' Becky screamed.

Boards splintered and were flung into the air by the relentless force pressing up from below. Soon, the whole cover was bouncing helplessly on top of a ten-foot fountain of water and mud.

Spray cascaded from the zenith of the fountain and fell to the ground like a kind of muddy rain. Becky was soaked, yet she made no effort to move.

I've failed, she told herself bitterly.

They would never be able to save enough of the works to start again now. Never, never, never!

'Come out of that, lass,' said a voice which seemed to come from far beyond the rushing water.

But Becky stayed where she was because it seemed important that she should – though when she thought about it, she couldn't really say why.

She felt a hand on her shoulder, and did not resist as it gently guided her out from under the downpour.

Once clear of the water and mud she looked up at her rescuer.

'Hello, Dad,' she said lethargically.

'What the bloody hell were you doing standing there?' her father asked in the sort of voice we only hear in dreams.

'Just watching,' Becky replied, as if she were dreaming herself.

She turned towards the chimney she had been so proud of – the one with her name on it. It was swaying – she was sure it was swaying. Or was it she who was swaying? And was the rest of the world really swimming by as it appeared to be?

'We've got to get you away from here,' Ted Taylor said.

'The works,' Becky mumbled. 'Have to save the works.'

'We'll take care of that,' someone called out.

For the first time Becky noticed the group of people who were standing just beyond her father.

There was that nice Mr O'Leary from the New Inn. Ha-Ha Harry Atherton who st ... stuttered and had once worked with Dad down the Adelaide Mine. Mr Hulse – but why hadn't he brought *The Jupiter* with him?

Scores of other faces were there, too – faces she knew well but couldn't put a name to now – scores of faces strangely fluid, forming and reforming, nothing definite ... nothing that really made sense ...

'Look at the state of her,' Becky heard her father say.

Becky winced with pain.

'Was that a contraction?' her mother asked anxiously.

'I think so,' Becky said.

'And how often are they coming?'

'I don't know,' Becky admitted. 'Maybe every two or three minutes.'

'We'll have to get her back home right away,' Ted Taylor said.

'There's no time for that,' his wife told him. 'She's already gone too far into labour.'

'But – bloody hell, woman – she can't have the baby in the middle of all this,' Taylor protested.

'It's less dangerous than moving her,' his wife argued.

'I suppose you know best,' Taylor conceded. 'You usually do.'

He picked up his daughter and carried her to the office. While he held Becky in his arms, Mary Taylor did her best to turn a functional place of business into a room suitable for the birth of her grandchild.

'Lay our Becky on that sofa,' she told her husband. 'And then you'd best get off and find that fancy doctor Michael's hired to look after her.'

'Bugger the fancy doctor,' Becky said through gritted teeth. 'Get me Ma Fitton – midwife to royalty.'

For the next hour – or it may have been a day, or perhaps a year – Becky drifted in and out of consciousness.

In her more lucid moments she demanded that her mother stand by the window and give her a running commentary on exactly what was going on outside.

'What are they doing now, Mam?'

'They're moving the timbers from the salt store. Working like madmen, they are. By, but he's stronger than he looks, that Mr O'Leary. And Wally Hulse isn't doing bad for an old 'un, either.'

'Make sure they get all the machinery out first,' Becky insisted. 'The machinery's the most ... most expensive ...'

Then she would be gone again, only to return to life a few minutes later with fresh enquiries and orders.

'Keep your mind on the main job, girl,' Ma Fitton grumbled. 'I've never had a less helpful patient than you and that includes my princess, who was used to doing *nothing* for herself.'

The contractions were stronger, the pain was growing worse.

'Where are you, Mam?' Becky called out in agony.

'I'm here,' Mary Taylor assured her. 'Right beside you, love.'

'Push down harder,' Ma Fitton urged.

And though she would never have thought herself capable of it, Becky found the strength from somewhere to give an extra push.

'I can see the head,' Ma Fitton said encouragingly. 'Keep going, girl!'

And almost before Becky realized it, the whole thing was over and Ma Fitton was holding the new-born infant in her arms.

'Is it all right?' Becky asked anxiously. 'Is my baby all right?'

'It's perfect,' Ma Fitton told her. 'A perfect little girl.'

'Perfect,' Mary Taylor agreed.

'And d'you know what you're going to call her?' Ma Fitton asked. 'Or have you been too busy worrying about other things to put your mind to that?'

'I'm going to call her Michelle,' Becky said.

There was a sudden loud crash outside.

'What was that, Mam?' Becky demanded.

Mary Taylor reluctantly tore herself away from her new grandchild and went over to the window.

'Well, I suppose it had to go in the end,' she said.

'*What* had to go?' Becky asked.

'I'm sorry, love,' her mother replied, 'but that was your chimney falling over.'

Becky took her baby in her arms.

'Fancy that, Michelle,' she whispered in the infant's ear. 'And your dad didn't want me to go Africa with him because he thought I'd be better off having you quietly at home.'

EPILOGUE
1891

Not-Stopping Bracegirdle and Dottie Curzon stood at the head of the alley which led to Mrs Bracegirdle's back door. The weather was mild for early November, but even if the ground been covered with frost they would probably still have stationed themselves on this spot. A kitchen, as Not-Stopping often said, might be cosier for a chat, but kitchens gave you no view of what was going on in the lane.

'I read in Thursday's *Guardian* that they lost six hundred thousand tons of water and forty thousand tons of earth down that hole near Michael Worrell's works,' Not-Stopping said.

'Sounds a lot,' Dottie Curzon replied.

'I should say it is,' Not-Stopping agreed. 'A sack of coal is a hundredweight and if I remember me schooling, there's twenty hundredweights to one ton, so it would be like tipping six hundred thousand times twenty sacks of coal down the hole, which is ... well, you can work it out for yourself.'

'Sounds a lot,' Dottie Curzon repeated.

'And now Becky Taylor-as-was has gone and called her daughter Michelle,' Not-Stopping continued, as if the two events were connected.

'So you told me,' Dot said.

'Michelle!' Not-Stopping said scornfully. 'Daft name, if you ask me. Sounds like Michael.'

'It's probably just a coincidence,' Dottie suggested.

It was one of Dottie's better shots, but it was completely wasted on Not-Stopping Bracegirdle, whose attention had been distracted by the clip-clop of horses' hoofs.

'Well, will you look at that!' Not-Stopping gasped.

Dottie did, and saw immediately why her friend had sounded so surprised. Coaches were not an uncommon sight in Marston

– gentlemen travelling to their country estates often passed through the village – but the coach which had just appeared on the crest of the humpbacked bridge was unlike any they'd ever seen before.

It was a coach from a fairy tale, the sort of coach in which Prince Charming might have searched for his Cinderella. Its body was elaborately carved and painted in gold leaf. It had a crest on its door. Liveried servants sat at the front and stood at the back.

'It's the Queen,' Not-Stopping said. 'It has to be.'

The coach passed the New Inn and drew almost level with them. By straining their necks the two women could just make out the passenger, who was not their monarch at all, but a florid, well-dressed man in early middle age.

The coach reined in directly in front of them. Over-awed, Not-Stopping and Dottie for once let embarrassment overcome curiosity and gazed down at the ground.

'Excuse me, plees,' said the man sitting next to the driver.

Not-Stopping looked over her shoulder to see who he was talking to, and finding no one she realized that, incredible as it might seem, she was the one he was addressing. Smoothing down her apron and adopting a genteel smile, she turned back to the coach.

'Yes, can I help you?' she asked in a voice she normally reserved for the Vicar.

'Ve are looking for a Frau Feeton,' the man said in a heavy foreign accent.

'Nobody of that name here,' Not-Stopping replied. 'Well, there wouldn't be, would there? Not in a little place like Marston?'

'He means Ma Fitton,' Dottie Curzon said. 'She lives just down the lane – at Number thirty-five.'

'Sank you,' the foreigner said, tipping his hat.

'I could have told him that,' Not-Stopping whispered sourly to her friend.

The coach rattled on and stopped in front of Number 35.

'I think I need to go down the lane to the post office,' Not-Stopping said.

'I'll come with you,' Dottie Curzon decided.

The Bracegirdle house was only five doors up from Fitton's, but by the time they had reached Ma's alley, both women felt in need of a rest. From their new vantage point they watched the servant open the carriage door and the well-dressed gentleman get out.

'I'd have worn me clean apron if I'd known anybody important was coming,' Dottie Curzon whispered.

Servant and master walked up the path to the front door and the servant rapped loudly on it with a gloved hand. There was some delay before there was the sound of bolts being drawn back.

'Probably not had her front door open since she buried her fancy-man, that Gilbert Bowyer,' Not-Stopping commented.

Finally, the door *was* open, and Ma Fitton stood there, looking very intimidated at the sight of such grand visitors.

'I haf been wisiting ze area because I haf much interest in the subsidence,' the gentleman said.

'Yes?' Ma Fitton replied, very perplexed indeed.

'It vas only when I vas in Norzwhich zat I learned zat ze woman who brought me into ze world lived close by,' he continued. 'And zen, of course, I knew zat I must come and see her for myself.'

Ma Fitton's mouth fell open. She tried to speak, but words failed her.

For perhaps twenty seconds the three of them stood in a frozen tableau on the doorstep, then the servant coughed discreetly and said, 'His Royal Highness would appreciate a cup of your excellent English tea.'

'Yes ... yes ... of course,' Ma Fitton spluttered. 'Come in – only you mustn't mind the mess.'

The three entered the parlour and the door was closed behind them.

'There you are,' Not-Stopping said triumphantly. 'I always told you she wasn't making it up.'

The doctor had prescribed at least a week's bed-rest, and it was from her bed that Becky heard the maid announce that her brother was waiting to see her.

'Jack?' she said.

'No, Ma'am, Mr Philip.'

Of course it was Philip! Becky told herself. She must still be half delirious to think for even a second that it could have been Jack.

Jack would never come to see her again. Jack was dead.

'Ma'am?' Daisy said anxiously.

'I'm all right,' Becky assured her. 'You can show my brother in now.'

Philip was dressed in his best flared overcoat and had a soft felt hat in his hands. He stood hesitantly on the threshold of the bedroom and looked nervously around him.

'For goodness' sake, come in and sit down,' Becky said.

Philip crossed the room and sat awkwardly on the chair next to Becky's bed. 'How much longer are you going to be stuck in bed?' he asked.

'The doctor says I can get up in a couple of days,' Becky told him.

'That's good, then.'

'Would you like to hold your niece for a minute?' Becky asked, pointing to the crib in the corner.

'Um ... yes ... of course I would.'

Philip picked up little Michelle and rocked her gently, but it was clear that his mind was elsewhere.

'I'm going to have to go away,' he suddenly blurted out.

Becky sighed.

'What have you done this time?' she asked.

'I was ... er ... involved in a bit of jewellery smuggling. I know it was wrong but ...'

'You only know it's wrong because you're in trouble again,' Becky said. 'Are the police after you?'

Philip shook his head.

'Not the police – this feller called Leech from Manchester. He was the one who was supplying the goods. But I've lost them.'

'Lost them? How did you manage that?'

'They were hidden in lumps of salt at the works. They're probably a couple of hundred feet underground now, buried under tons of mud.'

So Philip had abused his position in the works as he always abused whatever positions he held. Becky tried to summon up anger and found that she couldn't. Philip was Philip. The best you could hope for him was that, with guidance, he could be steered away from trouble most of the time.

'Well, if you're in some sort of danger, you'd better get moving,' she said. 'Try and keep in touch this time, will you?'

Philip gently replaced the baby in her cradle.

'I have got a *bit* of money,' he said. 'Not much – not enough to get Caspar Leech off my back – but a bit. If it would help to – you know – start rebuilding the works, then you can have it.'

'Wouldn't you be better returning it to the people it belongs to?' Becky asked.

'How would I find them?' Philip asked. 'Do you expect me to go around all the big houses in Manchester asking if they've had a robbery and offering to pay some compensation if the answer's yes?'

'I suppose not,' Becky said with a smile. 'So it's probably for the best if you keep the money, Philip. God knows, you'll probably need it more than I will.'

Philip gave her one of the impish grins which had never failed to melt her heart.

'I'm more bother than I'm worth, aren't I, little sister?'

Becky returned his grin.

'You can say that again,' she agreed.

The afternoon post brought a copy of *The Strand Magazine*. Becky hadn't ordered it, but on the front – in spidery handwriting – were the words, 'You just might enjoy *A Scandal in Bohemia*.'

Becky turned to the story.

'*To Sherlock Holmes she is always* the *woman,*' it began, '*I have seldom heard him mention her under any other name.*'

Becky quickly read the rest of the story, following Sherlock Holmes' adventures from Baker Street to St John's Wood, where the woman, Irene Adler, finally outwits him.

'*He used to make merry of the cleverness of women,*' the author wrote towards the end, '*but I have not heard him do it of late.*'

At the bottom of the page, in the same handwriting as on the cover, was a short message:

'The story I promised you has taken years in the writing. I hope you think it's worth it, and hope, too, that it will remind you of those few days we spent together so long ago – ACD.'

It *did* seem so long ago, Becky thought, yet she could picture it all as clearly as if it had been yesterday – examining the spot where Septimus Quinn was supposed to have died, following his footprints along the tow path, tracing the route Old Gilbert had taken to commit his murder ...

Becky laid the magazine aside. Dr Doyle had provided a temporary distraction, but it was the present and the future, rather than the past, which weighed heavily on her mind.

She wondered where Michael was at that moment. Was he somewhere on the River Niger, looking for signs of her dead brother? Or had he already met the same fate as Jack?

'No!' she murmured softly. 'He can't be dead.'

But if the river had finished off a man of Jack's experience, what chance would a novice like Michael have? And if was still alive, why had it been so long since he'd written?

'If Michael's dead, I'll never fall in love again,' she whispered into her pillow.

She'd said that once before, she reminded herself – after Richard had told her he wouldn't marry her. But that had been different. Her love affair with Richard had been built on the treacherous ground of his falsehood; her marriage to Michael rested on the solid foundations of love and respect.

'No, I'll never fall in love again,' she repeated, 'because if I live to be a hundred, I'll never find another man to measure up to Michael.'

Ted and Mary Taylor stood looking at the spot where the crack had opened up across Wincham Brook. The hole was no longer there – instead there was a circle of fresh earth, two hundred feet across.

It was not a neat, flat circle. It bulged and dipped with its own tiny mountain ranges and rift valleys, as if it were the work of a careless giant or an absentminded god. And through the middle of it, Wincham Brook was haphazardly cutting itself a new path.

'What do you think finally brought a stop to it all?' Mary asked.

'Muck,' her husband said.

'I'm not sure I'm following you,' Mary said.

'Think of the hole as a vinegar bottle turned upside down,' Ted told her.

'You mean wide at the top and narrow at the bottom?' Mary asked.

'Exactly,' Ted agreed. 'Now all the water that kept on rushing down the hole was carrying a load of soil it had torn from the banks, wasn't it? What must have happened in the end is that the narrow neck simply got clogged with muck so no more water could get in.'

'Well thank God it's all over,' Mary said.

'We've no guarantee it is yet,' Ted cautioned. 'There was a landslip only the other night. In Foundry Lane.'

'Foundry Lane!' Mary exclaimed. 'But that's nearly two miles from here!'

'The old mine workings run even further than that,' Ted said.

They turned round and walked back to what had once been the site of their son-in-law's salt works. Ted stopped, bent down and rummaged among the pile of bricks which had once formed the main chimney. When he stood up again, he was holding in his hands four bricks – still mortared together – on which were painted a white letter R.

'Our Becky,' he said.

'Do you think they'll ever be able to rebuild?' Mary asked. 'I mean if Michael ... if he ever ...'

'If he ever comes back,' Taylor supplied.

'You don't think he will, do you?' Mary said.

Ted Taylor's eyes misted over.

'Our Jack didn't,' he said.

For a while they stood in silence, then Ted said half-heartedly, 'Well, let's not get morbid — it may never happen. Come on, love, I'll treat you to a shandy at The Witch and Devil.'

Their route led them along the Dunkirk Road. There had been some subsidence there, too, and without the benefit of a stream to carry fresh earth to them, several gaping holes still remained.

A large number of sightseers had gathered round the biggest, a crater at least thirty feet deep and sixty feet wide, and a group of religious-looking gentlemen, standing at the very edge of the chasm, were conducting a service.

'Now, my friends, the ground you are standing on is the rottenest in the world,' their spokesman said. 'It may all go down with you in a moment while you stand listening to me, and if it should go as suddenly as it did last Monday, how many of you would go straight down to hell? When the end of the world does come, it will come as suddenly as this terrible accident, but instead of the water, there will be fire.'

'I think he's right,' Ted Taylor said.

'You mean about the fire next time?' his wife asked.

'I mean about this being the rottenest ground in the world,' Taylor told her. 'Listen, love, we've been talking for years about selling up the business and getting a boarding house in Blackpool. What say we finally set about and do it?'

'We'll see,' Mary Taylor said with a sad smile.

Richard Worrell looked down at his sleeping son. There was not a trace of the mother's pinched petulance in the infant's face, he thought to himself. Strip away the babyish pudginess and the features which remained were his own — the same handsome nose, the same cunning, ruthless eyes.

'You're mine, Gerald,' he said. 'All mine.'

He picked up the nightdress his son had been wearing earlier and held it in front of him.

Such a tiny garment! Such a tiny child!

'But you won't be like that for ever, young Gerald,' he said. 'You'll grow up, and when you're grown you'll always be on my side, won't you? Wherever I succeed, you'll build on my success. Wherever I fail, you'll see I'm revenged.'

Though she had fought against her misery for hours, Becky felt she could no longer make the effort. Tired and defeated, she buried her head in the pillow and let the tears flow as they wished.

The crying brought some relief — released some of the tension which had been building up inside her. After five minutes the pillow was sodden, but Becky was starting to feel a little better.

You have a child, she told herself, the most beautiful baby in the world. You have a trade to fall back on. And even if you'll never find love again, you at least know what it's like to have had it once.

The more she considered it, the stronger she felt.

There's lots of people worse off than you, she thought, so for heaven's sake stop feeling sorry for yourself, Becky Worrell.

She heard the bedroom door click open, but she didn't raise her head from the pillow.

'Please go away,' she said.

She was prepared to face the world — honestly she was — but not *quite* yet.

'Well, this is a fine welcome for a couple of heroes!' a voice said.

Jack!

Could it really be Jack?

Becky's head whipped up from the pillow, and as she twisted round she saw her grinning brother — and Michael standing next to him.

'You could have frightened me to death just turning up like that,' Becky said to her husband after the kissing and hugging were finally over.

She was trying to sound angry, but she knew she was failing miserably.

'You could have prepared me,' she pressed on. 'You could have at least written to let me know you were coming.'

Michael, cradling his precious baby daughter, looked into his wife's eyes.

'Would you rather I'd stayed in Africa a little longer?' he asked.

'Of course not!' Becky replied.

'Well, if I'd written, that's what would have happened. It was either us or a letter on the first boat back – and I thought you'd prefer us.'

Jack laughed.

'He's got you there, Becky,' he said.

Becky turned to her brother. Jack was thinner than she remembered him and there were heavy shadows under his eyes, but he seemed as cheerful as ever.

'What happened to you?' she asked.

'I was trading with the Brassmen,' Jack told her, 'that's a tribe from the Upper Niger – and they turned on me.'

'How do you mean? Turned on you?'

'Well, I've always been fair with them,' Jack said, 'but I suspect there's others that haven't been. Anyway, they must have decided that no Europeans can be trusted because one night they attacked my steamer. They took us all prisoner and sank the boat so Queen Victoria wouldn't find out what had happened. They killed all my nigger crew and ate them. I don't know why they decided to let us whites live. Perhaps they were saving us for a special feast later on. Or maybe they thought they'd get a good price for us when the slave traders passed through.'

'How dreadful for you,' Becky said.

'Yes, it was a bit,' Jack admitted. 'Anyway, they did let us live, but a pretty miserable life it was, tied up all the time and half starved. We'd almost given up hope when Michael arrived.'

'I think that's enough for now,' Michael said hastily. 'We don't want to tire Becky out.'

'I'm not tired and I want to hear it,' Becky told him. 'You get back to admiring your daughter while Jack finishes his story.'

Michael seemed on the point of arguing, then Michelle gave a little chuckle and he could no longer keep his eyes off her.

'You should have seen him, Becky,' Jack continued. 'He only had a couple of native guides with him but he walked straight into the village, as bold as you please. He was carrying a rifle, but he threw it on the ground to show he wasn't looking for any trouble and turned to face the Brassmen's spears completely unarmed. And was he impressive? Gordon of Khartoum couldn't have done it better!'

'He's exaggerating,' Michael said, managing to drag his attention away from his daughter for a second. 'It wasn't half as dangerous as he's making out.'

'Shut up, Michael,' Becky said. 'Go on with your tale, Jack.'

'So, him and his guide squatted down in the dirt next to the chief of the Brassmen and started talking to him. They were yammering away for over an hour, and all the time we were watching them and shitting ourselves. Sorry, Becky — but we were! And then Michael walks up to us — looking as cool as if he's just had tea and sandwiches with the Vicar — and tells us he's bought us, and we're free to go.'

'What did you pay for him?' Becky asked her husband.

'His own weight in M & R Worrell's finest salt,' Michael told her. 'And after hearing the way he's been talking today, I think I was over-charged.'

They chatted for a few minutes more, then Jack said, 'Well I suppose I'd better leave you two alone, hadn't I?'

It was the moment Becky had been dreading — the moment when she would have to tell Michael that his works — and with them, all his dreams — had come tumbling down.

'Put the baby back in her crib and come and sit by me,' she told her husband as Jack closed the door behind him.

Michael laid Michelle tenderly in her tiny bed and then sat down next to his wife.

Oh God, what can I say? Becky wondered. How do I break it to him?

'There's been an accident,' she said.

Michael smiled. 'An accident?' he asked. 'Is that a nice way of saying that we don't have a salt works any more?'

'You ... you knew already!' Becky gasped.

'I found out as soon as I set foot on Liverpool docks,' Michael replied. 'Bad news travels fast.'

Then how could he be so calm? How could he be taking it so well?

'I was there when it happened,' Becky told him. 'I saved as much as I could.'

'I know about that, too,' Michael said. 'By all accounts, you were very heroic.'

'But did I save *enough*?' Becky asked anguishedly. 'Can we start up again with what we've got left?'

'I won't know that until I've had a look at both the equipment and the site for myself,' Michael said.

'Aren't you worried?' Becky asked.

Michael looked across at the baby and then back at her.

'I was worried that I'd die in the jungle without ever seeing you again,' he said. 'I was worried that something would have happened to you or my child while I was away. How can a little thing like a salt works compare to that?'

He still didn't realize the full implications, Becky thought, but he had to be told — he had to be made to see.

'We might go bankrupt,' she said aloud.

'We might,' Michael admitted.

'We could never afford to stay here,' Becky told him. 'We'd have to move into somewhere much smaller.'

'Have you grown *very* attached to a life of luxury?' Michael asked, smiling again. He made a sweeping gesture round the room with his hand. 'Would it *really* bother you if we lost all this?'

'Of course not,' Becky said hotly. 'I'm used to living on the edge of poverty – I've done it for most of my life. But what about you, Michael? How will you cope with it?'

'After public school, it should be easy,' he told her. 'Besides, there's no reason why we should stay poor for ever. My father made his fortune from nothing, and with what you managed to save from the works, we're considerably better off than that.'

'If we can't re-start the works, what will you do?' Becky asked.

'I might go into partnership with your brother Jack,' Michael told her. 'I could invent something, like my father did. The world is full of opportunities, Becky, and I only have to grasp one of them for us to be rich again.'

He took his wife's hand and stroked it tenderly.

'Besides,' he continued, 'as long as we're together, does it *really* matter whether we're poor or not?'

'No,' Becky, said. 'As long as we're together, *nothing* else matters.'

Michael left Becky alone to rest.

But how could she rest on a day like this? she asked herself.

Her husband had come home safely – bringing with him her brother, back from the dead – and instead of being crushed by the news about the works, he was bursting with plans for the future.

'You have the most wonderful father in the world,' she told the little baby lying in the crib. 'And I have the most wonderful husband.'

The baby made a gurgling sound, almost as if she understood.

'You're going to have a marvellous life, little Michelle,' Becky said. 'I promise you are.'

Four miles away, in Peak House, Richard Worrell was just promising his son Gerald exactly the same thing.